# DON'T PUCK WITH MY HEART

## SARAH BLUE

Cover by - Maldo Designs

Editing by - Foxtale Editing

❀ Created with Vellum

# WHAT IS AN OMEGAVERSE?

An Omegaverse is an alternate universe where humans have a specific designation in a hierarchy based on their biology—**in my series they are not shifters**. You are either an Alpha, Beta or an Omega. Your designation determines specific traits of your physiology and personality.

**Alphas** tend to be aggressive, they're generally more dominant and hold positions of authority. Many Alphas form packs which increase their wealth and dominance. Alphas have a history of taking advantage of and abusing Omegas. Alphas who are assigned male at birth have a fleshy ring near the base of their penis that swells during intercourse called a knot. It allows them to "lock" into place with an Omega. While Omegas are the most physiologically compatible when it comes to taking an Alpha's knot, Betas (or even Alphas) can take a knot with practice. Female Alphas have a lock that clenches around the penis and holds it inside, female Alphas and male Omegas are a great fit for this. Female Alphas can lock with other designations.

**Betas** are the closest to everyday humans. Their scent and sense of smell are not as strong as an Alpha or Omegas. They tend to be the most level-headed out of the designations.

**Omegas** tend to be the softest and most gentle of the designations. Generally, they do not hold positions of power, are homemakers or have positions in lower standing. Their scents are extremely arousing to Alphas. Out of all the designations, Omegas are the most likely to be abused or treated poorly. Alphas have the most opportunity to reproduce with Omegas.

Omegas go through **heat cycles** during which they are the most fertile. At this time they're sensitive to light, noise, and scents. They require the comfort of a nest full of soft fabrics and textures. Their body requires a large amount of sexual stimulation during a heat cycle, and it can last for several days. If the Omega is with an Alpha, their Alpha or Alphas will do everything in their power to make sure they are cared for and comfortable during their heat. Going through a heat cycle as an unbonded Omega can be unsafe for their physical health and sometimes their safety.

**Scent matches** are basically your fated mate. No other Alpha or Omega will smell as good as your scent match. You are physiologically a perfect match for each other, in this universe this is a very rare thing to find.

Please note that my Omegaverse falls under a more sweeter category than dark. Though there are issues in the system of dominance in society my books lean on the sweeter aspects of society and not the darker side.

# SPOTIFY PLAYLIST

Download Here
Where Have You Been - Rihanna
Radio - Lana Del Ray
Fix You - Cold Play
Crawling - Linkin Park
fOoL fOr YoU - ZAYN
Captain Hook - Megan Thee Stallion
Landslide - Fleetwood Mac
Chasing Pavements - Adele
We Will Rock You - Queen
Perfect - One Direction
Electric Love - BØRNS
I Ain't Worried - OneRepublic
Eat Your Young - Hozier
Never Felt So Alone - Labrinth
Ribs - Lorde

Perfect - Alan's Morissette
I Want You - Kings of Leon
Needy - Ariana Grande
Anti-Hero - Taylor Swift
Congratulations - Post Malone, Quavo
I wanna Love You - Akon, Snoop Dogg

# CONTENT MESSAGE

Welcome back to the Pucked Omegaverse. If you need a refresher on what an Omegaverse is, please make sure to reference the 'What is an Omegaverse' page. It is recommended to read One Pucked Up Pack first, as there are many character cameos in this book.

For a full list of content please visit my website.
https://authorsarahblue.com/content-warnings/

# DEDICATION

*To the girls with a mean inner voice,*
*tell that bitch to stfu.*

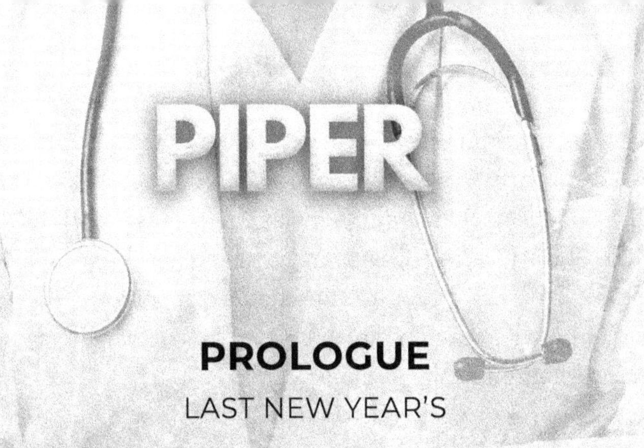


## PROLOGUE
### LAST NEW YEAR'S

Champagne is clearly the source of both good and evil. Even though I know I'll feel like shit tomorrow, I feel euphoric right now, like all the problems that phase me in my everyday life don't exist.

You know what exists though?

*Alexi fucking Bandnin.*

I've known him for years now, having been an NHL WAG's best friend and with how many games I attend with Charlotte. Now that I'm in my residency and Anders retired, my games have been less frequent. That doesn't mean I still don't appreciate everything that is Alexi Bandnin.

I've thought about fucking that man within an inch of his life at least a hundred times, but something always holds me back. It's probably the way he looks at me with his mischievous smirk or the way that everyone on the team seems to absolutely adore him.

It's not that I think Alexi is out of my league, I think that if I let myself indulge in that tall, big, future silver fox that I wouldn't be able to walk away. Not many Alpha males want an Alpha female in their pack... but Alexi, he seems different.

Like he's so confident in himself that no other Alpha would feel like a threat.

Charlotte sips her champagne as she comes and stands next to me. She's wearing this sparkly navy dress, and she looks adorable. You can't even tell she had a baby. I've witnessed—against my will—each member of her pack groping her tonight with how stunning she looks.

What does a girl have to do to get groped around here?

"See anything you like?" she says, taking another heavy sip. "I don't know, like a very tall man with a Russian accent who looks at you like he wants to eat you out from behind."

I smack her arm, and she spills some champagne over her fist. She laughs with her head flung back. I can't help but to smile, seeing my friend so carefree and happy. I was there during the darkest days of her life. It's amazing to see her so radiant and happy.

"Charlotte, you're supposed to be someone's mother," I joke, and she shakes her head.

"Being a mom doesn't stop me from getting railed every day that ends in Y." She cackles again, and it's contagious.

"How much have you had?" I ask, clinking her glass.

"Making up for lost time and future lost time," she says, slurring her words.

I arch an eyebrow at her and pat down my short black dress. I might be showing more leg than what most people would say is appropriate. And maybe I dressed this way because I knew Alexi would be here. Just because I shouldn't sample the goods doesn't mean he shouldn't know full well how hot I am. "What do you mean future time lost?"

"Meaning, my heat is coming up and I want another baby."

I smile and bump her hip with mine. "You're good parents, you know that?"

"I learned from the best," she says, her eyes watering as she smiles.

"Yeah, you sure did." Both of us are quiet for a moment, remembering Kathy and how pivotal she was to both of our childhoods. The moment of sadness is quickly forgotten as we watch Eli shimmy over to where we're standing.

Eli is absolutely wasted, his eyes heavy looking as he turns up the music and stumbles over to his Omega. "Dance with me, baby," he says, and Charlotte giggles as she takes his hand. I watch them dance, and other hockey couples follow suit and start dancing. The dancing is horrible, and I laugh as I watch men who can skate on blades dance with absolutely no rhythm. But the moment fades, and the sad and lonely part of my brain takes over. I'm not sure if it's the bubbles of champagne floating through my body or watching couples and packs dance together while I feel pathetically alone.

The countdown is about to start, and I feel like I'm intruding. It's hard to pinpoint exactly why, but I feel like this more often than I'd like to admit—like I don't belong in certain spaces. I have a hard time feeling like I belong in my surgical program, and sometimes I feel like I don't belong in Charlotte's space. She will always be my best friend, but things change when you get a pack. Me being an Alpha adds an additional layer to that.

I slip away through the sliding door of their kitchen. The champagne keeps me warm as I down the rest of my glass and look out into their perfectly domestic backyard. I would have given anything for parents like Charlotte and her pack. I smile to myself, thinking about how well-adjusted and loved their children will be. Eli and Mikael are breaking generational curses, and Anders and Charlotte are continuing their family traditions on their own. It's beautiful, and I'm more than happy for them, but I can't help but feel like maybe I'll never have that. Do I even want that?

The sliding door behind me clicks, and I assume that it's Charlotte.

"Charles, I'm fine. I'll be right back in."

"I think you look more than fine, Piper." I shiver at the sound. His deep timber does something for me. I spin around and tilt my head to look at him. Alexi always looks good whether he's in his uniform or suits after games, but I think casual Alexi may be my favorite. God, I'd pay good ass money to see him in a pair of sweatpants that are a size too small. I lick my lips and remember that I need to reply to his statement —his very flirty statement.

"Thanks for noticing."

"I always notice you." I clear my throat, and the thought of Alexi constantly noticing sends a pang of want through me—a want I shouldn't even be entertaining.

"Thanks," I say lamely, not knowing how to respond when his full attention is focused solely on me.

"For the champagne or noticing how beautiful you are?"

I down the entire glass of champagne he hands me, and he just grins. "Would you like another?"

"Yeah, we should go inside." He looks me up and down and stares at my legs. He takes a step forward, and he's close— close enough to kiss. It's cold as shit, and his scent is faint, but I can tell it's masculine and perfect.

"Are you cold? I could help with that."

Oh fuck, do I want this big huge man to wrap me in his arms and warm me right the fuck on up. He smirks down at me, and isn't it just a huge blow to my ego that he knows exactly what effect he has on me.

"You could get me another glass of champagne." He rubs his chin. His beard is short right now, and it's dark and speckled with gray. *It's hot.*

*He's hot. Is it hot out here now?*

"Are we going inside, or should I bring it out here?" he asks. He looks back down at my legs, and now I'm wet. Thank god it's cold and I'm not an Omega or else he would know my whole wet panty situation right now. "I'll be right back," he says to me, taking off his jacket and handing it to me. He looks like he wants to do more but doesn't.

He re-enters the house, and I wrap myself in his jacket, his scent permeated in the soft material, and I sigh at the scent. It doesn't make me lose control like an Omega scent might, but it feels comforting and warm nonetheless.

I hug myself, and the last two flutes of champagne hit, my skin buzzing and a sense of easygoingness flowing through me. It's definitely the drinks making me feel like a sex-crazed lunatic. If I had my wits about me, I definitely wouldn't be basically drooling as he speaks to me. But I needed a few drinks tonight, I needed to shut my mind off. Expectations of who I'm supposed to be are starting to weigh on me, and well, the champagne helps me forget about all the shit piling up in my life.

There are a lot of expectations of what a surgeon should be like, and I don't feel like I fit any of them. I know I'm smart, and I love helping people, but the job is more difficult than I imagined. What I need is an outlet, some place to let go and be me after spending so many hours meeting how others think I should act and portray myself.

*Shut the fuck up, and enjoy tonight,* I chastise myself as the door reopens. My body immediately responds to him as he holds an entire bottle of champagne up. "Thought the bottle might be the best route," he says while taking a swig and handing me the bottle. The bottle where his perfect fucking man lips touched. I take an even bigger sip than he does. We both just stand there in the cold night for a few minutes, the silence between us comfortable yet thick with sexual tension.

We haven't had many conversations alone—we're always in a group setting where I can ogle him but not act on it. Being alone with him feels different, charged in a way that I'm not used to.

It's the champagne, it's got to be the champagne. I take another sip, because what else am I supposed to do, open my mouth instead and tell him how I want to climb him like a tree but that's all? I can't handle a relationship right now, and as flirty as Alexi is, I don't think that's what he's looking for. I'm pretty sure he had his ho phase a while ago. I lick my lips, liking that he's older. All of the men—Beta men—I've dated before have been my age.

"That dress is something," he says, glancing down at me and looking at my legs that are likely to freeze off.

"It is, isn't it?" I say doing a little twirl and holding the bottle steady. He grins at me, and having his full attention on me feels more intoxicating than all this champagne does in this moment. I swallow thickly and turn my head toward the house.

The noise in the house is loud, and I can hear every number of the countdown. They're at the number five when I hand the bottle back to Alexi.

I'm not sure if it's all the champagne bubbles, but when I hear the cheers of happy New Year inside of the house, I abandon all doubts. I tug on Alexi's tight blue dress shirt and crash his lips to mine. He doesn't hesitate, his hands cradling my face as he kisses me. Alexi doesn't hold back; he moans into my mouth, and his tongue works against mine. He isn't rough with the kiss, more fervent than anything. My hands slide up his chest, and I can't help but grip his soft hair. I know he likes it when he kisses me harder and one of his hands slides down my back to grip my ass, hitching his massive thigh between my legs.

I've never been kissed like this before. Like I'm all consuming and Alexi will never get enough. Like I need this kiss more than I need to breathe, like no kiss in my life will ever compare to the way this man is holding me right now.

*It's completely fucking terrifying.*

"I want you so fucking bad," he says, kissing my jaw and down my neck. His teeth graze along the column of my throat. "I'd make you feel so good," he says, and damn if I don't know that's the fucking truth. "You should be *mine.*"

It's the last word that breaks the spell, my buzz faltering out of me just as quickly as it started. I don't belong to anyone; I don't have time for anything serious or the emotional capacity for it. My career is my focus right now. There's no room for someone who's larger than life like Alexi.

I take a step back and look up into his deep brown eyes, handing him his jacket. "My stomach hurts, so I think I need to get home."

"I'll drive you," he says.

"No, um… actually, I have a guest room here. I… thanks for the jacket."

"Piper," he says in an exacerbated sigh.

"Happy New Year, Alexi."

"Happy New Year," he says sadly, and when I see how disappointed he is, I realize I need to stay as far away from Alexi Bandnin as I physically can. I glance at him one last time. He's the kind of man you settle down with, who consumes your whole life. I have to stay focused. My life has always been planned out for me, and I can't let a man get between that.

Alexi is a one way ticket to domesticity I'm not ready for, so I do what I do best: I run away and don't take another glance back.

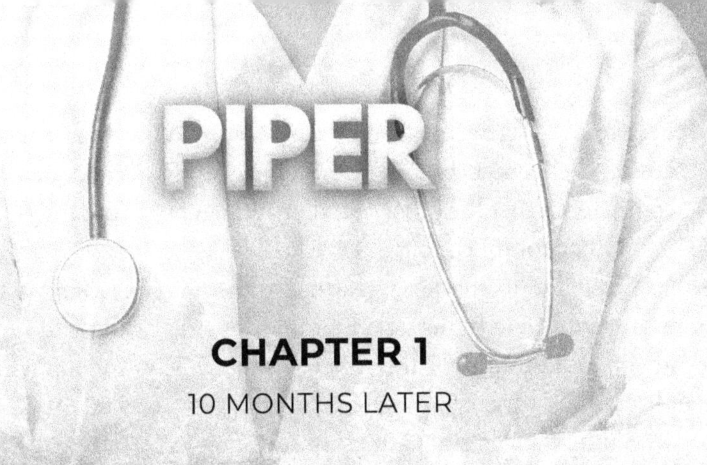


# CHAPTER 1

## 10 MONTHS LATER

I feel like I'm fueled by coffee, my need to be productive, and the chocolate chip muffin I ate this morning. This is my thirteenth day in a row working, and I wonder when it's going to feel like I belong in this surgical program.

I'm exhausted as I observe the anterior cervical discectomy. The other residents look on in awe, and I can't help the lingering feeling that this isn't where my skill set lies. I swallow that disturbing thought down. The years of my life I've dedicated to being here can't be for nothing. I've worked endlessly to stand in this operating room and observe, and that's what I'm doing, learning.

"Dr. Blake, can you tell me why we do this from the front of the neck and not the back?" Dr. Marsh, the attending surgeon asks.

"It reduces risk to the spinal cord, nerves, and neck muscle" He hums approval but there are no kudos. You don't get a sticker for knowing the right answer. But you do get belittled if you're incorrect.

"Dr. Hoft, what is the top risk?"

"Damage to the carotid or vertebral artery," Shuana says

next to me. Archnemesis might be a little intense for what we are to each other, but the sentiment stands. I can't help but compete against the other female Alpha in my program.

"Other complications?" Dr. Marsh asks.

"Damage to the laryngeal nerve, hematoma, injury to the esophagus." He hums again and decides that's the end of our lesson as he continues the surgery. Shuana is on suction while I observe the surgery from above, waiting to be called on.

Surgery wasn't a path I chose for myself, not really. My father, Doctor Peter Blake, basically told me this was my path. I'm his only child and, to his satisfaction, also an Alpha. It's been ingrained in me that I needed to take on a profession that is competitive with a high salary. He would have accepted me being a lawyer, but this is the path he set out for me, and I don't see me stepping off the ride anytime soon. Of course I had to make it more difficult by selecting one of the longest residencies and most competitive fields with neurosurgery.

I shift on my feet, making sure I don't doze off. I can't wait to pee and get another coffee once the surgery is over, I'm on hour twenty-two of a twenty-four hour shift. At least I have Charlotte's baby shower to look forward to tomorrow. I smile behind my mask just thinking about it. It's why I've worked so many days in a row, to have this one day off, to celebrate my best friend, something I wouldn't miss for the world.

The surgery goes off without a hitch, and immediately after, I'm handed a tablet and a to-do list of patients that I need to check on—post-op and pre-op patients.

This is the part of the job I don't mind, interacting with patients and reassuring them that everything is going to be fine.

I'm headed to Gill Florence's room when Shuana bumps into my shoulder. "Broken spine is mine," she says in her shitty little tone. Shuana is just as tall as me but with reddish blonde hair that she always wears in a high ponytail. We're both the only female Alphas in Neurosurgery, even if we weren't competing head to head, I'd probably still hate her.

"His name is Mr. Florence, and Dr. Paulson thinks she can possibly help him gain some movement with surgery."

"She's wasting her time, he's never going to walk again. But if she wants to do a kyphoplasty I call dibs."

That's when my competitive side kicks in. It's not about cutting for me, it's making sure that Shuana knows I'm better than her in every way. Also, that she needs to stop being such an unfeeling bitch to our patients.

I beat her to the room, but just barely.

"How's your pain today, Mr. Florence?" I ask before Shuana has the chance.

"I told you to call me Gill."

"How's your pain today, Gill?" I reask the question. He grimaces, and his wife Pam touches his shoulder.

"It's intense, especially on my side." He pulls back his blanket, and I do a quick examination before nodding and giving him a reassuring smile. His skin is purple and blue from where he fell, but the fact that he can feel that part of his body is a good sign. The fact that he still hasn't been able to move his toes, is not.

"I'll talk to Dr. Paulson about increasing your pain management. She should be in before five to speak to you about your options."

"Dr. Blake, is he going to be able to walk again? He's a handyman, so he needs to be able to get around."

"The trauma from your fall is severe, but Dr. Paulson will go over your options when she's in this evening." It's hard speaking around the truth and not making promises to patients. It's one of the first things you learn; you can't make any guarantees or promises. Thinking about Gill's future has me saddened, and as much as I hate Shuana, I know she's right. The chances of him walking ever again are small but Dr. Paulson is talented. I give Pam and Gill a small smile before noting his chart and updating the nurse about his pain level.

"Told you, I wonder if she'll let me do the injections," Shuana says before walking away. I roll my eyes and head to the next patient.

It feels like the day will never end, and I'm dead on my feet. But I persevere—*it's what a Blake does*, my dad's voice echoes in my head. The day consists of two more iced coffees, a Dr Pepper, and a mirage of snacks I shouldn't be eating until the day is finally over.

But it's not truly over. As much as I want to go back to my townhouse and pass out on the bed, that's not an option. My first stop is the dollar store where I buy all the pink and blue shit I can find, streamers, plates, balloons, and I find a bag of creepy miniature babies that I purchase. The next stop is the grocery store where I grab the fruit and cheese tray as well as the baby shower cake. I grab to-go sushi for my own dinner, and only then can I call it a night.

I might be busy, but there's no fucking way I'm going to fall behind on my best friend or aunt duties. That is something I will not slip, unlike many other facets of my life—like dating.

Who has time for dating anyway? I can do without the dinners, the courting process of the dating, but the sex... well, I'm really missing getting laid right now. The fact that I don't have energy for a good fuck is concerning.

I don't let it phase me though. This is all part of the process. Giving up a decade of your life for a very significant accomplishment... right?

I put the food and cake in my very barren fridge and eat the sushi with my fingers before showering and going to sleep.

*I've got this. I'm going to be okay.*

———

I'm barely through the door when the cake almost falls from my arms as my favorite tiny human wraps her arms around my leg.

"Auntie P!" she screeches. Anders shakes his head and scoops up his daughter.

"It's fine, why don't your daddies go get everything from the car while I hold my favorite girl." She holds out her hands, and I scoop her up, kissing all over her face dramatically. Anders, Eli, and Mikael all shake their heads but smile at their daughter before going outside and getting all the baby crap from my car. "Where's mommy?" I ask her.

"She's tired. My babies make her tired."

"I bet they do," I say, kissing her hair one more time before going into their massive living room. Charlotte is wrapped up in a blanket, like the quintessential Omega she is, as I approach. I put Katie down who scampers off to the kitchen, and I push Charlotte's hair away from her face.

"Hey, Charles," I say, sitting down on the couch next to her. "How are you feeling?"

"Huge, tired, and hungry."

I put a hand over Charlotte's. "But everything is good with the twins?"

She smiles and nods. "Everything is good. How about you? You look tired, Pipes." I hate the nickname Pipes, but it started so long ago; there's no turning back now. Charlotte is the only one who I'll let call me that.

"You know, it's just a lot of hours, I'll be fine." She flips her hand and squeezes mine.

"Piper—"

"It's fine, I'm fine, Charles. I promise."

"You really didn't have to do all of this for the baby shower, seriously," she says, shaking her head.

"I wanted to. This is what best friends are for. "

Suddenly, Katie comes running back in the room and tosses a string cheese at Charlotte. "Here go, mommy," she beams. Charlotte's eyes water as she scoops up her toddler, opening up the string cheese and eating.

"I hope your brothers or sisters are just as sweet as you."

I hug my niece and best friend before standing up. "I'm going to go help your Alphas set up. Knowing them, they won't even know what to do with a streamer."

Charlotte waves me off, grabbing Katie to take a nap on the couch. In complete amazement, I watch as they both sleep through us getting everything together for the party. Placing streamers on the ceiling, scattering balloons throughout the room, and setting out the food.

By the time we're done, I'm exhausted and wish I could take a nap like Charlotte, but there's still so much to do.

I decide to throw the creepy plastic babies into the punch bowl as Mikael walks by. "What in the fuck?" he says, looking down at the punch bowl.

I shrug my shoulders and toss an additional bag in there. "What, it's funny."

"Okay, if you say so," he says, rolling his eyes. Mikael and I still aren't besties, but I know how much he loves and takes care of my best friend, so I put up with him. Eli walks by next, putting cups and cutlery on the table.

He laughs at the babies in the punch, and I smirk. Eli has moved to the number one spot in pack Hodges for the day. Their massive dog, Hank, rubs his enormous head against my thighs while I put the final touches on the décor, and I can't help but to get down on my haunches and pet his cute, giant face.

Suddenly, the doorbell rings. One of Charlotte's Alphas answers the door. A bunch of people come crowding in. Most of them are hockey wives I haven't met, but I can hold my own in a crowd of strangers. Plus, between Hank and Katie, I have all the entertainment I need.

That's when I hear *his* voice.

The deep rumble of his greeting to Charlotte does something to me, and I stay down, petting Hank and hiding behind the couch.

It's pathetic, truly.

Alexi Bandnin, number eight for the New Haven Foxes and a man I kissed a year ago, and I can't seem to get it out of my head.

It was one kiss, one drunken night, almost a year ago. Yet, his voice does something to me, and I can't help but to hide from him anytime we're all in the same place.

"Fuck, Hank," I tell the Newfoundland like he has all the answers. He doesn't understand as he just drools on my jeans. "What do I do?"

"Dr. Blake?" I hear his voice and look up from Hank's head. There he stands, looking as gorgeous as ever in casual gray pants and a tight black T-shirt. I stand up to my full height, and I have to look up at him. I hate how much I like that, *that I like an Alpha.*

I mean, I don't like him, like him. But who can truly blame me? He's tall, muscular, has dark brown hair with graying edges. His beard is salt and pepper, and he even has all his teeth currently. He's so fucking hot it's unbearable. Literally, I can't bear to think about the kiss and how I felt when it happened. No kiss has ever made me feel that way. Charlotte would say it's because I only date safe Beta boys—men—I'd have no problem leaving in the dust. But kissing Alexi, I knew that if it went any further there would be no coming back.

"Alexi."

"Did you decorate for the party?" he asks, and I nod my head. "Smart, beautiful, and she throws her best friend a party." I'm thinking of my escape route when Katie runs right into Alexi's legs. He grabs her by the calf, holding her upside down high in the air. Fuck, it's so attractive to see him play with a child. "And what are you doing, *ptichka?*"

Katie starts making tweeting noises and flapping her arms like she's a little bird. I've got to get the fuck out of here before things get any more endearing.

"Uncle Lexi, let me down!" she screeches.

I swallow. "Uncle?"

He flips her, tossing her in the air for a moment before letting her down. Katie goes around the room collecting balloons and acting like a bird. Alexi shrugs his shoulders and looks at me expectantly. "She likes me."

Yeah, what isn't there to like? He rubs his fingers through his hair, and I remember the one time my hands were tangled in it, and I swallow thickly.

"Are you coming to any of the games this season?"

"Maybe," I say, knowing how hard it is to do anything with my schedule. But how convenient it is to admire him from afar while he's on the ice. This stupid crush is bullshit.

"Work has you busy?" he asks, and it's the first time I can sense that he doesn't feel as confident as he appears. He's shifting his weight from side to side and stuffs his massive hands in his pockets.

Now I'm thinking about his huge hands and how he cupped my face like I was something precious when we kissed.

Red-fucking-alert. I've got to get out of here. I scan the room before answering his question.

"Residency is hard."

"But you enjoy it?" he asks with an arch of his brow.

"Um, yeah. Of course. I'm going to check on Charlotte." He looks at me like he doesn't believe me but says nothing as I skitter away like a scaredy-cat.

I nearly tumble over a pregnant Charlotte as she smirks at me.

"Piper, I say this with love. You're being such a little bitch right now." I grab the cake out of her hand and shove a huge bite in my mouth.

"Fuck off, Charles." She laughs as I stuff my face with the grocery store cake that is dry as fuck, feeling overwhelmed. I've been in such a dry spell, and just being around Alexi has stirred something inside of me.

"He wants you too, you know."

*Oh, I'm well fucking aware, and that's the terrifying part.*

# ALEXI

## CHAPTER 2

I'm a patient man, but I think I've lost the battle of wills when it comes to Piper. I'm ready to make a move—again—whether she's ready or not. She basically couldn't get away from me fast enough as soon as she saw me walk into the party.

But I know she's not running because she's not interested.

Honestly, I don't know why she's running from this. All I know is that I've never actively wanted someone so badly. When I met her years ago, I thought she was beautiful but didn't think a female Alpha would ever be of interest to me. But as I've become closer to pack Hodges and got to know her, how strong, loving, and talented she is, I've become a bit of a man obsessed.

Last New Year's Eve is something I can't get out of my head. She wanted that kiss just as badly as I did. It might have taken a few too many glasses of champagne for her to lower her inhibitions enough to accept the kiss. But she was just as needy for it as I was. She tangled her long fingers in my hair and moaned against my lips.

Piper Blake wants me but refuses to act on it.

I've tried to get her attention in multiple ways, but nothing seems to be working. Charlotte told me that Piper said I was attractive. Maybe she just needs more time to get to know me. All I know is I'm willing to do whatever it takes.

Anders hands me a piece of cake, and I glare at him as I take his offering.

"Alexi, I told you I was sorry." We've been struggling this season without Anders. We can't seem to find a goalie that fits in well with the team—not like Anders did. "Mikael said they've recruited one from the Icemen."

I grunt and nod my head. "Supposedly."

"It was time for me to come home and be with Charlotte and our growing family. I'm sure the Foxes will figure it out."

I shrug and sigh. "You're right, sorry."

"You're competitive. I know how much you care about the team."

"I wanted this to be the year."

Anders clasps his hand on my shoulder. "You never know, Captain." I nod, but my hopes aren't high. I was with Dallas for so long, and I was even lucky enough to win a Cup with them. But I just can't help this need for one more Cup. One last major victory is what I need to leave the ice. My forty-second birthday is this year, and I'm an anomaly when it comes to hockey. To be able to play at this level for so long is impressive. But I can't help but to want it all. If I could lead the Foxes to victory, I could leave and give my body a break—at least that's what I tell myself.

Part of me thinks someone will need to break my kneecaps in order for me to leave the ice. I can feel it, all the years of hockey damaging my body, but I really don't give a fuck. I gave up everything for hockey, relationships, packs, heats. And now that I feel like I could have those things, it makes me want to leave the game.

The Cup and the pretty Alpha hiding in the kitchen from me would make retiring more than worth it.

"You know she goes to Alpha fitness on East Avenue," Anders says while his daughter runs to his legs and he picks her up. I arch an eyebrow at Anders, and he shrugs. "I owe Piper everything. If she's not willing to make the first step, I will."

I know most of their pack history; part of it is a huge reason why I'm so drawn to Piper. Charlotte has all but said that Piper basically saved her life when her world went to shit. I'm not sure how Anders, Mikael, and Eli got so lucky with this pack. I'm not usually a jealous man, but there's a tinge of it now. It's an overwhelming feeling, like I've missed out on something special.

I'm in amazing shape, I have a lot to offer, and I can't help but to feel like now is the time.

Charlotte walks up to Anders, kissing their daughter and her Alpha's cheek.

"She usually goes from 5–7 a.m.," Charlotte says.

Mikael comes over, taking Katie from Anders' arms as he shakes his head. "You two need to leave Piper alone and let her do what she wants."

Anders and Charlotte shake their heads. "Yeah, because you're so great at getting your own head out of your ass," Anders says.

"Daddy said ass," Katie says to Mikael.

"I know, *ma chouette*, let's go get cake," Mikael says, giving Anders a glare as he takes Katie to the kitchen.

"I'm tired," Charlotte says. She's small, minus the bump overtaking her form as she grabs Anders' forearm. I want that, but I don't need it. I like the idea of an Omega, who doesn't? Someone who needs care and attention. But I can't help but feel that I like how independent and successful Piper is. I can take care of her in my own way.

"Let's say your goodbyes and take you down to the nest," Anders says to his Omega. They both give me a smile before leaving the party so Anders can give their Omega the comfort she needs.

Part of me wants to go and find Piper again, maybe I can corner her to the point where she can't run away. That's when Eli comes up to me, handing me a beer.

"Are you ready for tomorrow?"

"As ready as I can be."

"I watched his tapes, he's good."

"We need great," I tell Eli, and he nods. Eli is just as hungry for a championship as I am.

"Maybe we can do some more defensive drills. I feel like that's where we're lacking. Better defense means less scoring opportunities."

"I'll talk to Coach Applegate."

"Good. Thanks for coming today, man."

"Of course. I wouldn't miss it."

Eli smiles, and someone ushers him to the kitchen. "See you tomorrow," he says as he walks away. I'm left in the living room with a drooling dog who wants my cake and the prettiest Alpha hiding from me.

Would it make me a stalker if I started going to her gym?

I walk around the house, and she's nowhere to be found, so I take the loss and head home. To my large, sparse, and lonely home that I can't help but wish was filled with a pack to come home to.

---

My shoulder is sore, and I already know I'm going to need to take an ice bath later today. I'm rolling my shoulder as I skate on the ice, hoping for the best but expecting the worst. Our starting goalie has been absolutely shitting the bed the last few games, and now we have a new backup, one I'm hoping can prove himself and turn into our starter.

The team stretches and Mikael is next to me. I'm sure he's just as skeptical as I am.

"He better be fucking good," Mikael says.

"No fucking kidding, *rebenok*."

"When are you going to stop calling me a kid?"

"Probably never, *rebenok*."

He rolls his eyes and continues stretching. Coach Applegate skates out on the ice. He's new, so he has a lot to prove. He retired from professional hockey about a decade ago, but he played even longer than I have. He has only coached in the college sector, until now. I'm not sure how I feel about the man, but I appreciate that he's hungry for a win.

"Men, I'd like to introduce Owen Connery. He's coming to us from the Icemen, and we're excited to have him."

He raises his hand in his full goalie gear. He's not a big man, and it's concerning to me. The more surface area he covers in the goal the better. We all acknowledge him with head nods and other greetings as he heads to the goal. He starts skating the crease and stretching.

"Remind me to punch your brother-husband in the face."

Mikael can't help the laugh that escapes him, and Coach Applegate gives us a dark look. We both shrug our shoulders, and the new goalie's eyes meet mine. They're light blue and menacing, and I find it very intriguing. In what way, I'm not sure yet.

"Let's see what he can do, Bandnin."

"If you can catch up, *rebenok*." I push his shoulder, making him go down on the ice. He curses but is quickly chasing me as the assistant coach lets loose some pucks so we can warm up. The new goalie surprises me with his movements. He may not be tall, but what he lacks in size he makes up for in his speed and alertness.

He saves some pucks that I'm not even sure Anders would have been able to save. I don't get my hopes up, not just yet.

"Alright, let's run a scrimmage. Our game against the Islanders is this weekend. They've been playing like shit, but that's no reason to go in confident. If anything, I want a high scoring game." Applegate pairs us off into two teams, and I have to grab one of the black pinnies to toss over my practice jersey. The new goalie is on the opposite side, and I can't help it, but the need to humble his ass is overwhelming. *Consider it a formal greeting to the team.*

Mikael and I are on the same team. We're usually on the same line, me, him, and Eli. But Eli is on the other team, and I can already tell they are playing more against each other than the other team during the scrimmage.

We don't play as rough as we would in a normal game, but it also doesn't stop me from pushing Luqvist into the boards or elbowing Pavelski as Mikael passes me the puck. I'm quick in seeing where I can score, and I realize I need to get closer to the net. As I do, I get pushed in the back, which sends me into the net, knocking down the new goalie.

I hear the *whoosh* of air leave his lungs as I land on top of him. Bright blue, angry eyes glare at me as I grab his face mask.

"Welcome to the team, *novichok.*"

He punches me hard in the side, and I roll off of him laughing. He doesn't say anything as we both get up, and he's back in his stance.

*Maybe the new guy isn't so bad after all.*

# CHAPTER 3

I'm not sure what type of introduction I expected from the team, but getting laid out by their massive left winger, Alexi Bandnin, wasn't it. I nearly thought he would notice something was off when he was so close to me, but he didn't. He just laughed like a psychopath and said something to me in Russian.

I knew it would take a lot to prove myself to this team. I'm twenty-four and just now getting picked up from a feeder team. It's not common, but there are reasons for it. Reasons I don't plan on disclosing unless they're absolutely necessary.

Coach Applegate seems pleased with my performance as he taps my helmet, which I remove as we skate off the ice and head to the locker rooms.

"You did good out there. Keep up the intensity and maybe you'll get some playtime during the Islanders game." My heart beats rapidly as he says it, and I take a deep inhale.

"Thanks, Coach." He nods his head and walks away. The concept of even getting to play in an NHL game always seemed so far-fetched. Even after all the lengths I've gone to get to where I am, I still didn't believe it would ever happen.

I make sure to hang back on the ice long enough for mostly everyone to finish their shower before heading into the locker room. The only people left are Mikael Martel and Alexi Bandnin, probably the two scariest fuckers on the team. I swallow thickly as I undress and head into the shower. Thankfully, they're empty except for me. I bring my own wash, deodorant, and scent blockers with me so I can put them on immediately after my shower.

The other guys don't bother me, and I shower quickly using all my own products. Fuck, I feel tired, but there's no time for that shit. Not when I've finally made it to the big leagues. I need to suck up any ounce of pain, discomfort, or internal struggles. I refuse to be what biology made me. I'm completely washed and have all my deodorizers on as I step out of the locker room. Bandnin and Martel are still talking as I head to my locker to get dressed.

"You did good, new guy," Martel says.

"Owen," I reply. "Or Connery."

"Confident that we need to remember your name?" Martel says, and Bandnin elbows him in the chest. "What? It's called hazing. You literally took him out during the scrimmage."

"And he took it well," Alexi says, and I swallow. I turn to my locker that doesn't have a name plate yet, dropping the towel and getting dressed.

"See you tomorrow," I hear Martel say as he leaves the locker room, and I'm left alone with Alexi. I don't know why I feel on high alert. My sweatpants are on and I'm throwing the henley over my head when he leans against the locker next to me.

"You're a Beta?" he says with his head tilted to the side.

"Yeah," I reply, grabbing a ball cap and throwing it over my semi-wet hair.

"Interesting."

"Plenty of Betas play professional sports."

"Of course," he says, nodding his head. He leans forward, and I swear to fuck he's attempting to scent me.

"The fuck are you doing?" I say to him, grabbing my shit off the floor and tossing it over my shoulder.

"Nothing, *sólnyshka.*"

"Alright then, bye." My tone is shitty, but I don't care. If I let these guys think I have something to hide or that I can't take the heat, it will all go to shit.

He waves his hand at me as I leave, I feel off-center from that weird as fuck encounter. I jump into my car and head to the Airbnb I booked for the month. My contract is very loose. There's basically no guarantee that the Foxes won't up and cut me tomorrow, so I wanted something flexible. So for the next month, this is what I call home.

It's a small basement apartment. The woman upstairs is elderly, and her daughter helped set this up so she has additional income. It's small and cozy in its own way. I feel exhausted, and my shoulder hurts slightly from that hit from Alexi. But there's no way that I'm going to let this slow me down.

I take a second shower when I get home, removing all the deodorizers and letting my own scent flourish. It's already subdued because of the amount of medication I'm taking, but sometimes it's nice to just be myself. Even if I might hate this part of me with every fiber of my being. It's a part of who I am, and I know that if I don't give into some of its facets, it will haunt me.

The bed in the basement apartment is comfortable as I lie down. I swear I sleep like the dead and don't wake up until my alarm goes off.

———

Practice isn't until ten today, so I take the opportunity to explore some of the town. The area I'm renting from is very walkable, and I find myself wandering down the street until I find a small café. The door chimes with my arrival, and I'm assaulted with the scent of fresh coffee beans and baked goods.

I wait in line and look over the menu while I wait. Suddenly, a tall woman runs into me, some of her coffee hitting my forearm.

"Oh, fuck, I'm so sorry," she says. Quickly she puts down her drink and her purse. She's wearing light blue scrubs, and her dark hair is in a messy bun on the top of her head. A fistful of napkins is in her hands as she cleans off my forearm before looking at me. "Are you okay? It didn't burn you?"

I shake my head and smile at her. She's clearly an Alpha, smelling like oranges and cinnamon; it's an extremely pleasant scent. Possibly on the verge of too appealing, but I shove it down. I'm extremely grateful for all the scent blockers that I'm on for my own scent, and it helps with my ability to scent others.

"I'm fine, seriously."

"I'm so sorry. I was looking at my phone and wasn't paying attention. Let me get your coffee."

"I'm fine, really."

"What would you like?" she asks, not taking no for an answer.

"A hazelnut latte," I say. She smiles and shakes her head. "What?"

"It's my best friend's drink of choice. Go take a seat at that table, and I'll bring it over," she says in a tone that warrants no discussion. I'm honestly still a little tired, and she's getting me a free drink, so I oblige and take a seat at the table she directed.

It takes a few minutes, but she comes back to the table with her drink, mine and two baked goods.

"Would you like the blueberry scone or the chocolate croissant?"

I give her a look that says she's being dramatic and take the blueberry scone. She smiles and takes the croissant. She dips a piece in her coffee before eating it.

"I've never seen you here," she says.

I shake my head. "Just moved here for work."

"It's a great area. I love it here. Oh, where are my manners? I'm Piper." She holds out her hand, and I shake it. Her hands are soft; her nails are short and have no nail polish on them.

"I'm Owen."

"Nice to meet you, Owen."

"You too, except for the third degree burn on my arm." She gasps and looks at my arm, and I shake my head and laugh. "I'm kidding. I'm fine."

"Don't make me take the scone back."

I take a massive bite of it, showing that her threat has no bite to it, and she shakes her head.

"So where do you work?" I ask her.

"At the hospital, I'm a surgical resident."

"Oh, wow, that must be a lot of work."

"Yeah," she says quietly as she stirs her coffee but doesn't drink it. I decide to not push that line of questioning any further.

"Since you're a New Haven expert, where are the best places to eat?" She lists off multiple places, most of them I will forget as I can't help but stare at her animated face. She's beautiful in more ways than I would like to admit. But if there was ever a time to not get distracted by an Alpha, it's now.

I plan my escape route, but I'm saved by Piper's pager. She

looks at the device, and her brows furrow. "I've got to head out. Maybe I'll see you around sometime."

I nod and give her a wave. I make a mental note to avoid the coffee shop with the beautiful, friendly Alpha in the future.

My phone buzzes in my pocket, and when I see the name, I groan and scrub my face. I sigh dramatically and hit the answer button.

"Hey, Mom."

"Owen Gregory Connery, what in the actual fuck do you think you're doing?"

I rub my forehead with the palm of my hand, and there's a massive pause of awkward silence. "Mom—"

"Do they know, Owen?"

"Mom—"

"You could get hurt, Owen. You could get so seriously hurt. I don't even want to think about all the medication you're on right now to hide who you are. Baby, you're perfect. You don't need to hide this. "

"You know if the NHL knew, they wouldn't let me play. I need this. I really fucking need this."

"Owen, you know I know how talented you are, sweetie. But what is the cost going to be?"

I sigh and rub my eye sockets. I love my mom more than I love anything or any person. But I really don't care to be coddled right now.

"I finally made it. I'm finally living my dream. Isn't that what you've always wanted for me?"

"I always knew you could achieve anything. But I'm worried. Can you blame me?"

"All of my medications are prescribed," I lie, and I hear her groan over the phone.

"But they don't know."

"They can't know."

"I swear to fucking god, Owen. If you so much as sprain an ankle, I'm driving to Connecticut and dragging you home. Or I'll tell them everything."

I groan over the phone, knowing she's completely serious. It's why I didn't tell her that I got bumped up to the Foxes.

"I promise I'll be careful. I'm taking care of myself."

I hear her click her tongue over the phone, and she sighs. "Okay. Don't make me drive out there."

"Well, I was hoping you would for a game."

"Such a smart ass," she says, and I laugh.

"Where do you think I learned it from?"

She sighs, and I know she's irritated with me. She loves me enough to know what a dream this is. I would never forgive her if she ruined this for me, and she knows that.

"I expect to hear from you at least once a week."

"Okay."

"And your brother would like to hear from you."

I groan, and my mother doesn't comment. I know it's not Max's fault that he got the better end of our genetics and got to live out my dream. But I can't help being a jealous asshole.

My mom breaks the silence. "You know, you'll run into him eventually."

The thought of running into him on the ice has me wanting to quit right now, but I won't. The chances of me playing during games aren't even that high right now. So we will cross that bridge if or when we have to.

"Then I'll see him when I see him."

"I really wish you two would get along."

"I know, Mom." I feel guilty. The fact is it's on both of us. I hate Max because he has everything I want, and Max hates me for hogging all of our parents' attention.

"I love you, and I better hear from you within a week."

"Love you too." The call ends, and my head is aching by the time I'm leaving the coffee shop. I've got about an hour to kill before practice, and the only thing I want to do is sleep, but I don't. Instead, I go for a light jog before I head to the training facility.

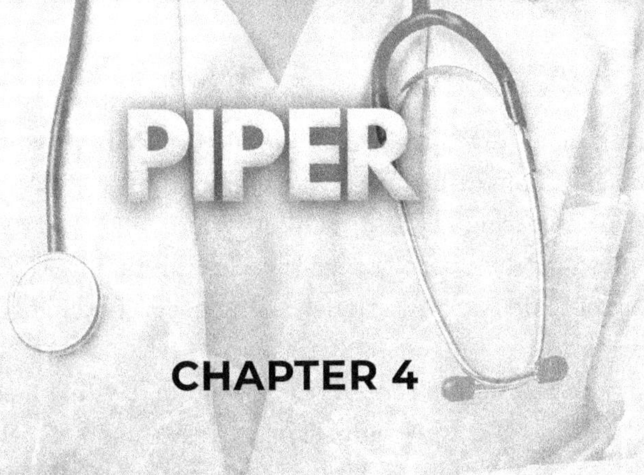

# PIPER

## CHAPTER 4

These last two shifts have been a true fucking nightmare. Not only have I been working with Shuana, but it seems like I'm so knee deep in paperwork that I'm not even practicing medicine. I do paperwork and spend less time observing and assisting in surgeries, hardly any patient care, which is where I know I should be.

Even though I'm feeling like shit, there's no reason to wallow in it. So I stick to my routine and head to Alpha Fitness. It's the one place I feel like I can clear my head. Besides staying in shape, I love the burst of energy working out seems to give me. I'm not overly fit by any means, but I've got a good amount of muscle at this point. I'm lean and happy with my appearance, so now it's all about maintenance.

I'm lifting, listening to *Captain Hook* by Megan Thee Stallion, when there's a hulking presence behind me.

*Alexi fucking Bandnin.*

I've never seen him here before. Why would he have a gym membership when I know for a fact he works out at the Foxes' facility? I do my best to ignore him, not glancing at him in the mirror or giving him any attention. Which is proving to be more and more difficult as I watch him lift his weights.

He's wearing a tight, white T-shirt, and I can see his nipples and the outline of his muscles through it. This is definitely not fair. Alexi is seriously using everything in his arsenal to break me.

I can't lie. Wouldn't it be nice to fool around with someone and release some of this tension? Having a few moments where my mind will just shut up and my body takes the wheel sounds like bliss. But I'm not sure it could just be physical with Alexi. Maybe I should go back to the coffee shop and run into that cute Beta.

It's not that I think Beta's are disposable. I love Beta men for many reasons, but none of them have captured my attention the way Alexi Bandnin seems to, and it's fucking terrifying.

I'm in the middle of doing a weighted squat, and I can't help but notice how much Alexi is looking at my ass while I do it. Should it feel as satisfying as it does? Probably not, but the way this man looks at me, *fuck.*

I drop the weights on the ground and spin around. "Alexi, what are you doing here?"

He puts his headphones around his neck, and I do the same. "I heard this gym was the best, so I wanted to try it out."

"Likely story," I say, about to turn around, but he takes a step forward, and while my mind is telling me to take a step back, I don't. I can't help but lean closer to him. Alexi smells like clove and ginger. It's masculine and thick, and I've never been so attracted to a scent in my life. He smells extra fucking good right now because he's been sweating.

"You know, there is a good smoothie place down the street."

"I'm not getting a smoothie with you, Alexi."

"Why not?" he asks with an arch of his eyebrow. The veins on his forearms and biceps are popping and fuck, I can't think around him. I've never felt less confident around a man in my life.

"It's not a good idea, Alexi."

"Why not, *malyshka*?"

"I don't have time for a relationship right now," I blurt out, and I watch as a huge grin slowly takes over his face.

"I was asking about a smoothie, not going steady." I shake my head at his outdated term. I know my face is probably red from working out, but he's just made it even redder. I'm not sure what to say, but he speaks again. "It's just a smoothie, Piper."

"Okay." I'm not sure why I give in.

Maybe it's because Alexi is endearing and extremely hot, or because I'm so uncharacteristically flustered over this man the answer just slipped from my lips. He smiles and puts his weights down. There's a nice trail of sweat from the collar of his shirt to his belly button, and it takes everything in me to not lick my lips. It really should be illegal for a man to be this big and attractive.

"I'll meet you at the entrance in fifteen minutes?"

I nod my head like an idiot, and with a parting look, we head to our respective changing areas.

I'm quick with getting showered and changed. I've at least been genetically blessed with thinner, pin straight hair. So I wash it and half blow dry it; it will dry on its own shortly. I debate putting on makeup.

Fucking hell, Piper. Get it together.

I'm wearing my scrubs so I can head right to work afterwards, and I look at myself in the mirror. It's hard for me not to notice the bags under my eyes or how pale I look. When's the last time I just spent the day outside? I shake off the feeling and compartmentalize everything, just as I always do.

Daddy issues are in their very own large box. The need to please is in another. My career box has been the most daunting box lately, but I keep it locked up tight. I'm already on this course. There's no way to… fuck.

I mentally wrap a chain around the career box and seal it tight. I take a breath and walk out of the locker room to the front door.

When I spot a wet haired Alexi smiling broadly at the front entrance, I can feel the relationship box rattling in my head. I smile back at him and wonder how I'm supposed to stop Alexi Bandnin from ripping that box wide open.

———

Alexi and I fight over who will buy the smoothies. He said that since it was his suggestion, he obviously should be paying, and well, I can't fight with that logic.

I got the espresso high protein vanilla, and Alexi ordered something extremely healthy. We sit at opposite sides of the table together, and I sip my smoothie, not knowing exactly what to say. He breaks the silence before I do.

"I like your scrubs," he smiles.

I shake my head and smirk. "I think you have the better uniform."

"Mmm… you might be right on that one."

"How is the season going?" I ask, keep it normal. Let's not drift back to uniforms. Because then I'll just think about how good he looks on the ice, and that is not a good way to keep the relationship box shut.

"It is still early. It's been a frustrating season, but I'm hopeful we will get it together."

"Anders is too humble to say it, but I don't think he realized just how good he was."

Alexi shrugs his shoulders. "He's doing something more important now."

My vagina and heart are in complete agreement over the preciousness of that statement, and I have to hold back from biting my lip.

"They're all really good dads. I'm glad Charlotte has them."

"She's just as lucky to have you as a friend."

I can't help the blush that takes over my face, and I shake my head. "I'm just as lucky to have Charlotte. She's saved me more times than I can count."

His eyebrows furrow, but I'm thankful that he doesn't pry. I'm definitely not ready to open that box. It stays tucked in that dark corner of my mind.

"What about you? Who's your best friend?"

"I quite like Mikael," he says with a shrug. "I've some friends in Dallas, but it's hard to stay close in this profession."

"And in Russia?" I ask, so curious about how he ended up here.

He smiles and shakes his head. "I go back at least once a year during the offseason. My ma wouldn't accept anything less. I still have friends from childhood there, but it's difficult."

I nod my head and wonder how hard it was for him to leave his home country to play in the US.

"Did you know English before you moved here?" Obviously his English is great, if not accented. Every now and then he says something odd, but it's more endearing than anything else.

"Not much, no. Luckily there were other Russians on the team. It took a while to learn."

I nod my head, and I appreciate how honest and easily he answers questions. *Why can't I be the same way?*

"How much longer do you have in your program?" he asks. I swallow and sigh.

"Probably another five years."

He whistles and takes a sip of his smoothie. "But you will be saving lives. It's a very important job." I shrug my shoulders, and he notices immediately. "I know a little something about giving up time for my career and nothing else, if you would like to talk about it."

I take a sip of my smoothie to give myself a moment to think. He's picked up on this small piece of me that I've been trying to hold back—even with Charlotte. I think she knows I struggle with this specialty but not the magnitude of just how much it's affecting me.

"I'm not sure if it's about the length of the program."

"Then what is it about?" His brown eyes are soft as he asks, and I have to blink a few times so I don't go and sit on his lap and tell him my whole life story. Getting smoothies was a bad idea. I groan internally, liking and hating how much I enjoy being around him.

My pager beeps, and I give him a soft smile. I look down, and it's non-emergent, but I've got to get the fuck out of here.

"Sorry, emergency," I lie, holding up the pager.

"Of course."

"Thanks again for the smoothie."

"Anytime, *malyshka*." Oh, I'm so Googling that shit later. I wave him off and nearly run out of the smoothie shop.

The cool air hits my face, and it's like a splash of cold water. I cannot let myself get cornered by Alexi again.

The walk to the hospital is short, and I put my stuff in my locker. I pull my hair into a ponytail, then put on my white coat and my pink stethoscope. I'm on my way to rounds when Shuana comes to walk right next to me.

"You missed a serious GSW to the neck last night. I thought he was going to kick it, seriously. Dr. Hugh performed an emergency surgery, and he let me close!" She's bragging, and I should feel jealous, and I am. But not about her closing the surgery, it's the fact that she got to save somebody. The adrenaline of being the first to touch that patient and be the deciding factor of them living—that is what I'm jealous of.

"That's cool, Shuana."

"More than fucking cool, Blake," she says, using my last name. "I saw him remove a bullet from someone's fucking vertebra."

"I believe you."

"God, you're no fun. What crawled up your ass?"

*You...* you did, Shuana. Now can you leave me the fuck alone?

We're luckily saved by Dr. Hugh handing out cases. "Blake, you're with Mayfield. Hoft, you're with me. Mann, you're with Dr. Paulson, and, Croxford, you're with Dr. Hess." There's no other direction. We just take our files and head toward our assigned attendings.

Shuana has a huge grin on her face from him assigning her to himself, like she's now the head of neurosurgery's favorite. Like congratulations for just being on call last night, you smug bitch.

With my files in my hand, I head down to the neuro unit. At least I'm with Dr. Mayfield today, one of the more tolerable attendings.

"Dr. Blake," she says with a smile as she messes with her tablet. "Today is going to be a rough one." I take a deep breath and nod, pulling up today's cases. She motions her hand for me to update her on what I know.

"Clara Henderson, age twenty-two, survived ovarian cancer three years ago. She now has a metastatic brain tumor. She's had radiation, which has made a difference, but it is pressing against the temporal lobe and needs to be removed."

"You will be assisting and observing the surgery. We're scheduled for tomorrow. Please check her vitals and make sure you are prepared for the craniotomy."

"Of course, thank you, Dr. Mayfield."

She nods, not even looking up at me as I head to the patient's room.

"Hi, Clara, I'm Dr. Blake. I'll be getting you ready for surgery tomorrow," I say softly. I make sure to leave the overhead lighting off as I speak with her. One thing I've learned in neuro is how horrific hospital lighting is.

"It doesn't matter," Clara says, looking out the window.

"How are you feeling?" I ask her.

"Like I'm going to die tomorrow," she says glumly. I'm already planning on staying the night at the hospital tonight, so I'll be ready for the surgery tomorrow. But another part of me wants to stay and monitor Clara's emotional wellbeing.

"Has Dr. Mayfield gone over the treatment plan with you?"

"It's for the best, you know. To just die on the table instead of having this come back. I can't even think straight," she says, tears welling in her eyes and gliding down her face.

"Hey," I say, touching her shoulder gently. "Dr. Mayfield is the best. If she didn't think she could get it all or improve your quality of life, she wouldn't do it."

"What life? I'm twenty-two years old. I'm a burden on my family, my life hasn't been normal since I was seventeen, what's the point?"

I take a deep breath, my heart breaking for her. How is one person supposed to take so much pain in such a short amount of time?

"Do you have anything you're passionate about?" I ask her. She blinks at me, not expecting the question.

"I really wanted to go to fashion school," she says. and I smile back at her.

"Then you'll go to fashion school. Dr. Mayfield is going to do your craniotomy tomorrow, and depending on the outcome, you might not need anymore radiation. But even if you do, we will monitor the tumor, and you'll be able to live a full life, Clara."

She shakes her head, and I know she needs a more positive outlook for tomorrow. It breaks my heart that she doesn't feel like she has a reason to fight. I know the surgery is not minor, that her tumor is large and so many things could go wrong, but I just want her to have something to look forward to. To not spend her last day before surgery feeling like life isn't worth living.

"Thanks for trying. But can you just take my blood and leave?" she says. I take a deep breath and nod.

"I'll have your nurse take your vitals and come and check on you shortly."

"Okay," she sighs and looks back out the window.

# OWEN

## CHAPTER 5

I'm on a serious high after practice. We drive to New York for the game tomorrow, and I can't help but feel like I'm going to get to play. No offense to Johannson—the current starting goalie—but I know I'm better.

While I'm nearly dead on my feet, there's no fucking way I'm cooking, so I head to the pho restaurant that Piper suggested. No, I haven't been thinking relentlessly about the tall, sweet Alpha. It would be nice to have a friend outside of the hockey team as well, but I'm used to being alone—but maybe I shouldn't be.

I feel like a sad little bitch when I open the door to the restaurant. It's small and cozy, only about five total tables. You order at the front and take a seat wherever you want. I order the pho with brisket and bubble tea. The waitress hands me my number, and when I turn around, I see her. Like I fucking manifested her with my thoughts. The circles under her eyes are dark, and her cheeks are stained red, like she's been crying.

I should walk past, go sit at my own table and act like I don't see her. But something is calling me to go sit down next to her.

"Is this seat taken?" I ask. She shakes her head no and gives me a watery smile. "Rough day?"

"Yeah, really rough."

"Do you want to talk about it?" I ask, not knowing what else to say. She looks at me questioningly. She wipes her face and stares down at her pho before looking up at me.

"I lost a patient today."

"I'm sorry," I say. What the fuck do you even say when someone tells you that?

"It's not the first time or the last. But… she was twenty-two. She was so defeated, and I… it's just hard."

"I can only imagine."

She eats her food, and she doesn't seem irritated by my presence, so I just sit in silence as my food comes. We're both just eating, two lonely people eating at a takeaway place.

"How is your new job going?" she asks, interrupting the silence.

"Really good, actually. I don't want to jinx anything, but we'll see how things go this weekend." Her smile is genuine. Even though she's in pain, she's still able to be happy for me.

"Superstitious?"

"Something like that," I say with a smirk.

"I know something about that. A lot of surgeons are very superstitious. Things have to be a certain way before surgery, special scrub caps, things like that. Some surgeons won't even perform a surgery if a patient tells them they think they will die. "

"And you?" I ask her.

She shakes her head. "No, nothing like that on my end."

"That's probably for the best if you're opening people up." She shrugs her shoulders while she stirs her pho mindlessly.

She changes tactics, clearly done talking about work. "You

know there's a Christmas market that starts this weekend. It's about two blocks that way." She points to the left.

"I'll have to check it out."

"If you need a friend to go with, let me know." *Friends are good*, I could use a friend.

"I'd need a way to contact you," I say.

She shakes her head. "Of course." She takes out her phone, and I give her my number. Then she texts me so I have hers. She gives me her full name, Piper Blake, and for some reason, at that moment, Connecticut becoming home feels a little bit real.

We finish up our meal. The conversation is light, and I'm thankful for it. I'm not being grilled by my mom or having an awkward conversation with one of my new teammates. Talking to Piper is easy. And while she may be beautiful, I think being her friend could be something I need to center myself in this new place.

It's an awkward half-wave for both of us as we part, going different directions on the street. I try to not let myself get too excited. This feeling of everything coming together for me, it almost feels too good to be true.

———

I take the backseat of the bus, feeling like an imposter as I look around at the talent. I give myself a mental pep talk. *I'm talented too, so I'm here for a reason.*

I expect everyone to leave me to myself, my headphones blasting Slipknot as Alexi comes and sits next to me. Out of respect for the captain, I take the headphones off and hear what he has to say.

"Hello, *sólnyshka.*"

"Are you calling me a prick or something?" I ask, and he belts out a laugh.

"No. Definitely not. Are you ready for today?"

"I'm just the backup."

He grunts and shakes his head. "You need to be ready, are you ready?" I nod my head, and I'm ready to put my headphones on when he speaks again. "You've done well at practice, but an NHL game is going to feel different than the minors. It's louder, the guys are bigger, it can be intimidating." I shrug my shoulders, even though he's inciting the fear of God into me right now. "Just treat the warm-up like you're playing, yes?"

"Yes, I can do that."

"Good boy," he says, nudging my shoulder with his. I swallow thickly, thankful as fuck that I can't perfume. Not only because it would be incredibly fucking embarrassing, but it would also ruin everything.

"I'll be ready," I tell him, and he smiles.

When I say that Alexi Bandnin is the most intimidating person I've ever met, I might mean it. It's not because he's mean or scary, it's because he's so fucking nice while being so goddamn big. Like, who gave him the right?

Eli and Mikael are sitting in the same row as us, and they are bickering when Alexi shoves Mikael's arm.

"Stop arguing with your brother-husband before the game."

"Shut the fuck up, Bandnin," Mikael says back.

"Well, if that's how you talk to your brother-husband, then I understand why he's irritated with you."

Eli laughs, and I have to hide one in the crook of my arm.

"When are you going to fucking retire anyway?" Mikael jokes.

"What and leave you all to your own devices? Never."

"Oh, okay, old man."

Alexi laughs and lets Mikael's insult roll of his back. Alexi is definitely one of the oldest players in the NHL, but it's wrong to call him old when he looks like *that*.

"Ignore him, Alexi. We will push you with a walker around the ice if we have to," Eli says, and there are another round of laughs on the bus.

Alexi grins and stands up, holding the headrest of the seat in front of us. "Would anyone on this bus like to challenge me to a duel?"

An eruption of laughter takes over the bus, my own included, and damn, it feels good to laugh.

"A fucking duel? We're not in the union, comrade."

"I don't see anyone raising their hands!" Alexi says with a booming voice, and that's when the laughter dies down. "Now, are we going to sing the fucking song or what?"

Mikael groans, and Eli smiles, standing up as the whole bus starts singing *We Will Rock You* by Queen. It's the most cliché thing in the world. But if it's a team tradition for away games, then it is what it is. I join in, belting out the tune and slapping my thighs to the beat. Alexi is still standing and gives me a gentle smile before continuing his awful rendition of the song.

———

We've just finished warm ups. The ice at UBS Arena is complete trash; it's watery, and I know the ice crew members will have to shovel the slush and ice off frequently. I'm on the bench, fully dressed, eager, and hopeful. Johannson wasn't looking too hot in practice, and I have a feeling if he lets in an unnecessary goal, then I might just get my chance.

My dream of playing in the NHL is solely based on me

wanting this guy to fuck up—which I know is wrong. But to be honest, I don't care. Johannson is an Alpha, so he's had the physical ability given to him genetically. I've had to work endlessly, destroy my body, and put aside everything for this. Not that Johannson doesn't deserve it, but it's so close, and I want it.

Coach wasn't kidding, the Islanders are playing like shit, and our front line is taking full advantage. Alexi on left wing, Eli at center, and Mikael is playing left defender. They are kicking the game off strong, showing we didn't come here to mess around.

Alexi emphasizes it early as he pushes the Islanders' defender against the glass, his shoulder pushed against the opposing team member's back. I can't hear anything from where I am, but I can tell that words are being exchanged.

Alexi wins the battle between them and passes to Eli, who slap shots the puck right into the Islanders' net. The guys on the ice huddle together to celebrate, and the announcer sounds off the goal. Fuck, I want that, I want to be a part of it so bad.

There's a lot of back and forth after the first goal. I can tell that the watery ice doesn't help. Most of the guys' shins are drenched in slush, and when Mikael goes tumbling on the ice with another player, his whole jersey is soaked when he's back on his feet.

There's a stoppage of play, and the ice crew skates on, pushing the slosh to the side entrance. Coach is talking in irritated tones about how he wants to finish the period with one more goal, anything less being unacceptable. The defense line gets kudos, and Johannson gets nothing because he hasn't had to do much besides prevent some icing and stand there.

Once the game is back in play, it's like watching a different opposing team. They're playing with more intensity—hitting harder and skating faster. We're keeping up, but the game feels a lot more even now. It's when they get a break away, two on one, skating fast down the rink. I see the shot before it happens, but Johannson doesn't. The puck hits the back of the net, and the buzzer sounds dramatically, and all the Islanders fans are cheering as their team boasts about the goal. There's only a minute and a half left in the period when Coach leans over to me.

"Get ready to go in," he says. There's nothing left to do but mentally prepare, and that's what I do. Hyping myself and getting ready to take this on, the thing I've wanted more than anything.

The intermission is short. Coach is hard as fuck on the front line for not getting more scoring opportunities. He doesn't even acknowledge Johannson, who seems to have already recognized his fate.

I'm a dick, but his loss is my gain, and we're taking it.

"You got this, *sólnyshka*," Alexi says, bumping his gloved fist to my helmet. I've really got to look up what that means, but I genuinely have no clue on how to spell it.

I'm in my net, cutting the crease and stretching. I'll be fucking damned if anything short of a masterfully placed puck is getting in this net for the rest of the game.

Music blasts in the stadium, and my heart races as the puck is in play. I don't keep my eye off it, always ready. There are a few moments that I think I'm going to see action, but our team is playing harder after a mixture of frustration and having our asses chewed out by Coach.

It's when number thirteen zooms down the ice that I know it's my time to finally shine. My defense is hot on his tails, and he shoots too early. I easily glove the puck, and I think I'm waiting for the ref to get the puck when number thirteen skates right into me, sending me to the ice.

I might be shorter than most of these guys, might not have

the genetic disposition to build muscle. But I've done everything I can to make up for it. I punch him in his helmet, but it's not only me who's on him now. Alexi hits him hard in the chest and curses in Russian at him. The refs break it up quickly, and no calls are made.

Rule number one of hockey: don't fuck with the goalie. And it's nice to know this new team has my back. I'm back on my skates when Alexi palms the back of my helmet with his gloved hand.

"Knew you were going to be a good boy, Connery." He taps my helmet one more time before giving me a massive grin and skating off.

Rule number two of hockey: keep your head in the game, and don't think about how fucking hot the team captain is.

## CHAPTER 6

I force my way to the back of the bus. We're all feeling the rush after winning the game, and coach promised us we could stop at Tomlinsons to get burgers, so besides celebrating the win, we're also hungry and tired.

Owen is sitting by himself—perfect.

His dirty-blond hair is still slightly wet and pushed back, and his navy suit is tight against his frame. He shifts uncomfortably, like he can feel me staring at him. The Beta really proved himself tonight. Not another goal was scored against us, and we scored four more. We're on a high, and he's a huge part of that.

So why does he look so glum?

"Cheer up, Connery. You fucking showed up today."

The left side of his lip tilts up, but he doesn't fully smile. "It was nothing," he says, waving me off.

"Nothing? You just played your first real NHL game and didn't let a fucking puck in." He shrugs his shoulders, so I take matters into my own hands. "Let's hear it for the fucking rookie! Zero goals in the last two periods." The bus erupts in barks, cheers, and hoots. I watch as Owen's pretty face goes pink. Not that Betas can't be beautiful, but the stoic goalie is something else.

I smack his shoulder and sit down next to him.

"You have quite the personality."

"That I do," I reply, stretching out widely so my knee is touching his. He doesn't shift, so I leave my leg firmly in place.

The new goalie has been an anomaly since we met, and something doesn't sit right with me. While I think he's proven himself at tonight's game, something still feels off. Like he's trying to not draw attention to himself, or he's hiding something.

I want to crack his shell. Just like I want to crack a very tall, beautiful brunette who I need to stalk at some point this week.

"So how do you feel?" I ask him quietly enough that the other players don't hear.

That small half smirk takes over his face, until he smiles. It's a soft smile, no teeth, but I'm intrigued by it nonetheless. "Fucking amazing," he says quietly.

"There we fucking go." I squeeze his thigh, and he stiffens under my touch. I remove my hand, and Owen clears his throat.

Coach is the last on the bus, his arms resting on the two rows as he grins. "That's what I'm fucking talking about. Let's get you boys some goddamn cheeseburgers." He grins before sitting down.

Eli and Mikael are sitting in the same row as on the way here. They have their phones out and are video calling Charlotte, Anders, and Katie. I smile as I watch them talk to their daughter. I'm not sure if I want kids of my own, but having a pack has been weighing on me hard lately. I think the only other thing that would make me retire, besides winning the Cup, would be solidifying a pack.

Right now, I know for sure Piper is going to be in my pack.

I don't care what the good doctor says, she's going to be mine. I'd be lying if I said the Beta next to me didn't stir something up as well. But I'm not really sure who is going to be the hardest to convince.

The good thing is, I love a fucking challenge.

————

I see why Piper goes to Alpha Fitness. I absolutely did not need a membership since I use the Foxes' facility, but this gym is top of the line. I'm nothing but persistent as I see her lifting weights.

She's so beautiful. I like her in scrubs and the few times I've seen her dress up. But Piper in tight yoga pants and a clingy T-shirt is probably my favorite. I have to use all my mental strength to calm my dick down as she bends over to pick up weights. Her long, dark ponytail nearly hits the floor as she bends. I've had too many thoughts about her ponytail.

I'm truly wondering when my persistence turns into something creepy. Nothing less than Piper telling me to fuck off will do.

I let her get most of her workout done. I'm lightly walking on the treadmill when I notice she starts doing squats—my favorite. I turn the machine off and make my way over. Her eyes connect with mine in the mirror before I'm even at the lifting area. Seems like my adorable Alpha might just be watching me too.

She takes her headphones off and spins around. I couldn't really see her face from where I was before, but when I look at her now, I'm concerned. She has signs of being tired, and she looks paler than usual.

Not being a complete moron, I don't ask her. I just arch an eyebrow at her.

"Need a spotter?"

She scoffs. "You'd love that, wouldn't you?"

"Very much."

"Has anyone told you that you're a huge flirt?"

"Not lately, no," I say with a smile and take the bench next to her, adding more weight onto the sides. I lie down on the bench and do a few repetitions. Am I being a sneaky fuck and making my scent thicker? Undoubtedly. The way Piper shifts her weight notes that she's not unaffected either.

"I can't get a smoothie today."

"Presumptuous. I didn't ask to get a smoothie."

"You know what—" She stops mid sentence and I drop the weight on the stand and stand up. I'm in her space, so close that she has to look up to speak to me.

"What, *malyshka?*"

"Oh, don't you *malyshka* me," she says, pointing at my chest. Her Russian is shit, and it makes me smile. "I looked that up. I'm not your baby girl. I'm an Alpha, and I'm no one's baby girl." My grin spreads even further.

"You could be." She sputters a little bit. I'm not sure what Piper is used to. Maybe male Betas who pander to her demands and don't give her shit? It feels like it as she blinks at me in annoyance.

"I told you, I don't have time for a relationship right now."

"What do you have time for?" I'm not proud of the line of thinking, but I'll take whatever she gives, and I'd be lying if I said I didn't think I could eventually convince her that we belong together.

"What?" she asks, looking at me suspiciously.

"What do you have time for, Piper?"

She blinks and licks her lips as she looks at me. "It's been a hard week," she says, and I'm not sure where the conversation is going, but I let her continue her thought. "I just want to not think."

My beautiful Alpha needs her head cleared. *I can do that.*

I grab her wrist and head to the men's locker room.

"Alexi, what are you doing?"

"What do you have time for?"

I look around the locker room. Luckily, Piper chooses to come to the gym before the sun is even out, which means the place is nearly empty. Her footsteps keep up with mine as I pull back the shower curtain and push her in first before blocking her in with my body.

"Do you want me to clear your head, *malyshka?*" She swallows, and her dark green eyes stare back into mine. "Do you want me to turn that big, beautiful brain of yours off?" I ask her, not touching, but we're so close I can feel her body heat.

She licks her lips, and I track the motion. She nods her head, and that's all I need. My hands are cupping both sides of her jaw as I press her back against the shower tile. Her lips are as soft as I remember, and she kisses me back eagerly, just like she did last New Year's.

Her one hand has my T-shirt in a tight fist, and the other is gripping at the hair at the nape of my neck. She smells amazing, her rich Alpha scent of orange peels and cinnamon. She's not an Omega which makes her scent being so thick even more appealing. She's not turned on because of her baser instincts or her hormones driving the show. Piper Blake wants me, and maybe it's not at the capacity in which I want her, but I'll take what I can get.

I know we don't have all the time in the world in this small shower, but I can't find the will to stop kissing her. As much as I want to touch her everywhere, kissing Piper gives me a purpose I haven't felt in a long time. I know that Piper doesn't *need* me. But fuck if I don't want Piper to *want* me as much as I want her.

A feminine moan escapes her as I press our bodies together as we kiss. Her strong thighs encase my larger one as I grind my hard length against her. I would do anything to sink inside of her right now, but that's not the plan. If I'm going to get Piper Blake to fall in love with me, I'm going to need her to keep coming back for more.

I press my thigh harder against her core, and her head lightly thuds against the tile, her throat beautifully exposed as I trail kisses against the exposed skin.

Her hand in my hair tightens as she grinds against my leg. Her eyes are closed, and I take a moment to stop kissing her throat and watch her. The way she moves against my body and how at this moment she seems so carefree. The stress I saw in her earlier ceases to exist as I glide my hand between us, separating her from my thigh and cupping her pussy, the clinging material hiding how wet she is from me.

"*Vy khotite priyti na moyu ruku, malyshka?*"

"What?" she says, opening her eyes and blinking. I realize I must have said it in Russian.

"Do you want to come on my hand, *malyshka?*"

"Please," she says sweetly. I can't help but to smile at the way I've made this Alpha putty in my hands.

With both hands, I slide her yoga pants down mid thigh. She has on the simplest pair of white panties on, and I like that. That she wasn't planning on getting finger fucked in the locker room, that she had no idea that this was how she would be starting her morning.

I keep her panties on and play with her outside of the material. I can tell she's enjoying my touch but wants me to move them to the side. But I don't give her what she wants, at least not right away.

My two fingers work her from the outside of the material until I can feel her wetness soaking them. I smile down at her, and her lips part, ready to say something, but I won't let her ruin this moment with any doubts. I cut her off by leaning forward and taking her lips with mine. At the same time, I push her panties to the side and finally touch her the way she wants.

I swallow her moan, and she bucks her hips against my hand.

I love that every drop of wetness touching my fingers is because I put it there. That I made her pussy this wet from touching and speaking to her. Biology plays a factor, but it's not the driving force. Just two people who are hungry for one another, it makes my cock even harder than it was before. But I can wait. I'll probably use the hand I finger her with to get myself off.

Piper holds my face to hers, and I can't help but smile as she kisses me like she doesn't need to breathe. I can't help but notice she's smiling too. Her smile turns to a moan as I slide two fingers inside of her and rub the heel of my palm against her clit.

Her hips are bucking into my hand, and her hands don't leave my face. Her eyes open as she stares at me. I can feel her cunt gripping me, and I want to watch as she comes undone. It's the only fucking thing I need.

"So fucking wet for me, are you going to come against my fingers?"

"Fuck," she says, throwing her head back and closing her eyes.

I tsk and slow down my motions, which makes her grip my hair harder in defiance. "Look at me when I make you come, *malyshka.*"

Surprisingly, she obeys, her green eyes on mine as I rub her clit with purpose. A new pool of wetness meets my hand as she milks my fingers and meets her release. Her pretty little lips are in an O shape, and her eyes glimmer with desire. She pants as her eyes search mine, my hand still deliciously wet on her pulsing cunt.

I watch as reality comes tumbling back to her. Piper looks down where I'm touching her. I remove my hand, and she winces from the overstimulation. She doesn't look at me as she rolls up her yoga pants. Once she's fully clothed, she swallows and finally looks up at me.

She opens her mouth to speak but sputters a little bit, like she's lost for words.

I just grin and take it. I knew Piper wouldn't just give into me after making her come. That something more is going on in that pretty head of hers. She's not an Omega who is begging for my knot or a woman looking for stability. She's independent, making a career for herself. Finding an Alpha isn't something she needs. Something about us potentially being together terrifies her. I don't push her, but I lean forward and kiss the side of her head. "You're welcome, *malyshka.*"

I don't look back as I leave the shower and gather my stuff to leave the gym.

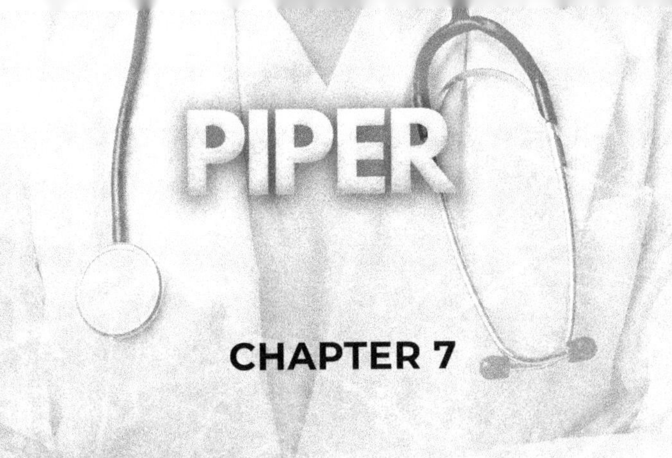

# PIPER

## CHAPTER 7

What in the fuck did I just do? My panties are drenched, and I'm standing in the shower stall like a fucking idiot. Did that man just make me come, giving me such an intense orgasm that my legs feel like jelly, in a gym shower? Not only did he make me come, he didn't ask for anything in return, and the last thing he said before he left was you're welcome. *Fucking you're welcome.*

He definitely did what I asked. For those ten minutes or so, every thought was gone, and all my stress and fears were alleviated. All I could feel was him and his all-consuming presence.

I'm not sure if I regret it or not. It felt good—no, it felt amazing. I've been in the world's longest dry spell, and that was exactly what I needed to help clear my mind. But it's Alexi.

This isn't some one night stand at a nightclub. This is the man I've actively avoided because I seem to lose every functioning brain cell when he's around. I take a few deep breaths and text the one person I know who can help me through this. I have a long shift, and I know I'll be dead on my feet. But if I don't work through this with someone, I'll probably over-think everything and go into an even deeper spiral than I am now.

S.O.fucking.S.

Charlotte: What? Are you okay?

I need a girls night. Tonight.

Charlotte: I have Katie, but we can order pizza and hang out.

I'll bring the booze.

Charlotte: I'm pregnant.

I'll drink for the both of us.

———

I'm with Dr. Mayfield again, and all I want to do is scream. All of her patients lately have been the most depressing cases, and I'm not sure how much more loss I can take. She seems to not even be affected, just onto cutting the next person's brain open.

I'm organizing her charts when she stands next to me. "You know I was in residency with your father?" she asks. I swallow thickly and shake my head. I don't like to bring up my dad, for more reasons than one. But I can't help but wonder if that's why she's been requesting me for her service as of late.

"No, I didn't know that."

"Peter has always been extremely talented. He reached out to me to see how you're doing." I try to hide any major reaction, especially because Mayfield doesn't give away much with her facial expression. "You know, you could use your name to get more around here."

"I don't want to use my dad's name," I reply, and Mayfield gives me a small smirk.

"Good. Now where are we with today's surgery?"

I hand the file over to her, showing that I've already checked with nurses and everything is good with his pre-op. It's another younger patient with an incredibly hard tumor to remove. I breathe in and out and think back to all of my training thus far.

Try to remain impartial, don't get emotionally attached, and stick to the medicine.

All three of those things are so incredibly hard and unrealistic. I'm not sure why I seem to be the only one in my program struggling this much. Shuana can talk about a casualty as if it means nothing, along with other people in the program. But every death, every near-miss, hits me right in the middle of my bleeding heart. It feels like every loss I've experienced while working at this hospital just keeps piling up.

The pain doesn't go away, and it just keeps getting worse. Like each loss is a brick and I'm inside as I build the structure; each loss is another step toward suffocating me completely.

But quitting isn't an option. My life was planned out for me before I was even born, and I have to stay the course. I've already put nearly two years of my life into this program, not to mention all my time in medical school. This isn't something you can just up and decide you don't want to do anymore.

I've got to find new ways to cope. At least that's what I tell myself as I walk into the patient's room.

Dr. Mayfield nods at me to present. "Mitchell Vermette, age twelve, was diagnosed with a pineoblastoma one month ago, and it has already increased in size."

"Are you ready for surgery, Mitchell?" Dr. Mayfield asks.

"I'm ready to fucking sleep," he says in a groggy voice. His mom tsks at him, but there's no heat behind it. The tumor he has is fast growing and specifically affects the part of his brain that handles natural sleep cycles. The pineal gland is right in the center of the brain, so it's going to be an extremely difficult and long surgery.

Mitchell's mom hands him a cup with a straw for him to take a sip, and I nearly lose it at that point, knowing the chances of his survival. He's older than most patients that we see with this tumor, and it's been growing rapidly. I give Mitchell and his mother a small smile before following Dr. Mayfield out of the room.

"How old is that scan?" she asks.

"Three days," I reply.

"Push him up the list. I need one more scan to make sure it hasn't grown any larger."

I nod and order the test, but I can't help the impending doom of going into surgery.

———

My feet hurt as I stand and watch Dr. Mayfield perform the surgery. She lets me assist minimally, but I do more observation than anything. We're going in on hour eight, and it's looking better than I imagined. Most of the tumor is removed, and she only has a little more to go.

I should be able to focus on what's in front of me. Blood and guts aren't the issue; I have no problem with it. It's just the impersonal function of surgery that sometimes bothers me. The callousness of some surgeons when someone's damaged body is lying on a table and hoping that we can fix the problem.

As I stand there and watch how remarkable Dr. Mayfield is,

all I can think about is Mitchell's mother and how relieved she'll be that her son is okay. I know my line of thinking isn't one of a surgeon. How do I change who I fundamentally am so I can handle this career?

Dr. Mayfield lets me help close, and all I feel is relief, but I still want to break down, and I don't know why.

————

Two bottles of wine and two large pizzas are probably overkill, considering it's me, my pregnant best friend, and her toddler. But I have faith that these two bottles will be enough to get me through this conversation.

I don't knock because I have a key to their house, much to Mikael's chagrin. "Hey!" I shout as I walk in the door and lock it behind me. Which is no easy task with two bottles of wine and two pizzas, but I manage.

"We're in the nest," Charlotte says, and I walk downstairs into their basement. Katie is jumping on the bed and doing continuous tumbles on the double king that's built into the floor. Eli installed a pull-down projector screen, and some cartoon with Australian dogs is on the screen.

Charlotte is lying on her side, a massive pillow between her legs. Her hair is in about fifty ponytails, and there's a smattering of makeup all over her face.

"Well, don't you look beautiful."

"Right?" Charlotte replies. "Do you know how hard it is to keep her occupied when it hurts to move?"

I feel Charlotte's forehead, and she wiggles in her seat, still not used to the way I care for her. I'm at least happy she lets her own Alphas do it. "How are you feeling otherwise?"

"Fine," she groans.

"Where's Anders?"

Charlotte smiles and shakes her head. "He found a rec league to play in."

I can't help but laugh. "That doesn't seem fair."

She shrugs. "He's like a god on that team. They're obsessed with him."

Katie waves her hands in the air. "Auntie P, watch!" She does a series of uncoordinated tumbles, but I clap and smile for her.

"You're getting good, Katie. Want some pizza?" She claps her hands and scoots off the bed. It's obvious that Charlotte has been bringing her down here a lot. Her pregnancies bring out a different kind of nesting for her.

I grab some paper plates and a cup for my wine from the mini kitchenette they have in here and sit down on the floor. Katie eats her pizza from the side and is preoccupied with the cartoon on TV. I nearly down an entire glass before Charlotte looks at me with an arched brow.

"So?"

I clear my throat. "So?"

"Piper, are you going to make me drag whatever it is you wanted to talk about out of you, or are you just going to tell me?"

I look over to Katie and then Charlotte, thinking of the best way to speak in code in front of my niece.

"Number eight... um, he..." I look back at Katie, and I watch as a slow smile takes over Charlotte's face.

"Oh, please, tell me what he did."

"Charlotte, I will f-u-c-k your s-h-i-t up if you don't stop smiling at me like that." She starts laughing and holding her stomach while she tries to control herself. She wipes the tears from her eyes and works through her laughter.

"You can't make me laugh like that. I'm going to pee

myself." She stops laughing eventually and motions with her hand for me to continue.

"He's been going to my gym," I say, and I watch Charlotte's cheeks heat. I glare at her but continue. "And well, you know that he makes me act like an idiot when he's around. I act like a simpering woman around him, and it's pathetic."

"It's not pathetic, Piper."

"It is. I'm an Alpha, I'm a doctor, for fuck's sake. He makes me… I don't know what exactly he makes me."

"Fuck is a bad word, Auntie P," Katie interrupts, my face going red as Charlotte gives me a look.

"Bad Auntie P, we'll make her pay into the swear jar." Katie claps her hands, and I glare at Charlotte who shrugs her shoulders. "She's going to be able to pay for college with that jar, I swear."

I pull out a five dollar bill and hand it to my niece, who smiles and goes back to eating and watching her show. "Little con artist."

Charlotte smiles and shakes her head, going back to our previous conversation. "He makes you feel like you're just Piper," she says nonchalantly and bites into a piece of pizza.

"What?"

She sighs and puts down the pizza. "The bar has always been so high for you, Piper. Your dad—" She thankfully stops and shakes her head, noting how uncomfortable I am. "I just don't think you're used to someone wanting you for you. He doesn't care that you're an Alpha or a doctor. He just likes you, and what's wrong with that?"

"I'm busy, so I can't handle a relationship. I've got to get through my residency, and things aren't going to slow down for years. Someone like Alexi wants a pack, wants an Omega."

Charlotte tilts her head as she looks me over. "You've never wanted to be an Omega."

"No, I haven't. But an Alpha male like him, he's going to want an Omega." Charlotte scoffs, and I blink at her. "Go ahead, say it, Charles."

"You want an Omega too."

"Yeah, in like ten years from now."

She waves me off. "Okay, but what are you freaking out about, exactly?"

I pour more wine and down it back. Katie is completely immersed in the show, so I talk in a whisper.

"He kind of, sort of, finger fucked me in the gym showers."

"What!" she shouts, and that gets Katie's attention. Charlotte waves her off, and Katie gives us a look of irritation before going back to her show and pizza. "How was it?" is her first question, and if she wasn't pregnant, I'd probably push her shoulder.

"That's not the point."

"Oh, that so is the point."

I sip more of my wine and shake my head. "It was amazing."

Charlotte smiles and lies back down, wrapping her leg around a pillow. "So what's the problem?"

"I can't be with someone in that capacity, not yet."

"So then how exactly did you go from 'I can't do a relationship' to the captain of the Foxes having his hand in your pants?"

I finish my glass and pour another. I guess we're going to be turning this into a sleepover tonight.

"I told him that I couldn't do a relationship, and he was all 'well, what *can* you do?' So I told him I just wanted to turn off my mind, and he definitely excelled at that."

"So you're hooking up?"

"I don't know?"

"Do you want to?" Charlotte says delicately.

I bend my legs and wrap my arms around them, resting my cheek on my knees. "Maybe, I think I could do just friends with benefits."

I can tell Charlotte is holding back, but instead she nods. "You deserve something good, Piper. You work really hard, and it's not an easy job. Maybe he can relieve your stress."

"It was really good stress relief."

Charlotte nods. "He looks like he knows how to fuck."

I toss a pillow at her, and Katie squeals as she picks up a pillow and tosses it at her mom as well. I can't help the huge smile that takes over my face as an impromptu pillow fight starts. The weight that was pressing down on me earlier seems to fade away. I don't have any answers, and I'm still not sure it's the right choice. Maybe Charlotte's right. What does it hurt to have a little fun? But the question is: is there a way to just be physical with no emotions attached when it comes to Alexi Bandnin?

## CHAPTER 8

I *'m a starting goalie in the NHL.*

I repeat it over and over as I leave the coaches' office, trying to not have a heart attack or actually show my excitement around everyone else.

Instead, I call the one person who I know will get it.

"Hey, honey."

"Hey, Mom."

"How are you feeling? Is everything okay? Do you need me to visit?"

"I'm starting. I'm fucking starting tomorrow."

She squeals over the phone, and I can hear her shouting to my stepdad George. "He's fucking starting, George!" I can't help the smile that takes over my face. I know my mom is worried about me, and she might not approve of the lengths I've gone to in order to get this position. But her genuine excitement is what I need right now.

"Thanks, Mom."

"I was going to watch anyway, but I'm going to record it. I think Sharon can show me how to do that."

"Listen, I've got to get to practice, but I just wanted to call you."

"I'm so proud of you, baby. But you better be taking care of yourself."

"I will, I am."

"I'm going to send you some new socks. I found ones with strawberries on them."

"Thanks, Mom, love you."

"Love you too."

I'm turning the corner and run into a large, firm chest. "Hello, *sólnyshka.*"

"Bandnin," I reply, trying to walk past him, but he doesn't let me.

"You're starting against the Canes?" he says as a question, though depending on how long he's been standing there, he already knows.

"Yes, I just spoke to Coach."

"Play like you did last game, and it could be more than just this game," he says. I'm not sure if he's trying to be threatening or giving me a pep talk. All I know is that it smells like ginger standing so close to him, and I need to get the hell on the ice.

"I think I've got it covered," I say in a shitty tone, and my captain's grin just widens.

"Oh, this is going to be so much fun."

He walks away, and heads towards practice. I smell my armpits and don't scent anything. I shrug my shoulders at the odd encounter and dress in all my gear.

When I skate onto the ice, I can feel Johannson's glare on me. He's shooting me daggers, but I ignore him. It was simple; I played better, and I got the spot. I'm not sure if he feels like the position should be his because he's been in the NHL longer or because he has a solid five inches on me. But nothing in hockey is just given to you. You have to work at it. I'm a testament to that. It feels like my life is finally clicking together, and piece by piece, this anger I've been holding on to is starting to fade away.

Practice is brutal, but I welcome the physical exertion. I'm sweating so hard I have to take my helmet off and squirt some of my water bottle into my hair before putting my helmet back on. I can't help but notice Alexi staring at me.

"What?" I ask him.

He shakes his head, and skates away with the puck. Bram Nilsen skates up to me. He's one of our best defenders. He's been in the league for a while and has been nice to me since I joined the team.

"The Canes have a player, Kristiansen. He's a fucking prick; he's always getting too close to the goalies. You need to be prepared to get physical tomorrow."

"I can do that," I promise with complete sincerity. Am I the biggest hockey player ever? Not by any means. But I can get rough when I need to be.

"Good. I'm hoping to get my hands on him too."

"Bad blood?"

"Could say that," he says, shrugging and dribbling the puck in place. "He's my cousin." Familial rivalry is something I can get behind, and I give Bram a curt nod of acknowledgement.

"I get it. Anything you need tomorrow, let me know."

"Knew I could count on you, Connery."

Every day it feels like I'm solidifying myself on this team, and I can't help but note just how fucking good that feels.

———

Am I getting pho in hopes that I'll run into a tall, smart, hot Alpha I haven't had the guts to call or text? *Possibly.*

Also, I absolutely love the food. It's the right mix of cozy, hot, and filling. I order my meal and sit at the table, waiting for my food. I'm looking up Canes' stats and players, even though we had a meeting after and during practice for what we should be looking for.

I also look at our schedule and sigh. I have a few weeks until we have a home game with the Sharks. I'm not sure how it's going to go down, what my mom has told Max, or how he's going to respond to me being with the Foxes. It's not that I give a shit. I think I'm more so worried about him blowing my cover.

My food comes, and I've lost hope that she's going to show up. I told myself that I just needed a friend, someone outside of the team. Someone I don't have to put a full facade on for. Well, that's a lie. No one can know, but there's something about Piper that allows me to put my guard down just a little bit. I haven't been able to put my finger on it, but it's addictive.

I'm about to leave when she walks in. Her gaze meets mine immediately, and she smiles. "Hey there, did you already eat?" she asks, and I lie, shaking my head no. I could always eat. We order separately and sit down and wait for our food. I don't miss the small smile Diep gives me when taking our orders. I'm just lucky she doesn't out me for being pathetic.

When we sit down, Piper looks much better than the last time I saw her. Lighter, like she isn't carrying around the same pain she was last time. I also note how much I like to see her in casual clothes. She hangs up her large coat and just has a large sweater and black leggings that accentuate her long legs.

"New job still treating you well?"

"Very well."

"Are you going to tell me what said job is?"

"Not yet."

"So mysterious," she says with a small smile.

"I take it work has been going better for you?"

"It has. I've been on the same rotation for a few weeks, and things have been going well. But I don't think neuro is for me," she says as Diep brings our food.

"Thank you, Diep," Piper says, and she smiles at us. "She's the sweetest lady ever." I nod my head and look over at Diep who gives me a wink. I have to shake her off before looking back at Piper.

"Why not neuro?"

"The stakes are too high. A lot of times, surgery is the last resort. So it can be all or nothing and very tricky. I don't know, I just don't like it."

"Do you know what you would like to specialize in?"

She shrugs and takes a bite of her food. "Mmm, not yet, but I have time." I nod and leave it at that. "Oh, did you want to go to the Christmas Market this weekend?"

"I'll be away for work."

"The mystery gets deeper. Pilot?" she asks, and I shake my head. "I'll figure it out eventually."

"No doubt that you will."

She smirks at me and eats a few more bites before tilting her head. "I know you're new to town. My best friend throws a Christmas party every year, and it's kind of a big thing. Lots of people will be there if you'd like to make some new friends."

"That would be nice, but I'll have to check with work."

"It's on Christmas Eve," she says, and I nod.

"I'm off."

"Perfect, then you can come with me." She points her spoon at me. "You have to bring a gag gift for the white elephant."

"For what?"

"It's like a gift exchange, but some of the gifts are terrible, and some are awesome."

"But why?"

"Because it's fun, I promise. You'll love it."

"Okay," I reply and try to hold back a smile. "Is your best friend an Alpha?" I ask curiously and wonder if she will be offended.

"Oh, no, she's an Omega. She has a pack and kids and the whole thing." She talks a lot with her hands, and I think it's cute. Especially when she has the pho spoon in her hand.

"Is that what you want, the whole thing?" I ask, using her language at her.

"I mean a pack, sure. The whole kids thing, probably not. I like being the cool aunt. Plus, the idea of being pregnant gives me shivers."

"Fair enough."

"What about you?"

"I don't want anything serious right now, but down the line, I could see myself in a pack or just with one person. I'd be content either way."

She smiles and nods her head. "Exactly, I feel like the pressure to pack up early has gotten a little intense."

"I would imagine as a female Alpha you get a lot of that."

She shrugs her one shoulder and takes a sip of water before speaking. "I feel like there are always expectations of me that I'll never reach."

I know I look confused as I look at her. She's a doctor, seemingly has her shit together, what does she mean she doesn't reach expectations? I'm about to open my mouth and speak when she beats me to it. "My job comes first right now, and until it doesn't, I don't feel like I can be a proper Alpha for anyone."

I gape at her and wonder why she feels like she needs to be someone's Alpha and not just herself, but I don't say that. "I understand that work comes first."

"At least someone does," she throws out there before moving the conversation. "Good luck with work. I've got a few long shifts ahead of me. But when you get back, can we talk more about going to the party?"

"Sure."

She smirks at me, picking up her jacket and bag. "See ya, Owen." I shouldn't like how she says my name. *Fuck. She's just a friend, she's just a friend.*

I watch as she leaves the restaurant and look down at my second helping of pho in front of me.

"Need a box?" Diep says, and I nod my head. She gets a to-go container for me and hands it to me. "Doctor Blake usually comes Tuesdays and Thursdays. She likes a schedule."

"I—"

"See you Tuesday," she says before walking away. I take my pho in hand and walk back to my basement apartment.

I'm not sure why I keep finding myself wanting to be in Piper's orbit. She's easy to talk to, and she's made it clear she isn't looking for anything right now. Does that make it easier for me to find myself in the company of an Alpha? I try not to hurt my head as I wrack my brain around why I specifically waited there today in hopes of running into her.

She invited me to meet her friends, and thinking about that makes me feel eager. Could this really be possible? Living out my NHL career and finally staying in one place long enough to make actual friends?

So what if my new friend is extraordinarily pretty, I can control myself. My medication helps with that too, thankfully. Or else I would probably become a chronic masturbator otherwise. Between the hot doctor who invites me to Christmas markets and parties, there's an even bigger Alpha who seems to have found his way under my skin in a way I don't quite know how to handle.

All I know is that I'm going to nurture this friendship with Piper. I'll eventually tell her I play hockey. I have to remind myself that right now she likes Owen, the supposed Beta with a mysterious job. There's no designations or preconceived notions in the way. We're just friends because we like each other's company. I can't help but wonder how she would feel knowing the real me, and if she would no longer be interested.

# ALEXI



## CHAPTER 9

Being on edge would be an understatement. A man can only jerk off so many times a day, and well, it's getting out of hand, or at least I wish I was getting off not by my hand.

I haven't been back to Piper's gym because I'm giving her space. I'm also hoping that by the time I do see her, she'll be missing me and my touch so much she'll let me touch her cunt again. I'll do whatever it takes for her to realize that she wants me back.

Then there's the grumpy, hot, little goalie. I like him, I've decided. Perhaps more than I should. I like how coy he's being about his excitement for playing and how subdued he is around the team. I want to see what's inside of that broody little shell.

I'm not sure when this urge hits me, but I can't help the overwhelming feeling of wanting Owen and Piper to both be mine. Sure, I've thought about pack life before; I've even had an Omega that I let get away to pursue hockey. Maybe it's my age or the lingering knowledge that retirement is happening sooner than later, but I want these two to be my pack.

Would I like an Omega? Sure. Do I need one? No. What I need are people who want to be with me and are eager for the possibility of having a happy life together.

When did I become such a fucking sap? *Fuck me.*

As soon as we get on the plane, I'm hanging up my suit jacket and unbuttoning the first few buttons on my dress shirt. The flight is short, so I don't change into something more comfortable. I sit next to Mikael, who looks grumpy as ever.

"What crawled up your ass?" I ask him.

"I just don't like traveling while Charlotte is pregnant." I nod my head in understanding.

"She still has some time?"

"Yes, but it's twins and—" He waves me off. "Anders is home, so I know it's fine."

I nod my head and take a few breaths before takeoff. I've been flying forever, but without a doubt, there's still nerves for takeoff and landing.

"We need to make a statement tonight," Mikael says when we're at altitude. I know the prick knows I hate it, but he doesn't tease me, which I'm thankful for.

"What kind of statement?"

"That we're making playoffs." I grin at Mikael. Both him and his packmate want the Cup just as badly as I do.

"Then let's give them something to talk about." Mikael smiles, and it's horrifying. I know the Canes are in for a rude awakening tonight.

———

The game is getting dirty, and I'm thriving off of it as I have this big fucker pushed against the boards and we're both going for the puck. Eventually I'm able to use my blade and kick it in the direction I need. I quickly pass behind the net to Eli, and he's tapping it into their goal.

The boos in the crowd are loud as I smack Eli hard on the ass with the stick.

"Ouch, fucker."

"Good goal."

There's a shove at my shoulder, and I'm spinning on my skates to see Kristiansen behind me. I've had far too many run-ins with the Canes' offensive linemen. Not to mention that Nilsen absolutely loathes him. "Fucker," he spews.

"You'll need to ask me nicely to fuck you, Kristiansen."

"Oh, go fuck yourself."

"Which is it? You're giving me mixed signals. Do you want me to fuck you or myself?"

It's then he hits me in the jaw with a gloved fist. My response is immediate, hitting him anywhere I can manage. There's a flurry of movement, other team members getting involved and the refs tugging me by my jersey. At that point I wrap my arms around him in a hug.

The refs finally pull us apart, and I raise my hands in the air.

"We were just hugging!"

"Fuck you, Bandnin," he says as he attempts to skate toward me again. The ref is pulling him back like a naughty toddler.

"Knew you wanted to fuck me!" I yell with a smirk. A few of my teammates are laughing, and the ref tugging on my jersey seems pissed.

"Stop acting like assholes, let's go," he says. I let him guide me by my jersey.

We get a double penalty, and we're in opposite boxes. He tosses a water bottle over the wall, hitting my helmet, and I can't help but to laugh. The fans in the stands are going crazy, cheering for the violence.

*I fucking love this sport so much.*

I take my glove off and make a dick jerking motion to Kristiansen, and he starts cursing in a language I don't know. As the clock counts down and four on four is about to end, I'm prepared to go back on the ice. I'm also prepared for this dipshit to retaliate

As soon as the countdown ends and I'm back on the ice, I avoid the rat nose fuck who, predictably, is skating toward me instead of his bench.

I try to be the bigger person. I also know Coach will shit a whole motherfucking brick if I get another penalty. I skate to our defending goal, and Kristiansen follows. I expect an illegal hit from the back, but that's not what happens. Connery leaves the goal on a glide, using his padded legs as a place for the fucker to trip and fall right over him.

Absolute mayhem breaks out. Every player on the ice has a jersey in their fist or is tangling with another player. I find myself stepping between Kristiansen, who is lying on the ice with Connery. I grip the back of his jersey and fling him off and go ham.

The whistles are blowing left and right, but it's nowhere near as loud as the echoing voices of the Canes fans who are absolutely losing their shit.

Things are broken up, and both teams are handed major penalties. Mikael takes Owens' spot in the sin bin, and it's two on two on the ice.

The sin bin is full as we all sit on the bench and can't help but to laugh at the situation.

"New guy seems alright," Mikael says next to me.

"I told him to take him out. He's one of us," Nilsen says next to us. He's a quiet member of the team but no less lethal.

The man can hold a grudge more than any person I know, and his pettiness does us well during games.

"Yeah, he definitely is."

Nilsen starts the chant, "One of us! One of us!" Which has Owen shaking his head from the goal as he pays attention to the few players on the ice. The ability for a breakaway to happen is high. And we immediately stop chanting when one of the opposite players gets that breakaway, but Connery is ready. Catching the puck in his mit, he saves us from making it an even game.

We all collectively lose our minds in the sin bin and over on our bench.

The penalty is over, but it's far from the last one during the game. But we walk away with a one–nothing win against the Canes.

———

We have a private dining room at this Italian place, and we're all hyped after tonight's win. Of course no drinking while it's on the NHL's dime. So I find myself slinking off to the main bar and ordering a vodka soda.

Owen shocks me by approaching the bar.

"What do you want?" I ask him.

He bites his lip and sighs. "Amaretto sour," he says. I try so hard not to say some remark about him liking sweet shit. I hold back and order it for him.

We both sip on our drinks in silence for a moment before I break it.

"You killed it tonight." He shrugs, and some Alpha part of me breaks. "Don't shrug that shit off. That was an intense, rough game. You saved fourteen shots on goal tonight. It's a big deal."

His fair skin heats, and I smirk while drinking.

"Okay, you're right, it's a big fucking deal," he says in the most excited tone I've heard from him yet. I'm not sure why he feels like he needs to act so unaffected around us. He's doing a good job, and he should accept the praise.

"There we go."

"It just doesn't feel real, ya know?"

"I've been playing for a long time, and it still doesn't feel real sometimes."

"Seriously?"

I nod and take another sip. "It's such a high though, isn't it?"

"I felt like my heart was going to beat out of my chest the whole goddamn game."

"Good, it should be like that."

"It felt so good to knock someone over too." That earns a laugh from me as I nod.

"Your first NHL penalty." I hold up my half empty glass, and he does the same.

"And more to come."

He smiles, and I realize I've got it down bad for the Beta more than I wanted to.

"You know, some of the guys throw a party for Christmas if you'd be interested in coming."

"What day?" he asks.

"Christmas Eve."

He swallows and looks down like he's really thinking about it. "I already have a party that night."

"Well if you can make it, just let me know."

He nods, and finishes the drink. "Thanks for the drink, cap."

"You're welcome, *sólnyshka.*"

"Once I figure out how to spell that, I'm looking it up."

"Be my guest."

He walks away, and I'm at the bar by myself. A pretty petite Beta female approaches me and sits down.

"Can I get you a drink?" she asks, and I shake my head.

"No thank you."

"Oh. Are you sure?"

"I'm sure." I've got two very difficult people I'm chasing right now, and I have no further interest in anyone else, even if my wrist is getting an exceptional workout.

The night at the hotel is lonely, and all I wish is that it was filled with two people who don't know each other and have no idea the lengths I'll go to in order to make them both mine. I am a patient Alpha, after all.

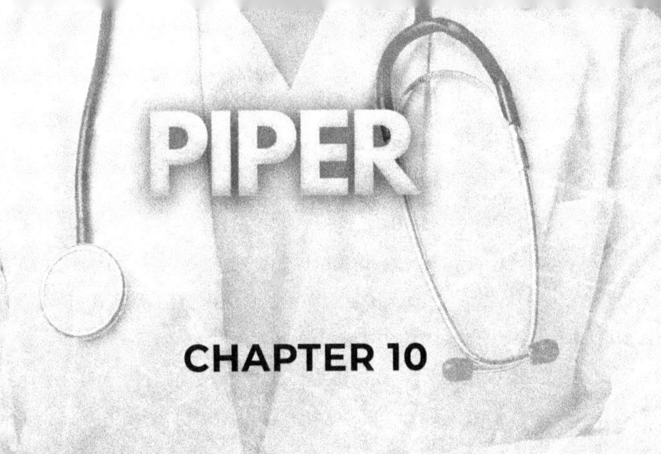


## CHAPTER 10

"Charlotte, what the fuck do you think you're doing?" I scold her as I take all the shit she was carrying out to the living room.

"Sorry, damn. It's just chips."

"It's just chips," I parrot in her tone. She rolls her eyes and sits on the couch. "You do look pretty though, Mrs. Claus."

"Shut up," she groans, lying back. "You look like that hot lady in Who-ville that the Grinch was in love with."

"I'm glad that's the vibe I'm giving off. It's exactly the look I was going for."

"Yes, because your daddy is going to be here."

"Oh, shut up, Charlotte."

"That's right, he finger banged and ghosted. Wait, no. You told him you didn't want anything, and now you're wishing you'd run into him sooner. He'll be here tonight."

"I know that, and I'm not thinking that."

"Mmhmm."

"Plus, Owen is coming."

She arches an eyebrow at me before rolling her eyes.

"That's right, your super hot Beta buffer. I'm sure this will go splendidly."

"He's not a Beta buffer. I like Owen."

"Do you like Owen because he's safe?" My heart sinks when she says that, and it's at that moment that I know it's not true. I don't see Owen in that light at all.

"Actually, I really like talking to Owen. He's peaceful."

"Hmm." Charlotte clicks her tongue like she's about to say something else. But her Alphas all come barging through the door first.

"Katie is with my mom," Anders says, leaning down and kissing Charlotte.

"I'm so happy they're here," Charlotte says, and I smile. They wanted to be here for when the twins were born. Knowing what she lost, to have Anders' family here has been helpful, even if it isn't permanent.

"When is everyone getting here?" Eli asks.

I'm sitting next to Charlotte, and I watch her soften next to her Alphas. Is it weird to want to provide that calmness to someone, but another part of me wants to receive it as well? Not the coddling that Charlotte gets, but just someone to tell me that it's going to be okay. I sigh to myself. Things have been okay lately. I haven't wanted to quit work fifty times this week, and I feel at peace. Though some feelings have been lingering, despite my best efforts.

I pour myself a glass of champagne, turn on the music, and make sure all the lights are on. Different hockey players, wives, and various neighbors start making their way to the house. Low conversation is taking place all throughout the lower level.

I keep watching the door and wonder who I'm wanting to show up more, Alexi or Owen. I shake my head. Obviously Owen, this will be great for him. He needs friends, and everyone is going to love him. In no way shape or form am I attracted to the blond-haired, blue-eyed Beta who is so calming and easy to talk to. I'm also absolutely not remembering Alexi's hands on me, nope, not even a little bit.

As the front door opens and I see the person's height, I know that it's Alexi. I down the rest of my champagne and go into the kitchen. I feel bad that I won't be front and center when Owen gets here, but he'll find me.

I switch to a Coke; I've got to have my wits about me. I say this to myself as I'm huddled in a corner with a plate of cheese and my soda. I'm opening the pantry door to restock the crackers when the door shuts behind me, and I jump.

"Fuck."

"Good seeing you too, Piper," Alexi says with a huge smile on his face. "Are you hiding from me?"

"No, I'm just getting crackers."

He points to the shelf on the opposite side I'm looking in. "Those crackers."

"Right," I say, grabbing the crackers close to my chest.

"You look very pretty tonight," he says. My heart absolutely does not beat faster. In fact, I don't feel affected at all. We're just friends. A friend who happens to touch my vagina so good that I can't think straight.

"You look nice too," I say, which he does. He's wearing tight gray dress pants and a white button up. The sleeves are rolled up, showing his sculpted forearms, and I swear I can see a few chest hairs sticking out of the top of his collar. No one should be able to pull off every single thing they wear the way he does.

"Sorry I haven't been to the gym. Season has been busy."

"Oh, I didn't notice." Such a lie. I catch his smirk in the dimly lit pantry. He takes a step closer to me.

"You know, this pantry is convenient. Dark, quiet, we're here… together."

I swallow thickly, and I'm trying to weigh the pros and cons in my head. He takes another step closer. His hand eagerly reaches out and grips my hip. He doesn't do anything besides touch me there, searching my eyes and waiting for my response.

I'm about to open my mouth and say something stupid like yes, when the pantry door opens. Alexi's hand is immediately off of my hip with a grinning Charlotte holding the door open.

"Uh, so Owen's here," she says, the blond Beta poking his head into the pantry. His eyes glance between me and Alexi, and it looks like his mind is working a million miles a minute.

"Connery?" Alexi says in a confused tone.

"You know Owen?" I ask.

"You know Owen?" he parrots, and my brows furrow.

"So I guess you've figured out my job now," Owen says with a shrug of his shoulders.

"You work for the Foxes?" I ask. Alexi shifts a little next to me, and Charlotte makes a noise in the back of her throat.

"I'm the new goalie."

"Oh, wow. That wasn't on my short list of what I thought your job was."

"This is fun and all, but why don't we get out of the pantry," Charlotte says. Good idea, I'm far too close to Alexi right now. And things just got awkward.

Alexi gives Owen a head nod, and I can't help but notice a tint of pink on Owen's cheeks. It's comforting to know the man doesn't just render me into a puddle—it's universal.

"So this was the party you were already going to?" Alexi asks him.

"Yeah, didn't know it was the same one, or that Piper had any affiliation to the Foxes."

"Piper is your date to the party?" Alexi asks with a mischievous smile.

"We're friends," I interject, and Alexi's smile widens even further.

"Piper is a good friend to have," Alexi says. Charlotte still hasn't left, and her pregnant ass is just standing there with a beaming smile like this is the most riveting TV show she's ever seen in her life.

"Piper is the best kind of friend," Charlotte says, and I've never wanted to drown her before, but there's a first for everything.

Alexi looks at Charlotte, and it's like they have a little moment. Both of them know too much information, and I don't like it.

"Owen, do you want to get a drink?" I ask.

Owen looks between Charlotte and Alexi and nods his head, then follows me to the drinks table.

"What was that all about?" Owen asks as soon as we're a distance away from Charlotte and Alexi. I grab two glasses and begin to pour a very full glass of champagne.

"Which part?" It would be a Christmas miracle if he could just drop it and leave it as it is, but if I were Owen, I would have questions too.

"Are you dating Alexi?"

"No, I'm very much single."

"It looked like you two were close in that closet," he says, and I'm not sure if I detect jealousy or not. Would I like it if he was jealous? Maybe...

"No, he's just a friend."

"I'm just a friend," Owen says with a smirk as I hand him his glass and take a large sip of my own. I shrug my shoulders and redirect the conversation.

"So you're the new goalie they've all been talking about, huh?"

"Subject change, classic, I like it," Owen says, taking a sip then swallowing. "Yeah, I wanted to make sure it was going to stick before I said it out loud to anyone."

"Didn't want to jinx it?" I say with a smile, and he nods his head. "Well, at least we don't have to do the awkward get to know yous. You should know everyone from the team, just not their neighbors."

I turn and look to the side. Alexi is talking with a few other players, but he keeps looking at me and Owen—often.

"This might be an awkward question," Owen says.

"Shoot." Does it get any more awkward than walking in on me standing in a pantry with his captain? His captain, who I was totally going to let finger bang me next to the crackers and apple juice in my best friend's pantry. Maybe I need another glass of champagne to get through tonight. Owen was supposed to be my buffer, but it seems like he's going to be a bigger complication than anything.

"Does Alexi usually stare at you like this, or is it because I'm here?"

I furrow my brows and look at Owen. "Why? Does he usually stare at you?"

He shrugs his shoulders. "Maybe."

"Hmm, then you're not alone. He's intense," I reply and sip my drink. I swear the big Alpha smirks at us across the room, and I swallow thickly. "Do you want to get some air? There's a fire out back."

"Yeah, a refill?" he asks. I don't even have to nod, I just hand him my glass, and he fills us both up before we go out the sliding door. "Damn, this backyard is something."

I laugh and shake my head. "Yeah, three hockey dads and a mom with an active imagination," I say, looking at the built-in trampoline, pirate ship playset, treehouse, and the spot where they blow up the bounce house when it's warm outside.

"So Charlotte, Mikael and Eli's Omega, is your best friend?"

I smile and nod as we sit on the chairs circling the firepit. No one else is out here, and it feels peaceful. The first time I've been able to quiet my mind since I got to this party.

"Yes, for as long as I can remember. She's my person."

Owen smiles and nods his head, taking a sip and looking at the flickering flames in the backyard.

"When you said you were the fun aunt, was it about their daughter?" he asks, and I can't help but to smile and think about how much I love Katie.

"I love Katie like she's my own, but I get to return her at the end of the day." I laugh, and he does too. I tap my fingernail against my glass and look at him. "What about you, do you have any nieces or nephews?"

He shakes his head. "No, I haven't really been around many kids, don't know if I want them either. But I think pack life is for me, down the road."

"Every pack needs a Beta."

"Oh yeah?" he says.

"Who else is going to keep everyone sane and in check?"

"Your friend doesn't have a Beta."

"True, but she has her hands full."

Owen laughs and shakes his head. "Mikael seems like a full time job."

I don't comment but take another sip of champagne. The bubbles are definitely starting to kick in now. I cannot let history repeat itself when it comes to champagne and Charlotte's deck, I remind myself.

"I'm sorry we never got to go to the Christmas market," he says.

"Oh, it's no big deal. I've been working a lot anyway."

"Shocked that you have off tonight."

"I have to work Christmas and New Year's Eve and day."

"We have a stretch of away games after Christmas, but maybe when I get back we could do something to make up for it?" he says. His cheeks are either pink from the chill outside or asking me to hang out. I can't tell if it's friendly or a date. But talking to Owen is easy, and I find myself wanting to spend more time with him. He's reserved, but I can't help but to feel there's something deeper to Owen. There's something about him that's always pulling me in, and I'm going to find out what that is.

"Sure, I'd like that," I say, not holding back my smile.

"Good. Okay. Once I get back."

I nod, and there's a rapping noise against the glass. Charlotte is waving us inside, and I sigh. "It's time for white elephant."

"Right," Owen says and gets up from his chair. We both bring our glasses inside with us. No more drinking tonight or I might say something stupid to a handsome Beta or let an Alpha rail me in my bestie's pantry.

"There's just enough room next to Alexi for you two," Charlotte says, pointing to Alexi, and I glare at my best friend who just claps her hands and sits on Eli's lap.

The couch is a tight fit with Alexi, and before I can even sit down, Owen takes the further spot, resting his arm on the couch rest.

*Just fucking awesome.* I gently sit down between them. Both of their thighs touch my own. Alexi's presence is loud and overwhelming in both his personality and size. Owen isn't small, but next to Alexi, he feels like it. With both of their thighs touching me, I'm back to not being able to think.

Alexi stretches out, his arm on the back of the couch, and I can't help but notice his thumb landing on Owen's shoulder too.

"You should try and get my present," Alexi says next to me.

"Why?"

Alexi shrugs his shoulders and leans a little closer. "Mine's the one with the candy cane wrapping paper."

I can tell Charlotte is eavesdropping on the entire encounter as I sit back and wait until I draw a number. I'm number eight, and I wait my turn as everyone goes before me. When I have to stand up, I have to hold my skirt down. I have to do the same thing when I bend over and pick the gift that is very specifically not Alexi's.

He just gives me a smile, knowing that there's a whole other round and he just so happens to be the last person called who gets to choose.

Owen grabs my gift, and I hope he decides to stay with that instead of swapping. It's the second round, and I stay with my gift. Charlotte is next, and the little meddler hands the candy cane papered gift right in my lap as she takes the gift from my hands. I look over to Alexi, who seems more than pleased with himself as the game concludes, and everyone is stuck with the gift they have either swapped or chosen.

We go in a circle opening the gifts. Mikael got a huge pair of panties, which his pack makes him put on. It gets a round of laughter and tears from the entire group. Charlotte opens up a pair of used hockey socks. And so forth it continues with a few gifts that are scratch offs or cash, but more often than not, they're gag gifts.

When we get to our couch, Owen opens his gift, which I brought. It's a pair of soft socks that look like kitten paws.

"They're cute, thank you," he says. I smile back at him and fuck am I so glad he's here.

It's my turn to open my gift. I give Alexi a cursory glance, and he's just grinning. As I rip the paper, I see what it is. "No you fucking didn't."

"Oh, what is it?" Charlotte says, which starts a train of people asking to see the item. I hold up the box and try not to let mortification fill my body or show on my face.

There's an eruption of giggles, and every fiber of me wants to elbow Alexi in the stomach.

"Honestly, Piper, they're expensive. It's a good gift."

Charlotte Hodges is about to get her best friend card revoked as I look down at the box in front of me. This man bought a vibrator in the hopes that I would be the one to pick it at this Christmas party.

Alexi opens his gift, and it's a signed puck by Mikael. "Great, my least favorite player's autograph." People laugh and start heading out to different parts of the house. Owen stays put, and I'm about to get up when Alexi says, "Didn't want you suffering while I'm away for games, *malyshka.*"

He's not quiet about it and even looks at Owen after he says it. Alexi sits back down casually, and as I get up, I can feel both of them looking at my ass, but I'm too flustered to care.

*Tonight did not go how I planned, not by a long shot.*

## CHAPTER 11

It's my first string of away games, and I'm feeling unsettled. It probably has to do with the fact that my hotel buddy for these games is none other than our insane captain. Besides the fact that he intimidates me in a way that borders between flirting and intimidation. It's also the fact that Alexi is far more observant than anyone gives him credit for. He might be goofy and enjoys being the center of attention, but the man is not an idiot. He's observant and calculating when it comes to the information he gathers. It's why he's so good at hockey, he's able to anticipate what other players are going to do before they do them. It's attention that I don't want, there's information I don't want him knowing, and there's a deep-seated feeling that it wouldn't take Alexi much to crack all my secrets wide open.

We just finished up our team dinner, and it's time to rest for tomorrow's game, but I feel on edge. Sometimes when you're keeping a secret as big as mine, you can't help but feel like everyone knows you're hiding something. All it would take is a major slip up, me missing a pill or not putting on the proper amount of scent blocking deodorant on. One simple slipup could ruin everything I've worked so fucking hard for. It's not even hiding my designation that's my biggest concern. It's the way Johannson has been looking at me lately. I know I took the guy's starting position, but he seems to be taking it hard.

"Don't fuck up tomorrow, Connery," he says passing by.

"Play better, Johannson," Alexi says to him before I'm able to say anything back. "Don't let him rile you up, roomie. Let's go."

"It didn't bother me," I reply.

"Either way, he shouldn't be talking to a teammate like that. Not when we should be working together."

I walk in step with him, and he smiles at a few of the team members as we make our way to the lobby. He pushes the button to our floor, and I can't help but feel the tension rise with each moment we wait. I can't help but wonder if this is one sided? Am I so fucking paranoid and devoid of human contact that I've deluded myself into thinking he's more friendly toward me than others?

The bell chimes, and a few older women leave the elevator. All of them give Alexi a once over before fully exiting into the lobby.

"Could have had one of those bitties," I joke, and Alexi laughs.

"Finding someone willing isn't a problem I have," Alexi says. It's not in a cocky way, more so matter-of-fact. I scoff and shake my head, believing that he has no problems finding someone to sleep with him.

"What's the problem you have?" I wonder if he's going to disclose anything to me. I noticed the way he flirted with Piper at the Christmas party. And while I think the man gives me attention, it's nothing like the way he looks at Piper. Which might be similar to the way I'm looking at Piper, and I don't know how to make myself stop looking at her that way.

How I can't seem to stop finding ways to run into Piper or spend time with her. It's overwhelming how much peace she brings me when I'm around her, and I can't help it, I feel like she's the only thing keeping the part of me I keep hidden sane.

"Not a problem that can't be fixed."

"Mysterious, I like it."

He smirks and keeps his distance in the elevator, and I'm thankful. He smells great, not even just his pheromones. Whatever cologne he's wearing only brings out the richness of his clove and ginger scent. It's times like these I'm grateful for all the medication I'm on. Besides allowing me to live a semi-normal life, they also prevent me from bending over in this elevator and begging this Alpha to fuck me because he smells so good. I bet Alexi has a massive knot.

I'm zoned out when Alexi clears his throat. "Coming?" he smirks as he asks. I nod my head and follow him down the hall.

The hotel is nice, and while I'm excited to be on the road for multiple games, sharing such a small space for a stretch of time is going to be difficult.

"You can take the first shower," Alexi says as he plops down on the bed and takes his phone out.

"Thanks."

If he thinks it's strange that I bring an entire carry-on sized bag in the bathroom, he doesn't let on. I use all of my products that I normally do, and I'm trying not to focus on the large hulking man just on the other side of this door.

My wishful thinking is for naught as my dick gets hard. Which doesn't happen often with all the medication I'm on, and well, it's not going to go down itself.

The risk is high, knowing that my scent will linger in the shower, but I can't help myself. Spitting down on my cock, I start with tentative light strokes. It feels so much better than it should, and I hope it doesn't become a common occurrence.

What kind of fucking Omega wishes their hard-on would go away? Probably the one who hides his designation like he's a government operative. I shake my head, draining these negative thoughts from my head, and go back to touching myself.

My mind wanders to the Alpha on the other side of the door and the one all the way back in Connecticut. They would look so fucking good together. I can't help but to think of the attention they would give me.

Piper locking her tight pussy around my dick while Alexi knots me is playing in my head like a movie. The way Alexi would be pounding me from behind, making me fuck our pretty Alpha who is underneath me. The way that Piper would look up at me like I'm special and not a complete disappointment.

The way they would lean over my shoulder and kiss each other while they use me and take what they want.

I groan as my strokes increase, my other hand holding myself up against the tile. Warm spray pounds my back as I fist my cock and release against the tile wall. I breathe heavily as I look at my cum splattered on the wall. Shame runs down my spine that I used Piper and Alexi to get off like that. More so how I embraced being an Omega and having them use me for their pleasure.

I hate myself. How have I gotten this fucked up? I wish I was okay with who I was—what I am. But the truth is, I'd rather be anyone else, and if Alexi and Piper knew what I am, I'm sure they would be disgusted by me and my lies.

I don't need Alphas to take care of me, I can take care of myself. What I need is to not lose focus and accomplish what I need to. If I don't, I feel like there will always be this gaping hole in my chest, the one where I store my self-worth.

With the sprayer in hand, I clean up my mess and begin washing myself. The water pours over me like the shame I carry with me everyday. I'm methodical when I clean, making sure there's no trace of my essence, which is difficult for me to smell because it's my own.

Once I'm sure that I've cleaned myself and the shower enough, I get out, apply my scent blockers, take my medicine, and brush my teeth.

I want to smack myself for bringing an entire apothecary to the shower and not my clothes. I wrap a towel around my waist and leave, a plume of steam following me. Alexi is already up and nearly bumping my shoulder to get into the bathroom.

He inhales and looks at me. "Is that your shampoo?"

"What?" I ask, blinking up at him.

"Smells like strawberry… strawberry lemonade?" He tilts his head and goes to lean forward to scent me more, and I back away.

"Must be my bodywash, I don't know."

"Can I use it?" he says, and I swallow.

"That was my last bit," I lie.

He raises a brow at me, and his gaze travels down my chest. I feel like I'm under a microscope, and I don't know how I feel about it. It's almost like he knows exactly what I did in the shower, and I feel sick.

"Okay," he says, shrugging and walking into the bathroom. I take a deep breath and collapse back onto the bed.

If I'm not careful, Alexi Bandnin could easily know all my secrets.

———

Exhausted doesn't even begin to cover how I feel right now. Even in my own head, I sound like a complaining bitch. But I can't help it. Physically, I'm not built for this exertion, but I keep pushing myself. Mentally, I know I can handle the strain, I can always push my mindset further. But my body… it wants to give up.

It wants me to crawl into a nest and get fucked until I smell like the Alphas taking care of me.

*Needy ass fucking Omega pheromones.*

The only reason I can hold this at bay is because of the medication I'm on, which has its own slew of side effects. Like the way I don't usually get hard, how it adds on exhaustion, how it makes me feel. I can't say that I've ever been a sunshiny person, but right now, right now I want to disappear, and it's a hard feeling to swallow.

I'm close to everything I've ever wanted. How the hell can I feel so hollow?

"You good, *sólnyshka?*" Alexi asks with a furrowed brow.

"Yeah, I'm just going to go to the room," I say, waving him off. We went to shoot outs tonight, and I'm barely able to even walk to the room.

I know that Alexi is going to come back to the room and see me, but right now I don't give a shit. Flinging open the closet door, I grab the additional pillows and blanket, tossing them on the bed. I rip off my suit and fall into the bed in only my boxers. I'm asleep in a matter of seconds, and for a few blissful hours, I feel nothing.

---

"Rise and shine, *sólnyshka.*"

I groan, tugging a pillow against my chest and waving a hand.

"We've got a flight to catch, Owen. Get your ass up."

"Fuck off," I say groggily.

"Well, I can't simply leave your ass here. So get up, or I'll toss your little ass over my shoulder and carry you to the plane."

"Okay," I say, holding the pillow closer to my chest.

I expect Alexi to argue with me more, but no. He grabs me by my ankles and drags me down the bed, making me groan and blink open my eyes.

Before I can even do anything, he's gripping me by my hips and tossing me over his massive shoulder.

"What the fuck?"

"Told you what I was going to do. You gotta tell me where you get that body wash," he says.

"Put me down, I'll get ready."

He swats my ass, and I feel myself getting hard against his shoulder. His scent thickens, and I know if I don't diffuse this situation soon, it's going to get out of control.

"Put me down, I'll get ready."

He smacks my ass one more time, and I bite my bottom lip to hold back a whimper. He drags me down his front, and when I look up into his brown eyes, I can see how dilated his pupils are.

"You have five minutes," he says, crossing his arms over his chest. I nod and quickly take my medicine, deodorize, and pack up my shit.

The one thing I truly hate about the NHL, besides the fact that I'm barred based on my designation, is the fact that we have to constantly travel wearing suits. I know mine is a crumpled mess on the floor and that I'm going to look like a mess on the plane.

But when I leave the bathroom, Alexi has my suit pressed

and left it on the bed. The team captain looks at me skeptically while he stands by the door of the hotel.

"Ready?" he asks.

"Thanks for ironing my suit." He nods and looks over my frame, like he's interested and analyzing me at the same time.

"Anything for you, *sólnyshka.*" He opens the door, and we leave the hotel. He doesn't say anything to me the entire trip back to Connecticut.

# ALEXI

## CHAPTER 12

Owen Connery is a fucking Omega, and he's hiding it. He's doing it well enough that no one else has caught on. But having shared a space with him, it's evident.

Beta my fucking ass.

Not only did I catch a small whiff of his scent, but the way he passed out with all those pillows around him, while adorable, was a huge red flag.

I'm going to keep the broody Omega's secret, for now. I'm not even going to tell him that I know. I have a feeling if he knew he had been found out, he would panic and things would just become worse. Plus, I can understand the motivation. He wants to be in the NHL, and Omegas are barred from playing.

It's not right, but I understand why. Omegas are seen as precious beings that need to be protected at all costs, they're smaller, more fragile. Not only that, it's a safety issue for everyone. It's fucked up to say, but it's a huge distraction when the majority of players are Alphas as well. I didn't say that it was right, just that I understand some of the rules.

Owen isn't tall, but he has a strong build, a body he has probably had to work ten times harder for than anyone else on our team. My heart hurts when I think about this weight that he must be carrying and how it's affecting him. He has to be on so many medications and deodorizers to pass as a Beta. He's doing a good job of it.

If I hadn't been around him when he was showering, I might have had my suspicions, but I wouldn't have known for certain.

I was drawn to him before knowing this information, and it makes me feel guilty. I liked that he was a Beta and was who he was, but why am I even more intrigued that I know his secret? I wonder if Piper has any clue. I would imagine not.

It's been on my mind for days now, and I've kept it to myself and made sure not to let Owen know that I'm on to his little secret.

The only negative to Owen being an Omega is his standing with the NHL. He's really fucking good and deserves to be here. I truly think that he can help bring us that Cup. Not only that, but I feel like Piper is only going to be more into him when she finds out his designation. There's only so much time he can keep this charade up for. I'm a selfish asshole for wanting it to be till the end of the season.

I'm a piece of shit for the way I'm thinking about him. I push my sweaty hair off my face and watch as Piper lifts weights at the ass crack of dawn.

I've given her as much space as I'm willing. But I've missed her, and something tells me that the Alpha needs a little relief, which I'm more than willing to give.

She knows that I'm here. She's glanced over at me a few times. She looks tired and withdrawn, and I can't help this urge to want to make everything better for her. I know she's strong, intelligent, and independent. But I have this gut feeling that no one has ever truly taken care of Piper. I don't want to coddle her. I want to be her person.

God, I have my hands fucking full. An Omega hiding their designation and a female Alpha who doesn't seem keen on ever asking for help. But if anyone is going to bring these two together, it's gonna be me.

She stops lifting, her chest rising and falling with exertion as she takes off her headphones and walks over to me. With her this close, I can see the dark circles under her eyes and the tension in her shoulders.

"What do you want, Alexi?" she says in a bored tone.

"I wanted to see you," I reply. Not wanting to joke around with her, she doesn't seem in the mood. A dusting of color meets her cheeks, and she shakes her head.

"Alexi," she sighs and shakes her head. I'm so obsessed with this girl I'm about to ask her if she wants me to go down on her to take away her stress, but I need more.

"Do you want to get breakfast?" I ask instead. She tilts her head and looks at me in a way she hasn't before. Like I'm a lifeline and not some dipshit Alpha who won't leave her alone.

"Okay," she says, wrapping her arms around herself. "Fifteen minutes?"

"I'll meet you up front."

She turns on her heel and walks to the locker rooms. I do the same, the fond memories of finger fucking her in the shower playing through my head as I watch her go. While I wish I could do that again, this seems more significant, the step that I've been wanting to take with her. I need her to feel more beyond the physical with me, and getting time alone is the only way to do that.

Both of us take the time to dry our hair with how brutal the weather is outside. She smiles at me when we leave, but it doesn't reach her eyes.

The walk to the diner is a quiet and cold one. I'm not sure where to start. What can I say to show her that I'm not just all jokes, that I'm serious about her, about us becoming a pack? I'm not stupid enough to bring up Owen, all in due time.

The diner is fairly empty when the hostess leads us to our table and puts the two menus down. Piper glances at it before putting it down. She orders a coffee, pancakes, and a side of bacon. I stick with water, an omelet, and toast.

"How were your away games?" she asks, breaking the silence first. Every ounce of me wants to blurt out how the Beta we both seem to be drawn to is an Omega and it's a sign from the universe that he should be ours and we're meant to be a pack. But I stick with a simple answer instead.

"Good, we only lost one."

"Is Owen filling Anders' shoes?" she asks, taking a sip of her hot coffee when the waitress drops it off. I smirk at her and take a sip of water before answering.

"He's nearly there. Just needs a little more confidence, I think," I answer truthfully.

"I could see that. He seems really hard on himself." Should I enjoy this conversation as much as I am? Both of us talking like we want to make our Omega's life better gives me a deep thrill.

"What about you? How's work?" I ask. As soon as the words come out, I wish I could swallow them back up. Piper's eyes meet mine, and she doesn't cry, but there's a slight glassiness to her eyes. She shakes her head like she doesn't want to answer, and I'm not sure if I should be blunt with her or continue pussy footing around the subject. "Piper, you can talk to me. If not me, you should talk to someone about it. Every time I ask you about work, you seem to shut down."

She sighs and looks out the window. Small white flakes are falling, and she tracks them with her gaze before looking at me. Her green eyes bore into mine, like she's trying to assess if she can trust me or not.

"I just haven't voiced it to anyone yet. I feel like if I say it out loud, I'm a failure, or maybe that I'll actually do something about it."

I sensed that she didn't like her program, but the thought of her ever thinking that she's a failure is absurd.

"You're not a failure, you never could be. You're the smartest and kindest person I know," I say. She blinks at me and looks back through the window before looking back at me.

"I was always going to be a surgeon. It's what my dad wanted. He funded my education, and he pays my rent so I can focus on my residency. The only thing he has ever been proud of is that his daughter is going to be a neurosurgeon. It has always been this way. It's what I was meant to do." She takes a moment and sips her coffee before looking at me. I'm not sure if she is expecting judgment or what, but whatever she finds in my face makes her continue.

"I don't think I'm cut out to be a surgeon. It's not even the long hours or the training, it's the emotional side of it, and I know that if I told my dad, his disappointment would be palpable. It's just so impersonal, the act of doing surgery. The losses seem to cut me deeper than anyone else in my program, and I don't know why. It makes me feel weak."

"You're not weak for caring about people. If anything, it makes you a better doctor. Could you switch programs?"

She gives me an unbelieving smile. "I'm already almost two years in, so it would be time wasted if I switched now." She sighs and rubs her hand through her hair. "I think family medicine would suit me better, but I would have to start a whole new residency, extend my timeline even further. Not to mention I know my dad would cut me off if I left surgery."

I want to punch Piper's dad.

The possessive part of me I can't seem to control when it comes to Piper is telling me to pack up all her shit and have her live with me. I have more than enough money to support a pack and to support her while she lives out her dream. But I know if I said that, I would spook her and we would be right back at square one. The fact that she's confiding in me at all is more than I can ask for at this point.

"What does Charlotte think?"

Her cheeks turn a delicious shade of pink, and she hides behind her coffee cup. "I haven't told her."

Now I feel more like a caveman. I know something that not even her best friend knows.

"Why not?"

She shakes her head, and the waitress drops off our food. Piper collects her thoughts and in between eating, she explains.

"Even though Charlotte isn't my Omega, she still is in our own way. I have this need to protect her and take care of her. She has so much going on between three Alphas, Katie, and the twins on the way. There's no way I can dump my bullshit on her."

I give her a look that says she's full of shit. And she scoffs. "I think if you told her, she would tell you to leave the program, and that makes it harder for you."

Piper glares at me, and I know it's because she knows I'm right. While I don't doubt that she doesn't like to burden her best friend, the bigger part of this is dealing with her own feelings on the matter.

"Maybe, but it's not that simple. It doesn't matter anyway. It's the middle of the year. New programs wouldn't open up until the summer."

"But you would stay in this one and suffer in the meantime?" I ask, being direct with her. Piper doesn't seem responsive to bullshit.

She spears her pancake like it personally offended her and puts it in her mouth while she chews and contemplates my words.

Once she's done eating, she sits back in the creaky booth and crosses her arms over her chest. "I haven't made a decision yet."

It seems obvious to me what she needs to do, but it's her career, not mine.

"Can I say something without you stabbing me like that poor pancake?"

"Fine," she says. The waitress refills her coffee, and she thanks her and holds the warm liquid close to her face, hiding her mouth.

"Life's too short to live for other people. You don't want to spend more time doing something that doesn't make you happy. If your dad wasn't a factor, if money wasn't an issue and it was only you that you had to think about, what would you do?"

Her eyes scan mine, and she puts the coffee back down on the table.

"I'd switch programs," she says plain as day, and I watch as everything starts clicking in her own head. I wonder if she's imagining how much better life would be if she made this adjustment. It's easy from the outside looking in, but I just want her to be happy.

"I'm here if you ever want to talk about it or need help with the rest."

"Why?" she says suspiciously at me.

"You know why, and when you're ready for that conversation, I'm here too." I put three twenties on the counter and stand up, looking down at her while she's still seated. "I'm always here for you, Piper."

Her mouth gapes open, and I leave the diner, feeling like my situation just got even more complicated than before. But at the same time, I can't help thinking I'm just one step closer to building this pack, and fuck it feels good. Now, I just need Piper to put aside this front that she doesn't need anyone and for Owen to realize he's attracted to me and I can keep his secret.

I have my work cut out for me, but I know they are worth waiting for.

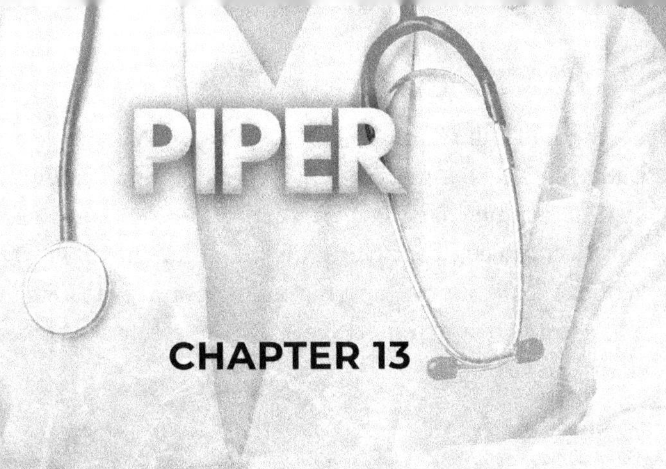



# CHAPTER 13

Fucking Alexi Bandnin and his sweet words. I'm not sure why I felt comfortable spewing all my problems to the hot-ass Alpha. It sucks even more because I know he's right. Having not said anything out loud has made things easier, and not voicing how miserable I am in my residency made it easier to put on the backburner.

Now that I've said it and the words came out of my mouth, I know Alexi is right, but I have no fucking clue how to act on it, or if I even can. Part of me feels like I just need to keep pushing through, that it's just a rough patch.

What's even worse? I liked talking to Alexi about my problems. It felt nice to have someone not judge me and wanting to help me. And I didn't feel like a burden expressing myself.

This is all just so completely fucked.

He could have tried to bang me in the locker room again, and I would have welcomed it. But somehow he tricked me into going on a date with him. He's a sneaky Alpha, and as much as I want to tell myself I need to stay away from him, the bigger part of me is hoping he stalks me at the gym again.

*I need simple.*

I would call Charlotte, but I know she has music class for Katie tonight. It's my one day off, and I don't know what it says about me that I can't be alone. I'm not sure what time Foxes' practice is, but against my better judgment, I text Owen. While Alexi is intense and makes me put my feelings under a microscope, being around Owen is like a calming force to the chaos.

Hey, you still want to hang out?

Owen: Yeah, I get off at four. Want to come to my place?

Sure, I'll see you at five.

Owen texts me his address, and I might dress nicer than usual. I mean, the man has only seen me in scrubs, workout clothes, and looking like a ho-ho-ho for Christmas. My brain, of course, is rattling about how I'm running to Owen the moment I feel insecure. That I keep saying I can't do anything serious, but there's something about this Beta that keeps pulling me in. Meanwhile, I'm running from my connection to Alexi. They are just so different in intensity. Deep down, I feel it, like the opposite side of a magnet, and no matter what I do, I can't fully escape.

I'm not sure what I'm trying to achieve by going to Owen's tonight. All I know is I feel like I'm floating into the abyss and I need to be centered. I'm not sure why Owen seems to be that person, but I'm so sick of floundering alone.

I'm scared, but more than anything, I'm lonely.

I sit on my bedroom floor and let that feeling sink in, let

it all sink in, and it breaks me. I'm surrounded by people every day, and yet I feel so alone. I have the bestest friend anyone could ask for, a career most people dream of, and yet it feels like none of it is enough. That I'm not enough. That these good things just happen to me and I don't deserve them. When will anything I do feel like enough? Will I ever feel deserving of what I have or who I surround myself with?

I've never felt so alone with my thoughts as I do now.

My whole life I've been good at keeping my chin up, shouldering the weight of other people's struggles and ignoring mine. But now it feels like that weight is catching up with me, and it's crushing me whole.

I consider canceling on Owen, not wanting him to be a crutch since he doesn't deserve that. But I know if I don't leave this house, I'll just feel fifty times worse. Instead, I wipe my nose, reapply my makeup, and put those thoughts in the back of my mind where they belong.

My reflection is overwhelming to look at, but I stare at myself.

*I'm Doctor Piper-fucking-Blake, and I will not break.*

———

The walk to Owen's place is cold, but luckily the chill seems to let my brain cells know to shut the hell up. He said to take the entrance to the basement, and I'm about to knock on the door when Owen swings it open.

His hair is wet, and his eyes are wide as he grimaces.

"Piper, I'm so fucking sorry."

"What?"

"Owen, honey, who is that?" I hear a voice in the background, and for a moment, my heart breaks. Owen has a girlfriend, of course he fucking does, he's so easy to be around and extremely attractive.

"Oh, it's okay. Um, see you around," I say, trying to save myself from any further embarrassment. Today really decided to kick my ass, didn't it?

"It's my mom," Owen says suddenly. "I didn't know she was coming by. You definitely don't need to stay if you'd rather go."

A relieved sigh escapes at me as I smile at him. "I can hang out for a bit." Owen looks nervous but takes my coat and hangs it up. The space is small but cozy. It smells amazing in here, and if I didn't know any better… I shake my head and notice the strawberry citrus candle burning on top of the stove. *Of course.*

The woman looks a lot like Owen, same blonde hair and blue eyes. She must be in her fifties and is definitely a Beta. She gives me a kind smile, and I sit down at the table she's sitting at. The same candle burns in the middle of the rounded wooden table.

"Hi, I'm Lori, Owen's mom." We shake hands.

"I'm Piper."

"Oh, I'm so happy my Owie is making friends in town."

"Mom," Owen groans at his mother's nickname, but I smile. This woman reminds me so much of Charlotte's mom, how warm and welcoming she is. I never had that in my family and always seemed to gravitate to people who embodied that. Maybe it's part of why I'm so helplessly drawn to Owen.

"Owen is easy to like."

Lori laughs, and Owen glares at her. "Sorry, of course he is. We were going to order food. Have you eaten, honey?"

"No, that sounds great."

Lori takes charge in ordering the food and places the call.

Owen looks completely mortified, and I can't help but to think about how adorable it all is. This is exactly what I needed to get my mind off of things.

"Piper, what is it that you do?" Lori says after hanging up with the restaurant.

"I'm a doctor," I say, keeping it simple.

"She's working to become a surgeon," Owen says proudly, and my stomach sinks. Of course when someone says you're a surgeon, there's always an impressive look on people's faces. It's what my father likes the most about being a cardiothoracic surgeon and why he wanted this path for me. Blakes are supposed to be prestigious.

"Isn't that wonderful. Your mom must be so proud," she says. I swallow thickly and plaster the fakest smile I can and nod. "Just like I'm so proud of my Owie. Have you had a chance to see any of his games?" Lori asks with a genuine smile on her face.

"Not yet, but I'm hoping to go to their game against the Penguins next week." Owen's face lights up with that information, and I can't help but enjoy it. I like knowing that Owen has this same connection to me as I do to him.

"You didn't tell me that," he says, and I shrug.

"It's still not a definite thing. I'll be coming off a twelve hour shift. But Charlotte invited me."

He nods, and I can't help but notice Lori's pleased expression on her face.

She claps her hands and smiles at the both of us. "I'm going to go pick up that food."

"Oh, I can do that," I tell her. I start to stand, but she pushes my shoulder down. Damn, she's strong for a Beta.

"You will not. You two can have a minute while I go get the food."

"Thanks, Mom," Owen says as his mom leaves the small

apartment. As soon as the door is shut, Owen gives me a shy look. "I'm so sorry, I didn't know she was coming. She loves keeping me on my toes."

"She seems like a good mom."

"She is, if not overbearing sometimes." He looks at me questioningly. "Piper, are you okay?"

"Yeah." I give him a small smile. He looks at me like he doesn't believe me, but he doesn't push me.

"I've missed seeing you," he says in a soft voice, and there's a small flutter in my chest.

"I missed seeing you too," I tell him honestly.

"This season is kicking my ass. I wanted to reach out sooner."

"You have a grueling job."

He scoffs and waves his hand at me. "Like you don't?"

"Right, two people with two very busy jobs," I say, and I search his blue eyes. I can't help that I've subconsciously moved closer. His mere presence pulls me in closer, like he has my body roped around in string and he's tugging me toward him.

"Right, no time to get distracted."

"No, we're both really busy."

He licks his lips, and I notice how he looks down at my own. "Right, neither of us can afford to lose focus."

"We're friends," I say, and he nods his head in agreement.

"Friends."

"Owen?"

"Yeah?" His gaze moves from my lips to my eyes, and I'm leaning closer.

"Why do I want you so bad?"

"Fuck." I'm leaning in, my lips so close to his when the door slams open. Owen's mom has her hands full with food, and the moment is broken when we're pulled apart.

"Fuckin' cold here. Christ, why couldn't you get picked up by Florida or something?" Lori complains, not even looking up.

Owen blinks at me, both of us realizing the spell that we were under. Lori clearly knows she interrupted something but puts the food on the table and grabs us plates.

There are far more lingering looks between Owen and I than I would like to admit. I'm about to excuse myself, even though that feels so incredibly rude when they just fed me, when Lori breaks the tension.

"Did you know Owen pissed the bed till he was eight?"

"Mom, fuck's sake."

I can't help the laugh that escapes me, and I have to cover my mouth. Owen glares at me, and Lori is cackling as she goes on with her story.

"Now, I love both my sons. But his older brother Max was a little shit toward Owen when they were little." Owen gives her a look that reads his brother never stopped being a little shit. "He would tell him stories or show him movies like *Jaws* before bed, and well, poor Owen would have nightmares and piss himself. I'm happy to say he's grown out of it, at least I hope so."

"How long are you staying?" Owen asks his mom.

"I was hoping you would get me tickets for tomorrow. Besides, I got a hotel, so you can chill the fuck out." Lori might curse more than any of the hockey players I know, but damn am I happy that she's here. Though she might have made everything awkward in the first place. It's better than staring at Owen or acting on what was about to happen.

Then I'd be even further in the hole with a Beta and Alpha I shouldn't want. That I don't have time for, that both keep trying to complicate my fucking life.

"Do you have any siblings?" Lori asks.

"No, but my best friend feels like a sister."

"Isn't that sweet."

"Her Alphas play for the Foxes."

"What a small world. It isn't that hot captain you've been talking about, right, Owen?" Owen's face is bright red as he looks over at his mother. At least I'm not the only one with an Alexi Bandnin hard on in the room.

"No, Mom. Can we stop talking?"

I pull out my phone and see the time. I need to be ready for rounds at five. "I actually have to get some sleep before my shift. Thank you for having me, Owen. It was nice meeting you, Lori."

"Of course, nice meeting you too, honey." Lori pulls out her phone and acts like she's ignoring us as Owen grabs my jacket and puts his own on. We're both in the tight little entryway outside of his door. It's cold and dark, and every part of me wants to fist his shirt and bring his lips to mine, but I stop myself. Starting something with Owen wouldn't be smart, right? My life is complicated enough, but as I look at him, I can't help but feel like there's something more here, something I can't explain.

"I'm sorry about her. Mom's always had a big mouth."

I shake my head and look at him, and while we're the same height, he's all muscle. Why do I like the fact that he's a Beta who could still toss me around. Shit, I'm in too deep. He licks his lips, and I sigh. "She was nice. I had a good time."

"Are we going to talk about this, Piper?"

"I can't right now," I tell him, and he nods. Both of us know that we shouldn't start anything. But damn, a deep-rooted part of me wants to.

He sighs and nods. "I'll see you at the game next week?"

"Hope so."

"Night, Piper." I can't help it. I fist his jacket and wrap him up in a hug, which he returns immediately. Holding on to him feels so right. He smells like his house, and I want more, but I stop myself. Owen deserves someone who can be all in, and right now, I can't. My life's a mess, and adding someone into it isn't smart.

His hand strokes down my back, and the hug is far more intimate than it should be. "Goodnight, Owie." He pulls back from the hug, and I can't help the laugh that escapes me. God, it feels good to laugh. When I clear the tears from my eyes and see the way he looks at me, I know I'm fucked.

I've got to figure my shit out. Because something tells me if I let Owen and Alexi go, it will be a bigger regret than any career decision I ever make.

"Go Foxes!" I say stupidly as I walk up the stairs and make the walk back to my townhouse. I'm not sure if I feel more or less helpless than I did this morning.

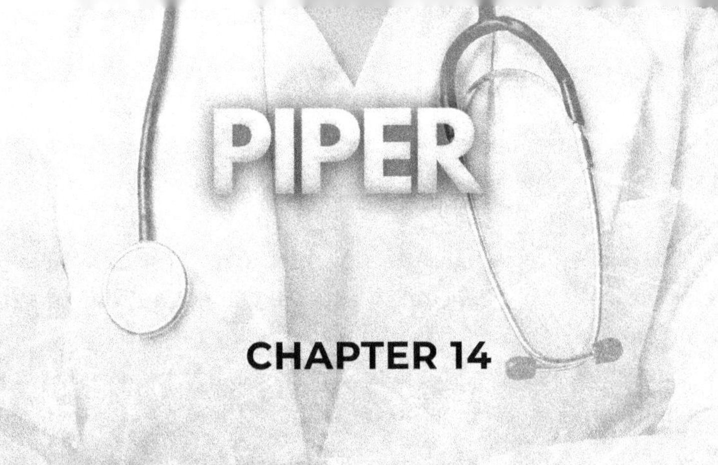


## CHAPTER 14

Anders, Charlotte, and myself are all in the fourth row watching pre-skate, and I can't help all the feelings flowing through me. Not only does Alexi keep smirking at me every chance he gets because the psychopath does his pre-skate with no helmet on. But Owen has squirted his water bottle over his hair twice, and I feel like I'm on edge.

I still haven't made a decision about work, not really. I can't just throw all my time away like that. I have to be absolutely sure. Not to mention the fact that both Alexi and Owen have been running through my head rent-fucking-free.

"Thank God you're not an Omega, or you'd be leaving a trail of slick in that seat," Charlotte says, breaking up my thoughts.

"She's speaking from experience," Anders says in my defense, and she smacks his chest.

"Yeah, Charles, glass houses."

"I just wish I knew who you were drooling over more, Alexi or Owen."

"Owen, goalies are better," Anders says, and Charlotte rolls her eyes. I'm sad Katie isn't here, but the fact is she gets bored before the first period is even over. Plus, Anders' parents have been trying to get as much time with her as they can while they're in the States.

Charlotte puts a hand on my thigh, and her pretty eyes search mine. "Piper Penelope Blake, are you hiding something from me?"

I swallow as I stare down at my small Omega friend. She has her moments of being intimidating. "There was a moment with Owen, well Alexi too."

"Are there more finger fucks you aren't telling me about?"

Anders has a coughing/laughing fit next to her, and I scoff.

"Anders, will you go get us some drinks?" Charlotte says to her Alpha.

"You got it, *kulta*." Anders leaves, and I feel like I can talk more freely.

"Alexi tricked me into going on a date with him, and I met Owen's mom."

Charlotte blinks at me, rubbing her belly. "These are things you tell your best friend, Piper."

"You have a lot going on."

"I never have too much going on to not make time for you, Piper. Tell me what's really going on."

I look out at the ice, intense brown eyes staring at me and Charlotte until his focus is moved to a rogue puck.

"I don't want to get into it here, but I'm working on it."

"Which part, that you hate being a surgeon or that you're in love with two guys."

"I'm not in love with them—wait—you know I'm not liking surgery?"

She scoffs and waves me off. "Piper, we've been best friends for as long as I can remember, of course I noticed. But I also know you, you have to come to terms with things on your own."

I blink at her a few times. "Charles, I don't know what to do."

"About the hot hockey men, or surgery?"

"Both."

"You want my real opinion or not?" I sigh and nod my head. "I think you need to stop caring what your dickhead father thinks and switch specialties. And as far as the guys go, I don't know Owen, but he seems kind and smitten with you. I think Alexi is perfect for you, and I've always known you would need an Alpha in your pack."

"And you were what, just never going to tell me this?"

She shrugs and looks out at the ice, smiling at her Alphas. Eli blows her a kiss with his gloved hand, and Mikael gives her a look that only they understand. "Like I said, you're hard headed. I love you, Piper. But you don't do shit unless you have the idea or want to do something. I know you would be happy with a Beta, and Owen could be that Beta. But no one has ever taken care of you." I scoff, and she grabs my arm and looks at me. "I'm not saying you need a nest or you need to be coddled. I'm just saying you deserve someone who you can share your burdens with, and I know that's hard for you."

Charlotte looks back at the ice, and I'm rendered speechless.

When I had breakfast with Alexi, that's how I felt. I felt understood and that I could tell him anything without feeling like a burden, and when I was around Owen, I felt lighter.

*Fuck.*

"But one thing at a time, maybe call the Colonel," she says. We both grimace at my dad's nickname.

"Maybe."

"I don't think you'll be able to go all in with the guys until you figure out what you want to do for work," she says, and I nod.

"What would I do without you?" I say, bumping her shoulder.

She smiles and rests her head on my shoulder. "I ask myself the same thing about you all the time."

———

The game is intense. There have been multiple penalties and power plays. The score is one nothing for the Penguins.

"They need to get their shit together," Anders says, his elbows on his knees as he watches the game. He always keeps some contact with Charlotte. It's obvious hockey is still something that he's passionate about, but Charlotte and their kids are more important. I'm so happy that they found the right balance. I can't imagine if Charlotte was doing this all on her own while all three of them traveled.

"Mikael is getting frustrated," Charlotte says, and Anders shakes his head.

"Our defense is letting too much slip through. The new guy doesn't stand a fucking chance unless they tighten up."

I watch Owen with all my attention. He's quick and surprisingly not afraid to get into the mix. I've seen him push multiple players and even trip one "accidentally".

Suddenly, there's a breakaway from a Penguins player, and it's two versus one, and they outmatch our defense. Owen barely has time to react and is too late. The puck hits the net, and the fans groan in unison.

I sip my beer. I've had far too many, and I'm getting concerned how much alcohol has factored into my days off. There's a girl wearing a Martel jersey in front of me who is starting to get obnoxious.

"Fuck, the new goalie sucks," she says on a giggle, turning to the guy on her left. He doesn't comment, and she doubles down on her statement. "They should really look at getting an Alpha for their goalie. He's too small."

I don't know if it's the beer or my need to defend Owen as I tap the guy's shoulder. "Maybe you should find a different date instead."

"Excuse you?" the woman says, glaring back at me. "No one was talking to you."

"No, but your loud and obnoxious voice carries, and since we all have to listen to you, I thought I'd put my two cents in. The goalie does not suck."

"We're down two nothing, he sucks."

"Not as much dick as you probably had to suck to get him to bring you to this game. He doesn't even seem interested." It's a low blow, and even I know that. But the guy she's with doesn't even step in.

"Piper," Charlotte says quietly and tugs on my shirt.

"Listen to your fat friend, and fuck off."

"Oh hell no." I know it's not very doctorly of me, but I'm up and jumping over the seat and getting in her face. I put a finger against her chest. "You got something to say, bitch?"

The woman's eyes are wide, and she does the dumbest thing possible. She pushes me. I've got about six inches on her and more muscle. So when I push her back, she bumps into the guy next to her, who accidentally spills his beer all over her.

To my absolute horror, I look up at the screen and see that the camera is zoomed in on our altercation. No sooner is a security officer dragging me along to the drunk tank.

"I'll have one of the guys fix this!" Charlotte shouts from her seat, looking both mortified and like she's trying to hold back a laugh at the same time.

"Let's go, drunky," the security guard says, gripping me by the arm and leading me up the stairs and down to level 1.

"Saw you were with Larsen. I'll do my best to not get you banned from the stadium, so what set you off anyway?"

"She said our goalie sucked and that my pregnant friend was fat."

The officer shrugs his shoulders and opens the gate to the tank. It's two long silver benches and sadly no TV to watch the game either. I have a companion, but he's sleeping in the corner. I find the most hygienic spot and sit down. I'm glad I left my stuff with Charlotte at least and wonder if she and Anders will be able to bust me out. It feels like my own personal sin bin.

I'm not sure what came over me. I'm embarrassed, but there's also a part of me that wants to go back and punch that bitch in her mouth.

Sitting in this stinky shell of a space has me realizing that I need to get my shit together. Charlotte is right; once I figure out the next step with my job, everything else will follow. I've got to grow a spine, deal with my dad, stop drinking on my days off, and deal with my shit.

It feels like I've been here for hours when I hear the security guard speaking to someone. "Of course, Mr. Bandnin, we'll make sure there's no record of any of this. Thank you so much for the signed jerseys. My kids are going to freak out."

"Thanks, Frank." Even if the guard hadn't said his last name, I would have recognized his voice. The guard opens the gate and gives me a curt smile.

"You're one lucky lady. Most people get a lifetime ban."

I give him a fake smile, and Alexi hands me my things. *Fucking Charlotte.*

Due to Alexi's meddling, I don't have anything to sign, and we're able to leave the stadium right away.

"I'm driving you home." I nod my head, feeling shame that he had to use his position to get me out of trouble. We're walking down a hallway I've never been in before, and the light hits him the right way, so I can really appreciate him. He's in a dark blue suit, and his dark hair is pushed back. No wonder why it felt so long, he must have done press and everything before coming to get me.

"I'm sorry you had to do all this."

"What did she say that set you off?" he asks, and my face heats. He saw the whole thing on screen.

"She said Owen sucks and that Charlotte was fat." He laughs so boisterously that I can't help laughing with him.

"You're full of surprises, *malyshka*." Great, *malyshka* is starting to grow on me, at least the way he says it.

He opens the door, and I realize we're in the locker room. The team has left, and he's grabbing his bag, and I can't stop myself from looking at his ass in his dress pants.

Fuck it all.

Maybe it's that he got me out of a jam, how good he looks, how he makes me forget. But when he spins around, I grab the lapels of his jacket and crash his lips against mine. I feel free.

If Alexi is surprised by my forward nature, he doesn't let on. He drops his bag, grips me by my ass, and is carrying me until my back hits a hard wall.

I groan, but neither of us stops, my hands roaming under his suit jacket. His massive hands knead my ass as he presses his hard cock against my core. He's fucking huge, and I need more.

Alexi kisses like I'm his oxygen, like he needs to kiss me or he won't survive, and maybe I'm starting to feel the same way.

"Make me feel better," I say against his ear. He pauses for a moment, and I hope that I didn't ruin everything. When he puts me on my feet, I take a deep breath knowing I've ruined the moment.

But when his big brown eyes meet mine and he unbuttons

my jeans, my heart races. He tugs them down along with my panties until they're about mid thigh.

"Hands against the fucking wall," he says in a deep tone. I swallow and immediately follow his direction. His hand squeezes my ass cheek before he removes it. There is shuffling behind me before I feel his large hard cock pressed against my ass. My nails want to dig into the wall for purchase, but all I can do is keep them laying flat.

The cold cement wall is the only thing I can focus on while I wait for him to do something—anything.

He grinds his length against my bare ass, his large hands gripping my hips roughly. "Is this what you need, *malyshka?* You need my cock to feel better?"

I don't answer him right away, and he smacks my ass. It stings, and my nails drag against the tile, flakes of paint chipping under my nails.

"I asked you a question."

"Yes, I need it," I say, hating how pleading I sound. Alexi just has this way about him that turns me into a begging, wet mess. I should hate it, I should be scrambling to take charge here. But I'm constantly managing everything in my life, so it's nice for someone to take control for once.

He slides his cock between my thighs, just rubbing the outside of my pussy lips.

"I didn't even need to touch your cunt to get you wet, did I? Maybe I should just fuck you like this. Maybe I shouldn't give you what you want."

"Please," I beg. It's dramatic, but I feel like I may quite literally die if he doesn't fuck me right now.

His one hand leaves my thigh, sliding up my stomach and chest. His hand grips my jaw, forcing the back of my head against his shoulder.

"But then how would I reward you for standing up for our

Beta?" he says, his cock ramming into my pussy with no other words. A ridiculously loud moan escapes my lips, and Alexi wraps his hand around my mouth, forcing me to shut up while he uses my body in the way I've been craving.

"This pussy needed me, you needed me," he says in a growl against my ear. I'm so thankful his big hand is covering my mouth, or I might let it tumble out how much I need him but don't want to. Or how this is the best I've felt all week, or how he completely consumes me when we're together.

Alexi's other hand leaves my hip, wrapping around and toying with my clit. I can feel his knot pressing against my entrance, and I picture myself fucking him so many times that I learn how to take his knot. The thought and his increased pace on my clit makes me moan against his hand.

"Lock my cock," he groans. He's fucking me roughly, and my face would be pressed against the wall if he wasn't holding it. I've never locked an Alpha, but I know if I do, I'll come right away. "Fucking milk my cock, show me how good it feels to be fucked by your Alpha."

All resolve breaks, and my cunt clenches around him, my walls spasming. His hand drops from my mouth and wraps around my chest. I'm not sure we could be any physically closer than we are now. With him no longer muffling my sounds, my moans echo in the locker room. My face feels numb, and my body holds Alexi's cock deep inside of me, making my orgasm last even longer. I'm shaking, and my cheek presses against the cold wall as I ride out my orgasm.

Alexi can hardly thrust, but my pussy does all the work for him. He moans against my back, his teeth grazing against my shoulder. "Fuck," he says, and that's when his chest starts to rumble.

It should be the fact that I locked him, that we fucked in his locker room, or even that he saved me from getting in trouble that should have me panicking.

But no, it's the purring of his chest that scares the absolute shit out of me.

My body releases his, and I feel a mixture of my wetness and his cum drip down my thigh. He doesn't stop purring, and he doesn't stop touching me. My head is spinning, and my flight response is on overdrive.

"You okay?" he asks, and I just keep my face pressed against the cement wall. Why am I like this? I feel like I'm about to cry and break down, but like I always do, I shove it deep down, where I keep everything else.

"I'm just going to get cleaned up," I say. I nearly have to pry his hands off of me. I don't dare look back and see his face as I walk over to the bathrooms in the locker room.

I clean myself up with shaking hands, both from the intense orgasm I had with Alexi and my overwhelming nerves over the fact that he's going to drive me home.

I'm trying to reason with myself the entire time that I get cleaned up. When I have myself in somewhat decent order, I walk back out to the locker room. Alexi is sitting in his locker, his elbows on his knees as he looks at me.

"Piper—"

"Can you take me home please?" He looks dejected, and I feel guilty about putting that look there. What is wrong with me?

"Yeah," he says.

The walk to his car and the drive is dead silent. I want to apologize for how I acted after, but there's a lot to dissect there. Alexi said a lot of things during sex that scared me. He mentioned Owen being our Beta, how he was my Alpha, I locked his fucking massive Alpha dick.

I rub my face and look out the window as he pulls up to my house.

Of course he knows where I live.

I'm about to just open the door without a word like an asshole. "Piper, can we talk?" I look back at him, his big brown eyes pleading with mine.

"Today has been a lot. Can we talk later?" I ask, I need time to process and not spew every single thing I'm thinking right now.

"You get a week," he says while still holding on to my arm.

"What?" I blink back at him confused.

"You have a week to think about this, and if you don't come to me to talk about it, well, I'll hunt your ass down."

I blink at him, and he smirks. Why do I both hate and love that this larger-than-life Alpha knows me so well?

"Alright, a week."

"Night, *malyshka.*"

"Night, Alexi."

## CHAPTER 15

I feel unsettled. Like the other shoe is going to drop and I don't know why. Having my mom visit was jarring. It always brings out a part of me I try to push down. She is the only person in the world who treats me like an Omega. I wish I didn't love it, but truly, when she's around, it's the only time I feel like my true self.

There's this guilt festering inside of me, not so much that I'm lying to the NHL, because honestly, fuck their rules. More so that I'm lying to Piper, and maybe a small piece of me feels bad for lying to Alexi. How I feel about Piper is unlike any connection I've had before. I can't deny that there is definitely an attraction to the older hockey captain either. But he is intimidating, but in a way that makes him alluring.

But now is not the time for a mental breakdown. I need to be stronger than ever. The game against the Sharks is coming up, and that might be the end of this all. If Max isn't willing to keep my secret, then my professional career could be over.

Part of me wants to call Piper and have her hang out again, but I know that if I do, one thing will lead to another. If we're both adamant that now isn't the time, the only thing we can do is stay away from one another. As much as I don't want that, I can't lose this focus, and Piper is on her own path that can't be disrupted right now. I wonder if she would change her mind if she knew I was an Omega.

I feel like a dick for even thinking it. She seems to like me well enough thinking I'm a Beta, but I wonder if she knew the truth, maybe she would change her mind.

Mikael breaks me out of my thoughts as he nudges my shoulder. "You good, rookie?" he asks, and I nod my head. "You sure?" he asks again.

"He's fine. Isn't that right, *sólnyshka?*" Alexi says while wrapping his arm around my shoulders and pulling me against his massive body. His thick scent nearly drowns me, but yet somehow comforts me at the same time.

I know that I should break away from his touch and act like I don't like it. But I stay put. My needy Omega nature wins this round. It feels nice to be held, and I hadn't realized how much I needed it until Piper gave me that hug last week. *Fuck.*

Alexi's hand pushes boundaries as he roughs up my hair and gives everyone a smile as they head to the ice for practice. Our game against the Caps is tomorrow, and this unsettling feeling is making it hard to focus. I go to follow everyone onto the ice, but Alexi holds me back, letting everyone else head to the ice while we're left in the locker room—alone.

He steps away from me to where he's looking down at me but doesn't give me a wide berth of space. He fists my jersey in a non-aggressive way, but it's still way hotter than it should be as I look up at him.

"What's going on?" he asks.

"Nothing, I'm fine."

"You're not fine. You seem tired and like your head is elsewhere." His eyes search mine, and I want to curse him for being so perceptive.

"I said I'm fine, so let's go to practice."

I go to walk away, but his hold on my jersey just gets tighter. "What do you need?" he asks, and my brows furrow.

"What do you mean?"

"What do you need to be more settled?" he asks, and my eyes widen. I rip his hand off my jersey and go to stomp away from him when he tugs me back. I smack his hand away, and he shakes his head. "I'm not going to tell anybody."

"Fuck." I tug at my hair, and Alexi shakes his head.

"I swear, Owen, I won't tell anybody. Just tell me what you need."

"Why would you keep my secret? How can I trust that you won't really tell anyone?" I ask him, my heart racing, and it feels like my stomach is going to sink out of my ass. Like everything I've worked for is going to go right down the fucking drain because this over analytical dick figured out my secret.

"Because the team needs you, and I think the rule is fucking stupid."

I blink at him but can't get a read on if he's telling me the truth or not. I shake my head. "You don't understand. I can't lose this."

His hands grip my padded shoulders, and he leans down to look me in the eyes. "I give you my word that your secret is safe with me. Just let me help you."

I don't buy his reasoning, and I shake my head. "You have no reason to really keep my secret."

He groans and shakes his head before he leans down and places his lips on mine. It's a quick little peck but enough to render me speechless.

"That's why, okay?" He backs up and removes his hands from me. "You don't have to feel the same way. It won't change anything. But I like you, and I like Piper," he says with a smile and shrugs. "You love hockey like I do, and you should be able to live out your dream. So let me help you."

I just stare at him, my mouth wide open and my lips still tingling from the brief kiss. He lightly smacks my jaw, bringing me out of my stupor while smiling at me.

"Just tell me what you need, and it's yours," he says. He gives me one last lingering look, like he wants to devour me whole, before walking on his skates and heading to practice.

My hand slides up my neck, and I touch my lips. I guess that was the other shoe I felt was going to drop this entire time, and I'm not sure how I feel about it or Alexi Bandnin.

--------

The plane lands in D.C, and I've felt Alexi's eyes on me the whole time, like he's just waiting for me to have a mental breakdown. I already told Piper that now isn't the time for a relationship, and now I have another Alpha who wants my attention. The Omega side of me preens at having two Alphas who are interested in me, but the other part of me is terrified.

On the one hand, there's an Alpha who knows the truth, who flirted with me before knowing my true designation, and has kept his word. Not to mention also happens to be into Piper just as much as I am.

I'm overwhelmed, and there's only one person I want to talk to right now. I feel like both a mama's boy and a needy Omega as I text my mom from the plane.

Hey, Mom.

Mom: Hey, sweetie. I have the DVR set for your game tonight.

. . .

I smile to myself and love my mom for her honesty. I know that she's in California right now and will be going to Max's game tonight. I always wondered how my brother felt about my relationship with mom and if he was jealous. Just like I was jealous of him being an Alpha and getting to live out my dream so effortlessly.

Does Max know?

Mom: No, I promised you I wouldn't tell him, and I haven't. Keeping this a secret is making me sick.

My captain found out I'm an Omega.

I see my mom is trying to call me, and I groan. As much as I want to answer, I can't right now.

I can't answer. I'm on the team plane.

Mom: Is he going to get you into trouble, Owie? Do I need to come back? Tell me what you need, honey.

He said he wants to help me.

Mom: You don't trust him?

He likes me more than just being his teammate.

Mom: Do you like him as much as you like
Piper?

I roll my eyes. My mom wouldn't stop talking about Piper after she left. About how pretty and smart she was, and how I was a dumbass for not telling her the truth so she could be my Alpha. Despite my mom's opinions on how I should be living my life, I do appreciate her support, and she always makes me feel a little less alone.

I don't know, Mom. It's all too much. I don't know what to do.

Mom: You let these Alphas take care of you. Stop being such a fucking dumbass. I love you. Call me later.

I sigh and put my phone away. Taking her advice is easier said than done.

———

The ice is sloshy, and we've gotten roughed up to the point where the tension is thick. The penalties are getting out of control, and Coach Applegate is one more power play for the Caps from having an aneurysm.

It's a tie with one goal for each team, and I'm nearly at my breaking point with exhaustion. It's times like this that the reality of how long I can play hockey hits—this is temporary for me. I can only do this for so long until my body breaks down. So with what time I do have in this arena, on this team, and in the NHL, I'm going to make the most of it.

There's a stoppage of play, and I take a swig of water and wet my hair. I squirt the bottle in the air and track the flow of the water, realigning my eyesight.

I'm not sure how I manage it, but I stay on my feet, I stay alert, and don't let another goal slip in. We end the third period at a tie, and I almost wish I would have let a goal in so we didn't go into overtime.

Multiple teammates clap me on the back, grab my face-mask, or slap my ass with their stick as we head back for a short break before coming back out and hopefully winning in overtime. The thought of going to shootouts makes me want to throw up.

I'm about to walk into the locker room when a fist grabs my shirt and drags me into an alcove.

I'm so tired that I just blink at Alexi as he holds me by my jersey.

"What do you need?" he asks, his eyes searching mine. At this moment, I can hardly give a fuck about the consequences. I just need… I need to be me. The person I shove so far away that most of the time I don't know who I am.

I answer truthfully. "I don't know."

He places his hand behind the back of my head and the other on my back. I wish we could ditch all the heavy gear, but there's no time. We've got to get back out there soon enough.

Alexi holds me tight against his chest as a purr rumbles out of him. His scent wraps around me like a cocoon, and his touch gives me purchase.

"You're doing so good out there. The team needs you, but if you can't do overtime, we can send Johannson in."

"No, I can do it," I mumble against his chest. He feels so

good next to me, and I'm somehow getting re-energized from his touch and words alone.

"I know you can. You never need to tell me how strong you are because I already know."

I want to laugh and tell him he's being ridiculous, but all I do is accept this kind comfort that he's giving me, what he promised me. That he wants to help me and that he will keep my secrets.

"This helped," I say, about to tug away, but he just holds me closer, like he doesn't want this moment to ever end. I'd be lying if I said I didn't want the same thing.

Eventually he lets go, not a word said between the two of us as we head back out on the ice. We clench the win with only two minutes to spare, and I sleep the short flight home. I'm so exhausted by the time we get to the practice facility that I worry about getting home.

Luckily for me, the decision is out of my hands when Alexi leads me to his car. I'm not sure how I get home, or how I end up tucked in my bed. But when I do wake up, all I can think about are the two Alphas who seem to be consuming all my thoughts and how much longer I can keep them at an arm's length.

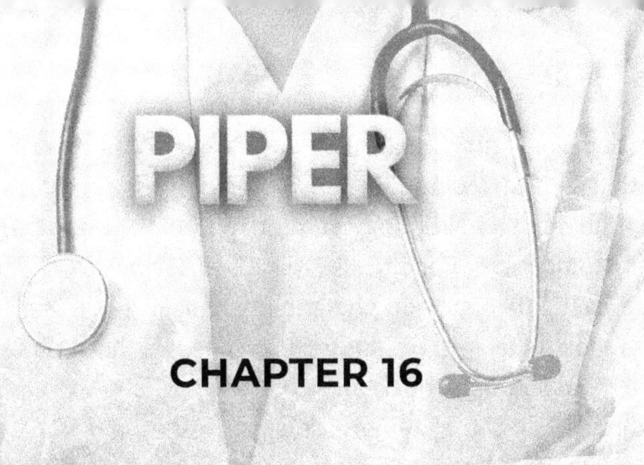

# PIPER

## CHAPTER 16

Did I let a week go by on accident? Maybe, possibly? All I know is that I'm barely functioning, and the thought of talking to Alexi about my feelings or reaching out to Owen feels like too much. No matter how much a part of me is craving both of them.

God, I wish I could stop being so fucking difficult. I wish that I could make these life changing decisions so easily, but I have to be sure. It's my first day off in over a week, and I plan on actually taking care of myself. Maybe I'll get a haircut and a manicure.

When my doorbell rings, my heart sinks in my chest.

My immediate thought is it's Alexi. He told me one week, and it's been eight days. But when I open the door, it's far worse.

My dad stands at my stoop with a disapproving scowl on his face. He's in his early sixties, though you wouldn't be able to tell. The man is an all overbearing Alpha. He still has a full head of hair—that he colors. It's dark like mine, and I can see a few grays scattered around his temples. While I'm the spitting image of him, when I look at him, all I feel is dread.

The only thing I feel from my father is his dissatisfaction with me. I'm looking at the reason why I never feel good enough. I wish I was brave enough to slam the door in his face, but I could never. Technically, it is his house anyway.

"Well, Piper, are you going to invite us in?"

I look to his left, and his girlfriend Tess is there. She's a Beta and kind enough, but I have no idea what she sees in my father besides his money. Personally, I don't think there's enough money in the world for anyone to put up with his ass.

"Of course, come on in."

"Hi, Piper." Tess waves at me. She's closer to my age than she is to my dad's. I give her about three more months. Dad's girlfriends usually only have a life cycle of about a year and a half until he gets bored or she gets too old, in his eyes.

My dad looks around the townhouse with a sneer on his face. It feels like he's making a list in his head of everything he disapproves of or thinks is tacky.

"I didn't realize you were in town," I say, breaking the silence first.

"Peter has a conference in New York, so we thought we would swing by and say hi," Tess says cheerfully. My father looks down at her like she's an idiot. Her expiration date dwindles down every time she speaks, the poor thing.

"Oh, that's great. I just wish I would have known you were coming."

"I had assumed you'd be working," my dad says. Ah, that makes more sense. He could just text me and say he attempted to stop by. Then he would be able to complain about how I wasn't around to see him. Nothing I do is ever good enough.

"Right, it's actually my day off."

"Then we should get dinner," Tess says. My dad glares at her. Oh, yeah, the poor girl is like expired milk at this point.

I swallow and look at my dad. "I could order in, or we could go somewhere."

"What would be faster?" he says, and I contain every ounce of frustration coursing through me.

"There's a pho place really close, and they're fast. I can go and pick it up."

"Very well," my dad says, sitting on my couch and turning on the TV. Tess looks around like she doesn't know what to do with herself before sitting down next to him.

They let me know what they want, though I know my dad will complain about the meal in some fashion as I call and place it.

"I'll be right back," I say. I barely even get a head nod or a grunt of approval before I leave the house.

*Some fucking day off.*

I treat the walk to pho like it's a death march. Diep looks surprised to see me here on a Friday but is friendly as always as she hands me my order. I might walk slower than necessary on my way home. The longer it takes me to get the food in, the quicker he'll want to eat and get the hell out of here. The sooner he leaves, the sooner I can breathe again.

I open the gate to my walkway when I hear my name being shouted, and I turn to my left to see a smirking Alexi.

"Fuck," I mutter, and he picks up his strides to meet me as I'm fumbling with my bag to open the door.

"Piper, it's been a week."

I sigh and look up at him, but he doesn't look pissed at least.

"You really like me?" I ask him, a plan in motion.

"I do," he says with a smile.

"Great, then come be a buffer between me and my dad." I give him no time to really let my words sink in as I open the door and nearly tug on his hand behind me. Alexi looks confused for a moment but gives a polite smile as I introduce everyone. "Dad, Tess, this is Alexi. He plays for the Foxes with Charlotte's pack mates."

"Ah, yes, your little friend," my dad says. Charlotte has been my best friend since I was five, yet he's never taken the time to learn her name. He's such an asshole.

"Lovely meeting you both," Alexi says, shoving his hands in his pockets. My father looks him up and down like Alexi isn't worth the dirt under his shoe, and it makes me even more angry than when he does the same to me. I ignore him the best I can and take out the food and place it on the table. I give Alexi half of my portion as everyone comes to sit and eat.

It's a round table, and Alexi is to my left, Tess to my right, and my dad is smack dab across from me. Here's to hoping they eat, leave, and I don't have to deal with my dad's judgements for long.

He eats slowly and methodically, like he does everything.

"They could ease up on the salt," my dad says. Tess hums in agreement, and I keep my mouth shut. The food is delicious.

"I think it's pretty tasty," Alexi says.

"You would," my father replies. I watch as Alexi's fist clenches under the table, but he doesn't reply.

My father takes one more bite before putting his spoon down and looking directly at me.

"I have another motive for stopping by." Of course he does. Peter Blake always has some sort of motive. It's not like I have a father who would stop by to say he loves me or that he hopes I'm doing well. I'm not sure my dad has ever told me he loves me now that I think about it.

"Okay," I reply. He looks over at Alexi like he's irritated that he's a part of the conversation, but he wipes his mouth and continues anyway.

"Dr. Mayfield has told me some troubling things, and I

thought you could use some more motivation, or we could discuss your current performance."

I know my cheeks are heating, mostly due to anger, not embarrassment.

"What did she say?"

"She said that you're too emotional and that you're getting too attached. She said that you show promise, but unless you get that under control, you'll fall behind in your program."

"I don't think I'm falling behind," I say, my appetite gone.

"I didn't ask what you thought. I'm telling you what your attending has told me. If you were my surgical resident, I wouldn't tolerate the way you engage with your patients."

"Well, thank fuck you're not my attending."

"Piper, that's enough," he says, arching a brow at my tantrum.

"I work extremely hard, and I'm a good surgeon. I think that caring for my patients makes me a better doctor. I'm sorry that I'm not detached from human emotion."

That one hits him deep as he glares at me. "Always such a disappointment, Piper."

Alexi's chair legs screech against the wood floor as he stands and places his hands against the table.

"That's enough. Your daughter is talented, intelligent, and compassionate. What else could you ask for?"

"I expect excellence," my dad says calmly, staring at me.

"I guess I'll just be a huge disappointment for the rest of my life, then. No one's perfect, Dad."

My father places his hands on the table to scoot his chair but stays seated one more moment before speaking. "If I get another less than perfect review from Mayfield, I will no longer fund your lifestyle while you finish your program."

"Well, let me make it easier for you. I'm thinking about switching to family medicine." It spills out of me like word vomit. I didn't want to bring it up, but he pushed me too far. It's almost like I want to truly disappoint him as much as possible.

"Pack up your things. I'm going to be renting this unit to someone else," he says calmly, standing up and directing Tess to do the same.

"What?" I say blinking.

"I said you're no longer welcome here. You want to throw away everything I gave you? Then fine, I'll give you nothing in return. The management company will be here tomorrow to make sure you're gone."

Alexi looks at me and then my father. I can tell he wants to say something, and I just shake my head at him.

"Fine, I don't need anything from you," I say to my dad, even though my heart is breaking. Sure, I knew how this would go, that I'd never really meet his standards. But there's still this small part of me that's always seeking his approval. This little girl who looked around at her dance recital and never saw her dad there. The little girl who danced with her best friend's dad instead of her own at the father daughter dance. The adult woman who just wants her dad to love her. He's asked everything of me, and I've done everything I could. I'm a child of a narcissist, and the wounds cut deep—far deeper than I ever realized.

"Wonderful, then I suppose I'll actually make a profit on this place instead of it operating at a loss," he says, looking me up and down. It breaks me, and I have no words left, my mouth gaping open.

Suddenly, Alexi's hand is on my dad's arm, tugging him out of the house. My dad's eyes are wide, and Tess is scrambling out the door. Alexi has him at the threshold, and my dad is about to say something, but Alexi speaks first.

"I'll pack her shit and make sure she's taken care of. Fucking asshole." Alexi slams the door.

I know it's not the right response, and everything is so fucked right now. But I can't help the laughter that bubbles out of me. Alexi called my dad an asshole, and his expression was priceless. I don't have a home anymore, don't know where my career is going, and I feel so emotionally stunted that I don't deserve any kindness.

But my dad being called an asshole, it helps the sting a little bit.

Alexi looks at me like I've absolutely lost my mind, and maybe I have. But I'm sure as fuck not going to break down because I know if I do, there's no going back. Now is the time to get my house—*ha*—in order.

"Piper, are you okay?"

I shrug my shoulders and grab a bottle of white wine out of the fridge. I know I told myself that I was going to cut back on my days off, but this seems fitting.

I sit on the tiled floor and flick off the cap. Alexi comes next to me, his long legs out in front of him as he holds his hand out. We pass the wine back and forth in silence until I finally sigh.

"Sorry for using you as a human shield."

He laughs and takes the wine bottle out of my hand before taking a sip. "This tastes like shit."

"It was five dollars."

He groans but takes another sip. "So are we packing your shit up?"

"Yeah," I sigh and clang my head against the wooden cabinet. "I could call Charlotte, but she has so much going on. Their house is full, and with the twins on the way, it's only going to be more chaotic."

"Stay at my place," he says. He's so nonchalant about it, like it was the obvious choice.

"I couldn't impose."

"I offered. I have three empty bedrooms, and I'm gone half the time for work anyway."

"I don't know, Alexi," I say. Our relationship status is already confusing, and living together would only complicate things even further. But what other options do I have? With Alexi, there's a guarantee of a quiet bedroom. At Charlotte's, she has three Alphas vying for her attention as well as a toddler and two newborns on the way. I know they would be more than happy to let me stay, but it would feel like walking on eggshells.

"You're sure?"

"Yeah, I'm sure." He takes the wine bottle and stands up and puts it on the counter. "We aren't packing up your shitty wine. Do you need me to go get boxes?"

"I can do it," I say, and Alexi shakes his head.

"Fuck, woman. Will you let me help you?"

I place my hands on my hips, and I want to tell him off. But I swallow it down. I'm not used to someone wanting to help me the way that Alexi does.

"Sorry, yes. I need boxes."

"Okay, I'll get some boxes, and you start packing up. I'm still starving, so I'll pick up more food on the way. And less shitty wine."

"Okay," I say softly, more than ready for a moment of peace by myself.

Alexi tilts his head and walks over to me and puts his thumb under my chin, forcing me to look up at him. "Your father's wrong. Fuck him for not seeing how perfect you are."

I blink up at him and his soft expression. The realty of

everything is hitting me, and Alexi must notice it. His hand drops from my face, and he gives me a small smile.

"I'll be right back." I nod as he leaves the house.

I start packing the kitchen first, and I'm thankful that I hardly ever cook, and I'll finish this space before Alexi gets back.

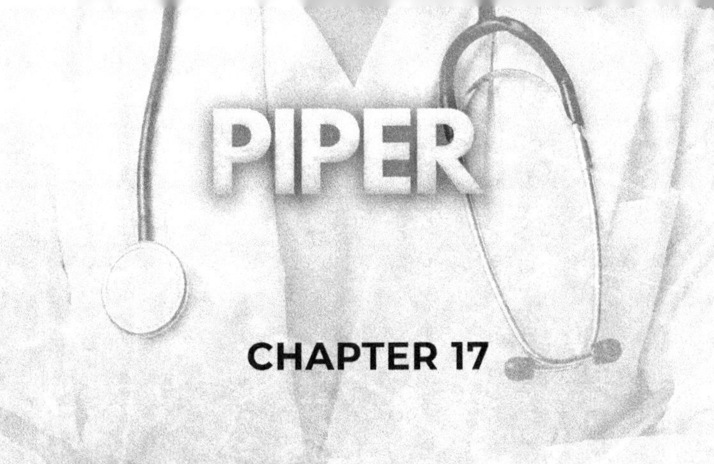


# CHAPTER 17

Charlotte is cackling so hard that if she doesn't stop, she's going to piss herself. I glare at her, and she waves a hand at me.

"I'm sorry," she says.

"You don't seem sorry, laughing at my expense."

"I'm not, you know I'm not. I wish I could punch your dickhead father in the throat. But the fact that of all people, you're moving in with Alexi. Piper, this sounds like a sitcom. The man is absolutely in love with you, and you still have no idea how to cope with your feelings." I give her another glare, and she wipes the rogue tears from her eyes from laughing so hard. "You know you can come and stay with us. You don't have to live here."

Eli places one of my boxes in the empty bedroom and kisses his Omega's hair before leaving us to go back out to the SUV. I nearly take her offer, but I can't help but feel like a burden and that I would be infiltrating their perfect little family.

"It's fine. It's not permanent anyway." Though I will likely need to find a roommate to afford a new apartment in the area,

I'll make sure I don't overstay my welcome. I need to find out where Alexi needs me to chip in.

Charlotte wraps her arms around me, her pregnant belly hitting my hip. "You're okay though? With what happened with the Colonel?"

"Yeah, I'll be fine."

"Piper," she sighs, and I squeeze her a little tighter.

"You just worry about incubating my nieces or nephews, or one of each. You don't have to worry about me," I say with a smile. Charlotte hasn't let go of me, and she sighs against my side.

"Just know that if you do want to talk, I'm here. I'll always be here for you."

"I know, Charles."

"Just don't do what you always do." I let go and look down at her with a raised eyebrow. "Don't act like you don't quietly suffer all the time. Your dad might be a piece of shit, but you have people who care about you, if you let us."

"I know," I say before giving her one last hug. Anders comes in with the last box, and I give him a small smile. "Thanks again for helping bring all my stuff over."

"No problem, if you need anything else, just let us know."

"Thanks, Anders."

Alexi walks in the room and claps Anders on the shoulder and looks around the room. "Do you need help unpacking?" he asks me.

I shake my head. "I'm good." He looks at the disassembled IKEA bed on the floor, looking unimpressed, but he nods his head anyway. "I was going to order in. Do you guys want anything?"

"No, I'm feeling pretty tired," Charlotte says. They woke up way earlier than she's used to so they could help me move, and it has me feeling slightly guilty.

"Are you sure?" I double check with her. She shakes her head and gives me one last hug. Eli and Anders both wave and do a little bro-shake with Alexi. Mikael is at home with a sleeping Katie.

I watch as my buffers leave the house, standing in the large living room. I look around Alexi's home—Alexi's extremely fucking nice home. I should have assumed the man who has had a professional hockey career for nearly two decades would have a nice home, but I guess I didn't realize how high end it would truly be. When he said he had a spare room, I was expecting maybe a ten by fifteen foot room. Not basically a whole owner-sized bedroom. It's bigger than my bedroom at the townhome. The bathroom is in the hall, but that's also bigger than the bathroom I had at my old place. The exterior has a historical look to it, just like my townhouse did, but he's completely renovated the whole interior.

I really wanted to renovate the townhouse, but I just never had time. Thinking about it makes my stomach sink, the way he just threw me out and didn't give me the chance to pay him rent. Just decided that because I wasn't meeting his standards, I'm not worth his time. I'm genuinely considering buying a fuck-ton of crickets and putting them in the townhouse so my dad has to pay to get rid of them and doesn't get a tenant right away. But I think enough damage has happened in the last two days. I only have four hours before my shift, and I'm hoping I can at least find my scrubs, favorite shoes, and enough time to put this fucking bed together.

Alexi shuts the front door, and I head over to the very sterile kitchen and open the fridge. It's nearly as barren as mine is at home.

"I can have whatever you need delivered," he says. I shut the fridge and turn around to face him.

"I can go shopping. I need to do something around here. Just let me know how much the rent is."

He shakes his head. "You don't need to pay rent."

"I do," I argue, and he crosses his arms over his chest.

"I own the place outright, so rent is not an issue."

I cross my own arms over my chest and stare at the larger than life Alpha. "I need to contribute somehow. I can't just live here for free."

"Why not?" he asks, and I huff. "Were you not living in your dad's home for free? At least at my place there are no expectations of you." My mouth gapes open, and Alexi scrubs his face. "That came out harsher than I meant, if you really want to contribute, food would be great. I eat out most nights."

This should probably be the time I tell him I can't cook for shit.

"I can do that."

"Alright, so we're all good then?"

"Yeah." I look around his nice house and how tired he is from helping me all night and then getting me moved this morning. "I appreciate all of this, Alexi, I really do."

He gives me a small smile. "You deserve better. Door code is 0880."

I blink at him. "You're kidding, right?"

"What?" he says, looking at me like I'm dumb.

"It's your jersey number forwards and backwards, Alexi. It's like you're asking to be fucking robbed." He waves off my very logical statement and walks toward me. He gives me no space as he grabs a bottle of water off the counter. His body doesn't touch mine, but it may as well be with the way his scent is wrapping around me.

As he goes to stand up straight, he lightly speaks. "Living here has no strings attached, I need you to know that. But I also need you to know that I want you, and you living here is only going to make me want you more."

My hands reach for his chest and glide down his ripped abs as I fist the bottom of his shirt. But his hand wraps around my wrists. I look up at him, and his gaze is intense.

"When I say I want you, I mean I want you to be my girl. I want to take you on dates, show you off, end my day with you in my bed." I swallow, and when I look at him, knowing that he's being completely honest with me, Alexi is all in. "I know you're not there yet, and until you are, I can't do anything else. It's… it's too much."

"I want to get there," I tell him honestly. Even if the thought of being with him in that capacity is terrifying. Deep down, I know I want it. I just need my life to stop spinning on its axis for just one moment.

"And our Beta?" he says like Owen is a done deal, like there's no other logical step than for him to be ours.

"I want to get there too," I say, and Alexi smiles. He tucks a loose strand of hair behind my ear. His calloused hand slides across my jawline, and all I want him to do is lean down and kiss me again. As much as I love how Alexi is able to shut my brain down, I know it's not fair of me to ask him for that when he needs a commitment from me.

I will get there, at least I hope. I'm looking at this beautiful man in front of me and wondering why I'm so broken that I can't accept everything he's offering me. I look away, and Alexi cups my face.

"I'm patient. Just don't make me wait too long, okay?"

I nod, and his thumbs trail under my jaw. He looks at me like he wants to kiss me so bad. My hands wrap around his wrists, and he sighs. Suddenly, a jolt to my side startles me. I look at my pager for work and groan.

"I've got to go."

"Okay, do you know what time you'll be home?"

"Probably late, sometime early tomorrow morning, don't wait up. I'll make sure to be quiet on my way in."

He nods and gives me one last lingering look. I have to dig through all the unlabeled boxes that I packed the night before. I find a clean pair of scrubs, and it looks like it's Crocs today. I look over at my mattress on the floor and sigh, knowing that I'll be sleeping on the floor tonight. It beats being homeless or the obligations that come along with living at my dad's property.

My shift starts absolutely horrifically by seeing Dr. Mayfield. I'd love to tell her how her little check-in with my father got me kicked out of my house. Or maybe I could just impulsively quit the program on the spot. The intrusive thought follows me throughout the day. Just ripping off my badge and quitting, telling Shuana she's a cunt and saying 'I quit this bitch,' but alas, I don't have the gall.

I don't have another job or program to transfer to. Until I have a completely solidified plan, I can't leave. Maybe there's still a part of me that doesn't want to let all my hard work go to waste, or admit I'm the failure my father thinks I am.

"Am I boring you, Dr. Blake?" Dr. Mayfield asks as I hold suction.

"No, of course not, Dr. Mayfield."

"You have great potential, but unless you really hone in your focus, I don't know if you'll make it."

How the hell do you respond to that? "Thank you, Dr. Mayfield."

"When I was a resident, I lived here. I never wanted to leave. You just don't see that with many new surgeons now."

I contain my eye roll. This ideology that you have to breathe, sleep, and eat medicine to be a surgeon is insane. Beyond the ridiculous competition and the low pay for the hours we work during our residency, the downsides of this profession are heavy. The most tragic part is just losing your identity and becoming this job completely, and if you don't, you're not trying hard enough.

Dr. Mayfield mostly performs surgery with little learning in between, so I just observe and daydream. Dream about working at a family practice and coming home in time for dinner with Alexi and Owen. I almost want to laugh at myself for imagining it. Alexi has made his intentions clear, sure. I have an obvious connection with Owen, but the idea of me having a pack? Deserving one? It feels foreign.

Dr. Mayfield lets me close, and I'm in the locker rooms changing into my clothes to go home in. Alexi's place isn't in walking distance, but it's a short ride in the metro or car service. With how late it is, I order a ride as I get changed.

Shuana is leaving at the same time as me and gives me a smirk. "You know, there's been talk." I ignore her, and she shakes her head. "They need to let some residents go."

"What?" I ask, not knowing if she's fucking with me or not.

"The hospital is making cuts. I heard at least two in each program might be cut."

"Who said?"

"Wouldn't you like to know?"

"Obviously, that's why I asked."

"Worried about your spot, Blake?"

More like hoping they let me go so the choice is out of my hands. "No, are you?" I say back in true Alpha fashion. While I might have a lot of internal struggles, there's no way I'm expressing them to Shuana of all people.

"Well, I think you should be."

"I think you should worry about yourself and your string of bad outcomes," I say back, and that has her glaring at me.

"Maybe you should worry more about becoming a decent

surgeon than relying on your name to get you here," she says. I want to say more to her, get into her face. But the fact is I'm tired, and the last thing I need is to prove myself to someone like Shuana.

"I guess we'll just have to wait and see."

"I guess so," she replies, tossing her bag into her locker.

I'm feeling like death as I get to Alexi's house. I put in his ridiculous code, and the lock swirls. My body aches, and I wish I would have put my bed together before going to work, but at least I have a place to live. I'm extremely quiet as I head to my room.

When I turn the knob, the last thing I expect is to see my bed on a frame, and for it to be made with clean sheets as well. I collapse on top of the soft material. Whatever detergent he uses is to die for. I'm not sure if it's everything piling up on me or this small act of kindness, but I finally let myself break. In the comfort of night and fully alone, I let the tears fall and soak into the beautiful sheets.

I just want to feel worthy, but I'm just not sure of what.

## CHAPTER 18

My bed feels hard, and my skin feels itchy. I know what I need, but am I even capable of asking for it?

It's nearly nine at night, and I'm caught up deciding who I should reach out to. Piper or Alexi. Alexi is easier. He knows what I am, and he's agreed to help me. I can't deny that there's something about Piper that centers me, but we both agreed that we can't start anything now.

The further we get into the season, the more I'm realizing that I won't be able to keep this up long-term. I'm coming to the conclusion that living out my dream for a season has to be enough. It's a lot to wrap my head around, but these last few weeks have been invaluable to me. And while I wish more often than not I was an Alpha and my body could handle this strain, it can't, and if I continue to push myself too far, the damage might be irreparable. Maybe I can find a job within the sector of hockey that doesn't tear me to shreds.

I have a lot of feelings about myself and my designation, but I want a future as a pack's Omega. I just need to do this for me first. I need to see the season through. Prove to people that

Omegas can do whatever the fuck they want. But more so to prove to myself that I'm able to accomplish something this significant.

This season is all I have, so I can't fuck it up. And right now? I need a fucking Alpha to help me stop spiralling. There's only a week before we play the Sharks, and the reality is, it might be my last game. I hop out of bed, throw on some sweatpants and a crew neck, and grab my jacket.

Alexi's house is farther than I should be walking this late at night, but at least the cold air clears my head. I should have texted him, but I guess part of me feared if I did, he would tell me that he's busy.

There's a heavy feeling in my chest of missing Piper, and it's odd. I don't truly know her, but it's like my body craves her. After the last time we were together, we decided to keep our distance. We're both too busy, focused on our careers. I have to shake her out of my head, knowing it's for the best.

I stand on the stoop for a ridiculously long time before I gather up the nerve to knock on the dark blue door. A few seconds pass, and I consider walking back home when the door opens. A sleepy, barely clothed Piper answers the door. I look at the house and make sure that my self-consciousness didn't just carry my feet to her house instead.

No, it's definitely Alexi's house.

"Owen?" she says, blinking at me. She looks beautiful, wearing nothing but a T-shirt and her hair in a messy bun on the top of her head.

"Is Alexi home?" I ask.

"Oh. Um, yeah." She waves me in and shuts the door behind me. She wraps her arms around herself, no doubt feeling the chill from outside. "Alexi!" she shouts down the hall.

"What?" he says, running down the hall in nothing but his

underwear. Fuck, that man can wear a pair of boxer briefs. Alexi looks between the two of us, taking a long second to appreciate Piper's appearance, which brings me some relief. They must not have been sharing a bed together. It's not even jealousy for a specific person. It's jealousy of not being in the middle of a really hot Alpha-sandwich. "Owen?" he says, blinking at me.

"Hey."

He looks at me and then to Piper.

"I'll just go back to bed," Piper says sadly.

"No, you don't have to leave," I say quickly.

"I've just got off a really long shift, so I need to get some sleep," she says. Her gaze stays on mine, and I swear I watch her pupils dilate before she shakes her head. She gives Alexi's bulge a glance before looking back at me. "Night," she says softly before retreating back into her room. My chest aches, and seeing her again only makes me realize how impossible it is for us to be apart.

When Piper's door shuts, Alexi's hand wraps around the back of my neck. "What's wrong?" I shrug my shoulders, and he leads me to his living room. It's nice, if not lacking in some personality. He holds out a hand for me to sit down on the soft navy cushions, and I do. He doesn't sit immediately but instead looks me over. I wonder what he sees? Does he view me as a pathetic Omega who needs someone to take care of them? No, I know that's not true. The way Alexi sees me is the way I wish I could see myself.

"Do you want anything to eat or drink?" I shake my head no, and he tilts his head before grabbing some soft blankets and plopping them on top of me. He sits down next to me, his arm and thigh touching mine as he turns on the TV.

"I should have called or texted you before I came over."

"I told you I'm here for whatever you need."

"Piper lives with you now?" I ask, and he groans.

"It's not exactly my story to tell, but she needed a place to stay."

"But you two aren't together?"

"Not yet," he says.

"Oh."

Alexi rolls his eyes and shifts his body so he's looking at me. "You're a part of that not yet," he says, and I blink at him. I mean, he told me he had feelings for me, and mine are growing for him too. But actually conceptualizing that me, Alexi, and Piper could be a pack doesn't seem real.

"She doesn't know my designation."

"I know," he says, shifting back to how he was sitting, except he slings an arm around my shoulder.

"She also says she can't handle a relationship right now."

"I'm more than well aware of that too. But she'll get there."

"I can't… I don't like the idea of becoming a pack when I'm hiding my designation."

"That's why were going to win the fucking Cup, and me and you are going to retire, and then the three of us are going to live our best lives."

"You've got it all figured out?" I joke, his fingertips trailing patterns on my shoulder.

"Someone has to, so I figured it might as well be me."

"And what if she doesn't agree?"

"She will."

"You're that confident?" I ask. Alexi leans down to whisper in my ear.

"Yes, I'm that confident." I can't argue with that. If I weren't on a slew of medications and deodorizers, I'd be filling this room with my perfume. "I can't wait to fully scent you and do all the things I want to do to you," he says softly.

*Fucking hell.*

"The NHL will probably kick me off the team if they know."

"I know, and that's why I'm going to keep your little secret. I'm sure Piper would too," he says.

"It feels wrong to distract her."

"I think our sweet Piper needs a distraction."

"I can definitely understand that," I say.

"Is that what you need, Owen? Do you need a distraction?" he asks. His hand moves from my shoulder to play with the hair at the nape of my neck. "Is that why you came here? You need your Alpha to make you feel better?"

My dick stirs, and it honestly baffles me how this man can have this effect on me. "My medication, it, um… makes things more difficult for me," I say.

"Just tell me what you need," he says.

"I don't know what I need."

"Let your Alpha take care of you."

A small gasp leaves me, and Alexi is tugging down my sweatpants and boxers. I'm on autopilot as he undresses me. I just stare at his bare chest scattered with hair and how his cock is getting hard under his boxers.

Without much effort, he lifts me on his lap, my dick half hard as he groans. The sound hits my brain before my cock responds, becoming fully hard. Alexi's hands rub up and down my thighs, and he just stares at my length while kneading my muscles.

"Do you need to come? Hmm, would that make my needy boy feel better?" I'm already feeling better having his skin against mine, and I can't help to press harder against his lap. "That's it. I'm going to make it better."

He takes his own cock out of his boxers. It's huge and weeping at the top. I can't help but to stare and briefly get a glance of his knot. Fuck, that would feel good inside of me right now. But letting Alexi knot me seems like it would solidify everything. That I'm his Omega, and while I want that, I can't have that right now.

"Soon, I'll give you my knot. I'll have you begging for it. Your tight, little ass dripping slick just begging me to fuck you."

I groan as Alexi spits down on his cock and raises his thighs, pushing me closer to him. I'm so close that our lengths touch. Alexi grips both of us, pushing us together as he strokes us in tandem.

His scent is heavy in the room, and I haven't been this turned on... quite possibly ever. The fear hits me of not being able to finish, but then Alexi is using one hand to stroke us together, and the other is rubbing my asshole. I involuntarily buck into his hand and moan.

"So good for your Alpha. I need you to come on me," he says. We're both angled toward his flexed stomach, and the imagery is too much. The fact that this Alpha wants me to come on him. Alexi has this way of making me still feel like a man while also allowing me to feel like an Omega. I could easily become addicted to it.

His pace increases, jerking us off together, and I can't decide what I like more, the press of his cock against mine, the combination of our pre-cum being used as lube, or how good his hand feels. He easily slides a finger into me fully, and I'm bucking into his hand relentlessly.

"Be my good boy, and show me how good I make you feel."

"Fuck." My hips stutter until I'm shooting ropes of cum onto his stomach. He watches in awe, but he doesn't finish. Immediately I slide off his lap onto my knees.

It's at this moment, I don't hate my designation as I look up into this Alpha's eyes and see how pleased he is with me. I dip my fingers in my cum on his stomach and drag it along his length before wrapping my lips around the tip and sucking him down.

Alexi's fingers tangle in my hair, but he lets me keep the pace. His pelvis bucks every time I swipe the underside of his head. I use one hand to toy with his balls and knot while I use my mouth.

"Fuck, you're so good."

I hum around his cock. How could I forget how much I enjoy being called good? How fucking unreal an Alpha's undivided attention could feel.

Suddenly he's groaning, his hand tight in my hair and his cock gagging my throat as he finishes. His cum tastes like his scent, and I swallow it down like the good Omega I am.

I sit up and look up at him as he blinks down at me.

"Stay the night."

I want to, but part of it feels like a betrayal to stay in Alexi's room while Piper is here. Like we're leaving her out. I look away, and Alexi sighs.

"At least stay in the guest bedroom."

"Okay," I agree, and Alexi smiles.

"Let's get you cleaned up first." He tucks his cock back into his boxers and stands before holding out a hand to me and tugging me up to my feet. "Do you want to talk about why you came over?" I grab my sweatpants and tug them on and grab my boxers, holding them in my fist.

"I think the hand job suffices." He smacks my ass, and I glare at him. "I really had to choose the two most emotionally stunted people to be in my pack."

"That sounds like a you problem."

He shakes his head like he realizes he has a type—hot and emotionally unavailable. Then he grabs me a bottle of water and walks me down the hall to the guest bedroom.

"Bathroom is down the hall, and my room is upstairs if you need anything. Like if you decide you want to talk about what's really bothering you."

I look down, needing to get it off my chest. It blurts out of me like word vomit. "My brother… he plays for the Sharks. I don't know if he's going to out me or not."

He looks at me like all the pieces click together for him. "Max Connery is your brother?"

I nod, and he runs his hands in his messy dark hair. "We're not close. I haven't spoken to him much in the last couple of years. I don't know how he's going to react."

"You really think he would out you to the NHL?"

"I'm not sure," I shrug.

"I've got your back no matter what."

That small reassurance helps my nerves, but the anxiety of coming face-to-face with Max on the ice is still daunting. Not that we'll really interact, but just seeing him there is going to send me into a spiral.

Alexi steps into my space. "I won't let him take this dream away from you."

"I'm not sure how long I can keep this up, Alexi."

He rubs the back of my neck. "I know, *sólnyshka*. I'll sort it all out."

I'm still one wrong move away from completely breaking down, but I can't help but trust in Alexi, and it's nice to have someone who has my back.

"I made the right choice coming here tonight."

He smiles and leans in, placing a soft kiss on my lips.

"Goodnight. Come to my room if you change your mind."

I nod my head, and he places a tender kiss at my temple before leaving.

It takes every ounce of me, but I stay in the guest room all night. Though deep down, all I want to do is grab Piper and take her into Alexi's bed with me.

What in the Omega fuckery is happening to me?

———

I wake up feeling like absolute shit. My head is throbbing, my body aches, and I have to take a serious piss. When I look at my phone and see that it's not even five in the morning, I groan, but I get up and drag my feet down the hall to the bathroom.

I'm already considering climbing into Alexi's bed after the bathroom. I swing the door open and find Piper standing in front of the mirror wearing only a bra and panties as she puts her hair into a high ponytail.

"Shit, sorry."

"You stayed the night?" she asks with a furrowed brow.

"I did."

"You stayed in the guest room?" she asks, looking even more confused.

I shrug my shoulders and start to close the door when she tugs it wide open. I try really fucking hard, but no amount of self-control will suffice as I look down at her perky breasts being cupped by modest pink fabric.

"Why didn't you stay in Alexi's bed?"

"It didn't seem right with you staying here too." She blinks at me, her hand on her hip. It's too fucking early for this. My head is pounding, and apparently, now I have to still piss with a half-chub, fucking awesome.

"Do you have any Tylenol?" I ask her, not wanting to talk about why it didn't feel right to sleep in Alexi's bed when she's not in it or how I've missed her. I definitely don't want to talk about how my chest ached when she went back to her room when she answered the door last night. These are lines we decided not to cross, and as I stare at her half-naked form, all I can think about is whether it's worth it? Should I just lay it all out there for Piper? Alexi is more than fine keeping my secret, and he made me feel good last night. I can't even imagine if I had both of them. But it's also not just up to me. Piper clearly has her own hang-ups holding her back.

"Are you okay?" she asks, opening the mirror and pulling out the medicine. I expect her to just hand me the bottle, but instead, she takes out two pills, fills a glass of water, and hands it to me.

"Just a headache, I think I'm a little dehydrated."

She puts her hand on my forehead, and the simple touch shouldn't feel as magnanimous as it does. Her soft skin pressed against mine feels calming and far more intimate than the action truly is.

"You don't have a fever. Is anything else bothering you?" she asks.

I want to say that my body hurts, that I ache everywhere, that some days I'm so fucking tired I don't know how I get out of bed. That I know I'm pushing every single boundary my body has and I know there will be consequences. Instead, I shake my head, and she hums.

I look down at her tits again like the complete pervert I am. "I've got to finish getting ready for work," she says softly, and I nod. I'll just go use Alexi's bathroom upstairs.

"Have a good day," I tell her softly, taking the Tylenol and placing the glass back on the counter. She sighs, and her arms wrap around me in a hug. This time, there are no coats between us. Her soft skin is under my fingertips, and her scent surrounds me.

I'm not sure if it's the Tylenol or her touch, but it feels like everything goes away for those few seconds.

"Bye, Owen," she says softly as we part. I back out of the bathroom, and she shuts the door. How in the fuck am I supposed to stay away from her? My head throbs again, and like the needy little Omega I am, I climb up the stairs and open Alexi's door. He doesn't stir, and I use his restroom and climb into his bed.

He doesn't speak, but he tosses his massive arm around my waist. It's more settling than I'd ever like to admit.

## CHAPTER 19

Max Connery can take a skate to the face for all I fucking care. If he would betray his brother in this way, he's a piece of shit. At least it's a home game. The idea of having to stay in California if shit went down would be brutal. If anything happens, I can just scoop my Omega up and take him home.

I smile to myself when I remember how pliant he was the other night. He wasn't stoic and broody, he was needy and vulnerable. The best part was that he came to me when he needed to be settled. He chose to be with me; he trusted me as his teammate and as his Alpha. Owen may not realize that's what I am. But one hundred percent that blond bastard is mine, and if anyone tries anything, I'll fuck them up, including his brother.

My hope is that Owen can help bridge this gap between Piper and I. But she's the most stubborn woman I've ever met in my life. It's part of her draw, how determined and focused she is. But she's also so critical and hard on herself, I just want to shut her mind down. I'm worried that if Owen can't get through to her soon, she'll move out and on. I can't let that happen.

I'm putting my jersey overtop of my gear as Owen paces in his full goalie gear. He's wearing socks with strawberries on them today, and it's fucking adorable. I make a note to get him more cute socks to wear for games.

"Chill the fuck out, Connery." Owen nods but doesn't stop pacing. "It's just the Sharks. They've been in the league for thirty fucking years and haven't won the Cup. We're good."

Owen gives Mikael a shitty look, and the Alpha throws his hands up in mock surrender.

Nilsen taps his chin a few times. "Connery…"

"What?" Owen snaps back.

"The Sharks' goalie is named Connery." Owen's face goes bright red in embarrassment, and I watch as his Adam's apple bobs. In any other situation, I would step in. But here, I'm his captain, his teammate. Off the ice is where I can be his Alpha, as much as it pains me. I know that Owen has the need to stand on his own two feet and be masculine.

"He is," Owen confesses.

"He is a cunt, yes?" Nilsen says, and that makes Owen and the others standing around us bark out a laugh.

"He is," Owen agrees.

"I'll send a message, don't worry. We have the better Connery," Nilsen says.

"What? You've already gotten suspended for getting rough with him before. Planning another?" Mikael says.

"If he tests me," Nilsen says. I shrug my shoulders, wouldn't be the worst thing.

"How do both of you fuckers have family members in the NHL, anyway?" Mikael says. Both Nilsen and Owen make non-committed noises.

"Same way you and your brother-husbands got on the

same NHL team," I interrupt, cutting through the tension. Owen gives me a small smirk, and Mikael gives me the finger, Eli just laughs and wraps his arms around Mikael in a hug.

"Get the fuck off of me," Mikael says to Eli.

"Charlotte would be so upset to hear you turn down my hug."

"Really cute, bringing our Omega into this," Mikael says but stops fighting Eli's arms around him. The ginger Alpha rests his head on his pack mate's shoulder and grins while Mikael scowls.

"I'd like an Omega," Nilsen says. I glance briefly at Owen, whose cheeks are back to being pink.

"And who would put up with your grumpy ass?" Eli says.

Nilsen points an arm in Mikael's direction. "Your Omega fell for this asshole. I should have no problem." Eli and I both laugh boisterously, and Mikael finally pushes Eli off of him in frustration.

"Do you have anyone in mind?" Eli asks with a grin on his face.

"Perhaps," Nilsen says. I swear this is the most he has spoken all season. He wraps his stick and doesn't give us any more information.

"What about you, cap? Are you going to retire off into the sunset and find a pack?" Eli asks

Owen turns away and acts like he's no longer part of the conversation. "Perhaps." I follow Nilsens lead and keep my fucking mouth shut.

"Perhaps a tall pain in the ass brunette is in your future?" Mikael asks.

"Ah, but you're already taken," I say with a wink, and Mikael rolls his eyes.

"I don't know how I put up with you fuckers," he says, standing and walking away.

"He's so emotional," I joke, and Eli is back to laughing again. I even get a rare smile from Nilsen.

There's a soft voice we aren't used to hearing in the locker room. Thank God we've all put our dicks away as this small woman approaches us. Her Omega scent is on full display and garnering everyone's attention.

"Listen up," Coach Applegate says, making everyone shut the fuck up and pay attention to what he has to say. "This is my daughter, Sloane. She is helping with our social media. If she asks you to jump, you say how high. If anyone of you fuckers disrespects her in any way, consider yourself dead."

There are a few clearing of throats, and Applegate takes a deep inhale to center himself. "Yes, Sloane is an Omega. If any of you can't control yourself, figure it the fuck out."

The small redhead waves her hand with a massive smile on her face.

"You got it?" coach barks, and there's mumbles of agreement and nodding of heads.

Sloane's cheeks heat as her father claps her shoulder. She gives her dad a smile and approaches our group.

"Hi, guys," she says with a wave. "Do you mind if I ask you what your favorite animal is for a video?"

"Mine is a sloth," Nilsen says, and Sloane beams at him.

"Thank you, Bram. I just need to record it this time, okay?" The Alpha nods his head as she records.

"I'm here for anything you need." Bram smiles at her. Eli smacks his shoulder, and he shrugs. "What?"

"Stop drooling over the coach's daughter." Nilsen wipes his mouth, and we all laugh.

"How about you, captain? What's your favorite animal?" Sloane asks while recording.

"Foxes, of course." She gives me a small smile and nods. She's tiny, probably about the same size as Charlotte, and I'm wondering why the hell Applegate would let his Omega daughter in a locker room full of Alphas.

She goes over to Owen, and he answers before pulling her over to the side. Standing next to my Omega, she looks tiny in comparison. I watch their conversation; Sloane is nodding, and Owen's voice is soft. She smiles up at him and taps his shoulder padding before making her way around the locker room, asking everyone the same question.

Owen comes and stands next to me, and I lean down casually. "What did you say to her?"

"That her scent is strong as fuck, and she needs to tone it down," he says.

"What did she say?"

"She said thanks for the concern, but she isn't changing anything about herself," Owen says with his eyebrows furrowed.

I sigh and bump my shoulder with his. "You're perfect the way you are too. Now let's go destroy your brother's team."

He inhales deeply and exhales. "Yeah, let's go do this." He heads to his locker room, and I see him take something before taking a swig of water.

———

The stadium is loud, and it's been made apparent that it's brother versus brother. Apparently Owen's mom is here, and he had no idea. She's cut two jerseys in half, one for the Foxes and one for the Sharks with Connery on the back.

Owen seems jittery on the ice, but he's performing well. I'm thankful that his brother is on the other side of the ice and that they won't have any actual confrontation—at least I fucking hope.

The game starts tame. We don't really have any beef with

the Sharks, well, besides Max Connery. I'm not sure what Nilsen's deal is with him, but every time we play them, he somehow gets a penalty.

I'm on the bench and watch as Owen has a fantastic save. But he shakes his head back and forth like he's trying to realign his focus. It's not one of his typical behaviors, and I can't help but watch him more attentively. It must just be the fact that he's playing against his brother and he doesn't know the outcome.

I'm on the ice with Nilsen and Mikael, and I know we're about to do damage. The three of us are a formidable force. None of us give a shit about getting physical, and we prove that as we get in formation and head toward the Sharks' goal. Mikael passes to me after he takes a hit to the shoulder. I can slap shot, or I can pass to Nilsen who is by the post. I pass to him, and he tips the puck in.

The buzzer goes off, and the crowd goes wild. My arm is up in the air, and I'm about to approach Nilsen for a celebration when Max Connery grabs Nilsen by the jersey. Nilsen gives him a shit-eating grin, and they start getting into it. It's absolute fucking chaos after that. Nilsen knows touching the goalie is a sure fire way to start an all out brawl, but apparently the Dutch dick doesn't give a shit.

I've got my hands on a Sharks jersey, tugging them off. The refs are blowing whistles, tugging men away like they're feral toddlers. But Max and Nilsen are still going at it. Both of their helmets are gone, and Max's lip is bleeding.

I'm expecting it to get broken up and squashed. But then I see Owen's frame skating down the ice and shucking off his gloves.

"Oh, fuck no."

I'm about to skate over to him and push him back to his goal when another player pushes me up against the glass.

We're in our own battle of wills when Nilsen lets go of Max and the opposing goalie sees his brother.

I can barely make out what they're saying.

"Go back to your side of the rink, Owen," Max says.

"Fuck you," Owen replies, and he swings, hitting his brother right in the jaw.

Max rubs his face and glares at his brother. "I'm not fucking hitting you."

Owen pushes against his brother's chest, and I'm trying to get this asshole to let go of my jersey to diffuse the situation. "Fucking hit me!" Owen says, pushing his brother again.

"Owen." His brother shakes his head. Owen hits his brother again, and it must make him snap. Because Max rears his fist back and hits Owen.

I've seen Owen take some hits, he's strong. But nothing will make your heart sink into your ass more than seeing your Omega hurt. I finally push the bastard who had a hold of my jersey off and skate over to Owen, who collapses on the ice.

His cheek is already turning a purple shade from the hit. But that's not the concerning part. It's the way he's clutching his fist against his chest and breathing heavily.

"Owen?" his brother shouts and gets down on his knees and shakes him slightly. "Owen?"

The fight stops around us as medical skates on. Owen's bright blue eyes are wide, and he looks at me. He grips my jersey tightly with his fist and drags my ear to his mouth. "They can't find out," he whispers. His breathing is thick, and it's terrifying.

"You're going to be alright. You hear me?" I tell him.

"I'm so sorry, Owen," Max says, Owen ignores him completely, so I do the same.

"I'll find you as soon as I can. It's going to be okay." Owen squeezes his eyes shut and nods his head. He's too fucking strong for his own good. I would kill his brother, but when I look over at the pain in his eyes, I refrain.

"I didn't want to hit him," he says. He doesn't give him up to the medic by disclosing his designation. I'm not sure what Owen's issue is with his brother, but it doesn't seem like the feeling is mutual.

Owen is taken off the ice on a gurney, and that's never a good sign. I look up at the clock. We still have ten minutes left in this period and a whole other period left, I have no clue how the hell I'm supposed to play when I know he needs me.

Johannson steps into the goal with Owen gone, and we lose three to one.

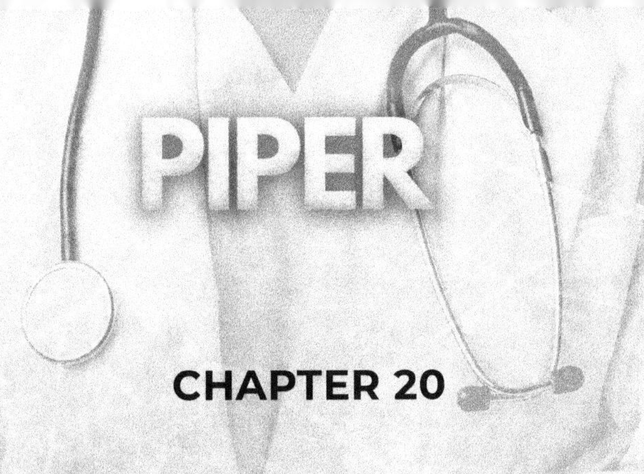

# PIPER

## CHAPTER 20

I'm headed to the E.R for a consultation. They have a patient who was in a motorcycle accident and they aren't sure if he damaged his spinal cord. Dr. Mayfield is in surgery, so I'm taking a look and reporting back. While I walk through the halls, I wonder if I could work in this department full time instead of surgery. No, I don't think emergency medicine is what I could do full time.

My head feels like a complete mess.

I've mostly come to terms with quitting surgery. My dad knows, and I'm not under his thumb. But there is still this lingering sting of failure and fear of the future. Not just when it comes to work, I know that if I keep getting in my own way, I just might ruin everything with Alexi and Owen, and I don't want to do that. I'm not sure why I can't get out of my own way.

"Oh, hey Piper. What has you down in the E.R?" Dr. Khan asks me.

"Consult, how have you been?" Lindsay and I both finished medical school at the same time, she seems a hell of a lot happier than I am right now.

"Good, minus having to take a splinter out of this girl's ass. When are people going to learn that public sex just isn't worth it?"

I laugh and shrug my shoulders. I think I would risk a splinter in the ass to have sex with Alexi again, but he's basically wearing a chastity belt when it comes to me until I can admit it's more than physical. Damn that sexy Alpha.

Especially because I could hear everything he and Owen did that night, and all it did was leave me longing and wanting. While at the same time feeling like I don't deserve either one of them.

A code is called and Lindsay gives me a curt nod as she heads to the next room. I'm a little turned around in the E.R. I think I'm supposed to be going to room 19. I pull the chart and begin to read it.

Heart palpitations, shortness of breath, collapsed during work, bruise to the cheek. It looks like Dr. Piebes is flushing his system believing it is some sort of overdose or drug misuse. He was admitted a few hours ago, and no blood has been drawn yet. I don't see anything neurological, and I'm about to put the chart away until I see the name.

Owen Connery.

My feet take me into his room faster than my mind can compute. I slide the glass door, and when I do, it's like I'm completely assaulted by his scent. His scent is clearly not one of a Beta. That scent of strawberries and lemons I smelled in his apartment, it wasn't the candles he had lit. *It was him.*

This tug that I've felt since I met Owen, it's clear as day now. I look at him, and his eyes meet mine, his blue eyes wide and his pupils dilating.

Owen Connery is an Omega, and he is my scent match.

My heart is racing in my chest, and I just stand there and stare at him. Every fiber of my being is pushing me to comfort him and make him feel better. But as I approach his bed, he shakes his head.

He swallows thickly. He's hooked up to fluids to help flush his system as well and a monitor to check his heart rate.

"Please leave, Piper," he says softly, and it's like my heart cracks in my chest.

I approach him anyway, his scent thicker, and I can't help the way I push mine out. Like I need him to realize we're scent matches, for him to accept me.

"Owen, you're my—"

"Please leave," he interrupts.

"What?"

"Leave."

"I'm not leaving you. What happened?"

He looks away from me, and I can tell he's trying his best to not scent me.

He's rejecting me.

I shake that thought out of my head. I know it's bigger than that, that it has to do with his career. He's clearly been taking a ridiculous amount of scent blockers, deodorizers, and God knows what else to be able to play in the NHL.

"Please just fucking go," he says, not looking at me.

"I'm your scent match. I'm not going anywhere," I say, reaching out and touching his arm, which he pulls away from me.

"Jesus Christ, Piper, get the fuck out," he says, raising his voice at me. "I don't want you here, seeing me like this." He holds up his arm connected to the saline, like being sick is hopeless or less masculine. "I don't want a fucking scent match. Everything I've worked for is gone. Now can you please just leave me to be miserable in fucking peace?"

"Owen," I sigh and reach out for him again.

"Get out!" he yells, and I startle, backing my way out of the room. My heart is racing, and I'm fighting back tears that are threatening to spill out. As I'm leaving, I see Lori and a tall man who shares some similarities with Owen, except they don't share the same blond hair.

"Oh my God, is he alright?" Lori says, and I watch as her face contorts. She must see the pain in my eyes and think that Owen is doing worse than he is. I shake my head and sigh, taking a deep breath and shoving Owen away in my mind.

"He's fine. He's in there. You can go and see him."

"Why do you look like you're about to cry, then?" Lori asks, perceptive as ever. I shake my head and shove my hands in my coat pockets. "What did he do?"

"You can go see him. I have another patient," I say. I walk away from Lori and whomever the other man was. I give the nurse from earlier a tight smile and open the door to the janitor's closet. I grab onto the shelves, and I break.

He told me to get out, that he didn't want me. That he didn't need me. I have a fucking scent match. If I'm being honest, I never thought that would happen for me. Charlotte and her Alphas are an anomaly, it's not the norm. But I have one, one I already had feelings for when I thought he was a Beta, and he doesn't want this.

A scent match. An Omega that I can call my own tops everything. My fears, my career, my stubbornness. I would throw everything away for my Omega. And he doesn't want me.

I let myself sit on the dirty floor, wrapping my arms around my legs. I feel completely undignified, but I'm not sure what else I can do but sit on this floor and linger in my own pain.

I'm not even sure how much time passes, but I'm sure patients are getting annoyed waiting to be seen by me. I should push my feelings to the side and be a doctor and do my job. I have a patient waiting for a consult, and I just can't pull it together.

All I can do is sit on this floor.

The door creaks open, and I'm ready to make an excuse when I see his hulking form. He shuts the door behind him and squats in front of me, his large hand cupping my shoulder.

"Piper?" I don't answer, I just press my forehead to his chest. "Piper, what happened?"

"Did you see him?" I ask, and he nods his head. "So you know what he is?"

He clears his throat and sighs. "I already knew. I figured it out after sharing a room with him for away games."

"He's my scent match," I say quietly, and Alexi's eyes bulge, and it's like he can't hold his own weight anymore and he sits down next to me. His long legs take up most of the closet.

"And he knows?" he says softly, his hand moving down my thigh, and I'm so thankful for the connection.

"I was assigned his case, and his scent hit me like a ton of bricks. He told me to get out."

Alexi groans and scrubs his face. "Come here."

"What?"

"Get the fuck over here."

"Why?" I ask, arching a brow at him.

"Cause I'm going to fucking hold you, and you're going to like it. We're going to figure this out."

"He didn't seem like he wanted to figure it out."

"Owen is complicated. Now get over here."

I groan and crawl over to him, straddling his legs and pressing my face against the crook of his shoulder. His large hand rubs up and down my back in a soothing motion, and it's like no other comfort I've felt before. I'm usually the one doing the comforting. This feels nicer than it should, I should probably stop. But I don't want to, this is the most centered I've felt in weeks.

"What are we going to do?" I say against his neck.

"The plan is still the same," he says gruffly.

"What plan?"

"Where I make the two of you mine," he says confidently.

"It won't bother you that Owen and I are scent matches and the two of you aren't?" He shakes his head and pulls me closer.

"No. I knew we were going to be a pack before you two, and now this just solidifies it." God, Alexi's confidence is something I wish I could bottle up and throw in a bathtub and soak it all up. How can he be so sure? So steady?

"He said he didn't want me."

"He just got taken away to the hospital, outed to you as an Omega. He's probably afraid he's going to lose everything he's worked for."

"And will he?"

"Not if I can help it. I think we might need to blackmail our Omega though."

I pop up from leaning against his chest and scan his face. "What do you mean?"

"We need to keep him close. His fucking scent match is a doctor, for fuck's sake. If he wants to get through the season, then he needs to take better care of himself. Figure out ways to hide his scent, control his hormones, and stay in check. It's clear that he's been suffering."

"I don't know enough about suppressants and what he's taking."

"Then do the research."

I swallow and nod my head. "Okay, but how do we get him to listen, to want to be around me?"

His hand glides up to the nape of my neck, and he

squeezes lightly. "He wants to be around you, Piper. You can't take what he said back there to heart, okay?" I look away, and he tilts my head back to him. "You want him?" I nod my head. "You want me?" he asks, his tone gentle and vulnerable. I lick my lips and drag my hands up to his chest.

"Yes, I want you both."

He smiles, and his hands drag back down my back. "Then let's go tell our Omega how this is going to work."

"I have to check on a patient first," I say, not knowing exactly how I can do that before seeing Owen. But I can't keep the patient waiting. Alexi gives me a nod and we both get off the floor. It's time to pull myself together.

———

"Like fuck I'm leaving him here alone with you all. Mom, you lied to me until the day of the game. This asshole knew he was an Omega and let him get hurt. The doctor can stay," Owen's brother says as we stand in Owen's hospital room.

Lori rolls her eyes. "I'm not sure what I did in a past life to have such dramatic sons. It was one thing to get into a god damn fight in the middle of a game, like I didn't raise you with a lick of fucking common sense. You two can sort out your shit later. Owen, do you want to speak with them?" Lori gives me a soft look and pushes her son's blond hair away from his face.

"Yeah. Max, you can go," Owen says, and I watch his brother's face fall. I know exactly how it feels being dismissed by Owen. Lori kisses her son's head and goes to leave the room. She grabs my arm and leans into me so only I can hear.

"Take care of him for me. I can't lose him." I give her a nod, and she sighs as both her and Max leave the room.

Owen looks away from us, and Alexi rolls his eyes.

"Here's how things are going to go," Alexi says, and Owen groans.

"I need to get some rest."

"After we talk," Alexi says, and Owen just looks out the window. "You're going to move in with us. Piper is going to help you monitor your medication better so nothing like this happens again. And I'm going to be here to help keep you centered and calm. We both want to take care of you."

Owen scoffs. "You're not even my scent match."

"No, I'm not. And treating your scent match like shit is a dick fucking move," Alexi says, and I'm jolted to standing a little straighter.

"And if I don't move in?"

"Then the team is going to find out you're an Omega. Or you can request to leave against medical advice, and Piper will sign off. We will let the team know that you had a bout of exhaustion and dehydration but you're good to go. Plus, you will now be living with a physician nearby to monitor you."

Owen looks at me. "You would do that?"

I nod and don't say anything. I'm not sure what I can say. Right now, all I can do is smell him, and every ounce of me wants to climb into that bed and cuddle him and tell him everything is fine, even if he was hurtful to me earlier.

"What's the catch?"

Alexi groans and inhales deeply through his nose. "There is no catch, Owen. Piper is your scent match, and I think I've made my intentions pretty fucking clear. So what's it going to be? Are you going to end your career now, or are you going to let us help you?"

"I can't go into heat," he says, looking at me with a mixture of guilt and relief.

"We will figure out all of that, but you need to agree to let us take care of you."

"Okay," Owen says softly.

"Okay then. Piper, can you get the paperwork started? Do you have anything to hide his scent to get out of here?

I nod, and I'm about to leave the room when Owen calls my name, and I turn slightly.

"I'm sorry, Piper," is all he says, and I'm not sure if he's sorry for the way he kicked me out of his room or if he's sorry that he can't accept that we're destined to be together. I sigh and leave, getting his discharge papers together as well as a topical cream to help with his scent.

I'm not sure what I just got myself into, but I think it's going to change everything.

# CHAPTER 21

I'm flooded with guilt by the way I treated Piper.

I panicked, there's no other excuse. I saw everything I worked for getting washed away. The years of bringing my body to the limit. All the years I could have spent actually learning to enjoy being an Omega wasted on this dream. In this feud I only seem to have with my brother, I've become obsessed with the idea of being a successful professional athlete. After the game and at the hospital, I'm realizing this sibling rivalry is all one-sided. I feel like shit.

Coach is making me take two days off the ice. He took Alexi's explanation well enough, but I'm not sure if he completely bought it. He's asking Piper to come down to the practice facility to meet in a few days, and that's why we're in New York.

It's why Piper is filling my paperwork out under a false name and why I'm consumed with guilt. Piper and I haven't talked much since that night. She got me a topical cream that helps with hiding my scent, and I'm back on my suppressants. It doesn't make it any easier though. I want her, and somehow, despite being a complete dick to her, she wants me too.

"Are you alright?" she asks. I don't deserve her kindness.

"Just worried about what they might say." There is an Omega Wellness Clinic in Connecticut, but I didn't want to risk anyone seeing me there, so Piper suggested we make the drive.

"We'll figure it out," she says softly. Alexi is at practice. He wanted to come, but I'm grateful for this time alone with Piper. I'm hoping I can apologize and clear the air. Not that there's much else to be done. We might be scent matches, but if I want to finish out the season, there's nothing we can do till it's over.

"Owen Bandnin," the receptionist calls, and I give Piper a glare.

She shrugs her shoulders with a soft smile, and we both follow her to the back. They do the routine blood scans, weight check, blood pressure, and a urine sample before sending us back into my own room.

The room is nice, far nicer than any doctor's office I've ever been in. Each room has its own scent diffuser, making it a more pleasant experience. Piper is opening up a pamphlet that was left on the counter and reading it. I sigh, feeling bad that this is how she is spending her day off.

"Piper?"

"Yeah?" she asks while not looking up at me.

"I know I said sorry at the hospital, but I need to make things more clear to you," I say. That makes her pause, putting the pamphlet down and looking at me.

"Okay," she says.

"I didn't mean to come off as rejecting you. I'm sorry for how I spoke to you. There's a lot of things I need to work through, but I'm not rejecting you. I need you to know that. I want this so fucking bad, please be patient with me?"

Her eyes soften, and she nods her head. "Thank you. I

know everything has been a lot, but that did hurt me. Thank you for apologizing."

"The regular season ends in a month and a half. The Foxes have done well, and I have high hopes for the playoffs. But I need this, Piper. I need to finish this season out. I feel like if I don't, I'll live the rest of my life with regrets. I've pushed my body so far, and I can't have it be for nothing."

She nods, and I have a feeling that Piper truly understands what I mean. I know she's having struggles of her own, ones I wish she would confide in me, but I guess I lost that privilege.

"Okay, then let's just take it one day at a time."

I nod my head, and every inch of me wants to slide off of this chair and wrap my arms around her, but I refrain. Piper goes back to her pamphlet when the doctor walks in the room.

"Mr. Bandnin, nice to meet you," he says, looking at Piper first to make sure it's okay to shake my hand. I like it more than I should. Piper gives him a look of understanding and stands up to greet him.

"Dr. Blake," she says, shaking his hand.

"I'm Dr. Horngale. It's a pleasure meeting you both." Piper sits back down in her seat as the doctor looks me over and pulls out his tablet going over all my results.

"It says here you had a vasectomy?" he questions me, and I swallow. Piper's eyes widen, but she stays quiet.

"I did."

"May I ask why?"

I take a deep breath and know that honesty is the only way I'm going to be able to get guidance. "I've been hiding my designation so that I can be a professional athlete." Piper rubs her hand down her face like I'm a fucking idiot.

"I see, and you thought that a vasectomy would help tamper down your need?"

"Part of it, along with the suppressants, deodorizers, Alpha scent blockers, and exhausting my body to the point of not feeling much." I chance a glance at Piper and immediately turn back to the doctor when I see the sadness in her eyes.

"Everything you say here is protected not only by HIPAA, but also the Omega Rights Act. Anything you tell me about your designation stays between these walls. I'm assuming you used an alias." My cheeks heat, and the doctor waves me off. "It happens all the time. Now let's get into it."

The amount of time I spend with Doctor Horngale is longer than any appointment I've ever had. He's thorough, understanding, and it's clear I'm not the only one in awe as Piper listens to every word he says.

"So the goal is what?" he asks plainly.

"I need to finish this season."

"Okay, and your heats?" he asks. *Fuck.* I swallow.

"I've never had one."

His eyebrows rise, and he rubs the back of his neck. "And you live with your scent match?" he asks, and Piper rubs her arm.

"That's recent." He hums, tapping away on the tablet.

"I think we can put you on medications that won't be so hard on your body, but with the caveat that once the season is over you need to make some serious changes. This is not a permanent solution by any means. We will have virtual appointments every week to make sure that you're doing alright and nothing happens like they did at your last game. Your body is overwhelmed. You've pushed it to the max, and the suppressants you were on are not for long term use. I am concerned about your heat in the long-term. But what I'm putting you on is FDA approved and has less side effects."

"What changes will I need to make after the season?"

"I suggest a vasectomy reversal, complete removal of all suppressants and deodorizers from your life. I wouldn't be surprised if the first time you go into heat is extremely intense, and it's something you both need to prepare yourselves for. I understand you're both unbonded currently. I don't see how, as scent matches, with an Omega who is nearly twenty-five going into heat for the first time how you will be able to keep the bond at bay."

"Why the vasectomy reversal?" I ask, and he clicks on his tablet before looking up at me.

"There's still research being done, but from what we've seen, male Omegas who have a vasectomy tend to have hormonal imbalances. Having it reversed can help significantly with your mood, heat frequency, libido, and general wellness. We can discuss other forms of birth control within your pack if that is the main concern."

Well, I guess that helps with why I've had such a hard time getting hard, except with Alexi.

His nurse brings in my prescriptions. "These are set for weekly refills. I'm not sending you out of this office floundering. Just because you're an Omega doesn't mean you shouldn't be given every opportunity, but you need to be smart with your health."

"Thank you," I say, and for the first time I truly feel seen by a doctor.

"You promise you will keep him in check?" Piper nods and smiles at the doctor. "Very well, the front desk will set up our virtual appointment." He leaves, and Piper and I glance at each other.

"This place is magical," she says, and I wonder who was more affected by this experience, me or her.

———

The drive isn't long, but it feels like it as Piper drives and I sit in the passenger seat like an Omega prince—in silence.

Fuck it. I've got to say something.

"I could see you working at a place like that," I say softly, and I mean it with complete honesty. Piper is so compassionate. She's great with me, her best friend Charlotte, she would be a natural.

"You think so?" she asks, and it feels nice to hear her voice again.

"Definitely. I've never felt so heard before by a doctor. He wasn't telling me to bond with you and shut the fuck up about what I want. He listened, adapted, and is going to actually help me."

"I'm sure they don't take on many residents at a place like that."

"Probably not, but they would be missing out if they didn't choose someone like you."

Her eyes leave the road for a moment to look at me, and then she's back to being quiet.

"I'm not sure I should live at the house. I think I should stay with Charlotte," she says softly.

"What?"

"You heard what he said. We can't do anything, and I could set off your heat at any moment. I'm trying so fucking hard to not hold your hand right now, Owen. How are we supposed to live together and keep our distance? I've never been allowed to have my own dream, and you do, and I want that for you so bad. I can learn to be patient, I can keep my distance so you can have this happiness that you need. But living together? I'm not sure I'm that strong."

I reach across the dash and take her hand in mine. I rub my thumb along the knuckles of her fingers and sigh.

"I'm holding your hand, and I'm not begging you to climb

over here and lock me. I'm not saying it's going to be easy. And I'm sorry that I'm putting you in this position. I'm being selfish, but please don't move out."

Her hand squeezes mine back, and she lets out an exhausted breath. "I'll stay. Plus, Charlotte is due in the next couple of weeks. I would feel horrible crashing in on their family."

"You know they wouldn't feel that way. You're never a burden."

She's quiet and contemplative for a moment before speaking. "I grew up in a house where I wasn't truly loved, I was a legacy. The only thing my father wanted from me was excellence and to make sure I didn't embarrass the family. Charlotte and her mom are the only people who have ever truly made me feel like I was loved and I was allowed to be myself. I'm working on it, but years of never being good enough doesn't happen overnight. The years of not feeling worth someone else's love don't just go away either."

I think about my own mother and how much she hates me playing hockey because I might get hurt. But she loves me so much that she supports me in my dream, how she's always been there for me through everything. I can't imagine not having that.

I give Piper's hand a squeeze and bring her knuckles to my lips and place a soft kiss on her skin. It was a complete risk, but I don't go up in flames or have the need to jump her—well, at least that's something.

I pull the bracelet out of my pocket. I had to pay Bram's niece twenty-five dollars to make these for me. I'm pretty sure he told her to gouge me for every dollar. As soon as I clasp it around her wrist she smiles. It's simple, stupid really, and I have its matching counterpart. Hers has lemons and strawberries on it and mine has cinnamon sticks and oranges.

"I know it's not much, but I'm all in, Piper. I'm so lucky to be your scent match," I tell her. It's at that moment that the distance I created before closes. The closure of the way I treated her and pushed away is forgotten. She squeezes my hand back and smiles as she drives. I feel a little bit lighter and like I can actually be the Omega Piper deserves.

"The feeling is mutual."

## CHAPTER 22

I deserve an award. One bigger than the Stanley Cup for my strength and patience for living with both Piper and Owen. The tension in the house… is something.

We just had another string of away games and I'm pretty sure the entire team knows something is going on between Owen and I at this point. But there was no way I was letting him room with someone else while we were gone. One, because I'm a possessive asshole, and two, I'm becoming addicted to the moments when Owen truly lets his guard down and lets his Omega nature shine through.

It's clear he's been so good at masking his needs, but when we're home or in a hotel room, he's able to truly be himself. Like right now as Piper reads something on her tablet and Owen is lying on her lap while she strokes his hair mindlessly like it's second nature. I rub my mouth and smile behind it. I'm not a psychic, but I'm pretty fucking sure I manifested this.

Are we doing everything a pack should be doing together? No. But again, I'm trying to be a patient man.

"What are you working on over there?" I ask Piper.

"Just looking up more information on the Omega Wellness

Clinic." I smile and nod my head and don't chime in at all. It's become clear to me that Piper doesn't like to be pushed. She needs to do this on her own. I can respect that.

"What do you want to do for dinner?" I ask.

"Oh, I bought groceries, so I'll cook," Piper says. I arch an eyebrow at her. It's been weeks, and she hasn't cooked anything. She has been buying a ton of takeout and snacks around the house lately, which I truly have enjoyed, but I'm not sure my oven has ever been used by her or myself.

"I didn't know you could cook," Owen says.

"Yeah, well, I'm full of surprises." She pats his head. "Get up, and I'll go get started," she says softly. Owen smiles up at her and moves. I'm not sure how they are both holding back, but they are. I had everything about his appointment parroted to me, and I get it. No matter how much I may fantasize about Owen going into heat, it needs to be at the right time.

Owen gets up only to flop his head into my lap, and I pick back up where Piper left off. His soft blond hair is between my fingertips as he closes his eyes and sighs.

Piper is clanging pots and pans in the kitchen, and it's at this moment I feel full. Full in a way hockey could only fill before. This… this is worth retiring for. I thought Owen's eyes were shut, but when I look down, he's looking at me appreciatively.

"What has that smile on your face?" he asks.

"Do I need a reason, *sólnyshka?*"

"I guess not," he says, closing his eyes, and I pet his hair more. I wonder if Owen just never embraced what he needed before. I don't want to bring it to his attention and have him pull back, so I just shrug my shoulders.

"I'm just really happy," I say, keeping it simple.

"I am too," he says softly, burrowing his face further against my thigh.

Piper's voice is low, but I hear her in the background and have to hold back a laugh. "Motherfucking cunt ass stove," she mumbles. I'm proud to say that I held strong and don't react, but Owen isn't and uses my leg to hide his laughter.

Somehow, despite all the noise Piper is making, Owen falls asleep, and I'm splitting my attention between Piper and some mindless show on TV.

"Are you sure you don't need any help?" I ask her. She blows a piece of hair out of her mouth.

"You know I've closed people's heads up after brain surgery, why is lasagna so fucking hard?"

"We could always just order in," I say, and there's more clanking in the kitchen.

"No, it will be done soon," she says.

"I'm sure it will be fine."

Piper makes a sound of disbelief but continues cooking. It smells good enough, and there haven't been any plumes of smoke, so I consider that a win in my book.

I rest my eyes, and I'm not sure how, but I fall asleep as well. It must be about another thirty minutes when Piper comes into the living room. She looks a little worse for wear but gives us a smile.

"Okay, dinner's done."

"Thank you for cooking," Owen says, getting up and lightly squeezing her hand before heading to the dining table. I follow suit as we all sit down.

We should have known by how hard Piper had to cut into the lasagna that it wasn't going to go well. But she cuts us each a square and plates it. The garlic bread is slightly burnt, but nothing that you can't scrape off.

Owen takes the first bite, and I have to prepare myself for how bad it's going to be. But when I hear an audible crunch come from him, I have to use every ounce of self control to not laugh.

Somehow Owen finishes his bite and smiles. "It's good, thanks, Piper."

She gives him a smile and looks at me. I take a deep inhale and refrain from cringing when my fork cuts through the crunchy pasta. I bring the bite to my mouth and school my features as I chew and swallow.

"Yeah, thanks for cooking."

Piper stands up, grabs the entire pan of lasagna and promptly throws it in the trash. "At least I know for sure that you both like me. That was horrible."

"What the fuck happened?" I say with a laugh and push my plate away.

"Apparently I bought one box of no boil noodles, but the rest you were supposed to boil. Who knew."

"Pho?" Owen asks with a smile.

"That sounds perfect," she says back, and I shake my head, wondering if this is the domestic pack bliss everyone talks about.

———

Both Owen and myself are completely exhausted after practice. We're working hard to clinch a spot in the Atlantic division. It's going to be tight between us and a few other teams, but it's possible. The Bruins all but have the top spot right now, the Red Wings and the Lightning are going to be our biggest competition. It's going to be hard getting that conference title, but fuck do I want it.

This season started off with me wanting to go out with a bang and end on top, but now it's turned more into giving Owen his dream and starting my pack. I can finally start to see the end of the tunnel. Leaving hockey isn't an option, but leaving the current level I'm at is an absolute must.

The drive home is tense. With Owen's new meds, by the end of the day his scent gets stronger. We've been smart about how we time things, but also make sure that he's being safe. My dick doesn't get this memo, however. I want to grab the Omega by his arm and hurl him onto my lap, but with how tired he looks, I can't possibly do that to him.

Not to mention our house is under an unspoken celibacy pact right now. My fist has never seen so much action in my life. I've been wanting to throw an idea out to the both of them, but I'm not sure how they would take it. The last time I did anything sexual was that night that Owen came over here in distress. I haven't touched Piper in weeks, and I've been craving it.

I was being honest when I said that them being scent matches doesn't bother me. I don't feel less than. Currently, I'm their solution. Neither of them will go into a pheromone filled spiral over me. Is it bad I want my roommates to use me to their content?

"Is Piper home?" he asks.

"Yeah, she should be. I think she got off around three, but she might be sleeping."

"I..." he trails off and shakes his head.

"What?"

He sighs. "Can I sleep in your room tonight?"

"You can have whatever you want," I tell him.

He rolls his eyes but smiles and gets out of the car. When we enter the house, there are already salads waiting for us. Piper sits at the table and smiles when we enter. Her smile quickly falters, and I can tell she's scenting Owen.

I'm drawn to Owen, I want him constantly, but I know the

draw for Piper is even more intense. If I'm patient, then she's in a whole other class of her own.

I look over at Owen, and his pupils are blown to hell.

"Fuck, I'll go to my room," Piper says, grabbing her salad and getting up like she's ready to leave.

"Wait," I say, and they both stop what they're doing and look at me. "What… what if I was the buffer for you two?"

"What?" Owen says.

"You've both been struggling. I mean, my right wrist is tired, so I can only imagine how you two feel."

"We shouldn't risk it," Piper says, the logical one in the pack.

"What if there were things in place to tone down some of the risk?" I say, and Piper puts her salad down.

"Like what?" That's what I thought. If she thinks we haven't heard the buzzing coming from her room in the middle of the night, she's delusional.

"I can touch one of you while the other watches."

"Touch Piper," Owen nearly shouts, interrupting the end of my sentence.

"What?" she questions him.

"There's too much risk in how we interact. Dr. Horngale basically said that if we give in, my heat will start. But if we don't touch, kiss, if I don't taste you…" His throat bobs, and he licks his lips like he's thinking about it. And now I'm thinking about it too, and my cock is hard and ready in my pants. "Then we should be fine. I feel guilty that I'm the reason everyone is holding out. It's not fair to you or Alexi."

"No, absolutely not. You're not blaming yourself. We all made a choice. Season is over in a few weeks." I arch an eyebrow at her, and she shakes her head. "Okay, best case or worst case scenario, a few months. I truly can't decide if I want you all to make it to the Cup or not." I appreciate her honesty and shake my head.

"Your Omega is telling you he wants to watch," I say, and she blinks at me.

"Owen?" she questions. He sighs and rakes a hand through his messy dirty-blond hair.

"Listen, I know I'm the reason we're not doing anything. But fuck, Piper. I want you. I want to see you come, I want to taste, fuck, lick, worship you, have you worship me. But we can't right now, so the next best thing is to watch Alexi do that for me."

She wraps her arms around her middle and looks between me and Owen and licks her lips. "You really think we'll be able to just stop there?"

"We'll have to," he says.

"What do you say, *malyshka?* You have been so good, so patient. Don't you deserve a reward?"

She narrows her eyes at me. "You were plotting this whole thing, weren't you?"

I shrug and take a few steps closer to her. "Can you blame me? Watching you walk around here in your bra and panties, showing me what I can't have. When I know it feels so fucking good?" I ask her, invading her space.

I look to my left, and Owen is already taking off his clothes. Piper looks at him wide-eyed, licking her lips before looking back at me.

"He needs it too," I say softly.

"I really fucking do," Owen says in a breathy voice and heads over to the couch where he tugs down his shorts and boxers, exposing his perfect cock. Piper's gaze locks onto where his hand grips the base of his dick.

"Do to me what you want to do to him," I whisper in her ear, and she shivers.

"You're sure, Owen?" she confirms with him again. I'm not sure why him stroking his cock isn't enough confirmation, but he answers her regardless.

"Please, Alpha," he asks. It's what breaks her, and I'm fucking happy for it. I try not to be a smug asshole about it, but it's difficult.

"Sit on the couch," she directs me.

*Fuck yes.*

I'm walking over to the couch, and she clicks her tongue. "You won't be needing your clothes," she tells me, and I grin, gripping the collar of my shirt and ripping it off before grabbing my shorts and briefs by the waistband and tugging them down.

"Fuck," I hear Owen groan from the loveseat. "Please get naked too," he begs Piper.

She looks over at him, and I know it's taking every ounce of her control to not just go over there and touch him and give into every desire. But being the strong Alpha she is, she shakes her head and looks at me. "Take off my clothes," she tells me.

Completely naked, with my dick hitting my stomach, I do as she says. I fist the hem of her T-shirt and drag it over her head. Her luscious dark hair hits her back, and I can't help but push it over her shoulders before placing a kiss on her collarbone before reaching around her back and unclasping her bra. Her arms fall to her side as the material slides down her skin. Owen groans, and both Piper and I can't help but to look over at him. The way he's biting his lip and stroking himself in a way to make it last.

"Her bottoms too," Owen says between strokes.

"Our Omega is impatient," I say, and Piper hums in agreement. I make quick work of untying the front of her shorts and pushing them off her hips, and the offensive cotton hits the floor. She steps out of her shorts, and her hands are on my chest. I'm proud of myself for not even making a comment about her not wearing any panties.

"On the couch," she tells me again. With a massive grin on my face, I sit on the couch, my legs spread wide and my arms resting on the back of the sofa. I feel like a fucking king, and the only thing that could possibly make this any better is if we were all able to touch each other right now.

But when I look over at Piper's naked body and the slight sheen hitting her thighs, I can't help but to feel grateful. I have her in my house, willing and eager to be with me. She understands the direction this is all headed toward. This isn't just a let me clear my head fuck, this is the three of us being a pack. We're solving a problem together, and she isn't running for the hills or overthinking anything.

I won't deny that I have a fear that she'll shut down after we finish, but I hope this is the start of a less skittish Piper, one who see's how important she is to me—to this pack.

Piper walks over to me, standing between my two legs, and looks back at Owen. "What do you want?" she asks him.

"I want to see you come," he tells her, but it feels like it's directed to both of us.

She turns back to me and arches an eyebrow. "Do you think you can make that happen?" she challenges with a smirk.

"*Malyshka*, you already fucking know I can make you come. The question is how long should I drag it out?"

"Don't drag it out," Owen says, panting in the corner. His knuckles are white the way he's holding is cock, and all I want to do is make it better. This is the best I've got—giving him the show he desperately needs.

"Come here," I tell her. Her cockiness is fading, and her need to be controlled and have her mind shut down is taking over.

She listens beautifully and even sits the way I want her to, with her back pressed against my chest and her delicious ass grinding against my cock.

"Play with her pussy," Owen says. The head of his length drips with pre-cum, and his sweet Omega scent lingers throughout the room. It's affecting both Piper and I in the most torturous way. At least we'll all get some relief from the situation.

Piper spreads her legs and puts more of her weight against my chest. I've been craving this, the way her skin would feel against mine. Everything we've done so far has been rushed and with too much clothing. But with nothing between us, it's more evident than ever we were meant to be together. That we fit perfectly, no matter our designation or the current situation we find ourselves in.

She presses her feet against the couch cushions and holds herself open for Owen's pleasure. His gaze rotates between her pussy, chest, and her facial expressions, then to mine. The way he takes us in together has me wanting to force his heat and find ourselves tangled and sweaty together. But I push that feral need deep down and just focus on the now. The way Piper's scent wraps around mine and the sweetness of Owen's scent driving our baser urges. The way her pulse thumps underneath my fingertips as I wrap an arm around her chest and hold her throat loosely.

My other arm wraps around her waist, sliding down her toned stomach to her pussy. My fingers drag down the short patch of hair until I meet her wet and ready cunt. She pushes her ass even harder against me when I touch her dripping center. Her head falling back on my shoulder.

Owen watches on with nothing shy of absolute desire in his eyes. His strokes are firm, and I know he'll be finishing quickly.

"You want to watch your Alpha come undone, *sólnyshka?*"

"Please. Let me watch him fuck you, Piper, please," he begs. His back arching off the couch as I slide two fingers inside of her pussy.

"I'll never get tired of how wet you get for me, Piper. You want my cock? You want to show our Omega what he has to look forward to? How crazy you make me with this pussy?"

Piper doesn't answer, she just lifts her hips higher. It's the best invitation I've ever been offered as I slide into her wet and eager cunt.

A low groan escapes me, and a feminine moan leaves Piper's lips as I thrust into her. My fingertips are tightly holding her hips as I fuck her from below. The only sounds in the room are all of us panting, the smacking of our flesh, and the little noises that none of us can hold back.

Owen is so close, his wrist turning and stroking as he stares at where Piper and I are connected. Like his salvation is in the mist of what Piper and I are doing for each other, like he wants it for himself.

"Someday I'm going to have you on your knees licking your Alpha's pussy while I fuck her. You want that, Omega?"

"Fuck, I want it. Fuck," he mumbles, his pace only getting faster as I wrap an arm around Piper's waist and play with her clit as I fuck her. I know I'm hitting the right spot as her pussy grips my cock and her breathing becomes more labored.

"I'm going to come," she says close to the side of my head.

"So's your Omega. Watch what you do to him." She lifts her head off of my shoulder, and it's magnificent as I watch them come together. Owen shooting ropes of cum over his rigid chest, and Piper dripping all over my cock as she milks me.

I fuck her brutally throughout her orgasm. I think she's nearly ready to tell me to stop as I pound into her, my knot pressing against her entrance, begging for entry. It expands outside of her as I thrust roughly until I fill her with my cum.

We all sit there a moment, covered in fluids and catching our breath after what happened.

No one knows what to say after the release we all needed, so I decide to break the ice. "We should all shower. You two can't touch each other tonight," I say.

Owen whines. He fucking whines, and my cock is hard again, and at the same time, all I want to do is give him everything he wants.

"Sorry," he says softly.

"Don't be sorry. This is harder than I thought it would be," Piper says, her naked body still on top of mine. I wrap my arms around her and kiss the side of her face, and she melts into my touch.

"I'm here for both of you. If you need a fix, I'm here. We can keep doing this, and we can rotate."

Piper laughs on top of me, and she jostles my knot. If she doesn't stop, I'll be bending her over the couch and fucking her all over again.

"So you're what? The house fuck toy?" Owen says, and I laugh.

I grin. "Damn right I am."

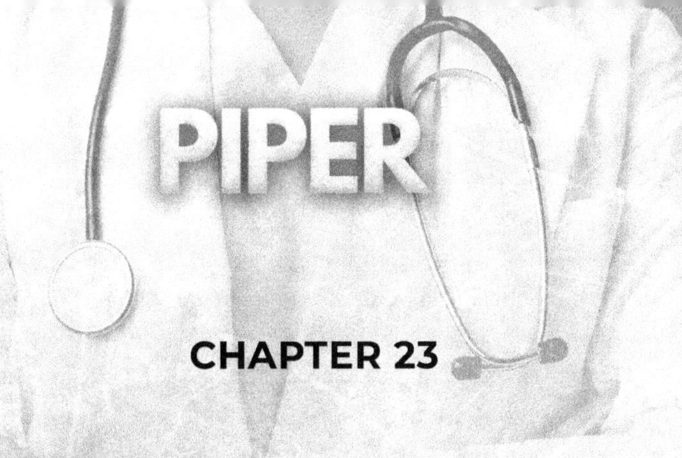

# PIPER

## CHAPTER 23

The scenting, the watching, and not being able to touch may kill me before this job does. I feel like I've been somewhat of a ghost at the hospital lately. Like my body is here, but my mind isn't. I've pulled up the application for residency at Omega Wellness at least ten times, but every time, I stop myself.

Why would a facility like that want me? Someone who couldn't hack it in surgery, a failure, a disappointment?

"Dr. Blake, do you have something else you would rather be doing?" Dr. Mayfield asks, and I nearly have to shake myself.

"No, sorry, Dr. Mayfield."

"If you're not able to focus during surgery, perhaps you should find a different specialty."

"I apologize again," I say, not wanting to say anything disrespectful to one of my superiors.

"I'm not saying that as your superior, I'm saying it as a physician. Dr. Blake, there's no shame in surgery not being your path."

"My father wouldn't agree," I say.

"Peter is an asshole," she says, and I blink up at her, only able to see her eyes with all her surgical attire on.

"I'm sorry?" I question.

"Peter was always judgmental. Yet did you know he had one of the highest bad outcomes in our year?"

"He never told me that, no."

"Of course he wouldn't. You could be a fantastic surgeon. I could make you one of the best. But the biggest thing is, you have to want it. So, Dr. Blake, do you want it?"

"I'm not sure."

She tilts her head and asks the scrub nurse for an instrument. "Then I think you have your answer."

"But what about the last two years in this program?"

"What's two years versus the rest of your life?" she says, and I'm nearly left speechless. "Unless you have another reason."

I shake my head, and she hums.

"The brain is such an interesting organ, it's why I became a neurosurgeon. It's the one organ we truly haven't mastered. Sure, we understand the functions of the brain, what specific parts do. Yet there are still so many parts yet to be discovered, but what is most fascinating is how the organ operates and how it is so unique to each individual. Something so delicate yet so expanse captures the essence of who we are. The brain is the center of everything."

It's the most I've ever heard her speak, and it's clear that she's passionate. She's not just a mindless cutter who likes doing surgery and pushing herself for no reason. Being a brain surgeon is her passion.

"Has anything ever spoken to you like the brain speaks to me?" she asks. I swallow thickly and nod my head. "Then you have your answer. It will be unfortunate to train someone who isn't as thorough, but I will find a way to survive," she says, and I swear that it was sarcasm, but I can't be sure.

"Thank you, Dr. Mayfield."

"We will keep this discussion between us until you make a decision."

"I appreciate your discretion," I say. This weight keeps lifting off my chest with each declaration. I can do this.

*At least, I think I can.*

———

I need to shower and sleep for a significant amount of time. I'm so tired that I'm not even sure how I'm functioning.

Maybe a bath with some bath salts will do the trick. I'm about to head into the bathroom when Owen leaves. We bump into each other, and automatically our hands go to each other's biceps. I give his muscles a tight squeeze. I love his body, and I wish I could touch more of it. He works so hard for the tone he has, and it shows; I want to lick every inch.

"Hey," he says softly.

We're about the same height, and I look into his beautiful blue eyes and sigh. "Hey."

We haven't talked about the other night or how it affected either of us. I can't decide if it was the right thing to do or not, but all I know is that it felt right. Alexi felt amazing, and having Owen's eyes on me made the experience even more thrilling. It's not something I've experienced before. I mean, theoretically I knew if I was in a pack, there would be sharing and watching, but actually experiencing it is a whole other story.

His hand slides from my upper arm to my neck. It's like a trail of fire where he touches me until he's touching my jaw. His scent is choking me, and all I want to do is finally cave and give into this undeniable, magnetic push and pull we've found ourselves in.

"Are you okay?" he asks softly.

"Shouldn't I be asking you that?" His brows furrow, and he shakes his head.

"It's something both of us ask each other. Isn't that what a pack does?"

"Are we a pack?" I ask.

"Maybe not a fully solidified one, but that's the plan, right? That's what you want?"

I may not know what I want to do with my life, where I see my professional future, but on this, I find myself feeling sure. "It's what I want."

His other hand cradles the other side of my face, and my hands automatically go to his waist.

"I wish I could be what you need right now," he says, and I shake my head. His hands don't leave their soft position against my jaw.

"You are. Is there something you need? Are you okay?" I turn the question back on him.

His thumbs rub against my flesh, and I can't deny how badly I want him at this moment. Not even in a feral way where our pheromones are running the show. I just want Owen. I want to be able to kiss, cuddle, and be casual with each other without this fear of what might happen.

It's not just that I sexually want Owen, no matter his designation or the fact that we're scent matches. I want him because I'm attracted to him, and I want to make him mine.

"I haven't felt this good in years. Between living here with you and Alexi and the new medication, I feel... less angry, less alone, and not as run down. You and Alexi gave me that, and I want to give you two everything back in return."

I smile at him and grip his waist a little tighter, and he groans.

Surely a kiss wouldn't set everything off?

Our faces are only a few inches apart, his strawberry citrus scent luring me in like a siren song and his touch bringing me so much comfort after my long day.

His thumbs rub my cheekbones, and he sighs, pressing his forehead against mine. We're even closer than we were before. One of us just needs to lean just a little closer, and we would be kissing. I would finally be able to taste him.

"We can't. I want to. So fucking bad. I swear I spend half of my day thinking about what it would be like to kiss you and touch you. Can you wait for me?" he asks.

I nod while our foreheads touch.

"You're worth waiting for."

He pulls back and smiles, his scent drowning me. While I was tired when I came home, all I feel is wired now, and I need some way to expel all this sexual tension.

"I think I'm going to go for a run."

"Okay, I think… I think I might need to spend some time with Alexi."

As badly as I want to watch, I fear I don't have as much restraint as Owen had the other night. Thank God we have Alexi in more ways than one. Part of me feels guilty that he isn't also Owen's scent match, but it's evident that he's the glue holding us all together. Without Alexi, there is no pack, regardless of me being Owen's scent match.

"He'll take good care of you."

"You… you could come up too," he says softly.

"I don't know that I could hold back. Go see your Alpha. I'm going to go for a run."

I drop my hands from his body, but he doesn't let go. "Soon," he says, and I sigh.

"Soon."

———

My heart is thumping in my chest. I really went on this run with no destination in mind, so I shouldn't be surprised I wound up in front of Charlotte's house. I'm a sweaty mess, but I'm already here. Clearly my subconscious knows I need my best friend.

I knock on the door because I don't have my key and I don't feel like dealing with Mikael's bitching tonight.

Anders opens the door. He cocks his head to the side but gives me a smile. "Hey, Piper."

"Hey, is Charlotte home?"

He nods and ushers me in. "She's in the nest with Eli, Mikael, and Katie."

"Oh, I can come back."

"You clearly ran here. She would be pissed if you came by and she didn't see you."

"Right," I reply, going down to the basement into the nest.

"Auntie P!" Katie shouts and runs to me. I grab her under her arms and hug her on my hip. I fucking love this little girl so much. It's probably because she's a pretty little clone of her mother with a touch of Eli in there.

"We can give you guys a minute," Eli says, looking down at his Omega with worry in his eyes.

"Everything okay?"

"If feeling like my vagina is going to fall out is okay," Charlotte says from her mass of pillows.

"Is vagina a bad word?" Katie asks.

"No, it's not," Charlotte says.

"Come here, *ma chouette,*" Mikael says, holding his arms

out to his daughter. Katie is skeptical, and Mikael sighs. "I'll give you back to Auntie P after she talks to mommy."

"Okay," she says, and she goes into her dad's arms.

I crawl into Charlotte's nest. Her mass of pillows nearly drown her, and I wrap an arm around her belly and feel my future nieces or nephews.

"You smell," she says, and I laugh.

"Sorry, I ran here."

"Why?" she asks, and I sigh. "I know you're holding back from me. No one is buying that Owen is just your friend, or whatever you want to call him."

"I know. You know if I could tell you, I would, right?"

"It's the only reason I haven't pushed you. I'd like to get to know Owen better."

"Maybe after you deliver these babies."

"Twins are supposed to come early, Piper. I'm eight hundred weeks pregnant," she sniffles, and I pet her hair softly.

"I'm sorry, Charles." Charlotte starts crying and mumbling about how much bullshit this is and how everything hurts and she just wants to move again. I stroke her hair and reassure my best friend. I'm not sure why being with her and comforting her makes me feel so much better.

"Oh, fuck," she says suddenly. Her sobs completely hushed.

"What?"

"My water just broke."

"What?"

"Go get everyone." I feel her stomach lightly. Having only learned about obstetrics in medical school, I have no clue what I'm doing, but I nod and run upstairs.

"Uh, so Charlotte is having the babies," I say to three shocked Alphas and a cheering Katie.

They all blink at me, and I give them a look that says 'what the fuck are you waiting for.' Suddenly, all three of them are rushing to the basement. Katie flings herself into my arms.

"I'm going to be a big sister."

"You sure are."

Mikael and Eli all but carry Charlotte up the stairs while Anders gets her to-go bag.

"My parents aren't answering the phone. Can you take Katie until I get ahold of them?" Anders asks.

"Of course, I did run here though, so can you drop me off."

"I want to go too!" Katie says petulantly.

Even though I can tell Charlotte is in a ton of pain, she smiles at her daughter and pushes back her messy blonde hair. "Having babies takes a long time, and it's gross. Don't you want them to be cute when you see them?"

"I guess."

"I promise either Auntie P or Mummo and Ukki will bring you to the hospital, okay?"

She hugs Katie tightly, and we're all ushered into their massive vehicle. Charlotte does a great job of hiding any discomfort in front of Katie. If anything, her Alphas are the ones absolutely losing their shit and fumbling over themselves.

They drop us off, Katie giving each of her parents a kiss before we go into Alexi's house. Luckily I made sure to pack some of her toys when I moved to Alexi's. But not as much as I had at the old townhouse.

When I open the door, Katie immediately runs to the living room where Alexi and Owen are sitting. Thank goodness they finished up what they were doing before I got back. I didn't even think about that, could have been fucking traumatizing, but they are both freshly showered. Charlotte and her guys would kill us if they had to have that talk early because we walked in on Owen and Alexi banging. Note to self: make sure your roommates aren't fucking before you bring a child into the home.

"Is that you, *ptichka?*" Alexi says to her, and Katie starts squawking like a bird.

"Does he have a nickname for everyone?" Owen asks.

"Basically," I reply and plop down on the couch. Owen's eyes dilate when he looks at me. I feel guilty with how heavy my scent is. But then I realize that it's Charlotte's scent that's bothering him. His shoulders are tense, and I can scent him stronger right now, like his pheromones are pissed that I dared to come home smelling like another Omega. It makes me feel supremely guilty, and I step away from him. He looks away in embarrassment, and all I want to do is comfort him, but I'm not sure how right now.

"Katie, do you want to watch a movie?" I ask, my eyes not leaving Owen, who seems to be at war with himself over scenting my friend on me.

"*Rio?*" she asks Alexi, not me.

"Of course. We need bird snacks." Katie starts acting like a bird, and Alexi puts the movie on for her before going to the kitchen and grabbing some snacks.

Katie stands in front of Owen and tilts her head at him. "You're like my mommy," she says inquisitively, and Alexi and I stop in our tracks. "And like me. We have pretty blonde hair," she says, and we both let out a soft breath.

Owen smiles at her and nods his head. "We do."

"My daddy says my mommy's hair is beautiful and so am I," Katie says with all the confidence in the world. I think we're in for a hell of a ride with this one.

Owen looks a little uncomfortable, like he doesn't have much experience with children, but he smiles at her. Katie scoots on the couch next to him as the movie starts.

"You went for a run and brought back a child?" Alexi jokes in the kitchen.

"I went for a run and ended up at Charlotte's house. She went into labor, and we ended up with her kid." Owen takes a deep breath. He's clearly battling between logic and his baser instincts, so I need to get Charlotte's scent off of me.

Alexi's brows furrow as he cuts up some cheese for Katie.

"That's a long run. Are you okay?" Always perceptive, my larger than life Alpha

"I'm fine," I say, feeling guilty for being short with him. Alexi sighs but says nothing. "What?" I ask him.

"Nothing, *malyshka*. Do you want to take a shower?"

"Yeah, I'll be quick." I look over at Owen, who takes a deep breath, and I realize I might need to adjust some of my actions with Charlotte. I'm not sure how I feel about that, but I have an Omega now, and I need him to be comfortable.

"We've got snacks and the movie covered."

"Thanks."

He looks like he wants to say something else or reach out to me. But instead I turn away and go to the shower.

*Why am I like this?*

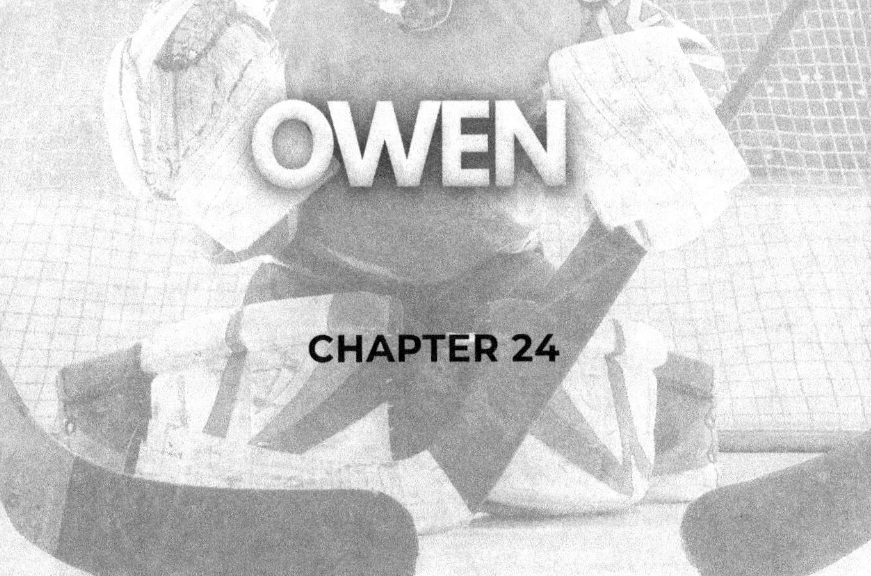

# OWEN

## CHAPTER 24

We're at the hospital visiting Charlotte and her twins. This is the softest I've seen Mikael since I started on the team. They had a son and a daughter, Andrea and Lincoln. They're so small and fragile, especially in their Alpha father's hands.

Piper holds one of the babies, and I stand in the corner. It feels like I'm intruding on a moment, like I don't belong here. Like they're all one big found family and I'm the outsider.

Piper stands next to me holding the baby while Alexi sits in a chair in the corner. Katie is beside herself when it comes to her new siblings. While I may not be used to being around children, I can feel the joy in the room, and it's the first time I truly get it.

Anders grabs Katie, and Piper and Mikael are directed to put the newborns in their cots. Charlotte looks exhausted, and I can't help but to feel like the Omega won't stop glancing in my direction, like she sees right through me.

"I'm ready for my sushi now," she declares, and Eli smiles at her and gives her a kiss.

"Let's go grab lunch. Do you guys want to come?" Eli asks, and we nod our heads in agreement.

"Are you sure you want to be alone, *mon sucre d'érable?*" Mikael asks, and she sighs.

"The babies are sleeping, and I need some sleep too. Go get lunch, and bring me all my favorites."

"Okay," he says, leaning down and kissing her forehead. Piper gives her friend a hug and tells her how proud of her she is, and then Charlotte looks up at me.

"Owen, can you stay for a second?"

I look around the room, and everyone looks confused. But you can't simply tell a woman who just had two children no. Piper gives me a small shrug and grabs Alexi by the hand and takes him out of the room.

I take a cautious step toward Charlotte. We've barely spoken besides the Christmas party, and obviously she knows that the three of us are living at the same house.

"Don't worry, Piper hasn't told me your secret," she says softly.

I blink at the small woman. "What?"

"I was trying to figure it out, what could be so important that my best friend would hide it from me. Then there was the intel I got from my Alphas about you being tired and the way that Alexi is with you."

"I—"

"Don't worry, they are too preoccupied with our family and hockey to notice. Your secret is safe with me. Just please don't hurt my friend."

"She's my scent match," I tell her.

Charlotte shakes her head. "Scent matches can hurt you the most."

"I promise, I won't hurt her."

"Thank you. Not that it matters, but you should be proud

of yourself, what you've accomplished. I don't know many Omegas who could keep up with an NHL schedule. No matter what happens, you should be proud of that."

"Thanks, Charlotte." I look over at her babies. "And congratulations."

She gives me a smile and a nod of her head as she lies down. I take that as my time to leave, but when I leave her room, I have multiple sets of eyes on me.

"What did she want?" Mikael asks first in an irritated tone.

"Hey, watch it," Alexi says immediately, and I scrub a hand down my face.

"Just reading me my rights as Piper's best friend," I say plainly, and her Alphas seem to accept that answer. Piper, however, doesn't buy it as she gives me a soft smile, and she places her hand in mine.

I'm not sure how much longer these soft gentle touches are going to be enough. But I take the small intimacies in any way I can.

———

We've just about got one of the playoff spots with our name on it. It's going to be close with the Lightning, but I know we can do it.

It's taking every ounce of my energy, but I fucking know we can.

Tonight is a special home game. Not only are we playing the Canes again, much to Nilsen's pleasure, but Piper is also attending the game. She hasn't been able to come to a game since we've officially started dating. Which I guess is the term I would use for it. You can't easily say I live with my scent match and we're in a vow of celibacy, but as soon as the season is over, I'm going to go completely feral over the woman.

Dating is a simple way to say it, but she's far more, so is Alexi.

Alexi, who seems not himself. He's fully dressed and ready for the game, looking sexy as he always does. The man is larger than life in both personality and stature, and I can't seem to get enough of him. It took finding Alexi and Piper, but I finally feel like I can be myself—almost. While I can't let my scent fully perfume or be as needy as I want to be, I'm not the same jaded, grumpy bastard I was when I started on this team.

I feel less angry at the world, and I can't tell if it's the shift in my medication or these two Alphas who have helped center me.

"You good?" I ask Alexi.

"Yeah," he says softly.

For the first time since we've met, I feel like Alexi is lying to me. I grab him by his jersey and take him to a small alcove in the locker room.

"What's going on?" I ask, seeing worry written all over his face.

"It's fine. We're fine."

"You look stressed, and you're not joking around like you usually do." I don't care that we're in the locker room, I place my hands on his chest, even though the padding stops me from touching his body.

He looks away from me for a moment before looking back. "Are you still going to want me after you can have Piper?" he asks. I've never thought that Alexi had any insecurities. He's always grinning and making jokes.

"Of course I want you. Nothing about that has changed. Did I do something to make you feel this way?"

He sighs and scrubs his hands through his hair. "No, you didn't do anything. We're just getting closer to the end of the season. I just worry that once you're with Piper, being with me won't be the same for you anymore."

I fist his jersey and tug him down so he has to look me in the eyes. "There is no pack without you. Don't you see it?"

"What?" he says, and I shake my head.

"You're the heart of the pack."

He shakes his head. "You're the Omega." He says Omega softly, so no one in the locker room hears.

"Sure, but without you, we're nothing. You've been there for me and Piper when we needed someone the most, despite not being a scent match. You've taken care of both of us with no expectations of anything in return. You were the one who was adamant that we would be a pack, and look at us now. You made this happen. You're the pack Alpha, and I don't want to hear any more of this bullshit again. I want you today, I'm going to want you tomorrow, and once this season is over, I'm going to want your bond mark just as much as I want Piper's, you got me?"

A wide grin takes over his face, and I take a relieved breath knowing that my Alpha is back to his usual self.

"I'm sorry," he says, shaking his head.

"Don't be sorry. You're allowed to feel however you want. Just know that it's not based in reality. I want you, Alexi, just as bad as I want Piper." Alexi and I haven't fucked, but we've done everything else. I'm too nervous to let him knot me and send me into heat. Even if he isn't my scent match and I'm still on a slew of drugs, it's a risk we can't take.

Right now, I'm about to throw risk to the wind to prove to this Alpha how much he means to me. I tug on his jersey again and bring his lips to mine. I'm sure we look ridiculous, both of us dressed head to toe in our uniforms, making out. But it feels right. He eases my nerves, and I've put his insecurities at bay.

There's a whistle, and Alexi shakes his head.

"You two gonna make out all day, or are we going to win this fucking game?" Mikael asks.

"Shut the fuck up. Let's go kick some Hurricane ass," Alexi says before swatting my ass, and Coach Applegate starts his speech.

"Let's go out there and clinch our spot in the playoffs. We're still in it if we don't win today, but securing a win tonight means we're going to the next stage. I know you're all hungry. Each and every one of you has worked hard this season. I need every single one of you to show that on the ice tonight."

There's banging of lockers, a group of us pushing each other and amping each other up. The locker room feels electric, and I'm ready for tonight. Every game we play, every day that passes, is another step closer to fulfilling my dream and starting the next one.

I've broken down my body, given everything I've got, and I don't intend to let it all fall through the cracks now.

"One more thing," coach says. "Be nice to the new mascot."

Suddenly, a dark haired Beta with a massive smile dressed as a fox with the head under his arm comes in.

"Hey, I'm Ethan," he says.

"No, you're Finnegan the Fox," Coach Applegate says next to him.

"Right." He nods and looks around, just happy as shit to be here. "Well, good game," he says, putting on the fox head and walking through the tunnel. I didn't realize tonight was the night they were debuting the new costume. The first fox they had looked like it had rabies and was on a bunch of antipsychotics. This one looks much more family friendly.

There's stick banging, butt taps, and loud music playing in the stadium before we skate out, and I can't help but feel like everything is just clicking into place.

I'm nearly out the tunnel when Bram Nilsen stops me. "Remember, fuck up Kristiansen any chance you get," he says.

"You know, Nilsen, you're kinda scary."

He gives me a feral grin, his mouth guard hanging between his teeth. Sloane walks by; she's taking a video of us for some app, and she shakes her head.

"Bram isn't scary, he's the sweetest." Her scent gets everyone riled up in the tunnel, but she doesn't give a shit as she smiles at him.

"See, I'm sweet," he says as he watches the Omega walk away.

"She's the coach's daughter."

"Semantics," he says, his gaze not leaving her while he speaks to me.

"You know he'll bury you alive if you touch his daughter."

"I'm looking, not touching," he says with an eye roll.

"Uh huh, sure."

"Big game when you're the one banging the captain."

"Oh, fuck off," I tell him, and he laughs and claps my shoulder.

"You know, I didn't think you would work out. I'm glad you did. Thanks for not being a massive disappointment," he says as we skate off onto the ice for warmups. If that's all the asshole wants to give me, so be it.

We're skating on the ice with music blaring and getting ready for the game when I look up at the box Piper is in. Charlotte is still recovering, so it looks like she's hanging out with Sloane and a few other hockey wives. I'm smiling at her when I look at her jersey. My face immediately drops, and Alexi is by my side.

"I'm going to redden her ass for that tonight."

"Beckford, really? That's whose jersey she wore?"

Alexi points up at her and gives her a naughty shake of his

finger, and she replies with a middle finger and a smile. Alexi is grinning and shaking his head, while he laughs animatedly.

"You two are going to be the fucking death of me."

"What did I do?"

Alexi rolls his eyes and skates back a little bit before swatting my ass with the stick. "Keep your head in the game, and don't let that," he points to the box where Piper is with his stick, "get to your head."

"It really just makes me want to punch Eli."

Eli skates over, and Alexi bumps his shoulder. "What the fuck did I do?"

"Why is Piper wearing your jersey?"

He looks up to the stands and shakes his head. "Did either of you assholes think about getting her one of yours?"

Mine isn't being mass produced, so I arch an eyebrow at Alexi.

"Still spanking her ass."

"Great to know," Eli says as he skates away.

"You good?" I ask Alexi, and he grins at me.

"Yeah, I'm really fucking good."

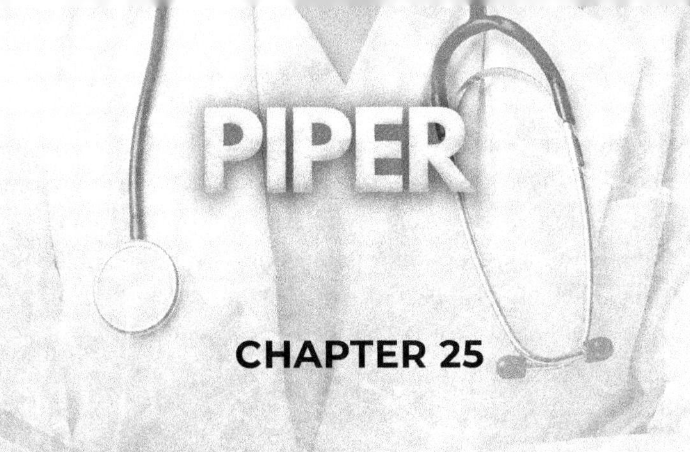

# PIPER

## CHAPTER 25

"Hi, I'm Sloane," the sweet voice next to me says. She's petite, gorgeous, and feels completely out of place. She's wearing a black T-shirt, not a jersey, and her reddish-blonde hair is down in loose waves.

"Piper, nice to meet you." I hold out my hand, and I'm instantly hit by her scent. She smells like peaches and sunshine. I look around and wonder who she's here with.

"I'm Coach Applegate's daughter. I've been managing some of their social media accounts. I'm not like the big wig marketing person, but I finally talked my dad into letting me help out, and well, it's been great," she says, just spewing out a ton of information. "Who are you married or bonded to?" she asks.

"Oh, um."

She looks at me and smiles. "You don't have to answer. But I am confused why you're wearing a Beckford jersey."

I give her a small smile. "Mostly to mess with Alexi," I say.

"Ah, so Alexi and Owen, good choices."

"Thank you." I'm guessing that Alexi and Owen haven't

been hiding the fact that they are seeing each other from the team, and a huge part of me likes that. Not that we aren't out as a couple, but when we are completely public, I want people to know the full extent of our relationship—with both of them.

"They have both been so nice to me."

"Has anyone not been?" I ask her defensively, ready to kick anyone's ass who decided to mess with the small Omega.

She smiles and shakes her head. "Oh, no. Some of them ignore me completely. I think I make them uncomfortable."

"They can control themselves and suck it up."

She snaps her fingers. "Exactly! That's why I refuse to hide my scent. I should be allowed to be who I am without worrying about someone hurting me or taking advantage of me. No offense, but I think Alphas need to be taught some more self control."

"No, you're absolutely right. It could be because my best friend is an Omega, so I've always been around scents. Some Alphas never learned how to handle themselves, not that it's an excuse. Do you have a pack?" I ask her, since apparently there are no lines during our conversation.

"Not yet, but one day. Hopefully soon."

"Are you on suppressants?" I ask her, and she arches an eyebrow at me. "I'm sorry. I'm a doctor. I've been considering specializing in Omega medical care."

That has her face relaxing. "I'm on a very low dose. Enough to keep my heat at bay. But I'm hoping I find a pack before I start seeing any signs of it coming."

"You know, it can really sneak up on you. You should have a backup plan, just in case."

She sighs and nods her head. "My dads have said the same thing. I definitely will."

The guys are warming up on the ice, and Alexi points at me and shakes his head. I furrow my brows, and then he tugs on his jersey, indicating he isn't pleased with me wearing Eli's jersey.

I give him a cheeky middle finger and watch him laugh on the ice. I fucking love when Alexi laughs. He throws his head back, his dark hair slightly damp and incredibly sexy. He laughs with his whole body, and even if he's pissed about the jersey, it was worth it. Besides, neither of them offered to give me one of theirs.

Alexi swats Owen's ass with his stick, and I have to bite my lip as I watch them together. God, I want to watch them together, but I don't know if I can handle it.

"Is Owen not out?" Sloane says casually.

"I think everyone on the team knows he's dating Alexi," I respond.

"I mean, that he's an Omega."

My stomach sinks into my ass, and I exhale softly. "I don't know what you mean."

Sloane hums under her breath. "Got it, secret Omega. Secret is safe with me."

"You can't tell your dad," I say to reiterate the most important part of this equation. The fact that Sloane is the coach's daughter, this could ruin everything for Owen.

"Pft, I don't tell him anything anyways. If he isn't smart enough to figure it out on his own, then that's his problem."

"Thank you," I say softly, even though my heart is racing inside of my chest.

"So… I'm guessing this is his last season."

"I think so," I reply, not wanting to give away all of our business to this Omega who I just met and is seriously good at making people feel comfortable.

"It will be a big loss for the team, especially if Alexi is leaving too."

"I don't know what Alexi's plans are," I say. I mean, he

talks a big game about us becoming a pack, and he's one of the oldest players on the ice, so I'm sure retirement is the plan.

"You're an Alpha worth leaving this for," she says quietly, her hand grazing my shoulder as she walks off. I blink while I watch her back as she leaves the box.

*What in the actual fuck just happened?*

———

Since the guys had press and a game recap, I decided to just come straight home. Especially since Charlotte wasn't at the game, and with no one to entertain me, I left right after. It was a tight game, but they won with a last minute goal with three minutes left in the last period. It's official, the Foxes are going to the playoffs, and I now have to stay celibate for God knows how long.

I groan, grabbing my favorite toy. It's squishy and locks perfectly inside of me, as well as a bulb at the end that vibrates and plays with my clit.

I know that I should do this in my bedroom and keep it to myself. But I'm feeling like a bit of a menace tonight. My need is so intoxicatingly heady. I only take off my jeans and underwear, leaving the jersey and the shirt underneath on.

I take up the same spot in the living room where Alexi and I fucked. The memories of him touching me and making me feel so good flash behind my eyes. It almost feels like I have Owen's eyes on me as I get wet and start teasing myself with the toy, rubbing the tip around my entrance.

The vision of it being Owen and what he would feel like inside of me is all consuming. Alexi behind him knotting his tight hole while I lock his perfect cock.

The imagery is nearly too much.

I know thinking about these things I'm not going to last long at all. The toy is halfway inside of me when the door slams open. My body stills as Alexi's and Owen's eyes immediately shift to where I'm frozen. My dildo is halfway in my pussy, and I should feel some mortification, but I just slip it in even deeper.

"You better take off that fucking jersey while you play with *my* pussy," Alexi says on a growl.

"Or what?" I taunt. I don't even bring up the fact that he called it his pussy.

Owen stands behind him. They're both dressed in their suits, and it just makes me even hotter. I don't take the jersey off and just continue fucking myself.

"You remember what I said on the ice, Omega?" Alexi says to Owen, who just blinks and stares at me as he loosens his tie. I think this is the most need I've seen in his eyes. He's been able to resist me for the most part, but right now, he looks like he wants to crawl on the floor and eat me out until I'm screaming his name and begging for his cock.

Alexi shakes his head, and his frustration is briefly paused due to Owen's cuteness as he looks back at me.

"Said I was going to redden your ass for wearing another man's jersey."

"You didn't give me one of yours," I say, even though the idea of a spanking sounds pretty awesome. I've had my ass grabbed during sex and maybe a light smack in doggy style, but a spanking to build up to a sexual release, I think I can handle that.

"We're going to play with fire tonight," Alexi says, ripping off his jacket, loosening his tie, and rolling up his sleeves. He turns to Owen and removes his jacket as well. "Take that fucking jersey off now," he tells me.

"Come take it off."

"I'm going to kill Beckford," he says as he takes a few big strides toward me. He's rough as he grabs it by the collar and brings his mouth to mine. His kiss is all consuming, and I'm nearly breathless as he heaves the jersey over my head. His irritation is even worse when he sees the shirt underneath is Mikael's number. "On your knees and hold on to the back of the couch."

I blink at him, and he grabs the shirt and pulls it over my head, leaving my bra on. He makes me hold this position in anticipation.

He swats my ass hard before walking away.

"I have an idea. Do you want to make your Alpha feel good and let her know she's only allowed to have our names on her back?"

I wish I could see Owen's face because he doesn't respond. But I see Alexi in the kitchen as he opens the junk drawer and takes out a pair of latex gloves. His eyes meet mine, and he winks as he walks back. He shouldn't look so fucking good in a suit, and he also shouldn't be able to turn me into a complete puddle because of the way he speaks to me.

Suddenly, Alexi is behind me, pushing his pants-covered cock against my ass and gripping my hips. "We might not be pack yet," he says while rubbing his hardness against me. "But you're going to learn tonight who you belong to, *malyshka*."

"That seems like a lot of talk and no action."

The audible crack of Alexi's hand against my ass shatters my brain. It hurts in the most delicious way, and I can feel myself getting wetter.

"How about I come on your back to teach you a lesson. Hmm? Put my cum where you thought it was okay to wear another man's name."

He slaps my ass in a string of three, and I'm gripping onto the couch for dear life. It should be degrading, right? Why does it feel like a completely possessive warm hug around my heart? Man, I'm fucked up.

"I want it," I say. He smacks my ass.

"I'm going to have your pussy dripping, and then our Omega is going to fuck you with your little toy while I stroke my cock and watch." The scene is broken completely as I turn around and look at him. "He's wearing gloves," he says softly.

Owen and I haven't even kissed, and he's about to fuck me with my toy. I look over at the Omega, who at some point took off everything and is completely naked, except for a black pair of latex gloves. His large toned muscular body is stunning, and I lick my lips as I stare at his hard cock.

"He's fucking beautiful, isn't he?" Alexi asks but doesn't let me answer as he smacks my ass in another set of threes. Alexi's warm hand slides from my tender ass cheek and drags through my wetness. "Fuck, Piper. I barely had to touch you, and you're dripping. You want it, don't you? You want to be claimed by your Alpha and Omega? Don't you, *malyshka?*"

"Fuck, please," I say, my face pressing down into the back of the couch.

"Be a good boy and make your Alpha come," Alexi says and I shiver. A latex covered hand grips my hip. A glove covered finger dips into my cunt, and I hear the most suffering masculine groan behind me. His other hand grips my hip with such force that I know he's going to leave a trail of bruises in his wake, and I welcome it. I want to rip the gloves off and have him devour me whole.

I have to remind myself that we're being cautious. That I can't just act on all my primal aspects. *I need to be good.*

"We can stop," I hear Alexi say softly to Owen.

"No," Owen replies, his fingers dipping inside of me, and I shudder before he replaces them with the sex toy.

"That's it. Look at how responsive she is to you," Alexi says to Owen.

"God, Piper. I…"

"It feels so good, Owen. You're so good," I tell him, turning around and glancing at him. His eyes meet mine, and I watch as he takes a deep inhale and shakes his head. His pace with the dildo increases, and a large hand presses down between my shoulder blades, pushing my face against the back of the couch.

The stretch of the toy and having both of them watching and touching me is enough to send me over the edge. But hearing them touch themselves, getting off on just watching me is what makes me come. My body shakes, and my pussy locks around the toy. Both of the men behind me let their pleasure be known by the noises they're making.

I hold the toy inside of me and turn slightly. I can only see Owen's lower half where Alexi is jerking him off, and Owen is returning the favor for him.

"You better hold that toy in your cunt until I give you what I promised, *malyshka.*"

He's really going to do it, and I find myself excited for it. I want to be claimed and marked by both of them. I do my best to get small glimpses of them touching each other and do as I'm told. Until there's a warm splatter on my lower back as I hear Owen reach his orgasm.

It takes Alexi taking over for Owen before I feel even more warmth against my skin. Alexi's hands knead my ass, and he groans before sliding his fingers in the mess and leaning over my back and gripping my chin with the other hand.

"Taste who you fucking belong to," he says in a soft tone,

slipping his large fingers in between my lips as I taste their cum mixed together.

*It shatters me.* The toy falls out of my pussy and lands on the floor as I spin around and look at Owen. I hadn't tasted him before, but now that I know how sweet he tastes, I need more. Alexi wraps an arm around my waist and tugs me against his chest.

Owen's pupils are blown, and he's still deliciously naked, just the gloves… covered in my release. I want him to dip them in his own mouth and feel as needy as me.

"Gloves off," Alexi directs. Owen looks between the both of us like his resolve is about the snap too. He doesn't listen, and Alexi barks the order again. "Gloves off."

Owen grabs the elastic around his wrist, flipping the gloves inside out and tossing them on the floor. "I-I—" Owen stutters and Alexi takes a deep inhale.

"Owen, go take a cold shower. I'll take this one upstairs."

"But…" Owen questions. He takes a step forward, and Alexi groans.

"I'm sorry, I took this too far. You two need to be separated. Owen, go get cleaned up, please." Alexi's voice is soft and pleading, and as scolded as Owen seems, he knows he's right. I know he's right. Because if Alexi wasn't holding onto me as firmly as he currently is, I would be on top of Owen right now.

"I'm sorry, Piper," Owen says softly before walking away and I feel… rejected… again.

"Come on," Alexi says, ushering me upstairs to his bedroom. His bathroom is the best in the house. But all I want to do is shove myself inside the smaller tub shower combo downstairs with Owen.

Alexi turns on the spray, and I wrap my arms around myself.

"I'm sorry, I took it too far."

I shake my head. "I instigated it."

He runs his fingers through his hair and fully undresses before wrapping his arms around me. There's a part of me that wants to run from the intimacy, but I'm also too worn down, so I accept his strong arms around me.

"No, it's my fault. I don't know what I was thinking—having you taste him. I just…"

"You just what?"

He shakes his head and opens the shower door for us to enter. He keeps his arms around me. "I think I just feel a little unsettled that we're all unbonded."

Hearing Alexi voice his insecurities makes me feel better. That's probably wrong, but it's nice to know I'm not the only one going through something when it comes to forming this pack. I rest my head against his chest. His breathing is even, and he strokes down my wet hair. I drag my nails down his back, lightly soothing the skin.

"Alexi, what are we going to do?"

"No more taking risks, I'll be better," he says softly.

I look up at him. There's definitely guilt and uneasiness in his eyes. "We'll get through it," I assure him, bringing his lips to mine. "Owen should sleep up here tonight," I tell him. I feel guilty that I'm the one who lost my shit and had to be separated. I can't imagine how needy Owen is feeling; he should have Alexi take care of him.

Alexi kisses me again. "One day we'll all share a big ass bed."

I smile up at him, over how sure he's been about the three of us this whole time. I wish I had a fraction of his confidence about us being a pack. It hits me then that I have to tell Alexi about tonight.

"Sloane knows about Owen."

Alexi groans and scrubs his face. "I had a thought that she

might. Seems like these Omegas have a fucking sixth sense." I laugh, and he shakes his head.

"She said she will keep his secret."

"We can only hope so," Alexi says. I lean into his body and just let the warm water hit me and his touch comfort me. It feels nicer than I'd like to admit having someone reassure me, and I'm not quite sure how to feel about that.

## CHAPTER 26

Looking at Piper is hard, being around Piper is hard, getting a whiff of her scent makes me so fucking hard I have to jerk off multiple times to calm myself down. It's only getting harder, and I can't help but to think it's only going to get worse before it gets better.

We just finished our last season game. I'm officially going to the NHL playoffs. We have about four days before our first game, and now is not the time to give in.

*But fuck, I want to give in.*

We haven't touched since that day where things went a little too far. Where it looked like if Alexi didn't hold Piper back, she would have taken me to the ground and fucked me senseless. I wanted it, I wanted to lick her cum off my gloved finger and be just as feral as her. But I didn't, and I regret it.

The medicine I'm on is waning, so I have to shower more often. I have to be even more careful during practice. One of the biggest benefits of being a goalie is just how much gear I wear that helps hide my scent. If we're going to the Cup, it could nearly be almost two more months of this, and the thought is daunting.

I find myself thinking often if winning the Stanley Cup is worth this much struggle. But then I think about what is two months versus a lifetime as a pack, and I settle myself down. I can do this, we can do this.

At least I fucking hope so.

My body is needy, and the way that Alexi keeps rubbing my thigh the whole drive back to the house has me about ready to let the man take control and do whatever he wants to me. He deserves it, really. Without Alexi, I wouldn't be sane, and I wouldn't still be doing hockey. He does it all with a smile on his face and a happy eagerness. This Alpha deserves the world.

"Don't worry, I'll take care of you when we get home," he promises with a smirk.

"Thank God."

He rubs my thigh again and squeezes it. "You did good today, are you feeling ready?"

"I'm ready."

"I'm going to get you that Cup."

"What about after?" I say curiously. I know Alexi has had a long career, and while his home is nice, he definitely didn't spend over abundantly on it.

He shrugs his shoulders and tilts his head. "I'm not sure, honestly. It's been hockey for so long. I think I'd like to still do something in the sport."

"I want to advocate for Omegas in athletics," I say, and Alexi smiles.

"Then that's what we'll do." He says it like it's no big deal. It's refreshing having an Alpha believe in me whole-heartedly. "Let's eat something and then go upstairs."

"Sounds good," I say, the stress of the game starting to hit me, and I'm feeling slightly tired. Not tired enough for Alexi not to go down on me though.

When we enter the house, Piper is in the kitchen, just staring at her laptop.

"What are you working on?" I ask her, and she shakes her head.

"Nothing, I was just about to close out," she says.

Alexi leans over her shoulder and reads what she's working on. "You're going to submit that, right?" he asks, and she goes to shut her laptop, and he stops her. "Piper, you need to send that in."

"I don't need to do anything," she says, taking a step back and glaring at Alexi.

Alexi then reaches over her and hits a button, which has Piper diving to her computer.

"What did you do?" she gasps and starts clicking around.

"You weren't going to submit your application, so I did it for you," Alexi says plainly.

Piper shuts the top of her laptop down hard. I stand in the corner, silently watching everything happen. Part of me wants to get in the middle and stop them from arguing, but another part of me feels like it's not my place.

"You had no fucking right to do that."

"I'm just trying to help. Everyone knows this is the perfect transition for you. You've been thinking about it for weeks. I couldn't just let you sit there and stare at the screen for hours doubting yourself. Now, you don't have to. It's submitted, and they're going to invite you into their program," Alexi says, like it's all simple and easy. But Piper's face is red, and she looks absolutely livid.

"This is my fucking future, I don't need a man or an Alpha coming in and telling me what I need to do. I don't fucking need you." She's breathing heavily and looks irritated with her choice of words.

Alexi crosses his arms over his chest. "You think I'm not

aware that you don't need me? That your life would go on without me? You've made it more than fucking clear with your actions."

"Don't turn this around on me. That wasn't your place to fucking submit that," she says back, avoiding what Alexi said.

"When was it due?" he asks sharply.

"It doesn't matter. It's my fucking life!"

"Your life that you don't let anyone into. Fuck, Piper. What else do I have to do to be your partner? Or will I just always feel like the Alpha you allow to share your space?"

She blinks at him and physically jolts like he smacked her. "I don't treat you that way."

"You're so in your own fucking head all the time you can't even see how other people see you. You're the smartest person I know, but right now, you're being so goddamn stupid. You should have filled out that form weeks ago. You should have quit surgery to focus on studying. You've been out from under your father's thumb for months. I've given you space, supported you, gave you a place to live, but I still don't feel like you want me."

"I do want you," she says softly, shaking her head.

"You have a funny way of showing it," Alexi says, storming past the both of us. He gives me a soft look before opening the front door. He sighs deeply, not looking back and just says, "I'll be back later."

The door slams shut, and I have to shake my head to take in everything that just happened. I look over to Piper who has her arms wrapped around herself. I've never seen her emotional before. But I watch as she breaks, tears streaming down her face as she slides down on the floor.

"Piper," I say softly as I get down and sit in front of her, opening my arms. I'm surprised when she takes the affection, wrapping her arms around me and placing her face on my chest.

"I-I—" she says between tears, and I pet down her hair and try to think of what to say.

"It's going to be okay."

"I didn't realize I was hurting him," she says softly.

"Alexi is strong, and he's upset right now, but he'll be back."

"I should have known that this would happen, that I would ruin everything."

"Hey, you didn't ruin anything," I say.

"Why can't I do anything right? I don't deserve you or Alexi. I don't deserve any of this."

I wish I could say Alexi was wrong, but it's clear that Piper spends a lot of time in her own head, and she's clearly in there pretty deep now.

I grab her face and force her watery eyes to look at me. "You deserve everything, and I'm so thankful you're my scent match." She shakes her head in my palms and is about to tug her face out of my hands.

*Fuck it all.*

I lean forward, bringing her lips to mine, and it's like the world tilts on its axis. She doesn't pull away, her fingers lacing in my hair as she kisses me back. All of these weeks of built up tension and need are behind the kiss. My heart is thudding in my rib cage, and all I feel is need.

Complete and utter desire fills every inch of my body.

I fist her hair roughly, and she whimpers, doing the same to me.

Piper pulls back, the green of her eyes almost completely taken over by her pupils. "Owen, your scent." I'm leaning forward to kiss her again, and her hands push against my chest. "Owen, baby, I think you're going into heat," she says softly.

"No, I can't," I say, leaning forward to kiss her again.

"I'm so sorry, Owen."

I lick my lips and try to gather my thoughts—I can't. My only thoughts are about my Alpha and how I want her to bite me, make me hers. I can't help the noise that escapes me when I realize Alexi isn't here. I need his bite just as badly.

"It's okay, I'm going to take care of you," she says. I blink at her, and some of the fog in my head clears.

It's over for me. I'm going into heat. Alexi and I will probably miss our first playoff game. I'm going to lose everything I worked for. I stand up and tug on my hair from the roots, the pain centering me before I walk back to my room.

"Owen," I hear Piper call, but I ignore her, shutting my door and locking it.

I've never been a destructive person, but right now, it feels like my only outlet.

I begin destroying my room, throwing everything off my dresser, removing the bedding from the mattress and flipping it. My fist connects with the wall, and I hear Piper pleading through the door. I tune her out.

I never wanted my heat before. I came to terms with it, knowing I'd be with Alexi and Piper, but it wasn't supposed to happen. I wasn't supposed to feel this hopeless and confused.

"Goddammit!" I yell, taking a picture of me from high school and throwing it against the wall. The glass shatters, and I hear Piper banging harder against the wall.

"Owen, let me in, please."

I sit on the floor of my destroyed room, but it feels small and suffocating. Maybe that's what I deserve. I take a deep breath, and that's when the pain starts to radiate through me.

It's worse than any hit I've ever taken on the ice. My abdomen clenches, and my stomach revolts.

*Hopeless, useless Omega.*

Everything I hated about my designation is all I can think of. Why I've suppressed it for so long, why I never wanted to feel like this. There's nothing I can do for myself. I'm completely hopeless without my Alphas.

*How fucking pathetic.*

Why would they want me? They were already fighting. There's no way for this pack to work. Everything feels hopeless: my career, this pack, my fucking traitor of a body.

*I just want it to stop.*

There's muffled noises behind the door when suddenly the door is off its hinges. A red faced Piper with tear stains down her cheeks and a furious Alexi who just used his shoulder to knock the door down. He looks around the room in disgust, and I crawl away.

"Fuck. Owen, *sólnyshka*, it's going to be okay."

I shake my head and wrap my arms around myself. Alexi approaches me like I'm a caged animal. "It's probably for the best that you destroyed this room. I have a better one for you anyway." He picks me up and tosses me over his shoulder and starts climbing the stairs.

A very quiet Piper follows us.

The pain has me grabbing on tightly to Alexi, and he soothes a hand down my back.

"We've got you. It's going to be okay. I'm going to take care of everything."

## CHAPTER 27

Should I have sent her application for her residency for the Omega Wellness Clinic? Maybe not. But I was just trying to help push her in the right direction. I've bit my tongue, watched her do this research and the way she lights up when she talks about Omega healthcare.

I knew it was due tonight by midnight. I also knew she would probably get in her own head about it and just not send it.

So I helped give her the push she needed. I didn't expect the blowup after or the words that came out of either of our mouths.

I was harsh, I know I was harsh, but I wasn't wrong. Sometimes I feel like I'm disposable to Piper, and I just want some indication that this is more than sex for her.

God, when did I become such a sensitive little bitch?

I'm halfway toward the bar when I turn the car around. This isn't who I want to be, the guy who leaves in the middle of an argument. That's not how shit gets resolved. I groan, knowing I'm going to have to make things right when I get home. Drinking whiskey or sulking at a bar isn't going to make this shit right.

I open the front door, fully expecting the cold shoulder or more anger from Piper. But all I hear is banging and Piper's pleas.

"Owen, please open the door. Let me take care of you." She's using her shoulder to try and bust down the door. In a few quick strides, I'm in front of her. Her face is red from crying, and as much as I want to dive into that, our Omega tearing his room to pieces is the priority.

"What the fuck happened?" I ask her. She blanches and shakes her head.

"I was upset, and he comforted me. We kissed, and his heat started."

"Fuck."

"He won't open the door," she says softly, and there's another loud bang.

"Back up," I growl, hoping that he listens before I take a step back and use my shoulder to fling the door down. It nearly falls off the hinges, and the chaos in front of me breaks my heart. He's completely destroyed his room and sits in the middle of the floor grimacing in pain.

"Fuck. Owen, *sólnyshka*, it's going to be okay," I plead with him, and he seems disoriented and just confused. I'm cautious with how I approach him. His scent is thick and calling to me like a beacon. All I want to do is make this alright. If I hadn't gotten angry with Piper, sent in the form, maybe none of this would happen. "It's probably for the best that you destroyed this room. I have a better one for you anyway," I tell him in a soft voice.

His gaze tracks me, and he makes a needy sound. I grab him gently and fling him over my shoulder. Piper follows without a word. I rub his back soothingly. "We've got you. It's going to be okay. I'm going to take care of everything."

I haven't shown either of them the nest yet. I thought it would make me look a little too presumptuous or that maybe Owen wouldn't like it. He's become softer around us, but he still has some hesitations about his designation.

The room is masculine while still being the perfect place for an Omega. Everything is set in a deep, romantic navy. I installed the best blackout shades I could find and added soft lamp lighting throughout.

"Playoffs," he mumbles as I place him down gently on the mattress that rests on the floor.

"I'm going to handle it. We have four days until the first game. Even if your heat lasts longer, we will still be okay. It's going to be okay, I promise you," I tell him.

Piper is still quiet and in the corner, her arms wrapped around herself. "Maybe I should go?" she says softly.

"What do you want, Owen?" I ask him.

"It hurts," he says. I can visually see that he's in pain, and what's even harder is how much he didn't want to admit how much pain he was in.

Piper's moves from her spot in the corner. "We're going to make it better. You're such a good Omega," she tells him. He whimpers as he reaches for his shorts and starts tugging them down. I help divest him of all of his clothes, and he immediately starts stroking his cock, the tip leaking, and I watch a small trail of slick soak the bed from his ass.

"Please. Please make it stop," he says.

I act immediately, wrapping my lips around his cock and tasting his sweet pre-cum on my tongue. His fingers tangle in my hair as he takes it. He isn't a gentle little thing as he fucks my throat, using my body in a way that feels all consuming.

Piper leans forward and kisses our Omega, her hands touching every inch of him as she whispers the sweetest praises to him. "Look at your cock in his mouth. Your Alphas love making you feel good. You're so good. We're going to make it go away."

He fists her hair and drags her face next to mine.

Not a demure Omega by any means.

The tension is thick between Piper and myself, but we put it all aside as we worship his dick. I slide up his shaft, my lips popping from the tip of his cock, and Piper takes over while I lick his balls and finger his tight asshole.

"So tight, *sólnyshka*. My knot is going to stretch you so good."

He thrusts into Piper's mouth, and she hums and gags around him, taking every inch. Suddenly, he's bucking into her frantically, hitting the back of her throat with each thrust as he holds her head down. He moans loudly, and I watch as Piper attempts to swallow everything, but cum drips from her lips and down his length.

His cock is still hard and dripping, and he continues moving his hips with my fingers inside of him.

"Piper, get on your back," I instruct her. She undresses herself and does as I say.

"Owen, go sink your cock in your Alpha's pretty pussy." He moans and acts immediately. His toned muscular body climbs on top of her. There is no preamble, no foreplay, no light kisses as he crawls up her body. He just climbs on top of her and thrusts in one go.

Piper grips the blanket and throws her head back in a light scream before wrapping her arms around his shoulders, her blunt nails making dents as Owen fucks her. He's frantic with no finesse; he just wants the relief.

Piper takes everything that he's giving and encourages him.

"You feel so fucking good, don't stop."

He groans, falling on top of Piper, his face next to her throat, taking in her thick Alpha scent. I've never been keen on another Alpha's scent. And while Owen's citrus and berry scent makes me feral, Piper's orange and cinnamon makes me feel nearly the same.

I'm spreading Piper's legs, and she whimpers slightly before making the adjustment. My hand is in between Owen's shoulder blades rubbing soothing circles. I look past him to Piper.

"Is it too much weight?" I ask, and she shakes her head no.

"Are you going to be a good boy and take a knot and a lock at the same time?" I ask him, my hand trailing down his back and squeezing his ass before slipping two fingers inside of him.

"Please, Alpha, I need it," he says against Piper's neck.

With my knees pressed against the bed, I use my slick covered fingers to lube up my cock before pushing into his tight and ready asshole. I groan, loving the feeling of him wrapped around me and the way he's keening and moaning into the mattress.

"Fuck," I hiss as I thrust into him, Pipers legs widening even further to accommodate both of us. "Are you going to take my knot, *sólnyshka?*"

He makes a noise against Piper's throat before he places ravenous kisses against the column of her neck. He licks and sucks her tender flesh. Piper's face is flush, and her breathing is labored as our eyes meet, our Omega between us and what feels like the weight of a million unsaid words as I pump into Owen.

I have to break the tension and press my face into his back as I fuck him. His slick drips down my balls and thighs.

"Shit, I've got to lock," Piper says before she moans. It's

nearly a domino effect. Her pussy clenches around Owen's length, and he isn't able to thrust anymore. So I fuck into him, jostling them as they're locked together.

Both of them are nearly incoherent as I use Owen for my release. I'm close, and I push my knot into his tight hole. He moans loudly, his hips trying to move, to fuck Piper more, but he can't. I make up for it by pushing completely into him. My knot grows in size as I pump into him, until I reach my peak, my knot fully inflated inside of him and cum filling up my Omega. His body is shaking, and he's making the sweetest noises against Piper's throat.

The three of us are locked together for God knows how long. Both Piper and I touch and soothe his body. His skin is hot to the touch, but he isn't writhing in pain anymore, and that's what's important.

Piper unlocks him first, but Owen is unable to move right away. So we all stay in place, Piper bearing the weight of Owen as I use my strength to stay off of her.

"You did so good. So beautiful, so perfect," she tells him as she plays with his hair. He groans and wraps his arms around her and presses his face in the bed. It's not long before a light snore leaves his lips, and Piper can barely breathe. Luckily my knot releases me at that moment.

The bed is a mess, we're all a mess. But all I can do is help wiggle Piper out from underneath Owen. Even as he's asleep, he doesn't want her far. But I'm at least able to shift him so that only an arm and a leg is on top of her.

"You good?" I ask her, and she nods. I'm about to walk into the bathroom when she grabs my hand and tugs.

"Can we talk?"

"Now?" I ask, and she tugs my hand harder.

I lie down on the bed next to her, and she faces me the best that she can. "When you left, I wasn't upset about the application. You were right, I was talking myself out of it. I was upset that I had hurt you. That I ever made you feel like I didn't care about you."

"I was frustrated. I shouldn't have submitted the form."

She shakes her head and squeezes my hand. "I'm glad that you did. That you believe in me when I can't. I… I don't think I truly realized how hard on myself I am until you came into the picture."

"Piper," I groan her name, and she shakes her head.

"All that time I ran away from this was because I knew if I gave in that my future was sealed. Because I knew you were it for me, and it scared the fucking shit out of me. You were right, I spend too much time in my head. I'm sorry for making you feel like I don't want you. I do want you, Alexi. I've wanted you for a long time, and I'm still so scared by how much I want you."

"But you never seek me out," I say softly and insecurely.

"Usually because I talk myself out of it, and I promise I'll work on it. On initiating and making sure you feel cared for. If anyone in this pack deserves to be cared for, it's you. Can you forgive me?" she asks, her eyes watery.

"I shouldn't have sent in your application, and I shouldn't have walked away," I say.

"I don't blame you. I want to be the partner you deserve. Let me try?" she says, and I shake my head, leaning down and pushing her hair out of her face before kissing her softly.

"I was never going anywhere, and you're exactly who I want you to be."

Her face pinkens, and Owen grabs her harder, tugging her against his body.

"I've got to do some recon and figure out what to tell the team," I tell her, a pit forming in my stomach.

"That can wait till tomorrow," she says, tugging my body down so I'm behind her and Owen is in front of her.

Everything is a mess, and all I can smell is delicious smelling fruit. But as I put one arm under her head and toss another over both of their bodies, I realize that everything I've ever wanted is in this bed right now.

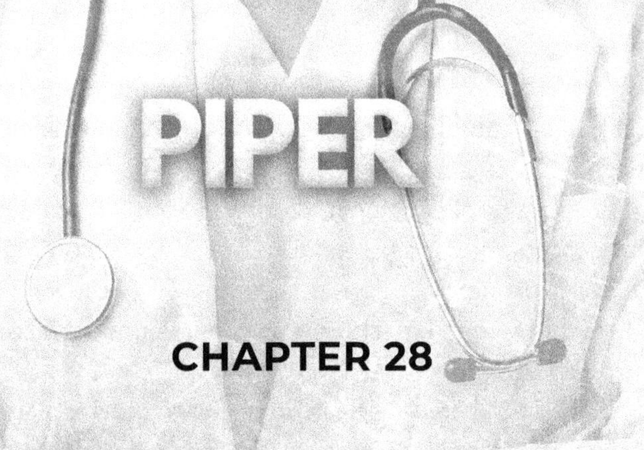


## CHAPTER 28

I'm able to sneak away for a few moments to make the dreaded phone call. I'm supposed to work the next six days straight, and that's definitely not happening.

The phone rings when the surgical chief answers the phone.

"Dr. Jenkins," he says curtly.

"Dr. Jenkins, this is Dr. Blake. Unfortunately, I'm going to need to call out for the next couple of days."

"For what reason?"

"My Omega is in heat."

"That's not a valid enough reason to miss multiple days in a row. Surely you have other Alphas who can assist during the heat while you come in."

"No, I don't. And even if I did, I wouldn't be able to leave him home in this condition."

"This is why we tell residents not to form packs with Omegas during residency. Your dedication needs to be to the program, not an adult-sized leech."

"What did you just say?" I ask in a shocked tone.

"Omegas' value in society is so low. You need to decide

what is more important to you, your future in medicine, or an Omega."

I'm silent for a moment, mostly because I can't believe what he said and I was wondering if I was just so tired that I heard him wrong.

"You're saying I have to choose? That you won't accept my time off?"

"Correct, I'd hate to see a doctor with so much potential go. But we've been making cuts as is. What is it going to be?"

"It's my Omega every single time. Thank you for the opportunity and the chance to learn at your hospital, but please send me my termination paperwork," I say and hang up the phone before he can reply.

This crippling weight that's been held over my head my entire life falls apart. It shrivels and crinkles and dissipates, and I feel like I can finally breathe. There's no more big choice to make. I've quit surgery. I did what I have been wanting to do for the past year.

I'm not even concerned about what people think about me, not even my father. I have two men in the next room who care about me, not what my profession or credentials are. They both like me despite my designation and even after all of this time of me being difficult.

That's more valuable than any job or residency program in the world.

I walk back into the nest. Owen looks adorable snuggled up to Alexi, who gives me a small smile.

"Everything okay?" he asks quietly to not wake Owen.

"I quit," I say softly.

Alexi jostles Owen in the process with his shock. "You what?"

"He told me I had to pick, be here for Owen's heat or come into work. I pick my pack every time."

Alexi grins at me and tugs me down to the bed before placing frantic kisses all over my face.

"Your pack, huh?"

"Yeah, my pack." I lean forward and kiss him, and he groans into my mouth, the noise waking Owen.

Owen is like a man unhinged during his heat, his sole focus to fuck and make the pain go away. I've read a lot about Omegas during their heat, but Owen seems very singularly focused, and he has yet to have a single moment of lucidity.

He's been completely naked the whole time, not wanting anything touching him. He barely even covers himself with a sheet or a blanket when he sleeps. Alexi just has on a pair of boxers, and I'm wearing one of his shirts and a pair of panties.

Owen kneels behind me, pulling my shirt over my head and tugging at my panties aggressively.

"Okay, okay," I tell him, pulling at the waist band and getting one leg out before the other. He pushes me down on top of Alexi. I have to catch myself on the bed, and Alexi laughs while he grabs my ass and spreads me out for our Omega.

Owen spits on my asshole and rubs his thumb around it before pushing his cock inside of my pussy.

"Fuck," I groan, my face pressed against Alexi's chest.

Owen leans forward, his body weight on mine again. I swear he wants to crush me to death, but when he nuzzles my neck, it's clear he just wants as much skin touching as possible. Alexi removes one hand from my ass to rub Owens neck as he fucks me.

I'm sure if Alexi hadn't just knotted Owen, he would be in on the action. Even still, his length is hardening underneath my pelvis as Owen fucks me.

Owen licks the side of my neck and barely holds his own weight on his elbows.

"I need you," he moans in my ear.

"You have me," I tell him between his thrusts.

"Please, Alpha. I'll be good," he says, and it's the most he's spoken since he started his heat. I'm sure the need to bond is riding him as hard as he's riding me right now. I've pushed it down. There's no way in hell I'm going to bond him when we haven't spoken about it. His heat was sudden, and I can only imagine the regret if we went that far. "It hurts, and I need you."

My heart aches, and I'm so close to pushing him off of me and putting him on his back so I can place my bite mark on his chest.

Alexi intervenes for the both of us. "Are you going to fill your Alpha up, Omega? Hmm? She needs it so bad."

Owen groans into the side of my neck, his forearm wrapping around my collarbone as he pulls me up. Alexi is beneath us and just watches in awe as Owen fucks into me. My tits bounce with each thrust, and Owen scents and kisses me as he takes what he wants.

Alexi reaches forward and places his thumb against my clit, rubbing in delicious circles, pushing me closer to orgasm with each rub.

"Do you want her to lock your cock, Omega?"

Owen thrusts into me hard, and Alexi continues playing with my clit, and it sends me over the edge as I lock his cock and I feel his cum flood into me. He not so gracefully takes me down onto the bed with him as we stay locked together, and his arm flops on top of me to land onto Alexi's chest.

Alexi lets out a *oof* sound and then laughs. "I don't think he realizes his size," he says softly, and I make a noise of agreement.

"Are you hungry?" Alexi asks, and suddenly my stomach grumbles. He leans forward and kisses my forehead before leaning over and kissing Owen's. "I've got to call coach and act like we're all still sick again, anyway," he grumbles while getting up and adjusting himself. He gives Owen and I one last lingering look before leaving the bedroom.

Suddenly, both of Owen's arms are wrapped around me, and my lock loosens, but he doesn't stop fucking back into me. Despite the amount of cum dripping out of me, or the fact that he's had four orgasms in the last hour.

"Please, Alpha," he mumbles in my ear. His teeth drag at the back of my throat, making me shiver. "Please."

I turn around in his hold and look into his blue eyes. His pupils are so large I can barely see a ring of blue.

"Soon," I tell him, stroking his face. He lies flat on his back and directs me to get on top of him, which I do. No matter how tender my pussy is, or how my thighs burn like a motherfucker. I climb on top of him and grab his messy cock and put it in me. "You're so good. Soon. I promise. You're mine."

He lifts his head, exposing his neck, the strong tendons flexing and completely tempting me. He whimpers as I slide down his length, his hands grabbing my hips for dear life.

"Make it better. It hurts," he says, and I break, fucking him as hard as I can, just wanting to make him feel good and take his pain away.

"You feel so good," I tell him. His hands leave my hips to wrap around my hair and bring my face to his throat. It's the clearest invitation I've ever been given, but I can't give in, no matter how much I want to. I can only imagine how good it would feel to bond, to no longer have this itching feeling of dissatisfaction when it comes to Owen walking around unclaimed. That there would be a visual reminder everywhere he went that he is mine.

Because he is mine.

He's mine in every way. He calmed me with his presence

before I even knew we were fated. And when I was aware of him being my scent match, everything clicked. Owen being mine is what gave me the strength to quit surgery, finally. Owen, Alexi, and I are a pack, and in the heat of the moment, with his delicious body pressed against mine, I can't think of any reason not to mark him.

He would feel so good, I would feel so good.

I'd always know he was okay, even while at away games. We would always be connected. I'd never have to worry about him when we weren't in the same place. He would be mine forever.

I need it. I need him.

"Bite me, I need it," he says. His pheromones choke me. His sweet strawberry scent fills up the room, traveling down my throat and into my lungs in an act that seems to completely shut my brain off. He fucks me from below, his hold on my hair tight as he uses me to get off. "Please. Please. Please." He's begging and pushing my lips toward his throat. "I need you."

"I need you too. Fuck, do I need you."

I continue riding him, my muscles contracting with each movement, and it's like everything goes hazy. Like all of my baser instincts are taking over. Every desire I've held back for weeks so that Owen could have his dream. But this is my dream, I realize. Having a pack, being mated to an Omega, it's more important than anything I could have ever imagined.

He starts begging again, and it breaks me. "Please make it stop."

So I do.

Without another thought or consideration, I lean forward as I fuck him and sink my teeth into his chest, avoiding his throat. It seems like the need for discretion of where his mark is placed is the only thing I'm able to comprehend.

The main focus right now is making him mine. I fuck him

as I leave my bite on him, my pussy contracting and tightening around his length, ensuring he fills me up with his sweet release.

We're both shaking and breathing heavily when I lift myself up on shaky arms and look at my mark on him. It's not even seeing it that makes it feel real. It's the contentment inside of my chest, the way I feel nearly whole being bonded to Owen.

I can feel his happiness, hunger, and tiredness through the bond. But pure bliss is the main thing I feel. He grins up at me and smiles. "My Alpha," he sighs dreamily.

I'm ready to kiss him when Alexi's voice booms from the door.

"What the fuck did you do?"

# OWEN

## CHAPTER 29

The tenor of my big Alpha's voice sends a shiver down my spine. I glance down at my chest and grin to myself when I see my beautiful Alpha's bite mark. *It's perfect.*

But I feel her guilt through the bond. We can't have that.

I grip her hips and slide her up my chest. Her pussy glides along my torso, marking me with her aroused scent. It makes me groan, and I grab her ass and bring her wet cunt to my lips.

"Owen," she says my name in both shock and intrigue.

"Piper, you need to stop. What did you do? You bonded with him?"

"It just happened. I didn't mean to," she says. I would like to render her speechless though. Her taste fills my mouth, and I groan. My tongue flicking and licking on her sensitive clit has her gripping the headboard and involuntarily shifting her hips on my face.

"We haven't even spoken about bonding. What if he's upset once he's out of his heat haze?"

I groan against her pussy and firmly squeeze and spread

her cheeks, trying to show him that this is what I wanted. I've never felt so content in my life.

"Fuck," she moans above me.

"Piper!" my male Alpha tries to get her attention.

"I can't talk to you right now. Not with his mouth on me like this. Are you going to tell him to stop?"

A noise rips through my throat, making it abundantly clear that she will not be taken away from me. She's marked me. I belong to her, and she belongs to me. Not even our pack Alpha can do anything about that. If he tries, I'm not sure what I'll do, but I'm sure I'll be able to convince him otherwise.

"Good Omega," my pretty, bonded Alpha says to me. It makes me work harder, needing to please her and show her how happy I am. That I'm rewarding her for giving me what I want. My touch on her hips is nearly brutal, and a visceral and needy part of me can't wait to see the marks on her skin.

Mark her, like she marked me.

I swat at her ass, and she leans forward as I suck on her clit. Her rich and heady Alpha scent fills my mouth and makes me need her even more.

There's shuffling in my nest, but I don't concern myself with it. My sole focus is pleasing my Alpha.

"Oh God, Owen, I'm going to come," she says in a soft breathy voice. My cock is weeping and brutally hard again. I'm thrusting up in the air when my other Alpha's lips wrap around my cock.

*Yes, that's what I needed.*

He is efficient and quick with his motions as he swallows my length. Like he can't get enough of my taste. I groan into my Alpha's pussy and fuck my other Alpha's throat as she breaks on top of me. Her wetness covers my lips and chin as she shakes over the top of my face and lets out the most contented and sexy sigh.

My Alpha is perfect for me. I love her, and she's mine.

I keep my hands on her, stroking up her sides as my other Alpha works my cock in his warm mouth.

When he massages my prostate while my dick is down his throat, I lose it, filling his mouth with my cum, which he swallows perfectly.

I suppose I can forgive him for barging in here and acting like we did anything wrong. We did what we were supposed to. What we're biologically programmed to do, bond and mate.

*Fuck, I need my Alphas again.*

The pain is dulled after having finished multiple times, but I still feel on edge. My abdomen is tight, and there's a lingering pain that throbs behind my eyes.

She tries to climb off of me, but I don't let her, wrapping my arms around her waist and pulling her close to me. Her stomach is in front of my face, which I place tender kisses against.

"Piper, what if he doesn't want this? This was too soon. You couldn't have stopped it?"

I feel her back stiffen at his suggestion, and I let out an annoyed huff.

"Can you yell at me later?"

"I'm not sure I can. We never spoke about it. I have no idea on how he views bonding. What if he wants the mark removed? He's going to have to hide that in the locker room."

I've had quite enough. I move Piper quickly off of me and stand from the bed. Both Alphas watch me as I grab Piper's ankle and drag her down the bed.

"Owen?" she asks, and I shiver. I grab her by the waist and pick her up. She automatically wraps her arms around my shoulders and her legs around my hips. "Owen, it's fine. No one is taking my bond mark off of you."

I look over to my large Alpha, whom I'm very displeased with for talking about me in this way. The way he scolded my Alpha and acted like I didn't beg her for her bite.

"You don't know that," he says annoyed. I glare at him and carry Piper to the bathroom and shut the door and lock it. I sit my body on the floor and hold my arms out for Piper to sit on my lap. Her size is perfect. She's tall but lean. She fits perfectly in my arms, and I'm never letting her leave.

She sighs and does as I want, sitting on my lap as her hands find my face. Her fingertips dance along my face and jaw.

"He didn't mean that. He's just mad at me." The look I give her must show my irritation. "I shouldn't have bonded with you without your consent." Hurt and anger floods me, but she shakes her head. "But I would never take it back. Being able to feel you and have this connection to you means the world to me."

"Good," I say softly.

Her hands stroke my face. "Owen, you in there?"

"Barely," I reply, and she smiles at me.

"You can't be mad at Alexi; he's just trying to protect you. He's a good Alpha."

"I know," I say, stroking her bare skin with the backs of my fingers.

"Do you need anything? How are you feeling?"

I groan, and the back of my head lightly hits the door. Even though Alexi hasn't knocked or tried to break down this door, I can sense him standing on the other side.

"Food," I say softly, not letting go of her. I may be having a moment of lucidity, but I'm still feeling possessive and frustrated. She tries to get up, but I grab her hips and tug her back down onto my lap.

"I've got to get up and get you food, baby," she says softly to me, her hands back on my face.

"Not worth it," I say, shaking my head.

"I'll grab some snacks," I hear Alexi's deep voice through the door.

"You can't stay mad at him, he didn't mean it like that," Piper says, and I nod my head and lick my lips. She leans forward and places a chaste kiss against my lips. "You're my bonded."

I squeeze her tightly against me, and she squeaks, making me lighten up on how tightly I'm holding her.

"I don't think you realize how strong you are during your heat."

The only thing I pick out of that sentence is that my Alpha thinks I'm strong. Somehow she ends up on top of my cock, locking me again.

———

I groan as I wake up. Every single inch of my body aches. I thought that I put my body through the ringer for hockey, but it's nothing compared to how I feel after my heat. I rub my hand over my chest and feel the healed bond mark Piper gave me and sigh in contentment.

"Thank fucking God," I hear Alexi say next to me, his big brown eyes trained on me.

"Hey," I say softly, and he pushes some hair out of my face.

"Hey, how are you feeling?"

"Like I got hit by a bus, but also better than ever."

"So you're not going to run to the doctor today to have your bond removed?" I give him a shitty look and a groan, and he laughs.

"I figured as much based on how you treated me during your heat when I brought it up."

I scrub a hand over my face and look around.

"Where's Piper?"

"Taking a shower."

"How many days has it been?" He swallows and looks away. "Alexi, how many days has it been?"

"Seven."

I blink at him. His face is blank like he's trying to not give anything away.

"We've missed two playoff games?" He nods but doesn't say anything else. "How bad is it?" He shakes his head like he doesn't want to answer. "Alexi, how fucking bad is it?"

"We're down two nothing in the series," he says dryly.

"When's game three?"

"Tomorrow."

I'm off the bed in a second, slightly disoriented, and Alexi groans.

"I've got to hydrate and get ready. We're not missing another game."

"You're exhausted from your heat. You barely ate and drank. I'm not even sure how you still are producing cum with how dehydrated you must be."

"I don't care. I'll get hydrated. I'll get an IV."

He shakes his head and scratches his beard. Now that we're in the playoffs, he won't be trimming or shaving it. I simply just can't grow much of a beard, so it's not an issue. It definitely won't be an issue if we don't figure out a way to make it to tomorrow's game.

"Wait, why does the team think we're not there?"

"Stomach flu," he says, shrugging his shoulders, and I tilt my head. Not the worst excuse to give.

"We're not missing game three," I say sharply, and Alexi

groans and flops back on the bed. He looks fucking exhausted, and I feel guilty.

"Okay, I just need some rest."

"Thank you for covering for me, and taking care of me, and always looking out for my well-being. That's what a pack Alpha does. I'm sorry if I was a dick to you during my heat."

He laughs and throws an arm over his eyes. "Besides when you were mad at me, it was the best week of my life."

I roll my eyes and get back on the bed. Sleep does sound pretty fucking awesome.

"You know, I would have been happy to have your mark on me too," I say shyly.

He moves his arms and shifts on his side to look at me, his hand going to the back of my head to rub the nape of my neck.

"Oh, I'm going to bond the fuck out of you. But not until I get you that Cup."

The man acts like winning the Stanley Cup is no big deal. I mean, I suppose he already has a ring, but he's so sure of himself, of me, and our team.

"And if we don't get the Cup?" I ask him, and he glares at me.

"You have to manifest this type of shit. But even if we don't get the Cup, you're mine. You're mine whether you have a bite on you or not."

"And you're not mad at Piper? About bonding with me, or before?"

"I'm still not happy she bonded with you the ten minutes I left the room, but I get it. About before, we're good," he says smiling. "I think we're all going to be alright."

"I think so too. Does Piper have to go into work?" I ask, shifting on the bed and shutting my eyes.

"Oh, about that. She quit."

"She what?"

# ALEXI

## CHAPTER 30

Piper exits the bathroom with her hair wet and her body wrapped in a towel.

"Oh, good, you two aren't fighting."

"You quit your job?"

"Yes, it was long overdue," she says, not telling him the complete truth.

He narrows his eyes at her and clicks his tongue. "Why does it feel like you're leaving something out? The whole reason my heat started was because you were arguing with this one over your application." He points his thumb at me, and Piper's cheeks heat. Owen tilts his head as he observes her. "I can feel your guilt. What aren't you telling me?"

"Fucking bonds," she mumbles and puts her hands on her hips. Did I just spend a whole week fucking her and Owen? Yes, but does a part of me still want her towel to fall down? Also yes. "I apologized to Alexi about what happened, and I apologize to you for starting you—"

"Let me stop you there," Owen interrupts her. "As pissed as I am for missing two playoff games, this is the best I've ever felt. I've never felt this much relief and contentment in my life.

Was the timing awesome? No, but I wouldn't change any of it."

I smile, and so does Piper. "Okay, so no more apologizing for that. But Alexi was right. I wouldn't have submitted it, and I would have continued in my current program because I'm scared of being a failure."

"You're not a failure," I say, and Piper smiles at me, and she nods her head.

"I know, I'm working on it." Piper looks back at Owen. "They gave me a choice. Come into work, or stay for your heat. I chose you."

Owen's jaw goes slack, and he rubs his face. "I'm not really sure what to say."

"There isn't anything to say. I think I finally have my priorities straight now. You, Alexi, Charlotte, and her pack. That's what's most important. Plus, we found ourselves a sugar daddy, so even if no programs want me, he'll take care of us."

She smirks at me, and I laugh. "Get your ass over here."

"I'd love to, but besides the fact that my vagina is literally sore, I have somewhere to be."

"Where?"

"Charlotte needs some help with Katie and the twins."

"I can come too," Owen says, and Piper shakes her head.

"No, if you want to be ready for the game tomorrow, you need to rest."

He gives her a lingering look but nods his head. She walks over to the bed, reaching over me and giving him a soft kiss. "Thank you for trusting us," she says softly. He swallows and nods his head, clearly lost for words.

She pulls back and runs her nails through my scruffy beard. "Are you done being mad at me?"

"Maybe, but a kiss might make it better." She grins, leaning down and giving me a kiss that I take full advantage of, adding some tongue.

"You two get some rest. I'll pick up dinner on my way home." I take a fist full of her towel and rip it from her body as she walks away. She shakes her head and her ass as she leaves the room. She seems so much lighter than she was a week ago, and it makes my heart feel full.

I grab Owen by his waist and tuck in behind him.

"Besides bonding, did anything else of note happen during my heat?"

I shrug against his back. "You just manhandled the shit out of Piper the whole time. I don't think in heat you realize how much bigger you are than her."

"I didn't hurt her, did I?" he says softly.

"You just saw her. That's the most relaxed I've ever seen her. She seemed to enjoy it, and I was around to lug you off of her when you fell asleep on top of her."

"Christ," he says, rubbing a hand over his face. "We're quite a pack, huh?"

"Fuck yeah we are." I snuggle up against my Omega and get some much needed rest.

———

"Welcome back, you lazy motherfuckers," Mikael says, slapping my thigh with his stick.

"Hello to you too, asshole," I say, grabbing his head and trying to plant a kiss against his hair.

"Get off of me."

"Your grumpiness only makes me want you more, Martel."

He rolls his eyes and sits in his locker. "I think you have your hands full enough."

"Oh?"

"I heard some details about your dick I really didn't want to hear."

I grin and lean against the wall. "Was my beautiful Piper telling your Omega how pleased she was by my performance? Was Charlotte jealous, wishing she had a well-endowed Alpha?"

Mikael rolls his eyes again. "You know damn well Charlotte has no complaints."

"Maybe I'll ask Piper to confirm."

"Oh, fuck off."

"You started it, *rebenok*."

"And I'm thoroughly regretting it. Is your boy ready to play tonight? Johannson has been shitting the bed."

I grin and look across the room to where Owen is getting ready. Piper put a *Lion King* Band-Aid over his bond mark. "Oh, he's more than ready." I wiggle my eyebrows at Mikael, and he scoffs.

"Can you please retire?"

"And leave you friendless? Never."

"We need to win tonight. If we lose, it's over before it even begins."

"We're going to win. And when we do, I'm going to go home and show Piper my appreciation with my impressive dick she can't seem to stop talking about."

He breathes heavily through his nose, annoyed with me. I love getting under his skin. "Is she coming to the game?"

"Yes, now that she doesn't have hours at the hospital, she's planning on coming to all the home games."

Mikael nods, and I can see some sadness written over his face. "The babies are way too small to be anywhere like a stadium. Anders came, and his parents are home with Charlotte and the kids. She said she would make any series final games she could."

Nilsen walks over to us and sits close so that only we can hear. "Word is that Gribko has a weak left side," he says softly.

"An injury?" I ask, and he shakes his head.

"Not sure. But shoot toward the left." Mikael and I nod our heads. "Good to see you back, cap. Was about to take your spot."

"Over my dead body," I say joking, knowing this will be my last season.

He arches his eyebrow. "Don't tempt me." I laugh, and Mikael stares at him as he walks away.

"On second thought, don't retire. Our team can't be left in the hands of that psychopath."

Coach lets a low whistle through the locker room and talks us up, stressing the importance of the win. Nerves and excitement tingle through me. There's nothing quite like playoff hockey to get the blood flowing.

"Let's go out there and show them what we got!" Coach Applegate says. There's hooting and hollering as we head out the tunnel for warm-ups.

The music is loud, and the atmosphere is magnetic and wild as we stretch and practice. Owen cuts the crease, and Johannson stands next to the goal, looking absolutely pissed.

I skate over to Owen and grab his face mask.

"You good?"

"Yeah."

"You fucking got this. Look, our girl is up there," I say, pointing up at the box to where Piper sits, smiling and waving to us. This time, she's wearing my jersey and Owen's last name sewed on it as well.

"Yeah, she is," he smiles, and I knock on his helmet again.

"Let's fuck it up," I say and dramatically kiss his mask. He shoves me off with his mitt, and I laugh as I skate away and keep warming up for the game.

It's a tight game, but we win, making this series competitive. Now we just need to do it all over again in two days. I have hopes that this series will stay clean enough; we can't risk any injuries or suspensions. But now that our team is whole again, I have no doubt in my mind that we can do this.

———

We get home later than I would like. Owen is exhausted and immediately goes into Piper's room and passes out—completely dead to the world. I smile to myself as I head into the kitchen, looking for something to eat, when Piper comes downstairs.

"Hey," she says softly.

"Hey."

"You guys played great. It was exciting watching you play in the playoffs."

"I'm just glad you wore the appropriate jersey. Now you have to wear it to every game." She smiles at me in agreement and takes a few steps closer to me.

"I have a surprise for you."

"For me? Should I wake up Owen?"

"No, it's just for you."

She grabs my hand and takes me upstairs, I assume to my room, but she turns into the nest. The nest that still smells like a combination of the three of us. But then I look around and see the small table and chairs set up, as well as the candles lit around the room.

"What's this?" I ask her with a smile.

"A date."

"Did you cook?" I ask, and she smacks my chest, and I laugh.

"No, I didn't cook. I went to the Polish place I know you

like." I wrap my arms around her, my fingers stroking her back before kissing the top of her head. Holding her right now feels different than before. Like she doesn't have one foot out the door ready to run away from me. She's fully present and eager to be with me.

"Thank you, this was really thoughtful."

"You know, we haven't been on a real date."

I gasp and grab my chest. "What do you call smoothies and gym locker rooms?"

"Not dates," she says as she heads to the table. I pull her chair back before taking my seat across from her.

She has some sparkling alcohol-free drink on the table and pours us each a glass.

I hold up my glass and ding it against hers. "To first dates."

"To first dates, though I think this is supposed to come before all the things we've done so far."

"Definitely not, threesomes before first dates always," I joke, and she smiles.

We start eating, and the food is absolutely delicious. I hum my approval, and she does the same. "This is fucking amazing."

"My mom used to make the best Kielbasa back home."

"Are you planning on going to Russia during the offseason?" she asks, and I scrub my face.

"I'm not sure. I might fly my mom out here. I just need to get her passport updated." She looks shy, and I reach across the table and cover her hand. "I know she's excited to meet you and Owen. I can't seem to shut up about the two of you."

"I'm sorry that I don't have a good family to bring you home to. Both of you have amazing mothers."

"Where is your mom?" I ask her softly. I knew the woman at her townhome that day was definitely not her mom. Her dad is obviously a piece of shit who loves dating women half his age who don't know any better.

"I don't have one," she says softly.

"What do you mean, did she pass away?"

She shakes her head and sighs. She looks at the sparkling juice, no doubt wishing it was alcohol. "My dad doesn't believe in packs. He doesn't trust Omegas, and he's just in general a possessive asshole. I was born via a closed surrogate birthing process."

I blink at her. "That man chose to have a child on purpose?"

"Even picked an embryo that had signs of being an Alpha. I will say, he's never been disappointed in my being female. Just disappointed in general."

"I can imagine growing up with him as your only parent was difficult."

"He had a lot of girlfriends, some better than others. But Charlotte's mom, she was the closest thing I ever had to a real parent."

I reach my hand out, and we hold hands, my thumb grazing over her knuckles. "I never met her, but the way Charlotte and the guys talk about her, she was obviously special."

She sniffs but doesn't cry. "She really was. It's funny. Owen's mom reminds me of her, but in a crass, no filter kind of way."

"She does seem like quite the character," I reply, excited to get to know her.

"What about your mom?" she asks me.

"She's a hardass, but she loves just as hard. I miss her."

"I'm excited to meet her. I love that you and Owen are willing to share your families with me."

I shake my head at her. "As if Charlotte and her pack aren't your family?"

"They are," she says fondly as we finish up our meal. "Alexi?"

"Yeah, *malyshka?*"

"I love you," she says confidently. Her eyes meet mine, and her cheeks are pink. She doesn't give me a minute to speak. "I just needed you to know that. I know I haven't been the best at expressing how I feel about you. We started off physical, but there were always feelings there on my end. That's why I was so scared to be with you. I knew we would end up packed up. I've never had someone believe in me the way you do. I not only love you, but you made me love myself again, and I'm not sure I'll ever be able to thank you enough for that."

I stand up and cross the table, getting on my knees and putting my hands around her face. "I love you too." I lean forward and kiss her, feeling lost for words about how I could possibly ever top that speech. We keep mumbling feelings in between kisses.

"Alexi?"

"*Malyshka?*"

"I need you."

I stand to my full height, and grab her thighs, carrying her over to the bed and tossing her down in the nest.

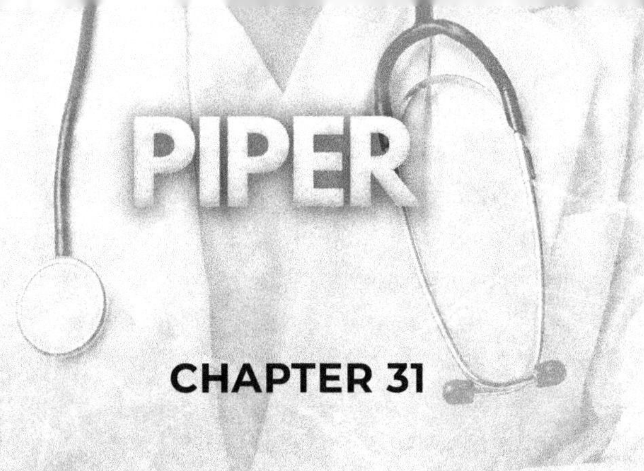



## CHAPTER 31

"Should we go to my room?" Alexi asks, and I shake my head.

"I ran it by Owen first." He smirks at me as he crawls on top of me, his large body boxing me in, and his scent fills the room.

"Our Omega was in on this?" His smile is contagious as I return it. His hand grips my hip as he surrounds me in the most intoxicating way.

"I told him I needed some time alone with you, and he understood."

"He didn't care that we'd be in his nest?" he asks with an arch of his brow.

"He doesn't see it like that." Alexi tilts his head, and I scoot back on the bed, my hands roaming the expanse of his built chest. "He sees his nest as a place for all of us. Where anyone in the pack can seek comfort."

"He told you this?"

"Somewhat." I shrug my shoulders. "I've been doing research on Omegas since we went to the clinic, and it seems like there are two spectrums of Omegas, ones who are really territorial of their nests, and the others who see it more of a place for the whole pack."

"I'm not sure if you talking about Omega shit is what is getting me hard right now, or how much you know about taking care of Owen."

"It can be both," I say, smiling up at him as he lays more of his body weight on top of me, supporting himself with his forearms and stroking his fingers through my hair.

Alexi leans forward, placing soft kisses on my face and playing with my hair leisurely. We've never been together like this before. It's always been a race to release or a fuckfest. It's never been slow and intimate.

The way he's touching me now tells me that's what he wants, and I'm craving it. Being with Alexi in a way I haven't been with anyone. Casual sex, fucking, is easy. Being vulnerable, telling someone I love them, that this is for the long hall is terrifying. Yeah, I'm bonded with Owen, and that's a connection that is beyond any intimacy I've ever experienced. But in a way, that wasn't a choice, that was destiny, a fate that we both couldn't overlook if we wanted to. But the man above me, he's a choice. Maybe the universe played a part in us finding each other, but me bringing down my walls to accept him as a pack —it's a conscious choice.

The way that Alexi is looking at me and touching me makes me feel like nothing else exists in the world except us.

There's no questions about my career looming over me, the mean voice in my head is quiet, and all I can do is get lost in this man who never once gave up on me. He knew without a shadow of a doubt that this is where we would end up. Alexi knew we were meant to be a pack before I even knew what I wanted, and I love him for that. If it weren't for his insistence and inability to give up on this pack, then I'm not sure where we would all be. Alexi Bandnin is the center of my recent happiness, and I need him to know how much he means to me.

I slide my hands overtop of his soft shirt; his body is a work of art, and all I want is his skin against mine. Feeling impatient, I tug at the hem of his shirt. He smirks at me before grabbing the neck of his shirt and tossing it over his head.

"So impatient for me, *malyshka.*"

"I need you," I say softly, and he looks down at me. His eyes go soft before cupping my face and kissing me softly. My heart races in my chest as his lips part and his tongue tangles with mine. The way this larger than life man can be so fucking soft for me has me melting into the mattress. His thumbs tenderly stroke my cheekbones as he pours his devotion with every sweep of his tongue and gentle caress.

I'm still fully clothed as his hand moves from my face, to my chest, to slide under my shorts. Alexi's fingers toy with the edge of my panties, and he groans into my mouth when he feels my wetness soaking the simple cotton underwear.

"I love how wet you get for me. Always ready for my cock, aren't you?"

I nod my head, and Alexi slips his fingers past the fabric. His large fingers circle my entrance and clit. His touch is soft, enough to entice and have me thrusting my hips into his hand, silently begging for relief.

He removes his hand from the waistband of my shorts, and a near whine escapes my lips, making Alexi laugh and shake his head. He removes his weight from my body, barring his weight on his knees as he tugs on my shorts and underwear impatiently. I help him take it off by shimmying out of the material. Instead of removing my shirt, he tugs the neckline down and uses my bra to prop my breasts up. He groans at the sight and leans down to suck my right nipple into his mouth. I can't help but tangle my fingers in his dark hair. His beard tickles my skin as his tongue lavishes my hard nipple.

With a free hand, I grip the waistband of his shorts, which he wordlessly removes for me. He continues giving my chest his complete devotion as I slip my hand between us. I use my thumb to drag his pre-cum down his length, stroking his cock lightly. He shudders when he sucks my nipple into his mouth sharply.

My fingertips graze his knot, and he groans, his forehead falling to my chest.

"You drive me fucking crazy," he says, nestling in against my neck, inhaling my scent, and placing reverent kisses up my throat.

Feeling emboldened, I wrap my hand around his growing knot and squeeze lightly.

"Fuck, just like that. You like my knot, *malyshka?*"

I swallow thickly and nod my head. I'd never really considered it before, but the idea slips through my lips before I have a chance to truly think. "I want to take your knot."

His body stills, and he pulls off my body to look down at me.

"What?" His expression is one of true shock as he blinks down at me.

"I think I could learn to take it."

He groans, his body falling back down on mine as he acts like a man possessed, his hands hovering over every inch of me as he kisses me.

"We would need to go slow and be careful," he says while placing a soft kiss behind my ear. He's right for more reasons than one; I don't want to hurt myself, and I can't even imagine what would happen if I locked him while he knotted me, it would likely be catastrophic. But the human body is adaptable, and it's not like I haven't seen Beta woman take a knot before in porn.

"Okay, I want it, I want you."

"Slow, and you tell me if it's ever too much," he says. His tone is serious as he pushes a rogue piece of hair from my face.

My nails drag along his beard as I bring his lips to mine.

"I promise. Please, Alexi."

My begging breaks him. His fingers are back to my pussy, making sure I'm wet and ready before he fists his length and slowly sinks into me. He exhales against the side of my face, one arm holding his weight as his other hand grips my ass tightly.

"I love this pussy so much," he says, and I can't help the small laugh that leaves me. He lets out his own as he hitches my leg around his waist to fuck me deeper. No doubt I'll have bruises tomorrow from how hard he's grabbing onto my ass. His strokes are deep and slow. My eyes meet his every time he hits the perfect spot.

"You want me to train this sweet, perfect pussy to take my knot, *malyshka?*"

"Please."

"Please, what?" he says.

"Please, Alpha," I say, and he clicks his tongue, and his next thrust is so rough I let out a needy moan.

"You want my Alpha knot? That's what you're going to fucking call me." His eyes bore into mine, and I moan, his dick settled deep inside of my cunt. This power dynamic between us is something I never knew I wanted or needed.

"Please, Alpha," I say quietly.

Alexi groans on top of me, his pace picking up. His hand comes to toy with my clit, and I can't help as my hips push against him and beg for more. Alexi grips my chin roughly and kisses me like I'm his next breath before pushing off of the bed and bracing himself on his knees. His large hands wrap around my thighs, situating me where he wants me.

His one thumb rubs my clit in a slow circular pace while his other hand teases where his cock is pressed firmly inside of my body.

"My brave, sexy girl, wanting me to stretch this sweet pussy," he says before pressing a finger inside of me. The pressure is light, a slight stretch with the addition of the finger and his cock. "Look at that. Fuck," he groans and starts fucking me harder. "You want another finger, *malyshka?*"

"Yes." His one hand leaves my clit as he smacks my thigh.

"Yes, what?"

"Yes, Alpha."

"Fuck," he hisses before adding another finger. The rest of his hand holds the base of his length. As he fucks me, his two fingers in addition to his already large cock has me shaking. When he returns to touching my clit, I break. My body shaking, my vision blurring, it feels like every nerve ending is firing off.

Alexi moans above me, his hips stuttering as my cunt wraps around him and his fingers. "Fuck," he nearly shouts, adding another finger inside of me, making me shout and my back arch off the bed. I fist the sheets from the pain and pleasure of the stretch. Alexi doesn't hold back, making me moan with each thrust. I can feel his knuckles hitting my entrance, and it makes me shiver with the thought of taking his knot and how badly I want to be with him in that way.

It has nothing to do with us both being Alphas; it has everything to do with me wanting him in every physical possible sense.

"Please, Alpha. I need it," I beg, and his thighs smack against mine as he fucks me.

"My girl wants to be full of her Alpha's knot and cum,

doesn't she? Such a needy, fucking thing." When I clench around his fingers, nearly locking his cock and fingers is what breaks him. He struggles to hold himself up while he fills me up with his cum.

I can feel his knot swell at my entrance and sigh when he moans out his release on top of me. He stays there for a moment before he pulls his fingers and cock out of me. We both make a noise of disapproval from the lack of contact.

Alexi plops down next to me and wraps his arms around my waist and tugging me toward his chest.

"Damn," he mumbles against my hair.

I make a non committal noise when the door creaks open.

"Are you all done?" Owen says sleepily.

I can feel heat on my cheeks, though there shouldn't be. The three of us were basically naked and tangled together for a week.

"Get in bed," Alexi says in a groggy voice.

Owen doesn't need to be told twice as he comes to sleep next to me. Alexi throws his arm over him and holds him by his bare waist.

"I take it everything went well?" he says, smiling at me. I lean forward and give him a small kiss before pushing back his blond hair.

"More than well."

"Smells like it. If I wasn't so tired, I'd do something about this boner," he says on a yawn.

"Maybe in the morning?" I say with a smile, my heart feeling full sleeping between these two men. It's not that I've ever felt the urge to be a center of a pack, it more so has to do with them. That they're both bigger than me, that they both want me. I feel cherished in a way I never knew I needed. Before I let negative thinking get in the way, I snuggle closer to the both of them.

The connection I have with Owen doesn't need words, and I know I need to voice them. When I look up at his half-lidded sleepy eyes, he gives me a ridiculously cute smirk.

"I know, Piper. Go to sleep, we'll talk about it later."

I always knew Charlotte loved her nest and that her pack sees it as a revered place, but this is truly the first time I really get it. This is more than a room, this is a place where I can be completely me with the two people who have somehow become my whole life.

# CHAPTER 32

By some fucking miracle, we've made it to the conference finals. It feels like I've been both completely absent and wildly honed in until now. My body is exhausted, but I'm trying to keep my mind focused. The away games have been more than difficult, and it feels sacrilegious to say that I wish the Rangers would have won the Metro division just so that Piper could have maybe traveled with us. I know it wouldn't have happened and that it would probably be a bigger distraction than anything.

I can't decide whether being bonded to Piper is better or worse in this situation. On the one hand, it's like there is a tether to her keeping us close, and the other very needy part that craves her at all times can be distracting.

The only reason I'm sane is because of Alexi. He's very respectful of how he treats me when we're around the team, but us being together is far from a secret. The only secret is the capacity of our relationship. We aren't simply partners, we're far more than that, and I kind of like that we have this secret. I've been able to keep Piper and Alexi to myself with no input from anyone else. Not that it's a secret how much Alexi takes care of me from the team's perspective.

Somehow Alexi has enough in with the coach, or the manager, to always make sure that we share a room during away games.

The Canes are the higher seed, so the first game is in Raleigh. It's nostalgic in a way, the Hurricanes being the team we're playing against, and they were my first ever starting NHL game. The first game is on Sunday during the day, so we flew out early and are getting dinner with the team.

Sloane is walking around with her phone taking videos, and she stops over by us. Nilsen is right next to me, and he beams as the Omega walks over. His smile is horrifying, but she doesn't seem to mind.

"Bram, there's a new dance trend. Do you think you could—"

She doesn't even finish her sentence. "Where do you want me?" She smiles at him and leads him to a corner of the restaurant as light music plays from her phone and she teaches him the dance moves. The rest of the team laughs at his expense. He throws a few angry looks our way, but then turns soft when he looks back at Sloane.

"Pussy whipped," Johannson says from the other side of the table. Alexi, Mikael, and Eli all stiffen as he says it.

"To be correct, it would be Omega whipped. Also, I don't think coach would like to hear you saying shit like that," Eli says, irritation written all over his face. He's usually incredibly easy going, but right now, he looks like he wants to bite Johannson's head off.

"Come on, I didn't mean it like that. It was a joke."

"Explain the joke to me," Mikael says in a flat tone. Johannson stutters slightly and shakes his head.

"Nevermind."

"No, you thought it was so fucking funny. Tell us, backup, what's so funny?"

Okay, for the first time since I joined this team, I get Mikael's appeal. He crosses his arms over his chest and gives Johannson a look that could kill.

"Everyone is so sensitive," Johannson says. *Wrong fucking thing to say.*

"No, you're just being an asshole. We have an Omega at home, as well as two daughters. Not that we even need that to be decent fucking human beings. You need to grow up," Eli says, standing and walking away from the table to leave.

Mikael stays seated, glaring at Johannson and forcing his hand. The backup goalie feels the weight of none of us wanting him around. He scoots his chair back and leaves.

"Fucking asshole," Mikael mumbles under his breath.

"No way Applegate keeps him next year," Alexi says. He was quiet during the exchange, but I know him well enough to know that he's pissed. I also think he is teaching Eli and Mikael how to take over the team for when he leaves.

"Of course not, especially when we have Connery," Mikael says, grabbing his water and taking a heavy sip. I look away from him and focus on where Bram is being given directions by Sloane, and he dances to the music like she tells him too.

When I look back at Mikael, he clicks his tongue and looks between me and Alexi. He makes a groaning sound but gets up from the table. He claps my and Alexi's shoulder before heading to his room for the night. Him and Eli always share, since they are pack mates.

"Do you think he knows?" I whisper to Alexi, who places his arm behind my chair.

"Even if he does, I trust him."

"I'm ready to stop lying," I say softly, his thumb and forefinger rubbing some tension away on my neck.

"I know, soon. Two more series, that's it. We're going to get you your Cup."

"Even just coming this far," I say, which is true. Who would have ever thought an Omega goalie could make it to the NHL, let alone the Eastern Conference Stanley Cup Finals? "I wouldn't have any regrets," I say truthfully. If we lost this in four games, it would suck, but to have played in the playoffs is more than I ever could have imagined for myself.

It's not that hockey isn't still my passion, that I don't love the sport. It's that I'm so fucking tired. Not only of hiding who I am, masking my true self, but my body aches. Omegas weren't meant to be built the way I am, nor to take the stress of this profession. I'm sure it has a lot to do with the medications I was on for years too. But I'm worn thin.

When I play my last NHL game, it will probably be one of the most bittersweet moments of my life. But I have more to live for than I ever realized. Two people who are more important than hockey will ever be.

"*Sólnyshka?*"

"Are you finally going to tell me what that means?" I ask him.

He grins and tilts his head at me. "It means sunshine," he says, and I feel loved and seen. I've been called an asshole more times than I can count, but I've never been compared to being someone's sunshine. I'm too stunned to speak when he says the pet name again. "*Sólnyshka?*"

"Yeah?"

"I'm getting you that fucking Cup," he says, leaning down and placing a gentle kiss against my lips, no care in the world who is around. Most of the team has left for the night. Bram and Sloane are too caught up in their own bubble to notice. I never thought I'd like PDA, but I almost wish there was more of an audience to see how much Alexi cares for me.

For the first time in my life, I'm okay with being a needy Omega in public, though most people in this room have no clue. I extend the kiss, and when we part, he grins at me.

"Let's go call Piper and call it a night."

"'Kay," I say, feeling breathless. He takes my hand in his as we walk to our hotel room, and I find myself eager to have more of these public displays of affection. He kisses the side of my head in the elevator, and all I feel is true and utter contentment.

———

It's the third period, and it feels like my legs are going to give out. The score is tied, and the last thing I fucking need is for this to go into overtime, or god-fucking-forbid multiple over times. I can feel myself getting sluggish, and that's the last thing the team needs right now.

In the middle of the ice, Kristiansen and Nilsen are going at it, and the refs are trying to pull them apart. Alexi was on the bench, but he skates out and motions for me to pull my helmet up. When he looks at me, I can see his worry written all over his face. His one hand is ungloved, and he holds up the smelling salts to my nose.

"Inhale," he says. I do, and immediately it hits me, my eyes going wide and my nose scrunching up.

"Fuck," I groan as I shake out my body and let out a cough.

"You fucking got this, how do you feel?"

"Like my fucking nose is on fire, but better," I say. Alexi takes my water bottle, spraying down my hair and the back side of my jersey, immediately cooling my skin down.

"Eight more minutes. All we need is eight more minutes, and then you can rest. I'll carry you to the fucking hotel, airplane, home. Wherever the fuck." He looks panicked, and

I'm not sure if it's the urge to win or to please Alexi that pushes me.

"I got it, I'm good." He grips my jersey to look at me, and I shake my head. "I said I'm fucking good."

He grins. "I should kiss that smart little mouth right now. Later," he says, skating back to the bench, where he puts his glove back on and tosses the smelling salts to Eli. He gives Nilsen a look, and the fight immediately stops.

That sneaky fuck instigated a fight in order to give me a break. I shake my head and smile to myself as I put my helmet back on.

*I can handle eight minutes.*

With Nilsen fighting his cousin, they both get penalties, and we're four on four for the next two minutes.

Each team holds their own.

*I can handle six minutes.*

Mikael takes a hard hit against the boards and is pulled onto the bench. Eli and Alexi are running the line and have a few good shots before the Canes turn it around on us. It's two close calls, but I don't let anything in.

*I can handle four minutes.*

Things only pick up in intensity, neither one of us wanting this to go into overtime. Both of us can taste the first win and set the pace for the rest of the series. The winner of the first game in a series typically has a sixty-five percent chance of taking the whole series. Those are the type of odds you want on your side.

*I can handle two minutes.*

Alexi and Eli get trapped against the boards, trying to dig out the puck. It's passed to Kristiansen who's on my left. I'm fast, but not fast enough as he scoops it in the net. The siren sounds, and the Canes' fans go wild.

"Fuck," I grumble, smacking my stick against the corner of

the goal and knocking it off the ice. The ref comes over and resets it while giving me a shitty look.

I can tell Alexi wants to skate over but instead gives me space. Anything is possible, and I know I can pull it together for overtime if we can rally and get a Foxes goal.

But we don't. We start this series at a deficit, and I can't help but feel like it's all my fault.

———

For what it's worth, Alexi keeps his promise, nearly carrying me to the hotel room and getting us food.

My phone buzzes, and I answer the call from bed, even though I'm ready to pass out.

"What's wrong?" Piper's pretty face asks, and I shake my head.

"Just a hard loss."

Her eyebrows scrunch, and I see her look behind me at Alexi. "It feels like more than just a loss," she says quietly.

"I'm just tired; it's not a big deal."

"You promise? Please don't bottle shit up. I promise you, it's not worth it." Her face is soft and pleading. Alexi grabs the phone from me as I sit there speechless and not sure what to say.

"Don't worry, *malyshka*. I'll take care of him."

"I know you will. I don't doubt that for a bit."

"What do you need, Owen?" Alexi asks me plainly. I blink at him, my emotions reeling through me. I'm tired, needy, and I feel crushing guilt from the loss of tonight's game.

"I think he needs you to turn his mind off," Piper says over the video call.

Alexi scoots closer to me, kissing my neck as Piper watches with interest.

"Is that what you need, for me to shut this pretty little head up?"

I nod my head and watch as Piper licks her lips over the call. "Yes, that's what I need," I tell him, and he makes a growling noise against my throat.

"I love it when you ask for what you want," he says.

"I want to watch," Piper chimes in from the screen, and Alexi laughs.

"Do you want praise for asking what you want too?" he says, and she places the phone on a table and starts rummaging through her drawer. "You better be bringing out my Christmas present, and you better put your phone somewhere where we can watch too."

"Yes, sir," Piper says. Alexi growls and places the phone on the nightstand before smacking my ass.

"Are you going to present that sweet ass for me, pretty boy?"

"Fuck," I grumble, and like the wanton Omega whore that I am, I tug my shorts off, I don't even mess with the shirt. Alexi doesn't even bother with his clothes, just tugging his cock out of his boxers and rolling his shirt under his chin.

I can see the way he's looking at my body on the phone and the way Piper can't avert her gaze as she starts to play with her pussy.

*I'm not going to last long at all. Fuck.*

"You should see how fucking bad he needs it, Piper," Alexi says behind me, his hand gliding over my ass before he slips a finger inside of me before adding another. I'm torn between shutting my eyes and letting the sensation of him touching me take over and the overwhelming need to see how Piper touches herself while watching us.

*Piper wins.*

Alexi's full attention is on getting me ready, which honestly won't take long. If he wanted to, he could thrust into me right now, and I'd thank him for it.

"Always so needy, so ready. How'd I get so lucky?" he says, fucking me with his fingers. I look over to the phone where Piper is lying down on her bed and touching herself while she watches. She has a tank top on, but her hair is mussed up, and her cheeks are pink. How can I miss someone so much when it's only been a day?

"You're so good. Fuck, I need you home and inside of me," she says through the phone, and I groan. My elbow holds my weight as I stroke my cock.

Alexi brushes the head of his cock against my hole before slowly pushing in and making me moan and press my ass closer to his pelvis. It's almost too much as I look up at the phone. The way Piper looks like she's already about to come, and how big Alexi looks behind me. I'm on the larger side as far as Omegas come, but being around Alexi makes me feel small. I think if you asked me months ago, I would hate it, but as he looks down at where he fucks me tenderly before smirking up at Piper through the phone, I realize I love it.

Never thought I would be into a man who could pick me up and manhandle me a bit, but now I can't imagine life any other way.

His grip on my hips tightens, his cock stretching me in the most delicious way. Alexi's knot hits my ass with each thrust but doesn't enter me.

My wrist is working overtime as I fuck my own fist.

"Please," I beg.

"Mmm, should I let our sweet boy come?" he directs to Piper, and I groan. Having my Alphas talk about me makes me feel feral.

"He has been so good," Piper says in her sweet voice, and I shiver.

"He has, he's such a good fucking boy," Alexi says, annunciating each word with a hard thrust. On the last word, he pushes his knot inside of me, and I shatter, spurts of cum hitting the mattress and trailing down my fist.

I'm only barely able to keep my eyes open as I watch Piper's back arch off the bed, her vibrator buzzing loudly as she reaches her peak as well.

Alexi continues rutting into me, making me whimper from oversensitivity. His knot stretches my asshole perfectly, and I feel like I might even come again. My cock doesn't go down, and Alexi reaches around me, his fist tangling in the sticky mess as he continues stroking me. My body quivers and shakes with each stroke.

I didn't think it was possible outside of my heat, but when his teeth drag along the side of my neck, I break. Squeezing him tighter inside of me and covering his fist with my second release.

He grumbles a string of Russian in my ear before I feel the warmth of his seed filling me completely. His knot holds us together as he kisses my back softly and he maneuvers us to our sides.

I wish I could talk to Piper more, thank her for helping calming me down, but my eyes are closing.

"I think that will need to be a new away game tradition," Alexi says behind me.

"He's asleep," Piper says softly.

"Next time, we need a bigger screen. I could barely see your pussy," Alexi complains, and Piper laughs.

"Be a good boy, and I'll give you your own private show," she says. Alexi squeezes me tighter against his chest.

"This won't be an issue soon," he says softly. I want to hear the rest of the conversation. The way they talk to each other is so different now. It's more of a mutual respect and understanding of one another. There isn't this big display of fighting over dominance.

Maybe it's being an Omega, but I can't help but to think I had some part in them figuring out their relationship with each other. It hasn't been easy, and I still don't think it will be. But loving them, that has turned out to be the easiest thing I've ever done.

# CHAPTER 33

This series going to game seven isn't ideal, but at least there is a game seven. We just tied it up at home against the Canes. The only thing standing between us and the Cup is this last game and then one final series.

I hate to admit it, but even I'm feeling the absolute fucking havoc that this season has plagued on my body. Maybe it's because I'm not just worrying about myself anymore, but either way, I'm fucking tired.

I already knew this season needed to be my last. But now my body is in absolute agreement with my mind.

Piper has been attending all our home games, but she heads home before us so she doesn't have to wait around for press and us getting dressed again.

We didn't even change out of our suits, and if Owen didn't look like he was going to absolutely pass out the moment we cross the threshold, I'd probably make him slip his cock out of those tight navy trousers and let me go down on him.

When I open the door to the house, the first thing that hits me is the scent of something burning.

"What the fuck?" Owen says, looking around. We walk

over to the kitchen, and I turn off the oven and pull out a burnt mess. If there wasn't a box mix for brownies on the counter, I wouldn't know what the fuck she was supposed to be making.

I fan it and close the oven and look around the room.

"Where is she?"

Owen scrubs his face, and his mouth turns down in a frown. "She… I think she's holding back her feelings down the bond. Can she do that?" he asks, panic showing over his features.

"If anyone's going to find a way not to share their feelings, it's going to be Piper."

I rub my hand down his back, the material of his suit soft. Not even having bonded yet, it's like his fear is radiating off of him in waves. As we walk down to the hall, I can hear Piper sniffle through the door.

I take a deep breath before opening it. Her laptop is open, and the screen illuminates her face in the dark as she looks up and Owen turns on the light.

"Piper, *malyshka*, what's wrong?" I approach her like she's a wounded animal. I've learned the harder I push her, the more she tends to push me back. Owen takes my lead, but I can tell he needs to be near her.

"I-I…" She covers her face and starts sobbing. I take the laptop from her lap and look at what she's upset about.

A grin spreads over my face. "You fucking got in."

She wipes her eyes and nods. "I did it."

"Of course you did. You earned this." She starts pulling herself together, and Owen takes that as his moment to swoop in and wrap his arms around her and bring her to a lying position on the bed.

She wraps her arms back around him, and it's low at first, but I hear her purr. I hadn't even heard it when they bonded. But now, as she holds our Omega, she's finally able to let go as the low rumble shakes through her chest, calming both herself and Owen.

"You burned the brownies," he mumbles into her neck, and she laughs. It's loose, and she throws her head back, tear stains down her cheeks, but the smile on her face radiates a happiness I've never seen in her.

She grabs Owens face, her fingers tangling in his hair. "I love you."

"I know," he smirks, leaning down to give her a kiss. "Just like you know I love you too."

She nods and wraps her arms back around Owen, holding out an arm for me to join. I was totally wrapped in watching them together, so I wasn't thinking about me in the slightest.

"It's really happening," she says, squeezing my hand. I wrap my arm around Owen and her, wishing I would have taken this fucking suit off before I got on the bed, but at this point, it's too late.

"What's really happening?" Owen asks softly, his eyes shut and his face pressed against Piper's neck.

"Us, our dreams, everything."

I pet down her hair, and she leans in against my hand. Fuck, my chest feels so god damn full that it might just crack wide open all over this room.

"When do you start?" I ask her.

"It starts in July."

"So we'll have a few weeks between winning the Cup to you starting work?"

"Oh my God. Congratulations on tonight's win. I made this all about myself."

"Things can be about you, Piper. This is a big thing. I'm so proud of you." She blushes, and as much as she might not want to admit it, the Alpha has a bit of a praise kink. Plus, I don't think Piper had enough people telling her how proud she should be of her accomplishments throughout her life.

"Owen," she says softly, pushing his blond hair from his face. He's out cold. Her brows furrow as she looks up at me. "He's been getting a lot more fatigued after games." She feels his skin and presses gentle touches along his face. "I'm worried he's pushing himself too far."

My hand leaves her hair as I touch the Omega between us. "He has. Around the third period, he's been losing gas. I'm not sure what else I can do. Smelling salts usually help give him a little bit more energy. But it's almost like clockwork."

Her eyebrows furrow even more, and she shakes her head. "It's just a little odd that it's hitting him now, and at the same time every game. We haven't changed anything with his medication."

"The games are closer together with playoffs, that's all I can think."

"Hmm," she says, looking down at Owen and placing a kiss on his forehead before leaning over him and taking a kiss from me as well.

"Happiness looks good on you, *malyshka.*"

"It does, doesn't it?" She grins, and I nod my head.

"Don't think I won't crawl over Owen and fuck you right next to him."

She bites her lip. "Do it."

I've never bluffed in my life as I untangle myself from Owen, who doesn't stir the entire time I show Piper just how happy I can make her.

———

"We did it. We really fucking did it!" Owen yells at me on the ice, our hands clenched on each other's jerseys.

All of our teammates are losing their absolute minds while the Canes' fans don't waste a second leaving their stadium.

"We fucking did." I don't give a single fuck. His helmet is off, and I swoop in and give him a soft kiss. I'm worried he'll be irritated when I pull back, but the eye roll and smirk are all I need to know.

"We're going to the motherfucking Cup!" Eli yells, his arm wrapped around Mikael, who is smiling. It's horrifying.

Owen seemed a lot more alert in the third period. I chalk it up to complete adrenaline as I wrap my arm around his shoulders, which turns into a complete dog pile of everyone on the team joining in.

After we've separated and shaken hands with the other team—well, everyone except Nilsen, who spits on his hand and offers it to his cousin, who refuses—we're back in our suits and ready to fly back to Connecticut.

"What time is the west conference final?" Mikael asks, scrolling through his phone.

"Should be starting soon," Eli replies. He also has his phone out, and I wonder if they have some sort of pack group text message.

"I'm hoping for the Predators," Nilsen says, closing his eyes and leaning back in his chair.

"Me too," Owen says softly.

"Hey," I say, squeezing his thigh. His blue eyes meet mine, and I give him a soft smile. "If it's his team, it will be okay."

"It would just be easier if it wasn't."

"I know. But let's just hold on to this win. Our girl is at home waiting for you."

"For us," he says, and I nod my head.

"For us."

———

"Do you two want to watch at our house?" Eli says, and Mikael gives him a look of irritation for having invited us, but I see that as a reason to say yes.

I look over at Owen to see how he's feeling, if he's tired and wants to go home and sleep, though I doubt he would be able to not knowing the game's outcome.

"We have to get Piper."

Mikael groans. "She's already at our house." He rolls his eyes, and Eli sighs at his packmate.

"We'll meet you guys there."

Their house isn't far from the airport, so we're there in under ten minutes. I grab both of our bags so we can change into something more comfortable once we get inside.

We somehow beat Eli and Mikael here. I go to knock on the door when Piper opens the door holding a small sleeping baby in her arms.

"We just got them down, so you're going to have to be quiet," she says, giving us a soft smile.

I shouldn't like how much I like her holding a baby. I'm not sure if kids are in our future or not, but I can't deny that seeing that side of Piper does something to me.

I lean forward and give her a soft kiss before stroking the small baby's blond, fuzzy head. "Which one is this?"

"Linc. Anders has Andrea."

"Where's Katie?" Owen asks, getting his own kiss from Piper.

"With Anders' parents, she's been eating up their attention lately."

"We're going to get changed," I tell her, and she gives us both a once over in our suits.

"Fine," she says, though her attitude says the opposite.

I shake my head at her but lead Owen to the bathroom for us to get changed. His posture is filled with tension, and I'm not sure what comfort I can offer him until we know the outcome.

After we're changed, we settle in on their couch, a very similar position to the Christmas party. Piper sits in between us, but unlike Christmas, she is leaning against both of us while she still holds the baby.

"Owen, baby, are you okay?" she says softly so that no one else can hear besides me and Owen.

"Yeah, I'm good." He wraps his arm around her shoulder, his fingertips touching my own shoulder, while my palm rests on Piper's thigh.

"I'm going to go put him down," she says, holding the baby up a little more.

"I'll take him up," Anders says with a smile, already holding one baby and taking the other.

I look around. "Where's Charlotte?"

"Also sleeping, so everyone needs to be quiet during the game, or else you will feel my wrath. Do you understand?" She points at each of us, and nearly everyone holds up their hands in surrender.

The game starts, and my stomach sinks immediately.

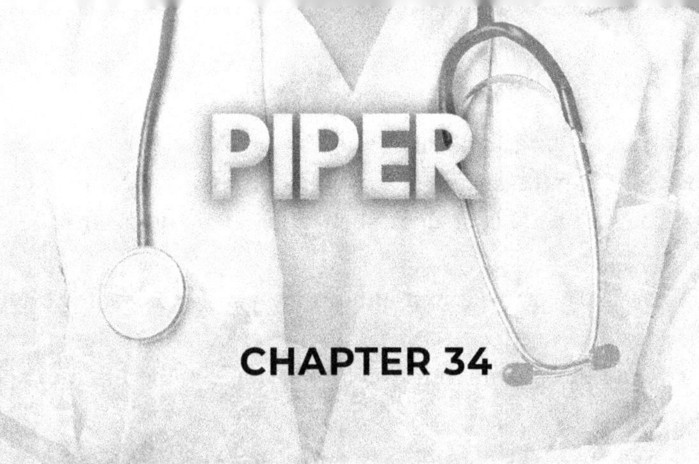


## CHAPTER 34

The Sharks win, and I can feel Owen's stress, fear, and anger through the bond. He gets up without a word, and the sliding glass door swooshes as he heads out to their back patio.

Alexi looks around and is about to get up when I pat his thigh.

"I got it," I say, leaning forward and placing a kiss against his hair. It's not that I'm opposed to Alexi helping, it's just that I feel like he fixes everything. I want to feel needed, and maybe there's this piece of me that still feels like I'm not a good enough Alpha for Owen. He's sitting on one of the large Adirondack chairs they have out here. His legs are spread wide as he rubs against his chin and looks out into their dark backyard.

I walk into his space and look between the empty chair next to him and his lap. Without a word, he holds out his hand, and I take it. He tugs me down onto his lap, and my hands are immediately on his face.

"Do you want to talk about it?"

"No," he says stiffly. I push his hair out of his face and just touch him, letting him know that I'm here. We don't need to talk about it, but he needs to know that I'm always going to be here for him if he ever does need to let something off of his chest.

"Are you worried about him outing you?" I ask softly. My curiosity and need to make things better outweigh the other half of me that wants him to tell me what's bothering him at his own pace.

Owen squeezes my hip before resting his head against the back of the chair.

"I don't really know what's bothering me right now."

"Have you been feeling okay?" I ask, touching his skin, and he sighs.

"Tonight's the best game I've had in a while. I don't feel as tired as I usually do."

"Did you do anything different?"

"I don't think so." He shrugs and looks away, his hand still on my hip.

"Maybe I could travel to California with you guys, even if I fly commercial or something," I say, and it's the first smirk I get since he got home tonight. He gives my hip another squeeze, and he turns his face to me.

"You would do that, wouldn't you?"

"I would."

He shakes his head. "I'll be alright." His phone buzzes in his pocket, vibrating against my ass and making me jump. He groans and digs it out of his pocket and sighs. Owen gives me a soft look before looking down at the phone.

"Hey, Mom." He pulls the phone away from his ear for a second. "I know. Yes. Okay."

He groans and hands me the phone.

"Hey, Lori."

"Piper, honey, how are you?"

I shift on Owen's lap. "Good, you?"

"Well, my two sons who don't speak to each other are both going to the fucking Stanley Cup Finals, so you tell me."

"Um, I guess you're doing great?"

"Is there enough room in that big Alpha's house for me, or do I need to get a hotel? I'm assuming my son can pull some strings to get his mother tickets. I know Max will do the same. I haven't had a chance to call him yet."

"We can set up a guest room for you."

Owen's head turns sharply toward me, and he gives me a long suffering look, and I shrug my shoulders.

"You've been taking good care of him?"

"Of course I have, he's my bonded."

"Your what?" Lori screams over the phone. Owen's eyes go wide, and he groans as I hand him back the phone.

"You didn't tell your mom that we bonded?" I ask, feeling more insecure about it than I should.

"Fuck," he grumbles, and I hop off his lap. I want to run. Deep down, that's all I want to do. I want to leave him in this backyard and go crawl into bed with Charlotte. But I don't, I take a long inhale and watch as he talks to his mom quickly on the phone.

I try to stay logical. He said he's happy to be bonded with me, that he's never felt so settled. But he's so close to his mom, so why wouldn't he tell her?

I'm completely tuning out his conversation with his mom as he hangs up the phone.

"Piper?"

"What?" I say more sharply than I mean to.

He sighs and stands up so that we're face to face. "I didn't tell her because my mother, as much as I love her, is nosey and insufferable when it comes to checking in on me. I wanted some time where it was just us."

I rub my arms and look away. His answer isn't as satisfying as I need it to be. "Okay," I say softly. The idea of saying all my feelings about how I'm hurt for feeling like a secret. How no one knows that he wears my mark on his chest, that he's mine. It fucking hurts more than I'd like to admit.

*Not good enough.*

*Disappointing.*

*I don't ask much of you, Piper.*

*Ungrateful.*

"Let's go get Alexi and go home."

"Piper," he says my name and tugs at my hand, but doesn't say anything else.

"I'm tired. Let's go home and get some sleep. You guys have practice in the morning."

He scrubs his hand in his hair and nods. As soon as we walk back in the house, I can feel Alexi's eyes on both of us. He doesn't say a word as we say goodnight to Charlotte's Alphas. We drove here separately, and I'm walking to my car without a word as a large hand wraps around my bicep.

"What happened out there?" Alexi says quietly as Owen continues to their car.

"Nothing, I'll see you at home."

"Piper," he nearly growls, and I shake my arm from his grasp. It's all too fucking much. Not only am I dealing with my own shitty emotions right now, I feel Owens as well. His frustration, anger, and now a dash of guilt, just fucking awesome.

"Are you sure you're okay to drive?" Alexi asks, his tone much quieter than before, and I nod my head and give him the fakest smile possible.

"We live five minutes away. I'm good. I promise."

"Okay, we'll follow you."

I want to roll my eyes, but the tenderness of him caring about my safety is enough to make me shut my mouth, nod my head, and get into my car. I don't let the emotion pour out. I bottle it in like I always have—like I've been taught.

*The least you could do is be grateful.*

*Make yourself scarce.*

*That's not how a Blake acts.*

*I spent a lot of money to have you, you know.*

I'm not sure who's meaner, my own voice in my head or the one that sounds like my father. He would be tragically disappointed to know that I was upset over an Omega, that I had bonded with one.

I've done everything he didn't want for me. I quit surgery, I'm in a pack, I bonded an Omega. These are all things that I want, and I was feeling good. Why is finding out that Owen didn't tell his mom about me such a blow? Alexi even told his mother in fucking Russia about me.

Alexi was probably right, I shouldn't have driven. Because, to be quite honest, I'm not even sure how I got from Charlotte's house to ours. But I'm now parked in the driveway and getting out. Alexi and Owen follow, and the tension is thick, and words unspoken follow us into our home.

I don't have the energy.

"I'm going to take a shower and head to bed."

"Piper," Owen says, putting his hands in his pockets and looking at the floor.

"I'll see you guys in the morning."

They both give me a look. Alexi's is curious and feeling out of the loop. Owen's look is more complicated. It's a look of guilt, but also irritation? I can't help but feel like I'm the source of it. I ignore both of them and head to my bathroom.

Crying in the shower is truly the most cathartic way to unleash your demons. The water flowing from the shower muffles my small whimpers, and the warm water loosens my muscles. I feel weak for breaking down, for caring, for letting such a small thing bother me this much. All these old feelings crept up on me like an absolute motherfucker.

I know it's not just about Owen not telling his mom. It's that I don't have a mom to tell, that my dad doesn't care. He kicked me out of the house for not doing what he wanted, and he hasn't spoken to me since.

Logically, I know that I have people that care about me, that Owen cares about me and he didn't mean to hurt me.

It doesn't make it hurt any less. This overwhelming feeling that no matter what I do, what I become, it will never be enough. It won't be enough for myself, my dad, my Omega.

So what's the fucking point?

I wrap my arms around my legs as I sit on the tiled floor and rest my cheek on my knee. My tears are starting to calm down, but my negative thoughts continue to run rampant.

The creak of the bathroom door has me wiping my tears, but I don't bother standing up. I hear what sounds like clothes being removed until the shower curtain is pulled back, and it's Owen, entering the shower fully naked, coming to sit behind me. His legs bracket mine as he wraps his arms around me.

*Fuck.*

I crack. I swear, I've never cried in front of someone so much in my life. It's the absolute worst. I would really rather drag my bare ass on hot pavement than to continually cry in front of my Omega at this point.

"I'm sorry," he whispers into my wet hair, holding me tight. "I love you. It had nothing to do with you and everything to do with me being fucking stupid. I'm fucking this all up. I… I don't know how to be an Omega. Hell, I don't know how to be somebody's boyfriend. I have a lot of growing up to do, Piper. You deserve more, I want to be better."

I nod my head, and his arms tighten around me further.

"When am I going to stop being such a fucking mess?" I say, and he kisses my shoulder.

"You're not a mess. You're a bonded Alpha, who got into an insanely competitive residency, who has so many friends who love her deeply. You're not a mess, Piper, you're just so fucking hard on yourself. And I certainly didn't help by not thinking things through. This isn't on you, it's on me. I'm so sorry, Alpha."

Great, more tears. The warm water pelts the both of us as I shift on the floor and wrap my legs and arms around him. His ownership of what he did wrong and that this isn't all on me is soothing and something I'm not used to hearing.

"Am I the needy one in this relationship?" I ask, trying to joke away all the emotion.

"No, that's obviously Alexi."

"Obviously," I say, pulling back and looking at Owen's face. He pushes back a wet piece of hair, and his fingers track down my face.

"As soon as this series is over, everything changes. No more hiding, no more secrets, I promise. I'm going to be a better man for you, I promise."

"I'm sorry for being so dramatic."

"You weren't. You were hurt, and this is how you've always acted when someone hurts you. Next time, don't run. I'm not going anywhere, and you know Alexi isn't either. I don't ever want to make you feel this way again. I hate seeing you cry and knowing I'm the reason why." He squeezes me tightly and inhales deeply.

"You're the Omega. You were upset first with your brother's team winning. I should have been there for you, not the other way around."

"We're a pack?" he asks me, and I nod my head. "Then it doesn't matter any of our designations. We're all going to be there for each other based on who needs it, and you were there for me. All this is new for me, I've never had to think about people outside of myself. I've never had anyone outside of my mom treat me like an Omega."

"What do you mean?"

He laughs and shakes his head. "You think I ever just casually lie on the couch and let someone pet my hair? Or that I would have ever trusted someone with my heat before? Fuck, I'd never even spent the night in someone's bed before I met you two. Let alone live with them or consider someone else's feelings. I'm learning to be someone's partner while also figuring out what it means to be an Omega. I keep fucking up when it comes to you." He pets back some of my wet hair and I sigh.

I blink up at him and tilt my head. "But you like it?"

"More than I thought I would. I like being seen as a masculine man, and sometimes being an Omega takes away from that. It's stupid, I know. But I never want someone to look at me and think that I'm hopeless or fucking can't take care of myself."

"Being an Omega doesn't mean any of that."

He strokes my back and nods his head. "I'm starting to understand that now. Sometimes things come naturally to me, and then other times they don't. I'm learning to adapt, we all are."

"You're the best Omega I could have ever asked for," I tell him softly and rest my face on his neck. Scenting him, the sweet strawberry citrus scent wafts off of him perfectly.

"How did we go from you being pissed at me to telling me I'm the best?"

I shrug and just soak him up. "It's hard to stay mad at you. You're too pretty to be mad at."

He laughs and shakes his head. "Are you ready to go upstairs and go to bed with your pack?"

"I guess this is what they mean when they say don't go to bed angry?"

"I guess," he says, standing up first and holding his arms out to me. "Just so you know, my mom is thrilled you're my bonded. She told me I seriously bonded up." I laugh and hold him tighter. Still hearing the little voice in the back of my head that I don't deserve this, I shut it down quickly and just try to savor this moment.

# OWEN

## CHAPTER 35

I'm thankful I made things right with Piper as soon as I did because there's no way I could function during this series without knowing we were okay—that she was okay. I never want to be the reason she cries ever again.

Not telling my mom was stupid, but God, that woman knows how to drive me crazy. I just wanted to enjoy being bonded and keep this a secret between Alexi and Piper. But it's clear that I was more than wrong. I'm sure I would have reacted similarly if I were in her shoes, if I felt like she wasn't proud to be my Alpha. It didn't click for me at the moment, but when I felt her rejection through the bond, it felt like my heart was being ripped out. As if I would ever reject her, I love her and need her. But it's become clear to me lately just how in her head Piper is.

I knew she was hard on herself, that she was an over-achiever and in general a very determined person. What I didn't know is how deep it truly is. I mean, I haven't met her father, but from what Alexi and Piper have mentioned, he's a fucking asshole. An asshole who made Piper feel unloved and undeserving for her whole life.

Well, I'm ready to remedy that. Along with all the other fucked up shit going on in our lives right now.

I'm happy that after our shower, I convinced Piper to come and sleep in the nest with Alexi and me. I'm not sure how other Omegas utilize their nest, but I just want to be here all the time with my pack. The room is filled with all of our scents, it's dark, cozy, and I love that Alexi made it specifically for me.

I'm learning more about myself every day, how to enjoy being an Omega, how to be in a relationship, how to be someone's bonded. So much of this is uncharted territory for our pack, and specifically me. It wasn't until recently that I've come to terms with the fact that being an Omega isn't a curse, and I actually like a lot of the stereotypical Omega things—and there's nothing wrong with that.

I'm trying to stay focused for this last series, but I can't deny that my heart is fully devoted to the people in this room. The idea of putting hockey in the same hierarchy of importance when it comes to Piper and Alexi is ridiculous. As soon as I have Alexi's mark on me, I know I'll feel complete.

Sure, having a championship title doesn't hurt. But this— being cuddled next to these two people, it's truly all I need.

"Morning," Alexi groans in my hair. His hand slides from where it was resting over Piper's stomach to squeeze my hip.

"We have practice today."

His forehead rests on the back of my head, and he groans. I have no idea how he's done this for so long. His hockey career has been beyond impressive, but I can tell that he's tired, at least physically. I think if the game was all about mental power, Alexi could play hockey for the rest of his life. But physically, while he's still in excellent shape, it's just too much. Hockey is so hard on the body, and Alexi deserves a high note to his retirement.

As much as he wants to win this Cup for me, the more I find I want us to win for him.

"We can stay in bed for five more minutes." His arm goes back around Piper, and he squeezes us all together.

Piper makes a throaty noise but settles back in against my chest.

"What are you doing today, Piper?"

"Probably go to the gym and then go to Charlotte's."

I nod my head and place my face in her hair. I have to remind myself that Charlotte is her best friend and nothing more. Can you blame me for having jealousy over my Alpha spending so much time with another Omega?

Piper must feel something down the bond as she spins in my arms. She pushes my hair back and places a soft kiss on my lips.

"Charlotte knows I belong to you. And it's never been like that—ever. She's my best friend, and I love her so much, but it's not like this."

"I know, really, I do. But apparently this possessive side of me doesn't."

"I'll make sure that there's no trace of her scent or anything before I come home."

I shake my head, and Alexi's arms tighten around us. "I'll be fine, I promise."

"I never want to upset you. So please just be honest when something is bothering you. Alexi and I always want to make sure that you're happy and we do our best to make sure you always feel confident and settled in our pack. Charlotte is my best friend, and I'll never give her up, but any way I can make you feel more content, I always will."

"Same," Alexi mumbles behind me.

"Just... can you not hold her, and I think making sure her

scent is gone will help. I like Charlotte and her pack. But when you smell like another Omega, I can't handle that."

She smiles and gives me a soft kiss. "I can absolutely do that."

*So this is what being in a grown-up relationship feels like?*

Piper kisses me again, and it's going to take every ounce of control to get out of this bed and not fuck her into the mattress before practice.

"You better go to practice," she says softly.

"I need this season to be over," Alexi groans, lifting himself up and plastering kisses all over mine and Piper's face. He smacks my ass before getting off the bed. "Let's get going, pretty boy. Have a good day, *malyshka,*" he says one last time before giving her a soft kiss and leaving the room to shower.

"I don't want to go."

"How long do you think it's going to take him to shower?"

"At least ten minutes."

"Get over here," she says quietly.

Immediately I'm crawling on top of her body. I love that Piper is strong but still smaller than me. I grip her waist, giving it a tight squeeze before pushing her shirt underneath her chin, exposing her breasts.

Ducking down, I take a nipple between my lips and suck. Her chest pushes against my face, and I suck harder.

"We don't have a lot of time," she says, and I groan. I want to take my time, lick her cunt for hours and edge myself to the point I'm dripping all over myself until I finally give in and sink inside of her.

Instead, I slide my hand into her sleep shorts, and my fingers rub against her clit before dipping inside of her and spreading her wetness around the small bud.

"Owen, I need you."

I shiver hearing those words from her lips. She needs me. Doesn't want me, Piper fucking *needs* me.

My dick is already hard, eager, and ready. But hearing her say those words has me nearly coming already. I remove her shorts and do the same with my underwear, not wasting a second as I fist my cock and push inside of her.

Being inside of Piper is unlike anything I've ever felt. I've always enjoyed sex, but being inside of Piper is my own nirvana.

"God, you feel so fucking good," I tell her. Her back arches, and her fingers glide down my back as she holds me tightly. Our chests touch as I brace myself on the bed and slowly thrust in and out of her.

"You make me so wet. I need you, Owen."

My hips move on their own accord, bucking into her and putting every ounce of effort into showing her how good she feels.

"You're fucking perfect," she says, praising me further. Her one hand tangles in my hair as the other digs into my back. "I need you to come inside of me."

My own desire to come is only overshadowed by my need to make her feel good, to please my Alpha. I adjust my angle so that with each thrust my pelvis is grinding against her clit.

"Just like that, so good. Don't stop," she tells me, and I obey. My thighs are shaking, and my pace is stunted, but when I feel her cunt lock around me, I lose it. Her moans spur on my orgasm, and I fill her up. My own release feels like it's never ending as she tightens around my length, making me let out my own noises of absolute pleasure.

I nearly collapse on top of her, and she wraps her legs and arms around me.

"I love you so much, Owen," she tells me with a tight squeeze.

"I love you too, Piper." We kiss, and the nest door opens.

"Can't leave you two alone for more than two minutes, I swear." Piper just shrugs her shoulders. She doesn't release me right away, though I know she could if she wanted to. She just holds us there. It makes me more happy than it should that my Alpha wants more time with me and she wants to start her day being marked by my scent.

"We need to leave in five," Alexi says, giving me a look that says I'm going to be spending the day smelling like Piper. At least between her scent and my suppressants, I won't have any issues today hiding my designation.

Piper rolls her eyes but unlocks me. A mixture of both of our releases drip out of her, and both Alexi and I watch with fascination. Piper is confident as she lies there with her legs open, letting us watch.

"That's just mean," Alexi says.

Piper laughs at his torture and slides her fingers down, dipping into her own cunt and presenting them to Alexi. "A taste for the road?" She arches an eyebrow at him in question, testing him.

He grabs her wrist in his large hands and unceremoniously pops them in his mouth, cleaning them dry, and his pupils widen. When he releases her wrist, he groans and adjusts his hard cock before turning around and walking out of the room mumbling about how we're the death of him.

I grin down at Piper and give her a kiss before leaving for the day.

---

The first game in San Jose has my nerves completely shot. Thank God for Alexi, or I would probably be curled in a ball having a panic attack about seeing my brother and the importance of this game. Sure, I had some nervousness during all the other playoff games, but this is the fucking big one.

Not to mention these are going to be my last games as a professional player. Though I'm ready for the next phase of my life, this feels bittersweet.

It doesn't help that I'm so over all the medication. My stomach has been hurting, and I feel so ridiculously tired; I'm not sure how I'm functioning. I'm constantly on the edge of needing a nap. At first I thought I was going to maybe go into heat again, but I haven't been nesting, and even though I pushed my first heat by such a significant amount of time, I don't think I would go into heat this soon.

It must just be the overexertion, being bonded and still on suppressants. I don't know. All I know is that I feel unsettled.

"You feeling okay, *sólnyshka?*" Alexi asks me while we wait to go on the ice for warm-ups.

"I'll be fine," I say, trying to motivate myself for this game. There's no time to be tired or to have a fucking tummy ache. I've got to go out there and perform, I can't let this team down.

Alexi fists my jersey the way he always does. If you were walking by, you might think it was aggressive. But I know it's Alexi's way of claiming me without being too over the top with it while we're at work.

He leans in so only I can hear his words. "I'm not just your captain, I'm your Alpha on and off the ice. You tell me when something's wrong, understand?" Alexi can joke around a lot, which I love. But when he's serious and intense, I nearly can't contain myself. He looks at me like he's analyzing me, and I sigh.

"I'm just tired, my stomach fucking hurts, and I just want to be home with Piper."

He gives me a soft smile and looks around. Instead of

hugging me, his hand comes to the back of my neck, and he squeezes softly.

"Thank you. Let's get you some Tums and Tylenol. After we win the game, we'll call our girl." I nod, knowing a call won't be enough. With the two first games being here, I'll be farther away from her than I'd like.

We're leaving the tunnels to go on the ice, and Johannson hands me my water bottle.

"Thanks, man."

"No problem," he says, skating out with me by the goal, both of us stretching and warming up with the team. I toss my water bottle in the back of the net. The effects of the Tums quickly wear off as I look at the packed stadium.

But what really makes my stomach sink is seeing my brother across the ice doing the same stretches as me.

While he hasn't outed me, there's this deep sick part of me that needs to beat him during this series. I don't know why I can't seem to stop this competition I have with him. But it's either going to be me or him with the Cup at the end, and I need it to be me.

# CHAPTER 36

Somehow we're up in the series 3–1. The Sharks took the first win, and if I'm being honest, Owen wasn't playing his best that game, and I was also distracted. But since then, we've been able to hold the lead. One win in San Jose and now two back to back wins at home.

But unfortunately, we're back in California. I'm hoping that we take the win here, but Owen seems off again. He's cutting the crease and stretching prior to the game. I never gave much thought to goalie stretches previously, but now I have to use all my strength to remain focused on my own task.

Piper and Owen's doctor seem confused by why he's so exhausted, but they are hopeful that once we're able to wean him off of his medication and he isn't doing such a high stress profession, he will have more energy and not feel sick all the time.

Knowing that he isn't feeling well eats away at me. I just want to make everything better. I guess that's the story of this pack, me wanting to fix everything all the time. But sometimes there are things I can't make better, and I need to learn to get over it.

Mikael skates next to me, leaving a wave of ice behind him as he breaks. "Your boy all set?"

I'm not sure what Charlotte's pack knows, but we don't vocalize it. Even if they know Owen's designation like their Omega does, they haven't said anything.

"Yeah, he's good."

"We're up by two, so if we don't win this game, we'll still be okay," Mikael says, and I narrow my eyes at him.

"Did you hit your head?"

"No, I'm just being nice."

"Well, it's fucking weird. Stop it."

Mikael shakes his head. "When I'm mean, I get yelled at, and now I'm too nice, and I'm weird. Can't win."

"I prefer you being an asshole. So bring that Martel out for the game, yeah?"

He rolls his eyes and skates away. Shoving Nilsen as he skates. Nilsen just grins and pushes him back against the boards.

I take a deep exhale, and as weird as Mikael's words were, they ring true. Of course I'd like the series to end now, take the Cup, and move on. But if we don't win tonight, we have a home game for game six. As long as we don't fuck it up, it's going to be hard for the Sharks to come back at all in this series.

We just need no injuries, and I need to make sure that Owen is healthy and can handle the pressure. We can do this.

———

We lost miserably. Owen played his worst game yet. It was so bad that coach pulled him and put Johannson in his place, which didn't help much. We lost four nothing and the whole team is feeling it.

There's still optimism rippling through the team, but the tension riding Owen is high. I keep quiet on the plane ride home, but I make sure to touch and reassure him in every non-verbal way possible. He doesn't shrug off my touch, which I'm grateful for, but he doesn't seem eager to talk either.

Thankfully, the tension falls away as he falls asleep the rest of the ride home. The rest of the team doesn't take the loss hard. We had a three game winning streak, and this is all a part of being a professional athlete and making it to this level.

No one blames Owen, and I'm thankful. Mostly because if anyone decided to talk shit about my Omega, I would probably find myself in jail or at least suspended from the NHL.

I thought at one point I'd get into a physical fight with Owen's brother, but the other Alpha seems different than I thought.

The man is definitely an asshole, but when it comes to Owen, he almost seems… sad. There wasn't a brawl like last time, and they didn't even speak during the game. But there's definitely still some major strain there.

I want to make it better.

I'm tired of Owen and Piper hurting and it being out of my control. It feels like the end of the season marks the end of all of our problems, and I'm yearning for it. I've worked so hard, beaten my body to shit, haven't had a solid relationship in nearly two decades. I'm so fucking ready to sail for this next phase of my life.

Owen wakes up enough to walk himself to my car, where he promptly passes out again. Once we get home, he doesn't stir when I carry him back to the house. While I can carry him over my shoulder, the man isn't light, and when I think about carrying him up to the nest—I give up, instead carrying him to Piper's room. She's sitting on her bed with her laptop when I lay him down and tuck him under the sheets.

Immediately, her hands are on his forehead, checking his temperature.

"He didn't look good out there," she says softly.

I shake my head and sigh. "I don't know what's going on."

She looks me over and tilts her head. "What about you?"

"What about me?" I say, shrugging my shoulders and sitting by her feet on the bed.

"You look tired too."

"It's part of the job."

"Do you want a massage?" My head jerks to her, and I raise a brow before giving her a smirk. "Not a happy ending massage," she says, rolling her eyes. "A normal one, to stretch out your muscles."

I give her a skeptical look but nod my head. I'm definitely not turning down an opportunity to have her hands all over me. She closes her laptop and places it on her nightstand and directs me to lie stomach down on the bed. I do as I'm told and jostle Owen a little in my movements, but he doesn't even stir.

Piper straddles my back, slightly sitting on my ass as she starts using her hands and arms against my back. I can't help the ridiculous noises she rips from my throat with each movement. My muscles are tighter than I thought, and she expertly finds all the knots in my back and kneads them with her thumbs at each opportunity.

"This feels so good, thank you," I tell her.

"You're welcome. It's nice to take care of you for a change."

I groan and just let her hands do their magic. If this is Piper's way of taking care of me, I wholeheartedly accept.

"I feel like you've been holding out on me."

She leans forward, and she's nearly pressed against my back as she whispers in my ear. "I don't think I could deny you anything, Alpha."

"Is that so?" I say with my face pressed against the pillow.

She hits a spot so good in my shoulder I can't help but to groan.

"Yeah, you deserve the world."

I shake my head and shift my body so that I can roll over while keeping her straddled over me.

"I have everything I want right here," I say, nodding my head to Owen who sleeps peacefully. I grab Piper's hips and stroke my thumbs over her soft skin.

"Well, if you ever want anything from me, all you have to do is ask," she says. The words are so reminiscent of the ones we tell Owen. To be honest and upfront about his needs. I'm so concerned about my pack that sometimes I feel like all I need is for them to be happy.

"Will you take my last name?" I ask her quietly. Once I bond with Owen and we register as a pack, I want it to be pack Bandnin, but I'm not sure how Piper feels about that, also being an Alpha. Not to mention she's a goddamn doctor and all the paperwork of changing her information.

She smiles down at me, her hands landing against the pillow on each side of my head. "I would be honored to become a Bandnin. I kinda like that you're claiming me," she says with a smirk.

"In any way I can," I joke, and she leans down and kisses my cheek.

"I'm ready for the beard to go."

"Hopefully one more game," I say, and she nods her head.

"One more game," she agrees.

———

The locker room is electric with excitement and nerves. I've been here before, I've won the Cup, but I'm still on edge. My heart rate is elevated, and I feel jittery, ready to get on the ice.

Owen looks like he's about to throw up.

He's fully dressed in his gear, sitting on the bench, and I come sit next to him. Our arms and thighs touch as I speak.

"What do you need?"

"I don't know," he says softly.

"Are you going to be sick?"

"I think it's just nerves. Once we get on the ice, I'll be fine."

"Don't push yourself." He nods. "Seriously, if you start to feel too sick, you need to know when to stop."

"I've got this," he says, amping himself up.

"Fuck yeah, you've got this. We're going to win this game, and then I'm going to take your sweet ass home, and I'm—" I lean forward so only he can hear "—going to bite that soft little neck and make you mine."

He swallows and looks at me. His pretty blue eyes are soft, a lot of the tension rolling off of him. "You mean it?" he asks.

"I think I've been pretty fucking patient."

"Tonight though, you want that tonight?" he asks.

"We don't have to, we can wait. I can plan something and make it special."

"You'd want that, tonight?" he asks again.

"Yeah, I don't want to wait."

He smiles and bumps me with his padded shoulder. "I think that was what I needed."

God, I want to grip him by the jersey and bring his mouth to mine, but I refrain from doing so in the locker room. My need to win tonight's game was already high, but the promise of making him mine right after is everything.

Nilsen walks by us and pats Owen on the shoulder. Honestly, he treats Owen with the most kindness out of anyone on the team. I've wondered if it's because he's a defenseman and Owen is the goalie, or if somehow he knows. Part of me is bothered by him touching my Omega, but I hold it down. After tonight, we won't have to hide it anymore, we'll be whole.

"Ready to kick ass, Connery?" Nilsen says to him.

"Yeah, man. Let's take it all tonight."

"Fuck yeah!" Eli shouts from the locker room, which makes more of our teammates chime in, which starts a cacophony of noise in the small space. There are three loud bangs when the speakers come on. "We Are the Champions" blasts, and I grin, starting off the song.

Owen shakes his head, but with the superstitions on the team, he joins in. Every man on the team sings the song, and we sound terrible, but this is it.

I know it's not smart to get your hopes up, but I just know this is my last professional game, and singing this song one last time is what I needed. I'm going to miss it, the comradery, the jokes, and the sport itself. But as I look down at the blond on the bench next to me, I'd give it all up for him in a heartbeat.

I end the song with the obnoxious last line, and we all cheer, the clanking of gear and sticks as we leave the locker room and take the arena.

*Let's fucking go.*

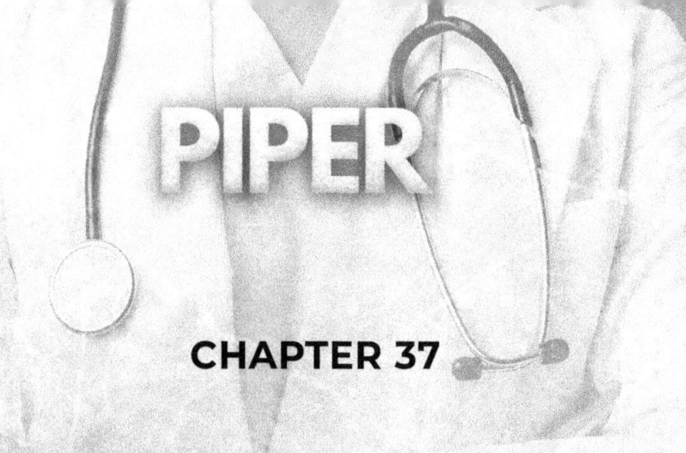

# PIPER

## CHAPTER 37

The arena is packed, and I'm lucky enough to be in the family box for the game. Charlotte dropped the kids off with her in-laws, and she sits next to Anders. Both of them are on the edge of their seats. I wonder if Anders feels like he's left behind, like he should be down there with his team. But then he looks over at my best friend and kisses her hair, and I realize that it's completely unfounded.

For the first time, I understand that. How a person can be the center of your world.

It hits me that I have that. Especially when my guys take the ice. I'm sure I'll miss this, being able to root for them and see them in their element. The way that Alexi takes someone to boards with ease, or watching Owen have complete focus and make a save when I couldn't even see the puck.

The crowd is losing their minds, and everyone is anxious for a win. A Stanley Cup win at home would be everything. Sloane takes her seat next to me and gives me a soft smile.

"Hey, Piper," she says and leans over, looking nervous.

"Hey, Sloane. Have you met Charlotte and her Alpha

Anders? Sloane is the coach's daughter, and she does some social media work for the team."

"Oh my God, you're the one getting Mikael to dance on PicTic?" Charlotte and Anders laugh, and Sloane blushes and nods her head.

"I'm actually surprised how much they're all willing to do."

"It's working, whatever you're doing. I mean, you've made people like Nilsen for fuck's sake," Anders says.

"He's just a misunderstood teddy bear," she says, perking up and watching the guys warm up.

"If you say so," Anders replies.

"Can you get Eli and Mikael to do a dance together?" Charlotte asks, conspiring against her pack.

"I'll see what I can do," Sloane agrees.

"Perfect," Charlotte whispers, looking down at her phone, and Anders shakes his head.

"*Kulta*, go call them. It's fine."

"I don't want to be annoying."

"You won't be annoying them. It's your first time away from the twins. It's okay, better to call now and not have any nervous energy down the bond."

Charlotte nods her head in agreement and goes to the back of the box to call Anders' parents.

Sloane is taking pictures and videos for some app, and Anders looks out into the arena attentively.

The game is intense and close. I sit on the edge of my seat the entire game. Between the loud screaming and clapping of the last ten seconds, I'm feeling so much pride and exhilaration for the Foxes and what they've accomplished.

But then I'm clutching my chest, feeling a pain incomparable to anything I've ever felt in my life. The pain feels like it's my body, but I know it's not. The pain belongs to the person who I have the deepest connection to—the person who owns part of my heart. There's only one thing I can think about, and it's getting to Owen as fast as I can. I look down at the ice, his helmet is off, and I watch as he falls face first into the ice.

Time ceases to exist, and I know I let out a pained scream before I'm on my feet and working my way down to him as the rest of the families are.

Just as fast as the pain starts, it stops completely, and my worst fear comes to life.

## CHAPTER 38

I feel good, better than good. The energy of the team and fans has me riled up. This is it, this is the game, this is everything. A game has never felt more exhilarating in my life. The tensions are high between us and the Sharks. Every now and then, I look across the ice to my brother. I swear he's been looking back at me, and I can't decide if I see the same resentment or pride.

Nilsen has a defenseman against the boards and scooping out the puck to pass to Martel. He doesn't let up as Martel passes the puck to his packmate, who scores the first goal of the game.

The cheering throughout the arena is nearly deafening as we celebrate the goal and take the lead for the game. Our chances go up with each goal scored, and I know the team is hungry for it. My energy is up, and my focus is solely on not letting a single puck in this fucking net.

Defense is on fire tonight; most of my saves have been easy gloved pucks. But as the game goes on the more desperate, they want to force game seven and take the win, just as much as we want to take the Cup tonight.

The moves get dirty, and more often than not, some stupid shit is getting called. They're trying to bait us into a fight and get a power play.

We hold strong, and eventually we break before the third period. When I skate off the ice, Johannson tosses me a bottle of Gatorade, and I catch it.

"Thanks, man."

"You're killing it out there," he says with a head nod. I'm not sure what flipped, but it seems like once we entered the playoffs, Johannson realized I was the best goalie for the team, and he stopped being such a dick. Goalie practice has been cordial, and we're more like a unit than enemies, it's been nice. It's more like what I had back with the Icemen. The backup goalie and I were close and cheered each other on. It's nice that we're ending the season on a high note and there's no longer this lingering tension between the two of us.

"Is there anything I should be working on?" I ask him, wanting an outside perspective. It's one of the biggest perks to having a backup who can help you specifically with the position.

"Just keep doing what you're doing," he says plainly.

I squirt the drink in my mouth and swish and swallow. This is it, the final countdown, the bookmark to an amazing season with the NHL.

Period three begins, and we're still only winning the game by one single point. It's a thin lead, and it's a scary fucking lead. We have twenty minutes to advance our lead or at least hold on to the one that we have.

The game is paused for the stadium to announce our fifty/fifty raffle and to pan around to different attendees at the game. I don't usually watch the screen, but something in me tells me to look up. When I do, I see my mom in a home-made jersey that is half the Sharks and half the Foxes. She's dancing with a pretzel in one hand and a beer in another. My stepfather George smiles up at her lovingly, and the wonderment of the moment only gets more real. Win or lose, I achieved what I wanted to, my mom is proud of me, I'm fucking proud of me, and I know my pack is overjoyed for me.

*I fucking did it.*

The cameraman goes to someone else dancing, and I look away, getting my head back into the game. I can't afford to get distracted now, not by anyone. I squirt my hair down with water and put my helmet back on as the game starts back up.

Eli and Alexi are passing the puck back and forth, trying to set up the shot. Eventually they find an opening, and Alexi slap shots the puck, shooting right past my brother and making this game two zero.

Alexi immediately skates my way, nearly knocking me over as we celebrate his goal. Nilsen, Eli, and Martel all come in for the dog pile to memorialize the next step toward our win. Once our teammates have dispersed, Alexi still has his arm around my shoulder, and we both look up at the box where Piper is.

She has a beaming smile on her face as she cheers for us. I feel her love and pride down the bond, and all it does is excite me more.

There are moments in your life that are core memories, the ones that follow you throughout the rest of your existence, and this is one of them. This accomplishment with the people I love next to me is everything.

The clock is waning, and we're about ten minutes into the period. Nilsen is following their right winger hard as he plows down the ice headed straight for me. He rears his stick back and shoots. The sound of the puck hitting the goal post and dinging is a relief. Defense hits the puck to the other side of the ice, and I take a moment to kiss the goal as a thank you for saving my ass.

Every moment ticks by, each minute feeling like the longest of my life. Until there's only about four minutes left. The Sharks pull my brother from the game, playing six men on the ice, and I'm more diligent than ever watching the puck.

Eli takes the puck from one of the Sharks players and pulls a long shot from our defensive side into the empty goal. He scores, securing our spot completely. The crowd goes insane, and my heart beats rapidly in my chest. The adrenaline of the game buzzes through me like an undercurrent, and it's like every nerve ending is on fire.

The next few minutes feel like a blur as we hold our lead and the final buzzer sounds.

Everyone is on the ice as we hold each other and music plays. Everything is so fucking loud it's nearly hard to think.

*We won the fucking Stanley Cup.*

Alexi is in my face, and we're holding each other, but I can't think. Something doesn't feel right. There's been no drop off of adrenaline; my heart is still hammering in my chest. My skin feels itchy, and all I want to do is peel off all this gear and take care of it.

I hold it together, thinking that it's just too much at once and my senses are fried. Alexi is speaking to me, but I can't hear, the noise being too much. Everything is too much.

My chest hurts, but I stay standing. There are some announcements as the Cup is brought out, and Alexi takes it first to do his rounds. He kisses it as he skates down the one half of the arena. The fans are loud, but it all sounds like a cacophony of noise in my head. It rattles around like one loud noise.

I can't think.

My chest hurts.

Alexi skates back to the team, and he hands me the Cup. Me. He hands me the Cup out of all the people on our team. My arms are weak, but I take it in my hands and skate the same direction he did. Holding the Cup up.

My vision is hazy. I can't see where I'm skating.

My chest hurts so fucking bad. I drop the Cup, and all I can feel is pain and the cold ice against my face.

# ALEXI

## CHAPTER 39

Winning the Cup with Owen is single handedly one of the best experiences of my life. I'm on a high after I hand him the heavy trophy and watch as he skates slowly over to his goal, and on his way back, I watch in absolute horror as he drops it and falls to his face.

I'm there immediately, and so is half the team. Family members are now on the ice to help us celebrate. With normal shoes on, Piper nearly busts her ass getting to us.

Medical has him flipped over; he's hardly conscious with his hand is gripped over his chest. I feel like I'm fucking dying as I look at him. What was one of the greatest moments of my life has suddenly turned to one of the worst.

Piper is barely functioning. Her hand is on his shoulder as the medical team calls an ambulance and discusses what to give him, getting a stretcher to get him off the ice.

"Owen, we're here. It's going to be okay," I tell him, and Piper sobs as she holds his hand. Owen isn't responsive, but he is breathing, even if it is labored.

He leans to the side and vomits. His face is clammy, and the medic is checking his pulse and his hands. I look at him questioningly as he glances at his fingernails and back at the medic.

"Give him Naloxone," the one medic says.

"He didn't do any drugs." Piper looks pissed at the medics, and I'm just feeling confused as to why they would assume he took something. Could some of his suppressants be doing this to him?

"It's our best bet before the ambulance gets here," the medic says, not saying that Piper is right or wrong, but trying to explain why they're doing what they're doing.

Owen groans as they administer it, and Piper chokes down a sob.

"I know it hurts. We're going to get you help, baby. Just hold on, okay?"

The ambulance is finally here, and Owen is getting carted off while they talk to Piper and I as they work on getting him stable. We go through the locker room and the back entrance to get to the emergency vehicle. It feels like time is moving at warp speed while also moving in slow motion.

"Is there anything else we should know?"

"He's an Omega, and he's on multiple medications."

We both go to shove ourselves in the back of the vehicle, and the medic shakes her head. "Sorry, we can only take one of you."

I meet Piper's bloodshot eyes and nod my head. She's already bonded to him, and she knows more about his medical history than I do.

"I'll meet you there," I tell her, and she nods.

"I'll take care of him."

The doors shut loudly, and I stand there in shock for a few minutes. The last half hour of my life seems to have happened at the speed of light. Some of my teammates approach me to get an update, but I'm in the locker room getting changed and collecting my things along with Owen's.

"Whatever you need, cap, just let us know," Eli says, a soft expression on his face.

"Seriously, let us know when he's okay," Mikael says.

"Do you need a ride?" Nilsen asks, and I nod my head. I can't think right now, let alone drive myself to the hospital.

I get other words of encouragement from the coaching staff and players. Noticeably, Johannson says nothing. If anything, he looks almost guilty.

I pocket that information for later. The only thing I'm worried about right now is getting to Owen. He has to be so scared and in pain, and I'm just here. I should have said fuck it all and bonded him regardless of the repercussions. I just wanted to make things easier for him during the season. But now I regret not marking him as mine. Maybe I would have noticed something was off?

Maybe not, Piper would have been in tune with him.

I feel so hopeless and worthless as an Alpha at this moment. All I want to do is make everything better. Nilsen is quiet as he drives me to the hospital. It's a swirl of color and lights, and the only thing I can think about is what if he's not okay. What if he had a fucking heart attack, what if this is the end.

Nilsen is the one to break me out of my panic.

"Your Omega is going to be fine, cap."

I swirl my head over to him and blink. Piper told the medics, but no one else was around. He shrugs his shoulders at me and sighs.

"I'm pretty sure the whole team knows."

"The whole team?"

"He hid his scent pretty well, but all the signs were there. I think we all agree that he's a good fucking goalie, so we didn't care."

I scrub a hand down my face and tug on my beard. God, I'm ready to cut this shit. "He… he didn't look okay."

"He's tough, and he's in good hands. They will figure out what's going on with your Omega."

I break.

I can't remember the last time I cried, maybe when my dad passed a decade ago. But I can't hold it in. I haven't even told Owen how much I love him, how much happiness he brings me, how I can't picture a world without him. I'm completely rendered speechless by the fear of losing him.

"Fuck," Nilsen mumbles next to me, but he doesn't say or do anything else, and I'm grateful. I'm not afraid of showing emotion in front of someone, but of all people, Bram Nilsen isn't the one I imagined.

He pulls around to the hospital entrance and hands me my stuff, which I take quickly and get out of the car.

"Let us know if you need anything, cap."

I nod and head through the doors and go to reception. It's all a blur as I give them his name and she takes me to a waiting room. I see Piper with her face in her hands as she cries, and my stomach drops.

"Is he?" I ask, but it's barely audible. Piper's red and watery eyes meet mine, and she shakes her head and motions for me to sit down next to her.

"He's having a procedure done," she says softly.

"Surgery?" She shakes her head and looks at me softly before she starts to explain.

"Opioids were in his system."

"We would know if he took something besides his normal medication," I say, interrupting her, and she nods her head.

"I agree, but he's in too much pain to talk about it. It

doesn't add up. But it seems like the amount he took and possibly in combination with some of his other medication developed an arrhythmia."

I don't bother asking for more information, but Piper must realize that I need more clarification.

"His heart is beating too fast. I thought he was having a heart attack, but luckily it didn't get that bad. They're trying to regulate his heartbeat so that doesn't happen, and they will also flush out his system. I know he wouldn't have risked his career on this, Alexi."

It feels like my brain isn't keeping up. All I can think about is seeing Owen, and now that I'm in front of Piper, I need to take care of her too. Our hands are interlocked as she squeezes my hand.

"I felt everything through the bond. He was shocked, scared, and in so much pain." She tears up again, and I take her in my arms. Both of us are a fucking mess over Owen being hurt and the fact that drugs he wasn't prescribed were in his system.

"He's going to be okay, he's tough," I say, repeating Nilsen's words from earlier.

"He is. They have to put him under for the procedure, and I can't feel him. I can't feel him anymore," she says, her tears soaking my shirt as I hold her close to my chest. My own emotions are coming to the forefront as I let go of my fear as well, trusting Piper to have me just as much as I have her at this moment.

We just hold each other, all the fear and unknown of Owen's condition eating away at us. Lori and Max both join us in the hospital room. Piper holds Owen's crying mother and consoles her even though she's nearly losing her shit as well. Max is quiet, but I can tell he's scared but just keeping it bottled up.

I'm not sure of all the details on why Owen and Max aren't close, but it's been evident in our small interactions that Max does love Owen—loving Owen is easy.

"I told him he would get fucking hurt. He never should have been hiding his designation. Fuck, Owen," his mom says. I don't think her foul mouth will ever be normal, but she gets it all out.

"Lori, I don't know what's going on, but I don't think this is Owen's fault. I'm diligent with him and his medication. Something isn't right."

"What do you mean?" Max says, the first time he's spoken since he got here.

"I don't know. I just know Owen, how seriously he took this, how good he was with his medication. This isn't adding up."

"You think someone did this to him?"

Piper shrugs, but the look on her face tells me everything. She thinks someone did this to our Omega.

"I'll fucking kill someone if they did this to my brother," Max says. Piper and I must give him a strange look, and he rolls his eyes. "Owen is the one with a problem, not me. I love my brother, and I want the best for him always. Can you think of anyone who would do this? Or anything out of the norm?"

Piper looks at me. "His fatigue during the third period at some games, his stomach. We were wondering if his medication was having some adverse effects."

"You knew something was wrong?" Max cuts us a glare, and Lori puts a calming hand on his forearm.

"It was just fatigue, and his stomach would hurt, but he was always adamant that he was fine. His physician even said that we were so close to the end of the season, and he would be weaning off his medications so we could just see if anything got worse."

"When would he start to feel sick?" Max asks

"Right around the third period," I say, which was always when he seemed to get the most tired and feel the worst. Sometimes it was different, but that was usually it.

"Someone on your fucking team did this," Max accuses, and my first thought is to tell him to fuck himself, but when I really think about it, it's the only thing that makes sense. If Owen wasn't taking the drugs, someone had to have been giving them to him.

"Fuck," I groan, and Max stands and paces around the waiting room.

"I should have never let him play. I should have told them he's an Omega," he says, shaking his head. "This never should have happened."

All four of us are riddled with guilt, feeling like we had a part in why Owen is in the hospital. A kind looking nurse in baby-blue scrubs approaches us and tells us that we can come back to Owen's room.

We're all solemn as we follow her to Owen's room in the Omega wing. His skin is pale, but he sleeps peacefully on the bed as we all approach, taking seats and just staring at him.

Suddenly, a male and female Alpha enter the room wearing their scrubs. The woman gives Piper a look before paying attention to the main physician.

"Mr. Connery is stable, and we are monitoring his heart rate significantly. We have regulated his heart rate and are currently using saline and other medications to flush out his system. He tested positive for opioids, and we're assuming that they were off the street. He also broke his nose on the ice with his fall. As long as he refrains from further drug use and takes medications as prescribed, he should have a full recovery."

There is a large sigh of relief, and Piper stands to speak to the male Alpha. He answers a few questions before leaving the room. The female Alpha stays behind and looks between Piper and Owen.

"Interesting," the female doctor says.

"You shouldn't even be here, there's nothing he needs neurologically."

"Just had to see the fall of the famous Dr. Blake. No longer in the surgical program and an addict Omega, looks like you win."

Piper breathes through her nose. If there's one thing I know about Piper, it's that there is a temper deep down in her. Especially when it comes to Owen.

"Shuana, if you don't get the fuck out of my face right now, I'm going to kick your ass." The doctor's eyes go wide, and she opens her mouth to spew more vitriol, but Piper takes a step forward. I'm up in a flash and my arm is wrapped around her waist.

"Owen is going to wake up soon. If you hit her, you'll be kicked out."

"Raincheck, then," Piper says, looking at the doctor and coming back to sit next to me.

"Oh, you're just perfect for Owen," Lori beams, the first smile out of all of this bullshit, and I can't help but to laugh. This woman is proud of Piper threatening to beat Owen's doctor's ass. The laughter is contagious until we're all laughing.

That is until a bright pair of blue eyes is blinking and looking around the room.

# OWEN

## CHAPTER 40

When I open my eyes and I'm not in the middle of the stadium holding the Cup, I blink in confusion. The overhead lights are harsh, and I wince at the throbbing pain in my head, nose, and wrist. My wrist is covered in a bunch of tubes, and I see a massive bag of saline and who knows what the fuck else.

I go to touch my nose, and a soft hand stops me from touching.

Seeing Piper gives me so much comfort. Alexi touches my leg, and I close my eyes and sink further into the bed.

They're here, they're here, and they're fucking scared, at least from what I sense from Piper.

"What happened?" I ask. My voice is dry and cracks.

My mom pushes my hair from my face and holds out a glass of water with a straw.

"What happened is you scared the fuck out of all of us, and I'll never know a day of peace again," my mother says, being dramatic as always.

"Do you remember anything?" Piper says sweetly. I

squeeze her hand and close my eyes as I try to remember everything that happened.

"I felt good for most of the game, but around the second part of the third period, my stomach hurt, and I felt dizzy. I was excited when we won, but that's all a blur. I just remember my chest hurting, I couldn't think straight, and then I fell." I go to touch my nose again, and Piper stops me.

"You broke your nose when you fell."

"Do they know why I fainted?"

Everyone looks around the room at one another, like none of them wants to tell me what happened. I look over to Max of all people; he won't sugar coat it.

He swallows and nods. "Opioids. They think you were taking drugs."

"I wouldn't. Piper is so strict with my meds, I would never risk this."

"I think someone drugged you," Max says, and Piper squeezes my hand.

My eyes close on their own accord, and I want to touch the bridge of my nose, but I stop myself. "Someone did this to me?"

"That's really all we can come up with," Piper says softly. Her hands are touching me everywhere. I can feel her relief down the bond still mingled with fear.

"Did anyone on the team know you were an Omega, or did you have a problem with anyone?" Max asks, not pussy footing around the situation.

"I don't think anyone knew."

Alexi clears his throat and rubs the back of his neck. "Apparently everyone knew."

"What?" I ask, wondering if it's because I'm out of it or if I heard him correctly.

"Nilsen said it to me in the car. He already knew. If he

pieced it together, I'm imagining more people on the team did."

"Do they know specifically what they gave me?" I ask.

"They don't, but now I'm concerned if you were given something more." Piper taps her thumb on my knuckle. "A few years ago, Charlotte was drugged by the guys' manager. It set off her heat and made her disoriented. Could that have been the goal?" she asks, looking around. I can tell how angry this train of thought makes Alexi and Piper both.

"All I know is I'm going to kill whoever did this to you, honey," my mother says, lightening the mood.

"When can I leave?" I ask.

"I'll find out," Piper says, leaning forward and kissing the side of my head.

Alexi moves and takes her place holding my hand. Max watches with… jealousy? No, there's no fucking way Max is jealous of me.

"Did we really win the Cup?" I ask, still feeling confused.

"We did," Alexi says plainly.

"I ruined the celebration."

"You didn't ruin shit," he says, pushing back my hair and kissing me in the same place as Piper.

"God, you're all so cute," my mom beams, and I shake my head.

"Mom, I'll call you as soon as we know something."

She purses her lips but looks over at my large Alpha and sighs. "Fine, I need to go find George anyway." My mom kisses my cheek, being careful of my nose, before pointing in my face. "If you ever scare me like that again, I'll kill you myself," she says before kissing me again. She gives Alexi's arm a squeeze before leaving.

"Can I talk to my brother?" Max asks, looking at Alexi and not me.

Alexi looks down at me, and I give him a nod. He squeezes my hand before leaving. I cross my arms over my chest and don't look right at Max.

It's silent for a few moments, but he breaks the silence. "Seriously, you just beat me in the Stanley Cup finals, and you want to act like I still have everything you want?"

My lips part as I look over at him. I really look at him, dark circles under his eyes, worry written over his face.

"Are you done hating me?" Max says softly. "I know I can be an asshole and I was a show-off when we were younger, but I just want to be in your life. If anyone is jealous, it's me."

I'm rendered speechless for a moment as I stare at my brother. "What?"

"You're an Omega, yet you achieved something I haven't yet. You're a great goalie, probably better than me. But besides the hockey stuff, you have them." He points his finger toward the door.

"You're jealous?" I ask, feeling completely flabbergasted.

"Yeah, I'm fucking jealous. You have a pack, a national title, and you did it all with the odds against you."

"I didn't think you wanted a pack."

"How would you know? You've spent your whole life hating me."

"I don't hate you, Max." He gives me a glare, and I shrug my shoulders. "Okay, maybe I felt jealous and competitive, but I didn't hate you."

"You thought I would tell on you to the NHL; you think the worst of me. Everyone does." He looks away, and it's the first time I see my brother as a vulnerable, real person. Not this pillar of success I've created in my mind. The goal was always to be better than him, and guilt crushes me at the realization that I've missed out on actually getting to know him because I was always so envious of what he had.

"I'm sorry, Max." It's the only thing I can think of to say.

"I don't need an apology. I just want to be a part of your life."

"Okay."

He arches a brow at me. "That it? Okay?"

"What do you want from me? It's not like we'll be competing against each other in hockey anymore."

He blinks at me. "You can't let this stop you. You're good, you deserve to be in the NHL, fuck the designation limitations."

"It's not about that."

His brows furrow, and he crosses his arms over his chest as he sits in the uncomfortable hospital chair.

"Then why? Why would you leave?"

"I have something more important now."

"You're leaving the NHL for your pack?" he asks, confused. Bless my stupid brother. I give him a small smile and nod.

"For my pack and for me. I've spent so long shoving down who I am. I wanted to be an Alpha in the NHL, and I pushed my body to the brink to achieve that. I want to be unmedicated and find out who I really am."

"So what, you're just going to be a stay-at-home Omega?" he asks, not being judgmental, but I still laugh and shake my head.

"I don't know what's next really, I just know Piper and Alexi are my whole world. Especially after this bullshit." I hold up my wrist covered in wires. "I need to rest, find myself, and just be."

"Okay, little brother."

"Maybe we could hang out during your off season."

He nods and rubs the back of his neck. "Yeah, especially since I don't know where I'm going."

"Your contract is up?"

"Yeah, I'm a free agent this year. I don't know if the Sharks want to pay to keep me on the team or not."

"They'd be stupid not to." My brother's eyes widen at the compliment, and I watch him hold back a smile.

"We'll see."

Piper and Alexi walk back in the room hand in hand. I smile at their affection for each other. I never gave much thought to pack life and handle not being the center of attention all the time. But I fucking love it. I love them individually, together, as well as us as a pack.

I should probably feel more disturbed about the whole situation, but it seems to have had the opposite effect. I feel grateful to still be here and have the life that I have. That my pack is here for me and that they love me and we will get through this and that I've made some sort of amends with my brother.

I'm sure that when the reality of everything hits me, I might feel more anger toward what has happened to me. But right now, all I can feel is happy to be alive and to be surrounded by people who love me.

"What's the verdict?" I ask Piper.

"They want to keep you overnight to monitor your heart rate and do some more blood work in the morning."

"What about him being drugged?" Max asks, and Alexi gives him a curt nod.

"I reached out to coach, and everything is a clusterfuck right now, but we'll get it sorted."

"Why is it a clusterfuck?" I ask him, and he shakes his head.

"Let me worry about it, you just worry about feeling better." I give him a glare, but I'm feeling tired. This has been enough excitement to last me a fucking lifetime. I haven't even had a moment to really let it sink in that my name is going to be engraved on the fucking Stanley Cup.

I'm trying to stay awake, but as Piper strokes my hair and Alexi kneads my calf, I'm all but lost to the need to finally let my body have the rest it deserves.

———

Mikael and his whole pack come to the hospital. Partly because Alexi needed his car and neither him or Piper have left my side the entire time. Max went back to California with his team, and my mom is still at her hotel with my stepdad.

When their faces are grim as they walk into my hospital room, I know something went down.

"What is it?" I ask, and none of them answer right away. Of all people, it's Charlotte who gives me a plain answer.

"The part about them trying to figure out who on the team did this to you, or how the NHL is freaking the fuck out over you being an Omega?"

"The NHL knows?"

Alexi sighs and scrubs his face. "It was leaked, but we don't know by who."

"Not gonna lie, Connery, the whole team knew your designation," Eli says in a calm tone, his hand laced with his Omega.

"Everyone?" I ask for clarification.

"Even coach apparently," Alexi says.

"He knew? But he didn't kick me off the team," I say in surprise.

"You're a fucking good goalie, and his daughter is an Omega. I'm sure he understands the need for bodily autonomy and being able to follow your passion," Eli says. My respect for Coach Applegate just went through the roof.

"I put my body through so much trying to hide it," I say, feeling annoyed that I didn't do a good job hiding the secret anyway.

"You did the right thing. If another team would have noticed, they would have outed you right away," Mikael says.

"What do they want to do?" Everyone looks around the room, and even Charlotte is quiet. "What do they want to do?" I ask again.

"They're considering stripping us of our win," Alexi says quietly.

"They can't do that."

"I don't think they will. They're just pissed a stupid rule was broken. I'll take care of it."

"You shouldn't have to take care of it. It was my choice to hide my designation. If anyone should be punished, it should be me."

"They aren't taking this from you," Alexi says.

"They aren't taking this away from us," I agree, and every head in the room nods. I thought that I would retire from hockey in peace, but it seems like there's more work to do.

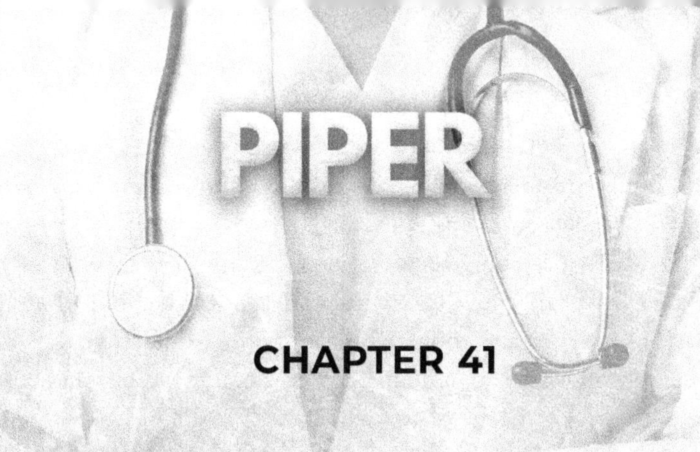

# PIPER

## CHAPTER 41

"Are you sure about this?" I ask Owen for what feels like the seventieth time.

"I'm not letting them drag the team down for my choices."

"Right, but the rule was discriminatory in the first place. I just don't want you being a martyr when you don't have to be."

I pull his tie up and straighten up his suit. He looks impeccable. His recovery has included lots of sleep and taking it easy, but he's adamant that this is something he needs to do.

"They're going to ask about the incident."

"I know."

"And?"

"I've got it covered," he says, cupping my face and giving me a gentle kiss. "I'm not going to break, Piper." He says it so softly, and it takes everything in me not to break apart right now and here.

"I felt all of it, you know. I just… I can't let anything bad happen to you ever again."

"I know, baby," he says with a grin, and I shake my head.

"That's my line." He sighs and wraps his arms around me. Without his suppressants, his scent is thick and comforting.

"This is something I need to do."

"Okay, I trust you," I say wholeheartedly. There are three people I trust with my life and that's Alexi, Owen, and Charlotte. We head to the room where the Foxes hold their post game interviews. The whole team is here in suits waiting patiently. Owen meets Alexi, who takes his hand, and they head to the stage to sit together.

I feel on edge because we still haven't had closure on who put Owen in this position in the first place. We have suspicions of course but no concrete evidence.

Reporters start hurling questions at Owen, and Alexi looks incredibly pissed like he might toss the table when Owen clears his throat.

"I think I'd like to speak first, and then we can keep any questions for last." There's murmuring throughout the crowd, but they all seem to lower their voices and let Owen speak.

"The reports of me being an Omega are true. I hid my designation from the NHL with a combination of suppressants, deodorizers, and other legal methods. No one on the team knew I was an Omega when I was recruited from the Icemen."

He adjusts in his seat, and I know that Alexi has a calming hand on his thigh to help him get through this. God, I love that man.

"I was driven to hide my designation because the NHL does not permit Omegas to play. I have to ask why that is? Is it because you think Omegas only have the purpose of being in a pack? Is it because I'm not physically strong enough? Or is it because I would be a distraction to other Alphas? It sure isn't because I have any advantages over the Alphas and Betas in the league.

"I have had to work ten times harder to gain the muscle I have now. Most of the Alphas on my team are exhausted after games, but sometimes I could barely even walk. I put my body through Hell to get to where I am today because I love this sport, and I knew that I would be great if given the chance. Omegas are not a designation that can be pigeonholed, and frankly, I'm sick of the biases in our society when it comes to designations and professions.

"I definitely wasn't a distraction on the ice as no one else even knew about my designation. So I have to ask if the NHL is mad because they're being called out for their prejudice finally. Or is it something else?"

He looks so fucking confident up there as he speaks. Pride swells in me over his confidence. He takes a brief pause before beginning again.

"My being on the team, if anything, was a disadvantage. For the NHL to even discuss the possibility of stripping us of our title is a demonstration of cowardice and an effort to cover up the real problem in professional sports. In our society, Omegas are perceived as delicate and desirable, and I'm telling you that we are far more than that. I believe I proved that a week ago when I was a part of us winning our first Stanley Cup. I will not stand by and let my team or my designation get dragged in the mud. I will remove my name from the Cup before I let any of the men behind me have their hard work stripped away, but I hope the league can understand where I'm coming from and understand the hurdles I overcame to play the sport I love so much.

"Hockey has been my life for so long, and I'm incredibly grateful to the Foxes and the NHL for letting me live out my dream. I hope that I've been able to open some minds and shed some light on my circumstances to help you understand that changes as a whole need to be made. Thank you."

Alexi smiles at him and rubs his shoulder. The questions are all over the place, and Coach Applegate takes control by pointing at reporters to have them ask their questions one at a time.

"Have you been medically cleared? What happened after you won the game?"

Owen sighs and looks around at his teammates. "I have been medically cleared. I had a heart arrhythmia that caused me to faint." He leaves out the part that it was possibly caused by one of his teammates.

"Are you attempting to return for another season?"

"No, this is the end of my professional career," Owen replies.

"If it weren't for you being outed for your designation, would you still play?"

"No, as much as I advocate for Omegas to follow their passions, especially in athletics, this has been extremely diffi-cult on my body, and I can no longer play at this level."

"Wouldn't you say that's a reason for Omegas not to be in the professional sector? You're advocating for the right, sure, but you just said yourself that your body can't handle it," the sleazy reporter with a cheap suit and a balding head asks.

"I played for the Icemen for nearly four years, and sure I didn't have as many issues with them as I did in the NHL, but I'm also twenty-four. Did you know the ECHL also prevents Omegas from joining, as well as most minor league sports? While still strenuous, playing for the Icemen was not as exerting as for the Foxes. Not to mention that ice hockey is one of the most physical and demanding schedules of all sports. So no, I don't see the parallel you're trying to make here."

I'm so impressed with Owen, the way he deflects or redi-rects each question. I swear if I didn't know him and was looking at him now, I would assume he was a politician or in public speaking.

"What are you going to do with your retirement?" the female reporter from MSN asks.

"I'm going to enjoy time with my pack and go from there."

The reporters go wild, wanting more information. But he waves them off, and Coach Applegate takes the stage and lets them know that questions are over. There is grumbling in the crowd, but they accept that the interview is over.

Alexi and Owen are whispering on stage, and I can only imagine what he's telling him. I'm smiling when a shoulder bumps into me.

"Sorry," he says.

It's Johannson, the back up goalie. The one Alexi and I suspect. We hadn't said anything to Owen yet because he's still having a hard time wrapping his head around the fact that one of his teammates drugged him. The outcome could have been so much worse. Even thinking about what could have happened makes me feel physically sick.

"Johannson, right?"

"Um, yeah."

"Are you excited to be starting goalie again?"

"I guess," he says, rubbing his freshly shaven jaw.

"All it took was putting a little something in Owen's water bottle. I hope you're able to sleep at night." I'm going completely off my gut and hoping that he's shocked enough that he backs himself in a corner.

His eyes go wide, and he shakes his head. "I didn't... I just wanted to make him tired."

*I see red.*

My fist connects with his jaw before I can even think, and I'm shaking out my hand as he cups his face. A large arm wraps around my waist and picks me up off the ground, so I can't take another step forward.

"What the fuck are you doing?" Alexi nearly growls in my ear.

"He admitted it. He is the one who was drugging Owen."

Suddenly I'm dropped and Alexi is pushing Johannson against the wall. Owen is in shock, I expect anger, but all I see is sadness. I take a step on his other side and hold his hand with my good hand, happy that I'm no longer planning on being a surgeon. Injuring your hand is a big no no.

Alexi has Johannson by the suit jacket as he pushes him against the wall. "You could have fucking killed him!" he screams in his face. Cameras are flashing, and teammates are rushing over to attempt to pull him off.

Johannson looks over at Owen, guilt written all over his face. "I really just thought they would make you tired and you would get pulled from the game and I'd get to play."

Alexi grips his jacket harder, pulling him away from the wall before banging him against the cement. His head makes an audible thud against the surface. As Alexi's hand slowly starts to wrap around Johannson's neck, I'm thankful for Coach Applegate, Mikael, and Eli intervening to pull him off of the piece of shit who dared to hurt my Omega.

Alexi's chest puffs up with each breath as his teammates tug him away, and Johannson sinks to the floor.

"I've already called the police," Coach Applegate says, looking down at the traitor. Clear disgust is written in his expression. "Connery, you good?"

"Yeah," he says softly, and their coach rubs his eye sockets with the palms of his hand.

"Winning the fucking Cup shouldn't be this fucking stress-ful," he groans as he looks back at my Omega. "You did good with the reporters today, but you're fucking crazy if you think

I'm letting them take your name off this win. You deserve it just as every member on this team does, probably even more for being the goalie. I'm not going to let anything else fuck up this win for you. Your name will be on the Cup, and this piece of shit is going to jail," he says in disgust.

"Thanks, Coach," Owen says softly, his eyes not leaving the other goalie who sits on the floor with his face in his hands. He squats down to get on his level, and the man looks at my Omega. I swear to God, if he tries anything, I'll end him. When I look over at Alexi, I can tell he's on the same page. "I would have done anything to make my dream come true. But I would have never harmed someone else. I hope you figure yourself out and find a way to live with what you did."

He doesn't forgive him or say anything else, he just stands and straightens out his suit jacket, looking at Alexi and me. "Let's go home," he says.

Alexi wraps an arm around his shoulder, and I take his hand in mine. All of us leave the stadium knowing that it's the last time either of them will leave as players for the Foxes. I know it's hard for both of them, but I can tell there's a lightness in their step, an eagerness to move on.

"How's your hand?" Alexi asks. I stretch out my fingers and wince, but movement is everything.

"Probably just bruised."

"I'd say we need to work on your violent tendencies when it comes to our Omega, but I don't think it will do much good."

I squeeze Owen's hand in mine for reassurance. "It sure wouldn't."

"You know that was way hotter than it needed to be, both of you," Owen says, and I shake my head.

"You can't go around saying things like that, you remember what your doctor said."

"Of course I fucking remember," he grumbles.

"Only a few more weeks."

"Yeah, well, tell that to my dick," he says, making Alexi and I laugh. "It's not funny. I've had a hard on twenty-four-seven, and he tells me no sexual activity until he knows my heart is good to go."

"That's right," I say, also feeling the strain of wanting to be with him, especially with how good he smells now that he's completely unmedicated and fully accepting who he is.

"I swear the universe is just fucking with us in making us go celibate again."

"I'm more than open to becoming the house fuck toy again," Alexi says with a smirk.

"I bet you are, big guy." He wiggles his eyebrows as we all get to the car and head home. A few things might be left in the air, but where we stand with each other seems more solid than ever.

---

It takes two weeks to get a decision from the NHL, but they don't change anything about the Foxes winning the Cup, and there are discussions of changing regulations regarding Omegas. My Omega helped make this change, and I'm not sure I've ever been more proud of a person in my life.

We throw a huge celebration at our home to celebrate, which is long overdue. Owen never got the chance to truly celebrate his Stanley Cup win, so we go all out. Everything is hockey themed and Foxes gear. The team is overjoyed at the celebration, and while I watch Owen smile and joke with the team, I can't hide my own smile.

He used to be so closed off, so afraid of being who he was meant to be, when he was perfect all along. I catch Alexi watching him the same way I do, and it's at that moment that I can't wait for Alexi to bond with Owen, for the three of us to be connected.

Alexi must feel my gaze on him, then he puts his beer down and walks behind me, an arm wrapping around my collarbone as he kisses the side of my head.

"You know we wouldn't have made it here without you, right?"

"No, it was your team, how talented you all are."

"*Malyshka?*"

"Yeah?"

"Don't sell yourself short around me. You're a big part of why this happened. You may not have been on the ice, but you helped Owen get his meds regulated and supported the both of us. I love you for it, you know."

I kiss his forearm. "Are we going to be one of those sappy packs that is obsessed with each other and is always saying overly cute shit?"

"Yeah, I think that's exactly who we're going to be."

# ALEXI



## CHAPTER 42

Nervous doesn't even cover how I feel right now. You know when you hold something off for so long that the task becomes near daunting? That's how I feel about bonding with Owen. I want to make it special and memorable.

Piper wraps her arms around my waist from behind and squeezes. Her head is pressed against my shoulder blades in a show of support and comfort.

"It's going to be perfect."

I take a deep breath and turn around in her arms. "I just want it to be special, he deserves it."

She wraps her arms back around me, resting her head on my chest. "So do you, you know." Resting her chin on my chest, she looks up at me. "You deserve the world too, Alexi."

I don't say anything, instead I just lean forward and kiss her forehead. I might have went a little overboard in the nest, but Piper didn't say it was too much. There are candles every-where, including rose petals on the bed.

"I've gone overboard," I say, looking ridiculous in the room.

"You did, but he's going to love you for it."

"You sure you don't want to stay?"

"I'll come in after. You two deserve this moment together."

"But we're a pack."

Her hands glide over my chest, and she smiles up at me. "We are that, but as much as we're a pack, we also have our relationships between each of us. Enjoy your moment with our Omega, and I'll come in and join in the afterglow.

I push her hair from her shoulder, and part of me wishes I could mark her.

"I know exactly what you're thinking, and I already have plans."

I laugh and arch an eyebrow at her. "Oh yeah, care to share?"

"Mmm. I think I'll keep this a secret for now." Piper walks away, and I swat her ass as she leaves the room, and I follow, looking for Owen.

When we get down to the kitchen, I notice he's done a significant amount of cleaning. Right now, he's removed everything from the refrigerator and putting it back in.

"Owen?" Piper says, and he makes a humming noise. "Owen?"

"Yeah?" he says while still digging in the fridge.

"You alright?"

"Yeah, it just needed to be cleaned. It was bothering me." Piper gives me a look, and her eyes widen.

"I can finish that, baby. Why don't you go up with Alexi."

He gives Piper a look like she's absolutely not capable of rearranging the refrigerator. But then sighs. "Okay. Let me just go put a different shirt on," he says, and Piper and I look at each other.

"Do you want my shirt?" I ask, and his face lights up.

"Yes," he says immediately, holding out his hand. I grab

the neck of my shirt and take it off and hand it to him. As soon as he puts it on, he smells the collar and smiles. "Let me just get my phone, and I'll meet you up there."

"Okay, *sólnyshka*," I say with a smile. As soon as he leaves the room, I nearly whisper shout at Piper, "Already? How is he going into heat already?"

She shrugs and bites her lip. "I mean, he's fully off his meds, and he had his first heat so late. His body must be overcompensating. He's nesting, so I think he will be lucid for a bit. Definitely enough time for you to bond."

"You're sure he'll remember if we do it now?"

She smiles and takes my hand in hers and squeezes. "He will absolutely remember. Go bond our Omega. Stop working yourself up." I lean down and give her a kiss, which she returns eagerly. Once we part, I take a deep breath and turn. Piper smacks my ass as I head up the stairs, and I wonder again if I have gone completely overboard for bonding.

When Owen walks in the nest and his gaze sweeps over the nest, I wonder if he's just going to want to clean and rearrange now that he's nesting.

I'm so ridiculous.

"I can clean it up if it bothers you," I tell him, and he shakes his head.

"You did all of this for me?" I nod, and he smiles. "What exactly did you have in mind?" he says, coming to stand in between my legs on the bed. My hands wrap around the back of his thighs as I look up at him.

"I was thinking you and I would finally bond. That I'd finally give you my mark and make you officially mine. What do you think?" I shouldn't be as nervous as I am asking the question. I know he wants it, but so much has happened.

He doesn't use words, he just wraps his hands behind my neck, and his lips meet mine.

"I think that's all I need," he says between a broken kiss. I have to rein myself in, I want this to be special and memorable. I'm not sure if it's more for me or him, but it doesn't matter. All that matters is that this moment is for the both of us.

Owen bends back down to give me a kiss, and I start undressing him while our lips touch. His hands are cupping my face as he takes over the kiss. His tongue is the dominant one as he shows me how much he wants us to bond. I love how demanding he can get. Owen may be the pack's Omega, but he's also the one truly in charge of this pack. Piper and I would do anything for him.

My breathing hitches when I think about the fact that we'll all be connected once I bond Owen. We'll truly be a pack, and I'll carry a piece of them with me in every moment of my life.

I have his shorts and underwear off, and I tug on the hem of the shirt while we kiss, letting him know what I want. Owen quickly tugs my shirt over his head, and he is deliciously naked before me. It's been a few weeks since the season ended, and he's not as cut as he was during the season. I think I might even prefer this more, mostly because he's truly himself and no longer pushing his body to the limit. His muscles are still strong and defined, and I can't help but to lick the tense muscles on his abdomen, making him groan.

My hand wraps around his hard, weeping cock, and I squeeze lightly. His scent surrounds us, and all I want to do is taste him. I want Owen to take over every one of my senses.

"I think you have on too many clothes, Alpha," he says.

Pleasure ripples through me as he calls me his Alpha. It's always something I've wanted, but the timing was never right. Now I can completely commit to Owen, to being a proper Alpha, and I can't think of anything more precious than this.

"Why don't you help me with that, then?" I say, and he

smirks. He's working on my pants, and I shimmy up to help him and roll them down my legs.

"Much better," he says once we're both completely naked. I slide over on the bed, and he joins me, both of us lying down on our sides.

I cup his face and give him a smile that he returns. My attempt at trying to steady my hand is for naught as he covers my hand with his own.

"I want you to mark me where people can see," he says, and I blink at him. My heart is thumping in my chest, and all I can feel is absolute devotion for this amazing man before me. When I think about everything he has accomplished and overcame, it's hard to not be completely enamored with him. I'm still in complete awe of how he's mine.

My hand trails down the side of his face, grazing his sharp jaw. My thumb glides down his sleek neck, and my thumb presses against the side of his throat.

"Right here?"

His breathing hitches, and he licks his soft lips. "Yeah, right there."

I scoot closer to him, our bodies now touching completely. His dick is leaking pre-cum against my stomach, and I have to stop myself from trailing my fingers in the mess and tasting him. Instead, I crash his mouth against mine, tasting his tongue and pushing his body against mine.

My fingers dig into his toned back, and he whimpers into our kiss, his hips bucking into my body, begging for me to touch.

"How do you want it, Omega?" I kiss his cheek and move down to his throat where I suck the flesh into my mouth, my teeth only grazing the tender skin. "Should I stroke your cock until you're a writhing mess and bite you as you come all over me?" He shakes his head, and I smile. "No? Mmm... should I take you from behind? Fill up that tight, sweet ass with my knot and bite you while you come all over my fist?"

"That one," he says breathlessly.

"Are you slick and ready for your Alpha?" I ask him.

"Always, always want you. I always need you," he says, and that sends me over the edge. No more sweet touches and promising words. I need him right now like I need to fucking breathe.

I'm on my knees in an instant as I flip him on his stomach. He's so needy and eager as he gets on all fours, his ass glistening with slick, ready and waiting for me.

"You're such a good boy for me." I watch as his flesh pebbles at the praise. I'm usually patient, but with how ready he is, I don't fuck around with any foreplay. I line my cock up with his tight hole and slowly push inside of him.

Both of us groan, me from how tight and warm he is. Owen keens from the stretch and pushes his ass back against my pelvis. My one hand is tightly gripping his hip while the other pushes his shoulders against the bed.

Owen's hands are balled into fists as he clutches against the sheets. My speed is slow, making sure he adjusts, and maybe some part of me wants him to beg for it. Each thrust is tame and measured, just exploring his perfect body.

"Harder," he says, his cheek pressed against the mattress.

"Mmm, you can do better than that, *sólnyshka.*"

"I want you to fuck me harder, Alpha. Please."

"There's my good Omega. I love this needy ass." I accentuate the point by giving his ass a light smack. He moans against the sheets. Though he isn't as into it as Piper is, he likes a light smack from time to time. "You want my knot, Omega?"

"Yes, please."

I wrap my arm across his chest and heft him up so that his back is now pressed against my chest as I fuck him.

"Touch yourself," I tell him, wanting to come at the same time as him but needing him to get started.

Our flesh connects with each thrust, ricocheting throughout the nest. But the sound of him stroking himself is what sends shivers down my spine. It makes me fuck him harder, which only makes him increase his own speed. Wanting to be the one to make him come, I move his hand away and realize that I want to see his face.

I pull out, and he whimpers.

"Fuck, you drive me crazy," I say. "On your back." Owen listens immediately, lying on his back and spreading his legs. "Have I told you what a good boy you are?"

He smirks and strokes his cock again. I lick my lips before gripping his thighs and dragging him down the bed. I'm on my knees as I push back into him. His eyes close, and his lips part as he moans in relief.

"Yeah, I like seeing you like this. I need to see your pretty face when I make you come."

My thrusts pick back up, and I take over rubbing his needy length. His tight hole is wrapped around me like a vice as I push in and out of him. The noises he makes with each thrust and stroke of his cock only spur me on even more.

"Fuck, Alexi. I need you."

"You have me," I groan between each snap of my hips.

"I'm gonna…" he trails off, and his delicious scent is nearly choking me with how heavy it is. I push all the way inside of him, my knot expanding inside as my hips stutter. Both of us are panting, and I lean forward while still stroking him. We're panting against each other's lips as we attempt to kiss, but we're both so close to meeting our release.

Owen comes first, his cum dripping down my fist as his eyes close and his body shakes. His scent is the richest I've ever smelled, and I moan as my own orgasm reaches me. The instinct takes over as I lean over and kiss his throat before opening my mouth and taking the soft flesh between my teeth.

I mark Owen Connery as my Omega, and as the bond snaps in place while my orgasm subsides, I decide this is the best moment of my existence.

We're both nearly convulsing from the aftershocks and excitement. I lick my bond mark, cleaning it and staring at the wonder of what we just did.

I pull back and look into Owen's beautiful blue eyes, and I feel it all.

Owen's love, trust, devotion, and pure happiness. That's what's at the forefront of everything, but lingering to the side is Piper. All I can feel is contentment, eagerness, and excitement.

My lips part to speak before I close them and swallow. "I love you, Owen. Thank you for trusting me to be your Alpha and for the gift of being your bonded."

His eyes water, and he nods his head. "I love you too." The words are quiet, but he wraps his arms around my back, dragging me down, and I blanket his body. "I feel…" He burrows his head in my neck and inhales deeply. My skin is covered in goosebumps from the action, that he loves scenting me and that us bonding and completing the pack is just as monumental for him as it is for me.

"Complete?" I supply the word, and he nods against my throat.

"Pack Bandnin," he says with so much tenderness I swear I'm about to lose it. I'm not sure when I turned into such a sentimental sap, but I don't really give a fuck. I'm allowed to feel overwhelmed by this moment and just how amazing my partners are.

"You're sure?" I say pulling back so I can look at his face. I know I asked Piper if she would take my name already, but if

Owen wanted the last name to be Connery, I would change mine in a heartbeat.

"I'm positive," he says softly, and I have him wrapped back up in my arms. We lie there for some time, my knot holding us together and both of us just soaking in this moment. My knot releases us, and the mess that leaks out of him shouldn't make me want to fuck him all over again, but it does.

There's a light tap on the door, and it takes a moment to compute that it's Piper. "Come in," I say. A beaming Piper opens the door, and I can tell she cried, but not from sadness, from happiness.

She looks at both of us, and it seems like words leave her.

"Get over here, *malyshka.*" Her smile widens, and I'm not sure she could have gotten to bed any quicker than she does. Owen is squished between the two of us as she looks at this throat and smiles.

"He gets a visible one?" she says on a mock pout.

Owen shrugs but smiles. "If you want, you can bite me somewhere else?"

Piper just smiles and places a tender kiss on his new bond mark. When she kisses the place where I marked him, I have to rub my chest for a second, my heart too full to handle this moment.

"We're a pack," she says in awe.

"Always were, now it's official."

"Pack Bandnin," she says, trailing her finger over her own bond mark now. "I like it."

I grin over her, and Owen kisses her shoulder. "This moment is amazing, but this nest is a mess, and I'm going to need the two of you to help me clean it up," he says, breaking up the moment.

"Owen, baby, I think you're nesting," Piper says, and Owen shakes his head.

"No, I just had my heat not that long ago."

She pushes his hair off of his face and kisses his forehead. "I know, I think this is your body making up for lost time and adjusting to not being on any medication. It will be okay, we'll take care of you."

"I know," he says softly. We both look at him cautiously.

"You're not upset?" Piper asks.

"No, I'm ready to really let loose this time," he grins. "But first we need to clean all the shit up in here." He looks over at me with a soft expression. "I loved it for the moment, Alexi. I don't want you to think I don't appreciate it. But it has to go."

I just smile. My Omega feels comfortable telling me his wants and needs, and it's more than I could have ever asked for. "You've got it." I kiss him and get off the bed, still naked as the day I was born, as I blow out the candles, and Owen grimaces.

"Yeah, you need to air this fucker out. I'm going to take a nap. Come on, Piper."

He drags our beautiful Alpha to his room and leaves me to clean up my romantic gesture. I smile to myself, feeling like the luckiest Alpha who ever lived.

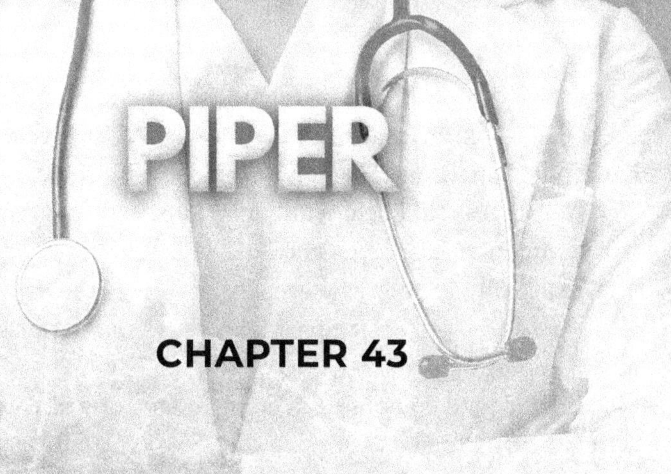


# CHAPTER 43

I almost forget that my last name is now Bandnin as the doctor calls us back to see Owen. The circumstances were completely different than the last time I was in a hospital setting waiting to see how my Omega was doing.

"You know, you're lucky I love you so much. Changing my name was a pain in the ass."

"I know, Doctor Bandnin," Alexi snarks, taking my hand in his.

When we walk in the room, Owen looks less than impressed and groggy.

"He may be a little out of it, but the procedure went well. It should help with his heat cycles, making them shorter and less frequent."

"Cream pies are going to take on a whole new meaning," Owen says, and I have to stifle a laugh in my elbow.

"The anesthesia should wear off soon, and he'll be good to go home."

"Thank you," I tell the doctor as Alexi and I go to his bedside.

"How are you feeling?"

"Like an old man just fondled my balls." This time, Alexi barks out a laugh, and I can't hide my own amusement.

"Well, this should help with your heats."

"Mmmhmm, can I get some Reese's?"

"Yeah, baby, as soon as we leave."

"No babies, just creampies," he says, and I squeeze his arms.

"Time to get you home. I'm going to take care of you until I start work on Monday."

"We're both going to take care of you," Alexi says, and I nod in agreement. Alexi and Owen have just been enjoying retirement so far. I can tell they don't like being cooped up in the house all the time, so I know it's only a matter of time until they plan out their next move, but for now they are content.

Everything has been moving at what feels like warped speed, and it seems like starting my new program has creeped up on me. It's bittersweet. I love being at home with the guys, but I'm someone who needs to work and have structure. I'm excited to go back to having a daily schedule each day.

"Doctor, I think I need my balls checked again," Owen says with hazy eyes, and I shake my head while Alexi laughs.

"Let's get you home."

"'Kay," Owen says, closing his eyes.

"I'm going to get his discharge paperwork," I say, and Alexi kisses the side of my head before I leave.

The nurse at the station hands me everything I need, and I'm filling it out when a familiar voice speaks next to me. I know a lot of people in this hospital, but this voice doesn't belong here.

When I tilt my head and see my father speaking with the head of cardiothoracic surgery, my heart sinks. I drop the pen on the counter and just stare. He doesn't break eye contact with the other surgeon throughout their conversation. Only when the other surgeon is done speaking does he look at me.

I'm not sure what I expect, a confrontation, another speech on how disappointed he is in me? But what I get is complete indifference, and I can't decide if that's better or worse. All I know is that when I look at him, I'm no longer seeking his approval. Who gives a shit what this heartless man thinks of me?

All I care about is my pack and my future. It's clear that Dr. Peter Blake is no longer a part of that future. I'm not sure what I thought about my father being in my life again after he unceremoniously made me homeless for not going down the path he wanted me to. I'm still not sure how I feel about the possibility of having my own children, but I know I would never have turned my back on my own.

I would never make a child feel like a constant disappointment or force them to do things that they didn't want to for my own selfish reasons. But most of all, I would never cut contact from my child simply because they wanted to carve their own path.

"Mrs. Bandnin, are you okay?"

My father looks at the nurse who just called my name and shakes his head in disappointment as he walks away.

"I'm fine, I'm done, thank you." I hand the clipboard back to the nurse and walk back to his room.

A few months ago, I would have broken down or done something self-destructive after the encounter with my father. But all I feel is a sense of closure, a door I can finally shut.

I no longer seek approval from Peter Blake, and as far as I'm concerned, the only family I have is my pack and Charlotte. Walking away completely from a toxic family isn't a light decision, and maybe it wasn't truly my choice. But accepting it and moving forward with my life is my choice.

"You okay?" Alexi asks. I'm sure he's feeling all the emotions down our shared bond with Owen.

"Yeah, everything is more than okay." I give him a kiss, and for the first time in my life, it's not a lie. I really am okay.

———

My first day at the Omega Wellness Clinic is like a kid going to Disney for the first time. I'm so in awe of all the physicians here and all the good work they are doing for Omegas and packs alike. It's so liberating knowing that I made the right choice and all facets of my life seem to be finally clicking together.

My main mentor is Dr. Gwynn, and I couldn't be more thrilled, his approach to patient care is amazing, and I know that I'll become a better doctor under his wing. I spend most of the first day learning the lay of the land and meeting everyone at the clinic.

This program will have a lot of hands-on experience as well as studying. There's so much to learn about Omegas, far more than I ever realized. It's actually quite shocking that some of what I'm learning isn't general knowledge. But that's the clinic's main goal, to spread awareness while also giving exploratory care to Omegas and support for packs.

I'm almost over-excited when Dr. Gwynn tells me that I'm going to be sitting in during a consultation. "I just want you to observe. No notes, this isn't a test, I just want you to see how we speak to patients and what a standard consultation looks like."

She holds the iPad in her hands as we walk into the room, and I see none other than Sloane Applegate sitting on the table waiting to be seen.

Her eyes don't widen, but she does give me a small smile.

I'm so thankful that she doesn't say she knows me as Dr. Gwynn starts the physical.

Mostly everything is standard as she discusses Sloane's weight, diet, pack status, and how she feels on a daily basis.

"Besides your standard physical, what brings you in today?"

Sloane looks at me and then back to Dr. Gwynn. "Can I get pregnant outside of my heat?"

Dr. Gwynn listens patiently as she responds. "The chances of you getting pregnant outside of your heat are low, but not zero. If you are with a Beta, the chances are extremely slim, but if an Alpha knotted you, the chances are small, but again not zero."

"Oh, okay then."

"We also did your blood work, and you're not pregnant."

"Oh, yeah, of course not. I haven't slept with him yet." I shouldn't be as curious as I am when it comes to who Sloane is sleeping with, but I am intrigued.

"Would you like to discuss birth control options?"

"No, I don't want to go on any medications."

Dr. Gwynn nods and looks over the iPad again. "You're on no suppressants, deodorizers, or birth control currently?"

"Very low dose of suppressant to be functional, but no to the rest," Sloane says proudly.

"You've also not had your first heat?"

That makes Sloane blush, but she nods her head.

"You've just turned twenty-one a few weeks ago, so the likelihood of your heat coming is high, especially not being on a higher dose of suppressants."

Sloane smiles weakly. "I know."

"Do you have plans for your heat?"

"I'm working on one right now," Sloane says.

"And what would that plan be?"

"I don't like to count my chickens before they hatch, but I think I know exactly who I want for my heat."

"Are they aware of this?" Dr. Gwynn asks.

"Not yet, but I'm working on it."

"I'm going to give you some literature on suppressants, Heat Haven, along with some other heat information so that you're prepared. If you are ever in danger, feel unsettled and need help, the clinic is here to assist in any way. I understand your decision to be unmedicated, but there are dangers with being fully unmedicated and unbonded."

"I'll work on the bonding part too." Sloane smiles at Dr. Gwynn, who smiles right back.

"I'm sure you'll have no problems. I'd still like to check in with you frequently to see how you are doing and to make sure that nothing changes."

Sloane nods and hops off the table. "Thank you."

Dr. Gwynn hands her all the material she needs, and Sloane gives me a conspiratorial smile before leaving the office completely.

"You didn't push her to take a higher dose suppressant?" I ask Dr. Gwynn as we head back to her office.

"No, I didn't. The world constantly tells Omegas that they know what's best for them, and that couldn't be further from the truth. Omegas function based on instinct, and people could learn a lot from listening to what their body tells them. Ms. Applegate is completely secure in her designation and who she is. I don't doubt the first Alpha she tells to bite her won't take the opportunity in a heartbeat. More physicians need to listen to the patient before jumping to conclusions. If she finds it's too much, she will come in for suppressants. Our job is to put the patient's mental and physical health above all else. Someone like Ms. Applegate is likely to not do well on suppressants."

"But what if she goes into heat?"

"She has Alphas in mind already, and if that doesn't work out, we've given her secondary options. Our job is to provide information, make sure the patient is safe, never to force our opinion on them. Like I said, their body knows best, and we should trust it."

I smile and nod. This is the type of medicine I want to practice. Actually listening to the patient, getting to understand their lives, and making choices based on multiple factors. This is where I belong, and I wouldn't be here if it weren't for everything that had happened in the last few months. I make a mental note to thank Alexi in every way possible for sending in my application when I get home tonight.

———

I'm ready to jump my Alpha's and Omega's bones as soon as I walk in the door after my first day, where I get home at six in the evening and not some God awful hour like when I worked at the hospital.

Instead, I'm greeted by a congratulations banner and all our family and friends in the room. Charlotte, her pack and kids, Sloane, some guys from the team, Lori, and Max. But front and center are Alexi and Owen who engulf me in a big hug.

"I really hope you had a great first day, or this party is super fucked up," Owen says, and I grab his cheeks and give him a massive kiss.

"It was the best first day."

I grab a fistful of Alexi's shirt and bring his mouth to mine. The kiss is far more salacious than it should be, but when he pulls away and blinks down at me, I smile.

"You're going to be a very happy Alpha tonight," I whisper as I pull back and go to greet our guests.

"Oh, honey, you're glowing. Did you have a great first day?" Lori says, giving me a big motherly hug. I hold her tightly before nodding. I give Sloane a look over my shoulder who shrugs before she goes and stands next to Owen's brother Max, introducing herself. The Alpha looks more than pleased to speak with her. I shake my head, and then a familar scent of maple and sugar finds me.

Charlotte wraps her arms around my waist and squeezes. Owen has gotten a lot better about her scent, but I know I'll need to at least change before the night is over.

"I'm so fucking proud of you, Pipes."

"Thanks, Charles."

I pull back from the hug, and my petite best friend's eyes are watery as she looks up at me. "Seriously, Piper. Look how far you've come. Not even just your new job, but look at you. I don't think I've ever seen you this happy."

"I am really happy," I say, smiling at her.

She holds my hands and squeezes. "You deserve all of that, you know that, right?"

"I think I'm starting to." She squeezes me one more time before heading back to her family. Well, except for Katie who runs up and hugs my legs. I pick her up and kiss her cheeks.

"Hey, pretty girl."

"Auntie P, this party isn't as good as my birthday party." I laugh and nod.

"That's true. Your princess party was pretty amazing."

"Is there cake?"

"I'm not sure," I say, walking over to the kitchen.

"Of course there's cake, *ptichka*." Katie squawks like a bird like she always does with Alexi. "You can't have a party without cake," Alexi says. He cuts her a massive slice and hands her a fork, telling her to eat in the corner where her parents can't see her.

"Her parents are going to blame you when she's running around all over the place."

Alexi laughs and wraps his hand around my waist. "Sounds like that's a problem for them."

I laugh, and the smile on my face nearly hurts. All the people I care about are in one room. I don't feel sad over the people who should be filling the space, I just feel whole. For the first time in my life, I feel like I deserve the life I have, no mean voice telling me otherwise. This is my life, and it's spectacular.

"I can kick them out though. I didn't know you would be eager for me, *malyshka*," Alexi whispers in my ear.

"Kick them out in an hour," I say, just as ready to give him everything I promised as he is to receive. I leave him dumbfounded as I make rounds to our family and friends.

# PIPER

## CHAPTER 44

Alexi finishes cleaning up downstairs after the small party while Owen drags me to the nest. His excitement and happiness is palpable. Even if we weren't bonded and I couldn't sense this down the bond, his body language tells me everything I need to know.

"What has you so excited?" I ask. I know they're both proud of me, but this seems like more.

He spins me around and kisses me. One of his hands tangles in my hair while the other holds my chin where he wants me. "Once Alexi is here."

"Oh, are you two keeping secrets from your bonded?"

He kisses me again, and when he smiles against my lips, I nearly melt. "We just found out today. But this day was about you."

I rub up and down his chest. The fabric is soft, but all I want is his skin under my fingertips. My hand cradles his jaw as I look at him.

"You're different, you know?"

"In a good way, I hope."

"In the best way. You smile more, you don't seem as tense,

you're more confident," I say, loving that us being a pack is what has made him this way.

"I feel like I'm finally me," he says softly, bringing his lips back to mine. The kissing goes from sweet to passionate as his tongue slides against mine. His hands are borderline rough on my scalp as I fist his shirt to hold him close. Strawberry and citrus floods the room, and I don't think I'll ever get tired of his scent or what it does to me.

There's an overwhelming feeling of belonging and how mine he truly is, just as I'm his.

Suddenly, a throat clears and breaks our kiss. Everything had been tuned out up until that moment. When I look to my left, Alexi is propped against the doorframe, smiling at the two of us together.

"I thought we were going to wait to tell her?" He arches a brow at Owen.

"I didn't tell her."

"Are we done being secretive yet?"

Alexi comes to stand behind me, so I'm sandwiched between the two of them. Alexi wraps his arms around me, one of them holding strong against my hip and the other holding Owen's hand.

I face back to Owen, who is grinning. His hand is on my other hip, and I feel so deliciously boxed in. If they don't tell me what's going on soon, I might just say fuck it and have them both naked and ask them about it later.

"The Foxes are taking us on as coaching staff. Owen will be the goaltending coach, and I'll be an assistant coach for power plays."

"I'm going to be the first open Omega to be on the coaching staff."

I smile at Owen and nod. I'm a little taken by surprise because I didn't know this was an option for the both of them.

"And traveling?" I feel selfish, but the idea of them being gone so much during the season is a little daunting. I know I'll be busy with my new program, but my hours are standard, and I want to come home to the both of them.

"Nowhere near as much. Owen won't be traveling with the team. Now that he isn't on medication, it doesn't seem as safe. He will be using deodorizers while he coaches. Owen is coming in to get the new goalies into shape, whoever they are. Having two new goalies on a team is going to be a nightmare, and now that I'm out of the lineup, they need to work on a new power play."

I bite my lip, feeling nervous, and Owen uses his thumb to free it. "It's not going to be anything like last season. I'm so thankful to have a normal life where I can be myself, and I'm not putting my body through fucking hell. But the idea of leaving hockey all together—I'm just not ready."

I nod. I can understand that, and when I look back at Alexi, I can see it in his eyes. He was fine letting hockey go to some degree, so this is more for Owen—I can appreciate that. He truly only got one year in the NHL, and it was hectic to say the least.

My eyes meet Owen, and I give him a genuine smile. "Congratulations, baby. You're going to get them into shape, I know it."

Relief washes over him as he circles me in the best hug he can manage with Alexi at my back. "I was worried how you would handle it. I'm making history taking this job, and I was ready to stop playing, but it feels right to stay with the Foxes and watch them continue to grow."

"They're lucky to have you."

"Just as lucky as we are to have you. I was promised a good time tonight," Alexi says, not mincing words.

"You were, weren't you?"

"What does that entail?"

"The thing you've both been wanting to do," I say, and Alexi groans behind me and kisses my neck. I love that his beard is neatly trimmed. I truly hope that the no shaving rule doesn't apply to coaching staff. I smile when I think about Mikael having to call Alexi his coach; that makes it all worth it to be honest.

"Which thing? I've got a whole list," Alexi says, and I scoff.

"Well, then I guess you pick." My hands glide up Owen's chest, and I feel like they are mentally communicating what they want to do with me. I like it far more than I should.

"You think you can fit both Owen and I in that pretty pussy? I have been training you to take my knot," Alexi says, his voice low and dark in my ear. The hair raises on my arms as I nod my head in agreement. Alexi groans behind me as he rubs against my ass, his hard length pressing against his pants.

Nervous would be an understatement, but I think I hold my composure together as Alexi starts undressing me. Owen lets him handle that while his hands are tangled in my hair, and we kiss like we're each other's oxygen. I help Alexi as I step out of my scrub pants, and I'm working on divesting Owen of his own clothes.

Alexi waits for no one as he tosses his own clothes around the room with abandon. Eventually, we're all naked and standing there. Owen in all his glory in front of me, and Alexi behind me. I don't stop kissing Owen as Alexi plasters kisses down the side of my throat and shoulder. Or when he wraps his hand around my waist and slides down my abdomen and starts playing with my pussy.

Owen devours the moans that leave my mouth while Alexi brings me pleasure. The man is incredibly good with his fingers, and it doesn't take long until my thighs are shaking.

My bare ass is pressed against his hard cock, and I'm begging with my body for him to let me come.

He obliges by inserting two fingers inside of me and rubbing my clit with his palm. His hand is relentless. It's only mission is to make me wet, and I'll need to be incredibly wet to take both of them.

Together Owen and Alexi hold me up as my orgasm hits. My head falls back on Alexi's shoulder as he makes me convulse against him.

"Always so responsive, *malyshka,*" he says in my ear. He removes his hand from my cunt and rubs the release on Owen's dick. It shouldn't be as sexy as it is.

Alexi kisses the side of my neck before opening the night-stand drawer and taking out a bottle of lube, then sitting it on top of the table. He lies on the bed first and strokes his cock. Both Owen and I lick our lips at the same time. Alexi takes the lube, and we both watch in fascination as the liquid drips down his cock.

"Get over here, Dr. Bandnin," Alexi says with that smirk I can't seem to get enough of. I do as he says and crawl on the bed, straddling his length. "Owen, get that pretty cock ready for our girl," he says to Owen while he fists his lubed up cock and slides deep down inside of me.

The wanton noise that rips through my throat has him smiling as he grips my hips. His right hand is tacky with lube as he squeezes my flesh. I control the pace, but I like knowing that if he wanted to take over, he could.

I lean forward to kiss him, my clit grinding over his pelvis, and each thrust there's the sucking sound of my pussy taking him. Wetness covers me everywhere, and the obscene noises our bodies make as we connect has me shivering. I kiss him before holding his head and using him as I see fit.

"Mmm, our Omega is going to stretch you so good. You'll

be able to take my knot, that's what you want, isn't it, *malysh-ka?*" His teeth graze my throat as more words spill from his mouth. "You want my knot so fucking bad. Your cunt is begging for it."

I moan as a second pair of hands grab my hips. I halt my movements, and Alexi's hands move from my hips to my ass cheeks where he spreads me for Owen.

"Fuck," Owen says behind me.

The hands on my body are deliciously rough and the pressure is nearly instant as the head of Owens cock pushes into my entrance. I shout and press my face into Alexi's neck. One of his hands moves from my ass to cradle the back of my neck.

He says something in Russian, and I just moan against his throat as Owen pushes himself deeper inside of me.

It hurts with an edge of pleasure. I can't help but want more. The idea of my pack using me for their pleasure together is the ultimate satisfaction. I want to give them every piece of me, including this.

Owen is nearly fully inside of me when they both start moving. The movements are slow but enough to send me into a frenzy. Thinking about both of them rubbing against each other inside of me, that this is the ultimate way for us all to be together at once, is everything I could have ever wanted.

I'm not even sure what noises I'm making in Alexi's ear, but his hand never leaves my head. Neither one of them stop holding me or telling me how good this is for them—how good I am.

"You should see how fucking sexy you look taking both of us. I'm not going to last," Owen says.

"You need to come inside of her so I can knot both of our cum in her sweet cunt," Alexi says, and I shiver. "What do you need to come?" Alexi asks me, and I just moan in his neck.

The stretch feels good, more than good. it's intense but in a way I could see becoming nearly addictive.

Owen presses his hand on my lower back, forcing my pelvis down onto Alexi's, who has stopped moving. Owen takes control of the motion, eager to reach his own pleasure. In the process, he's making my clit rub against the roughness of Alexi's firm abdomen and hair.

I'm not sure what comes over me as I bite Alexi's neck, his grip on the back of my head tightening as he moans. Owen's hips stutter behind me, and he thrusts harder than he has this whole time, his cock hitting me so deep beside Alexi's.

The orgasm is all consuming. My face goes numb, and my toes curl as I clench around both of them.

"Fuck," Owen says as I feel his warmth fill me, and he promptly pulls out of me. I can feel some of his cum on the back of my thighs. I'm whimpering from the loss, and my orgasm starts to subside. But when Alexi pushes his knot inside of me, I cry out against his neck. My orgasm crescendoed back to the forefront. I close my eyes so tightly that I see stars, and I have to remind myself to breathe.

"That's it. Good girl. Fuck, look at you taking my knot. This Alpha pussy was made for me," he says. My body shivers, and I can feel Owen's softer hands rubbing my back. I have to hold back my need to lock Alexi, but it's easier with the stretch, like my body knows it's getting what it wants. Alexi's knot holding his and Owen's combined cum inside of me, the need to lock him is dissolved, and I just enjoy the intense stretch.

My nails are digging into Alexi's skin, and I hadn't realized. I slowly loosen my hold, and he groans.

"You were right," Alexi says.

My communication skills are lost somewhere in the recess of my sex coma brain, so instead of speaking, I blink at him. He grins and thrusts his hips, making me moan and my pussy clench, causing him to groan and smile. He tugs Owen down next to us, who looks just as blissed out as me.

"I'm definitely a happy Alpha." I sigh against his chest, and the only thoughts running through my head are how I'm the luckiest woman in the world.

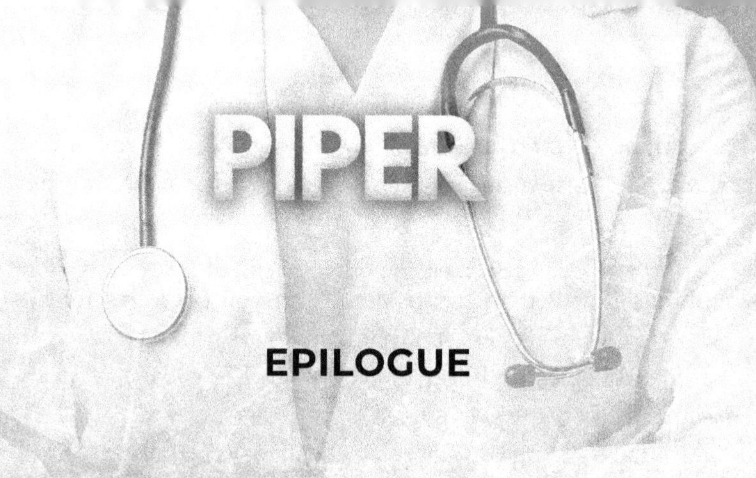

# PIPER

## EPILOGUE

It's the New Year's party, and everyone from the Foxes is here. It's been two years since that kiss I had with Alexi. I smile when I think about his persistence and how we got here. If he hadn't pursued me the way he did, I would probably be at a job I hate without the loves of my life.

My found family is all here, and I can't wait to see what this year brings us. Charlotte holds one of the twins while Mikael holds the other. They are growing so fucking fast, and it seems like time won't slow down for anything.

Katie is running around with some of the other players' kids. My Omega's hand is wrapped in mine when his brother approaches us, and Owen groans lightly before looking at his brother.

"Hey," Max says.

"Hey."

While they might have come to terms with some of their issues, Owen becoming his Alpha brother's coach didn't help things. They went from staying completely away from each other to now being forced to see each other every day—things have gotten tense.

"Happy New Year's, Max." Max gives me a warm smile. I think I'm his favorite in our pack, seeing as I never tell him what to do.

Suddenly, curly red hair pops up in front of us. She's holding a Dr Pepper up to Max. "Can you open this for me, Maxy?" Owen snickers, and I hide my own grin.

Max blushes as he opens the drink for Sloane, and she seems to ethereally skip away.

"What's going on there?" Owen says with an arched eyebrow.

"What do you mean? I was just opening her drink for her."

"Okay, Maxy."

"Oh, fuck off," Max says, storming off, likely to go sit in a dark corner by himself. His reception to the team hasn't been a warm one.

"Your brother is a real cock sucker, you know that?" Bram says to Owen.

"Yeah, I know," Owen supplies back.

"Are you sure you don't want to come out of retirement?" Bram says, shooting a dirty look over to Max.

Owen pinches the bridge of his nose and breathes heavily. "Yeah, I'm sure."

"Maybe I'll accidentally kill Max, and then we can get a new goalie." Owen and I both give him startled looks as he laughs like a maniac. "I'm kidding, fuck's sake." He shakes his head and walks away, noticeably following behind Sloane. I truly wonder what her plan is here. She seems to have multiple people wrapped around her small Omega fingers.

"They are going to make me go gray early," Owen says.

Alexi is wrapping his arms around both of our shoulders, and I poke him in the stomach, still as firm as ever. "I don't know if I can handle two silver foxes in this pack."

"I'm not a silver fox," Alexi says with a pout.

"You definitely are," I supply, and Owen nods his head.

"You two keep this up and you won't have a New Year's kiss."

We both let out mock gasps of shock, and Alexi shakes his head. "Fine, I'm bluffing. I only have a little silver though."

"You keep telling yourself that, *malysh*," I joke, and suddenly his mouth is against my neck, his beard tickling me and making me laugh. He grabs my wrist and kisses my tattoo with the letter A. He has the same tattoo on his wrist, except for P. Besides taking his last name, this was the other plan I had to bring us together. We might not be able to bite each other the way we did Owen, but it was a way to let each other know we belonged to one another. He doesn't immediately give me my wrist back, but looks me in the eyes.

"You two drive me fucking crazy," he says with a smile.

The countdown begins, and the three of us look at each other as the numbers get lower and lower. When the ball drops, we're a tangle of limbs as we kiss each other at the same time before parting. I kiss Owen first for his own kiss before switching to Alexi, then the two of them kiss.

"Happy New Year!" we shout out in unison with the rest of our friends. Charlotte is going down the line kissing all her packmates and her children. I can't help but notice Sloane sneaking a few of her own kisses from the corner of my eye.

When I focus back on my own pack, my chest throbs. They are my everything, and I wouldn't have had this without putting my heart on the line and getting out of my own way. I found my scent match randomly at a coffee shop, and the Alpha who holds me so tightly never doubted us for a second.

If I've learned anything it's that happiness isn't guaranteed, and the road to getting there is always going to be rocky. Letting pieces of your heart walk around outside your body is the hardest thing I'll ever do, but loving Owen and Alexi is easier than breathing.

My negative thinking could have ruined everything, but thankfully I have all these people around me who were looking out for me even when I wasn't. I'm whole because of them, and I can't wait to see how we grow together.

This life is nothing but what you make it, and I plan on making mine incredible with the people I love by my side.

**Puck Around & Find Out - Date TBD - 3rd installment of the Pucked Omegaverse**

# ACKNOWLEDGMENTS

**Stephanie** - Thank you for the medical help and feeling for Piper just as much as I do.

**Lindsay** - The medical help was so helpful and you helped me elevate the story so much.

**Leisha** - We both know Alexi is daddy without being called one.

**Nikki** - Thank you for always pushing me to keep going. And she is who you can thank for Alexi coming on her back.

**MJ** - Thank you for reading early and pushing me to continue writing Omegaverse

**Ice Planet Hoes** - The hoes always support, and I support the hoes back.

**Sandra** - For my beautiful cover and listening to me rant about my rogue plot points.

**Sam** - For being my hockey buddy and always supporting this dream of mine.

**Kim** - Thanks for hopping in and doing an early read for me and finding pesky typos.

**My ARC team** - You make the world go round, I love each and everyone one of you.

**My PA Val** - For teaching me how to ask for help and getting m organized.

**Content Creators** – To anyone who posts an image, a comment, or a video about any of my books just know I absolutely adore you. The work that goes into creating content is one of passion and it really warms my heart that you liked my book enough to post about it. Thank you for your hard work and effort.

# ABOUT THE AUTHOR

Sarah Blue writes contemporary sweet omegaverse, erotic, why choose romances. She loves romance in nearly any genre. When she isn't writing you can find her nose buried in a book or lit up from her kindle. She loves the sweeter side of romance and creating interesting characters while adding adventure and spice. Writing strong female characters and male characters willing to show weakness is something that makes her gooey on the inside.

Sarah lives in Maryland with her husband, two sons, and two annoying cats. If she isn't reading or writing she is probably working on a craft project or scrolling on Tik Tok.

# ALSO BY SARAH BLUE

**Pucked Up Omegaverse**

One Pucked Up Pack

Don't Puck With My Heart

Puck Around & Find Out - Date TBD

**Heat Haven Universe**

Heat Haven

Omega's Obsession

Protector's Promise

Too Tempting

Heat Haven Holidays

**Want to take a walk on the paranormal side?**

Charming Your Dad

Charming the Devil

Charming as Hell – Coming October 2023

**The Carlson Brothers**

Swallow Your Pride

Forget Your Morals - Coming 2024

www.ingramcontent.com/pod-product-compliance
Lightning Source LLC
Chambersburg PA
CBHW060611300726

48975CB00005B/1532